Cover art by Elizabeth Best. See her art on Instagram

@artoferbest

Logo and Chapter Headings by Omni Jacala. See his art on Bluesky

@artsyomni

This book, its cover, and all the internal art was lovingly created by a human, not generated by A.I.

Content Warning. This book contains: Violent, bloody deaths, physical and mental abuse, suicide ideations, body horror, dead family, mild swearing, and violent injuries. Please take care of your mental health if you find yourself struggling with the contents of this book.

Discover other titles by R. A. Meenan

Black Bound

Golden Guardian

Shadow Cast

White Assassin

Brothers at Arms

Umber Sky

Gray Matter

Mage

Angel

Facets of Color: Vol 1

The Hidden Archives: Vol 1

Greetings From Earth: Zyearth Tales Vol 1

Dedications

To my dear friend Randy, who sadly passed away while I was writing this book. I'll miss your smile, your passion for writing, your unwavering support, and the amazing story world you brought us into. May your soul live peacefully among the Lifted.

To my writing group members – Linda, Ambrelle, Heather, Chris, Jill, and Victoria. You always make my writing better!

To my beta readers, particularly Jordan and Joe.

To those whose devotion led to great sacrifices. You are seen, you are loved, and you are celebrated.

"I have found the secret, you see. To become a superhero, all you have to do is want it badly enough." – Nathan Fillion

ZYEARTH CHRONICLES

Judgement

Book Five

From the Four Sisters Archives

By R. A. Meenan

Starcrest Fox Press

CHAPTER 01

WEDDINGS. WITH AN "S."

"I know this is uncomfortable Neil," Ouranos said, holding one end of the *osaa* in his hand. "But please try to stand still while I get this on you."

Neil lifted his arms higher and stood as still as possible while Ouranos wrapped the long colorful strip of fabric around his chest and torso. The wrap felt like a goddamned mummy suit in a corset, making it hard to breathe. He looked silly enough with the long baggy pants and diamond loin cloth of the Athánatos, but putting on the *osaa* made Neil feel like he was putting on an offensive appropriated costume rather than getting ready to be married. His whiskers twitched. "How do you wear this stuff?" Neil said.

"Practice," Ouranos said, taking a brief moment to adjust his own *osaa*. He wore a slim silver chain with gemstones matching his eye color across his shoulders as well, as a mark of a royal. His arms, face, and stomach had complicated designs painted in silver on his fur. "I have worn this for every important ceremony since I was a child. And at my age, that is a very long time, even considering the war." He tightened a part of the fabric on Neil.

Neil winced. "I shoulda just worn my Marine dress blues and been done with it."

"You are about to become a Basileus of Athánatos," Ouranos said, wrapping the end of the strip around Neil's back and tucking it neatly in place. "Something no outsider has ever done. You should attempt to look the part. Show the Athánatos people that you care and respect them."

Neil glanced behind him, frowning, his heart pumping. "...Do they think I don't?"

Ouranos chuckled. "Sorry, perhaps a bad choice of words." He made micro adjustments to the fabric. "They know you care for their wellbeing. You have made that abundantly clear. But show them you also respect their culture."

"I hope they know that already," Neil said quietly. "We've been living here over three years, and I've lived by their rules." He glanced at the rotating fan in the corner, powered by one of the dozen Gem-based generators, graciously donated by the Fawns and fed by Defender-donated jewels. "Well. Mostly."

"The palace dwellers appreciate the use of electricity," Ouranos said. "Using technology is not a breech of tradition. This, however..."

"Alright, alright, I got it," Neil said.

"Besides," Ouranos said, standing. "Remember the real reason why are you are doing this. Your spouses."

Neil pictured last night with Natassa and Dami, one of love, intimacy, comfort, and peace. Something gentle and familiar before diving into a new role and navigating what it means to be Basileus... and married. A pleasurable shiver ran up Neil's spine, fluffing his fur slightly.

"You three will stand out not only as trio united in marriage, but as the future of Athánatos," Ouranos said smiling. "I cannot imagine a better union." He finished adjusting the *osaa* and took a step back. "There. All finished."

Neil glanced in the full-length mirror. Long pants with the diamond cut fabric, *osaa,* and beautiful red patterns painted over his fur. Every bit the Athánatos… on a puma. It still felt wrong. Like he was playing dress up rather than honoring tradition.

Just over three years had passed since Neil and his friends had beaten down Ackerson and his Angels and recovered Jaden and Embrik. It had been a hard-won peace, one that still felt temporary.

Like when Leah and Jaden had been missing, an underlying sense of dread stuck to them because they still hadn't found the missing Prinkípissa Alexina, despite all their efforts. The Fawns had pooled all their resources to send search parties, Commander Reddy pulled all kinds of favors to get help, and Jaden led teams into Canada whenever he could, exploring the last known area she was in.

No dice.

Jaden was hurt, but… oddly patient. She was clearly out there still. Otherwise Zeke would have her snowy owl summon Kyrie, and so far he still only had the golden eagle Archángeli.

Plus, their local time-traveling cryptic, the Black Cloak, had been involved. That had to mean something, no matter how much Neil didn't trust him.

But despite everything, they all felt Alexina's absence. Even Neil, though he had never met her.

The exploring and investigations had helped Neil build bonds with Jaden though, and Zeke, and Leah, and even Ethos, who was fully Ana now. The name change suited her as she grew into something brand new.

Something Neil found himself doing too, whether he liked it or not.

Good friends, a hell of a lot of therapy, and a new role in life as he prepared to get married and take on the title of Basileus to Natassa's Basilea, had allowed Neil to shed who had had to become in order to protect himself after the war had ruined him.

But it came with both good and bad. Good, because he had finally recovered so much of what he had lost in his youth. Bad, because it gave him a new outward vulnerability that he still had trouble coping with. Gone was the façade of the tough guy, and in its place, the quieter, softer, less standoffish puma Neil had been before the war. And this costume dress-up didn't help him deal with this new version of himself. "I look like a clown. Like… I don't belong."

"You look like a powerful Athánatos warrior," Ouranos said, gripping Neil's shoulder. "Brave and true, ready to lead his people into a new and wonderful life." He wrapped his arm across Neil's shoulder blades and gave him a gentle squeeze. "You belong, brother. With Natassa and Dami. With the royalty of Athánatos. This is your home." He butted his head against Neil's. "Cherish it, as you are cherished here."

Neil relaxed slightly. In the last five years or so, Ouranos had become the older brother Neil never had. Someone Neil could trust to the fullest. But despite Ouranos' reassurance, this still felt wrong. He sighed. "I suppose."

Another Athánatos, the royal biographer Abrax, walked up to them, clearing his throat loudly, holding a book and quill in his hand. "This idle chat is all fine and good, but can we please get back to chronicling your history? I would rather not spend all day."

Neil winced. It was bad enough that the wedding required a biographer, but why the hell did it have to be *Abrax?*

Neil had first met Abrax in a dungeon full of Athánatos prisoners, right after he had had a terrible PTSD moment from fighting off a dozen zombie-like Drifters. Despite the fact that Abrax was trapped, hungry, cold, and clearly abused, his immediate reaction to Neil, an outsider, had been nothing but hate. And even after Neil had fought off more Drifter sentries and freed the Athánatos prisoners, Abrax still went running to Ryota, tattling like a child.

Ryota had responded by turning Abrax into a Shadow Cast. That wasn't a scene Neil would forget any time soon.

Even after being turned back, and even though most of the rest of Athánatos saw Neil as a hero, Abrax had always been cold to him. Neil tried his best to forgive him. After all, if he could forgive Ana and the other Fawns for all the shit they pulled, he should be willing to forgive Abrax. But the little bastard made it difficult. The Fawns had been apologetic which helped when they were rebuilding their relationship, but Abrax had yet to apologize for anything.

Neil glanced back at him. Abrax had refused the finery that a wedding chronicler should have and instead wore the long, plain robes of his profession, using the excuse that since he was chronicling Neil's entire life, the wedding finery would just get in the way. But Neil knew it for what it was. Protest. Despite everything, he never approved of this union. Though he at least had the courtesy not to say it out loud.

Neil sighed. "Sure. Where'd we leave off?"

Abrax tapped the book with his quill, squinting. He adjusted the long sleeves of his robes. "Your valiant battle at… DC… fighting a roaring wind."

Neil ran a hand down his face. "Wasn't anything valiant about it. I went insane."

"But you lived," Abrax said. "And you have proof of your heroism. As I do myself." He lifted his robe and pointed to his left foot - his middle toe was missing. "I lost this fighting a wild beast."

Ouranos crossed his arms. "You lost that toe teasing one of the mule deer fawns in your youth," he said. "We all know the story, Abrax. The stable hands still use it to scare the apprentices and avoid further accidents."

Abrax narrowed his gaze. "Hrmph. They were not there, so they can believe their stories all they want. The fact remains is I live and that beast does not."

"Yes, such a terrible beast that lost its life to old age and comfortable living," Ouranos said, rolling his eyes.

Abrax snorted. "The story does not change. History is written by the victors."

"I wish it was written by the *facts,*" Neil said.

Abrax went back to his book and pen. "I intend to leave your, ah, *heroic* victory over the Drifters intact," he said. "But you must expect some embellishment on events I did not witness."

Neil winced. *Embellishment.* Abrax made it look like Neil had won the whole goddamned war by himself. Instead he had crumbled into a puddle of PTSD and suicide ideations. It was a wonder he had survived at all.

"Lord Ouranos." Eris walked in, pushing aside the curtain separating the dressing room from Neil's big bedroom. "Has Lord Neil finished dressing?"

Neil flattened both ears. "Eris, please just call me Neil. We've been over this."

Eris pushed aside the curtain and entered the room carrying a big, ornate box with a smaller box on top of it. Her forest green pants and light gray top contrasted her pure black fur nicely. "Apologies, Neil," she said, smiling. "But for today, it must be Lord, as the people expect. But if you would rather I not use it, then I will save that title for public appearances only." She put down the boxes and adjusted the long, braided quills running down her back. "Take comfort that we will only need to use the term for a day. Then it will be 'business as usual' as you have said."

Neil took a deep breath. "Thanks, Eris."

"Of course." She glanced him over. "Excellent work, Lord Ouranos. He looks as fit as any Basileus."

Abrax flipped through the book and scribbled something. "Fit… for… a… foreign… Basileus."

Neil shot him a glare, though Abrax didn't seem to notice. He sighed and turned back to the mirror. "I don't feel it."

"Perhaps because you are missing the most important pieces." She turned to her boxes and opened the biggest one. She lifted a long gold chain with red, teardrop jewels hanging off it on shorter chains. "Your jewels."

Neil stared at it. It was gorgeous. Delicate and thin, it was drastically different than Theron's. On purpose of course. No one wanted Neil to have any resemblance to Theron, so instead of his thick gold band and blue jewels, Neil went with a chain and red jewels.

Eris smiled. "This was inspired," she said. "Even the artisans say so." She walked to Neil. He leaned his head down and she draped it across his shoulders. She adjusted the hanging jewels, then reached back into the box and pulled out the matching arm bands. Ouranos helped her fasten them around Neil's upper arms. She spun him around and had him face the mirror.

Neil stared. He ran his fingers over the chain and jewels.

Eris squeezed his hand and Ouranos patted his back. Eris grinned, ear to ear. "This is a king I am happy to follow," she said. "Though so is the king who wears a green jacket, speaks with his citizens as his equals, cooks for the staff, and plays games with the palace children." She glanced up at him. "No matter what you wear on the outside, your heart has not changed. Our people know this, and this is why they celebrate you."

Neil took a deep breath. "Thank you, Eris. I needed that."

"Of course," Eris said.

Abrax slid in front of him. "Stand still so I can sketch this."

Neil stood stiff. Just what he wanted. A sketch of this moment, forever embedded in some ancient history book.

Abrax furrowed his brow. "I will have to add the Ei-Ei jewels later I suppose."

Adrenaline ran up Neil's spine. The Ei-Ei jewels.

"Here, Neil." Eris walked over and picked up the smaller box. She opened it and showed Neil. "Your Ei-Ei jewels, for the ceremony."

Neil glanced at them. After decades of hating himself and wishing he could just end it all, the idea that he was okay getting Ei-Ei jewels, jewels that made him immortal, still carried an echo of dread. He had so much more to look forward to now, so much to live for, but those suicide ideations never fully went away. But... the fact that he could willingly wear them was a good sign. He was healing. Hopefully.

The yellow diamond. The red arrow. And the triangle, currently colorless. "And this will take on my eye color."

"It will," Ouranos said.

"And... I'll get magic," Neil said. "Like you and Natassa."

Ouranos smiled. "That is the belief, yes. Control over all the elements. And likely one of Natassa's summons will join you. It is custom for their bond."

"Excelsis has a particular fondness for the *foreign,*" Abrax added.

Neil shut his eyes a moment. Did he have to keep bringing that up?

"Perhaps I should remind you that *all* the Phonar are foreign," Eris said, shooting him a glare. "They were allies from the mainland who gave their lives for summonhood. It is no wonder that any one of them would 'favor the foreign.'"

"Irrelevant," Abrax said. He scribbled a bit more. "Just try not to burn the palace down as your red friend almost had. We cannot afford more repairs."

Neil formed fists. "Abrax, I know Ryota did a lot of damage here, but he *died* saving Trecheon's *life*. Hell, if he hadn't turned against Theron, destroyed his lab, and helped us get the cured Cast to the mainland, we never would have beat the Basileus down. Show some damn respect."

Abrax flicked his ears back, but didn't say anything. He scribbled something else in his book.

Neil pinched the bridge of his snout. Goddamn it all.

Though he had unlocked one more new fear. Did Neil have what it took to wield magic? Could he actually keep his powers under control? Matt had all kinds of stories about his magic going wild. What if he did that? What if he actually *did* burn the palace to the ground?

Or worse… what if he didn't get any magic at all? What if neither of Natassa's summons joined him?

Would that mean he wasn't actually the Basileus?

Damn it, why was this so hard?

Ouranos gripped Neil's shoulders. "Courage, brother. The Phonar already recognize you as Basileus. So do the Archons. You will earn your magic, and you have an army of mages willing to help you learn how to wield it, Athánatos and Defender. You will not face it alone."

Neil twitched his whiskers, desperately wanting to think about something else. "But we still don't know if this will also change my fur or inner ear color."

"Time will tell," Eris said. "But I noted it did not change Prince Zeke's when he was bound to his jewels, nor did it change Jaden's in marriage, so it may not change yours either."

"Jaden's case may not be the best example, however," Ouranos said. "His was not an official Athánatos marriage. If they choose to go through with that ceremony, that may change."

"Regardless," Eris said. "We are unsure how the Ei-Ei jewels will change you, Neil."

Neil scrunched his snout. "I'm not sure how I feel about that. Like… if I should be happy or hate it."

"Time will tell that too," Ouranos said. "But for now, admire yourself, and picture your spouses in similar outfits. While this is a ceremony for Athánatos, it is also a ceremony for love. This is your reason for doing this at all, is it not?"

Neil turned back to the mirror. His mind flashed images of Damianos and Natassa, his soon-to-be-husband and wife, wearing the same outfits. His ears flushed and he smiled. "God, they're gonna be gorgeous."

"Good, you'll match," Matt said. Neil turned. Matt leaned against the door frame by the entrance to the room wearing a similar, less ornate version of Neil's outfit. He crossed his arms, a smirk on his face, and glanced over Neil. "Looking snazzy, hot stuff."

Matt and the other Zyearthlings had come back to Earth just over two months ago. The Master Guardian gave them all a six-month leave to Earth, labeling it a diplomatic meeting since Athánatos was getting a new king.

Matt had confided in Neil that even Lance said it was just an excuse to give them all more time together around Neil's wedding, especially since he was planning on calling Sacha and Leah home after this. One last long trip to Earth before visits became scarce.

Every visit now was just a little bittersweet. After having the Defenders around for over two years, particularly Matt and Izzy who Neil had grown closest to in that time, these short visits just weren't enough. But still, six months was better than six days, so Neil clung to it as much as he could.

Even when Matt was badly flirting with him.

Neil raised an eyebrow and placed a hand on his hip. "You've been spending too much time with Trecheon. Save the dirty talk for him."

Matt laughed. "Yeah, he does bring out the flirt in me. Though I'd hardly call that dirty."

Neil grinned. "That's cuz Trecheon gets all the dirty talk, doesn't he, *nephew?*"

Abrax scribbled furiously again. "Azure family… connections…"

"Don't forget to include what an amazing lover Jaden is," Neil said grinning.

Matt slumped. "Tell me you're joking."

Abrax narrowed his gaze.

Neil winked. "Where do you think *my* dirty talk comes from?"

Matt pressed his eyes shut, grimacing. "Lightning and *air,* Neil, could you *not?* The mental image alone…"

Neil just laughed. "You talk a mean game, Matt, but you can't actually take it, which I'll never get bored of." He turned to Abrax. "For the record, I am actually joking. Jaden only has eyes for Alexina."

Abrax snorted and ripped a page out. "I have wasted more paper on your jokes than any other Basileus in *history.*"

"My legacy," Neil said laughing. His face softened and he turned back to Matt. "Speaking of Trecheon… He still hasn't said anything to you, has he?"

Matt's face grew serious and he glanced at the floor. Trecheon had clearly been crushing on Matt for a while, but for whatever reason, he hadn't told him, so the whole thing just kind of hung awkwardly in the air, and everyone felt it. Matt twitched an ear. "No, he hasn't."

Neil frowned. "If it bothers you that much, you could just bring it up first."

"I know," Matt said. "But… I still don't really know how I feel about him yet either, and it doesn't seem fair to initiate the conversation just to turn him down." He leaned back and took a deep breath. "He's… kind of slowed down his flirting with me lately."

"I've noticed," Neil said, frowning. "Wish I could tell you why, but he hasn't mentioned anything to me. Or anyone, really. He knows that we're all aware that he's got the hots for you, but he pretends like we don't." He met Matt's gaze. "You okay with that? You haven't slowed down a bit. Hell, I actually think you've ramped it up."

Matt flattened his ears. "I think I have, subconsciously. Maybe trying to get Trecheon to flirt back the way he always has, just for normalcy. Feels like something's breaking." He sighed. "I wish I had the guts to just dive into a relationship and see what happens, but the thought of it scares me to death."

"Don't do that to yourself," Neil said. "Better to take things slow than to force something. You're already too much of a people pleaser."

"I know you're right, but sometimes it feels like it'd be easier. Or at least less stressful." He smiled, though it was somewhat broken. "Anyway, the rest of the gang is out here waiting for you. Including your special someones." He winked. "Better not keep them waiting."

Neil smiled. "We'll be out there soon."

"Do not fret over your relationship with Trecheon, Matthew," Ouranos said. "The best relationships happen naturally, and you have many years together to find out what you two need."

Matt smiled and nodded. "Yeah. Thanks." He gave an exaggerated bow, then walked out.

Neil watched him leave. "You're in his head, Ouranos," he said. "Think they have a chance?"

Ouranos flattened an ear, his tail twitching. "I think Matthew already knows what his feelings are for Trecheon, but he fears opening a door to a room he has never visited."

Neil turned back to the mirror, looking over his outfit, and holding the Ei-Ei jewels in his hand. He pulled the jewels close to his chest. "I know the feeling."

Ouranos wrapped an arm across Neil's shoulders. "We cannot help Matthew navigate his feelings for Trecheon, but we can help you navigate your new role. A role, I might add, that you have been playing in everything but name for the last three years. Longer, even, if you count your time on Athánatos before your official engagement, which I know many of our people do. The only thing that changes today is your title with Athánatos and your official connections with Damianos and Natassa. You are not here alone, brother."

Neil smiled. "Thanks." But he couldn't draw his eyes away from the mirror.

Abrax snapped his book shut. "If we are done with the terrible joking, I will take my leave for now and wander the crowd to get some eye-witness accounts." He left.

Neil sighed.

"Give him time, Neil," Eris said. "He is a good man at heart. He is just… stubborn."

Neil tightened his jaw. That sounded familiar. Much like him or Trecheon. Maybe time would heal it. It wasn't so much Abrax as it was the negative associations around him and this ridiculous biography. After all… Abrax was making him relive his time in the War of Eons.

A memory of Carter flashed in his mind.

After the Battle of DC where Neil watched Trecheon's arms get shot off, he, Carter, and Trecheon had somehow made their way to a field hospital just outside the city. Neil had spent days scared out of his mind, unable to sleep, unable to eat, with only one thought on his mind – end it all. End the pain. The fear, the trauma, the bombs overhead, the deep scent of gunpowder.

Trecheon's blood on his clothes and hands.

Neil had tried killing himself multiple times before they started sedating him. In a lot of ways, that was worse. Losing the last of his control in a war that had already took so much away from him threatened to break him entirely.

But then Carter showed up. Sat on the bed with him, held him, gave him a sense of peace, of… normalcy. Whatever normalcy came with war. And he said something that stuck with Neil for the rest of his life.

"Someday, Neil," the distant, dead, toneless voice of Carter echoed in his head. *"Someday you'll get better. You'll hone your skills. Face down a dragon. Marry a princess. You'll get the fairy tale ending you deserve."*

Neil wasn't sure he deserved it. But he was getting it anyway. He should cherish it, like Ouranos said. If only Carter knew how real his prediction had been. He found himself wishing his old combat buddy was here. *Godspeed, wherever you are, Carter.*

Well. No use pining for the dead. He puffed out his chest and drew as much courage as he could to his mind.

"Welp. Let's do this."

THE WEDDING(S) PARTY

"Hey, there's the puma of the hour," Matt said, grinning.

Neil entered one of the massive atria on the edge of the palace grounds, near the walkway to the Four Sisters statues where the ceremony would take place. All the guests of honor, Athánatos, mainlanders, and Zyearthlings alike, had gathered there, helping each other dress in the ceremonial clothing and elaborate body paintings of the Athánatos. Many snacked on cheese pastries, bread laden with olive tapenade and garlic, and a variety of sweet cakes, courtesy of Izzy, who had spent the last three days baking with the cooks in the kitchens for the celebration.

Everyone glanced up when Matt called out Neil's name, big smiles on all their faces. The joy wrapped around Neil like warm hugs, and his fur stood up slightly, radiating his excitement.

He never would have imagined this possible after his time in the war. Getting married to two loving people, having a job and title where he could do amazing good alongside his partners, and being surrounded by dozens of loving friends and family. God, he had lucked out. Now he just had to convince himself that he belonged here.

Philip glanced up and stood. He had just turned fifteen a few weeks ago and had grown fully into his adult coat, looking more like Neil's twin every day. He grinned and ran up to Neil, arms wide. "Haha, wow, look at you! You're like a king already!"

Neil hugged him tight. The last three years had been quite a journey for them, especially as Philip entered his teenage years, but Neil couldn't imagine anything better. His little piece of heaven. "Thanks, kid."

"Papa Electrik helped me with the ceremonial painting since I'm going to be one of Damianos' escorts," he said. He stepped back and showed off the gold and blue paint decorating his fur. "What do you think?"

Neil smiled. "Looks great, Philip."

Izzy grinned at him now. "Hey, Basileus, looking fancy!" she called. She twirled, letting the multiple diamond shaped strips of fabric hanging off the belt around her skirt twirl about. The bright white paint on her fur and quills reflected the beams of sunlight. "Gotta love how fancy these ceremonial outfits look, huh?" She adjusted the *okaa,* the feminine version of the *osaa,* and ran her hands over her bare stomach.

"It does make everyone exceptionally nice to look at," Darvin said, grinning, shaking his antlers and activating a bit of his Shadow Cast form, turning the silver tips black and inky. He wore the Athánatos pants, but he and his brother Roscoe had forgone the *osaa* and instead wore long, ornate cloaks that covered their shoulders and torsos. Both stags were painted with elaborate designs complementing their fur colors. He eyed Sami, who also wore one of the cloaks, forgoing the *okaa.* "Some more than others, perhaps."

"Har har," Sami said, smirking. She lay a plate of food on the big buffet table, shaking her white, fluffy tail and wiggling her foxy ears. "Save it for our own wedding, Mr. Stag."

Darvin frowned. "I haven't even *asked* you yet."

"Better get started on that then," Roscoe said. He carefully hung some simple gold jewelry off the tips of his copper antlers. "Neil's gonna one-up you today."

"Chadwick and I already one-upped you," Andre said, grinning. He held up his arms as Chadwick painted his dark skin with an ornate gold paint. Their matching gold wedding bands twinkled in the light.

Chadwick turned to Andre, smooth and smarmy, twitching his long black tail. "And what a one-up it was."

"Not a topic for polite company, babe," Andre said and he winked.

Darvin's ears flushed. "Come on. It's not a *race*."

"But if it was, you'd be dead last," Sacha said, laughing. She painted complicated black and gold decorations on her biomechanical arm. Trecheon sat next to her with drinks and food. She gave him the side-eye. "Except maybe one, perhaps."

Trecheon tugged at the *osaa* around his chest and pulled a jacket on, hiding his biomechanical arms. "Darvin and Sami have known each other since before I was *born,*" he said. "They've had far more time to actually get married. And my situation's more… complicated." He shot a quick glance at Matt, but didn't say anything more. Matt flicked an ear back and looked off.

Sacha chuckled. "Only as complicated as you make it, hun." She went back to painting.

Neil frowned slightly. Something really was… off, about Trecheon lately. He had been standoffish, quiet, and more reserved than normal. And he had taken to hiding his biomech again, though in really unusual ways.

Several years ago, Matt had fabricated some convincing covers for his arms, which Trecheon had taken to wearing regularly in public. But lately he hadn't be wearing them at all. No one knew why and Trecheon wasn't telling. Why he chose a jacket instead of the covers was anyone's guess. Neil'd have to chat with him when he could, see what's up.

"I could always scry if a future marriage in the cards," Angus said, pulling out his mirror and waving it at Darvin, smirking. He waved his wings, highlighting the glittery cloud and wind imagery painted on them.

"*No,*" Darvin and Sami said together.

Ethos… no, Ana, walked up to Neil, frowning. Her outfit was much simpler and she had refused the body paint. Said she didn't deserve to be here at all, considering their past, let alone be allowed the paint that marked her as a special guest.

Neil disagreed, considering all they had been through in the last three years, but he didn't want to force her. God knew they had both had enough of that shit under Ackerson.

She met his eyes. "You, ah… you look fitting. It suits you." She shook herself. "There is so much I want to say, so much I *need* to, after everything leading up to this, but…"

Neil smiled softly and drew her into a hug. "Ana. Enough of this huh? Quit beating yourself up over the past. We've moved on."

Ana hugged him tight. "I still don't know how you could forgive us for all the hell we dragged you through."

"Patience and determination," Neil said. "And a hell of a lot of therapy. I refuse to become Theron. Just as you refuse to become the Matron. And you could use the break. You faced the same trauma I did."

Ana gave him a little squeeze. "Yeah." She stepped back. "Pathos and Logos send their apologies about not being here, but we need someone in charge while mopping up Ackerson's mess. But uh, we wanted to talk to you about our… wedding gift, if you could call it that. We're working on trying to create a magic grid throughout the palace so you can have standard electricity. No more generators. We've got our best engineers on it, and we're hoping we can start groundwork in a couple of weeks, with permission, of course."

"Really?" Neil grinned. "That'd be great!" He paused and turned to Ouranos. "If the Athánatos are okay with it, of course."

Ouranos smiled. "I am sure they would welcome it with open arms."

Ana smiled. "Glad you like the idea. If it works well, we can implement it in the Archons and villages too."

"I like it as well," Ouranos said. "A good start to your rule as Basileus. And it will certainly make you stand out against Theron's rule."

Jaden walked up to Neil, smiling ear to ear. Over the last three years, Jaden had warmed up and became like a father to Neil. The kind of father he could kick back a couple of beers with and talk about anything life threw at them. It wasn't the same as therapy, but there was something deeply healing about talking about the war, about loss, and about Athánatos with Jaden. For both of them, it seemed.

Jaden patted Neil's back. "You wear the jewels well, Neil. Every bit the Basileus we need. I'm sure Eris and Ouranos agree."

Neil smiled carefully, his joints stiff. "I can only hope."

"Have more faith in yourself," Zeke said, standing next to Jaden.

Neil met Zeke's gaze. Like Matt, Zeke wore a similar outfit to Neil's, *osaa* and all, though fit for the royalty, with bright colors and a simple, silver chain across his shoulders, dotted with green jewels matching those striking, familiar green eyes all Azures seemed to have.

Unlike Neil, who struggled with every step trying to get used to this damn outfit, Zeke relished in it. The last three years had been transforming for him while he got to know his Athánatos family. Talk about a role reversal. This time three years ago, Zeke was asking Neil how to fit in.

Now Neil was the uncomfortable one.

Leah ran up now and threw her arms around Zeke's stomach, hugging him from behind. Zeke grinned, reached behind him, and wrapped an arm around her, pulling her next to him. Neil's heart warmed.

She stepped back from Zeke. "Embrik says the Archons and other important guests have gathered at the Four Sisters. Are we ready to go?"

Neil frowned. "Where's Dami and Natassa?"

"Here, love," Natassa said. Neil turned.

Natassa and Dami stood off to the side in all their wedding glory. Natassa wore a white skirt with gold accents and a thin gold chain like Neil's, but with purple jewels instead, matching her eyes. Her *okaa* was white with accents of gold and purple. She had delicate gold paint in complicated swirls on her belly and arms.

Damianos wore striking black pants with a black and silver *osaa*. His chain was also black and less ornate, with simple silver teardrops hanging from it, and his silver body paint outlined where the black and gold parts of his fur met. Both of them wore huge grins.

Neil grinned back, his chest swelling, and his eyes burning with building tears of joy. All the fear, all the nervousness melted away. Because this was why he was getting married. These two amazing, beautiful, beloved quilar.

Because his past hadn't stolen his ability to love.

The pair of them walked up to Neil and they all shared a deep hug. The world seemed to come to a halt as he held them. His future, right here. He still wasn't sure he deserved it, but if he didn't now, he'd make sure his actions as Basileus made it so he did. He kissed each of them. "I love you both so much."

Damianos snuggled into Neil's fur, laughing quietly. "I never expected this day to come. And yet, here it is."

"Hey, I promised you peace, didn't I?" Neil said.

"A promise well kept," Damianos said.

Natassa planted a kiss on Neil's forehead. She traced her finger over the jewelry across Neil's shoulders. "The chain fits you well, my heart."

Neil's face fell slightly. "Doesn't really feel it."

"Give it time for you to grow into it," Natassa said. "There is a reason why the chain fits loose around your shoulders instead of tight on your head as a crown or hanging around the neck like a traditional necklace. It symbolizes room for growth. It can move and change and adapt to whatever situation is needed, as a good leader should." She ran a finger down his chin. "You have already shown you can adapt and change. Just as you had in the past, you will do so now."

He took a deep breath and smiled. "Yeah."

"Here. A warrior needs his blade." Damianos held out a belt with a sword and sheath attached. A sword Dami's father, the Archon of Electrik, had had made for Neil weeks ago as a wedding gift. Long, sharp, and well-balanced, yet with a simple hilt, it was purposefully battle ready, though Electrik said he hoped Neil would never have to use it. Dami reached around Neil's waist and attached the sword belt. Then he wrapped his arms around Neil and planted a gentle kiss on the side of his head. "My Emerald Prince."

Neil hugged him back and leaned his head against Dami's.

Charlotte, Matt's sister, came up behind them, smiling. She was decked out more so than most of the other guests, wearing a simple chain with colorful beads across her shoulders, because she was going to be one of Natassa's escorts. The Athánatos didn't believe in "giving away" their brides. Instead, escorts were chosen. Friends and family attached to the quilar they escorted, as a reminder that marriage wasn't just to one person, it was to the network of people who loved them.

A tradition Neil appreciated. So much of his life now was because he had the support network he did. That wouldn't be possible without Natassa and Dami.

Natassa had asked Charlotte and Matt to fulfill that duty for her. Izzy and Trecheon would be Neil's escorts and Philip and Electrik's husband Taras would be Damianos'. A good mix of their friends and family.

Charlotte gave Natassa a squeeze, then turned to Neil. "I know you're nervous," she said. "But don't let anyone tell you that you can't be. It's normal."

Neil tilted his head back and crossed his arms. "I know you're right, but convincing my brain to believe it is another thing entirely."

Charlotte smiled softly. "You'll get it." She turned to Matt and Izzy, her long white and blue lined quills shaking, and held up two velvet pouches. "Matt, Izzy, I've got your beads here."

Embrik appeared now, in his full regalia as well, with Melaina at his side. "The guests are ready. Is everyone prepared for the ceremony?"

Neil closed his eyes and gripped Dami and Natassa's hands. *Remember why you're doing this. Because of these amazing quilar that you love. Because you can help them do so much good and make up for all the bad in your life. This is right. This is... home.*

Dami and Natassa squeezed his hands.

Neil opened his eyes, shaking slightly, but smiling. "Lead the way, Embrik."

THE BLACK CLOAK

Embrik led the group to the edge of the Four Sisters' Grove, which had been cleaned and manicured for the ceremony. Athánatos representing all the major Archons, plus the Archons themselves, wandered under the crystal-laden trees, chatting, laughing, drinking good wine and mead and eating Izzy's amazing pastries.

Neil swallowed hard and turned his attention to the scenery.

Beautiful crystal shards hung off the trees, painting rainbows and shimmers of light on the ground. Colorful blankets, all hand-woven, covered the ground in haphazard patterns, save for one golden path to the Four Sisters statues. Each of the seven large tapestries had been woven by top artisans in the seven Archon realms, displaying symbols and color accents for each house. The Four Sisters Grove would be the staging area where Eris would officially bind Neil and his betrothed.

Neil's heart threatened to burst out of his chest. He squeezed Dami and Natassa's hands. He eyed the Archons – his royal court, ready to receive them. All laughs and smiles, relaxed and happy.

Except Mistik. While they didn't look *angry,* they didn't share the same laughs as the others, standing isolated among the crystal trees, slowly nibbling at a pastry. They didn't even have their family around them. Whether they were absent as a way for Mistik to protest, or whether they simply didn't want to be around Mistik while the Archon pouted, Neil wasn't sure.

Neil flicked an ear back. Mistik had openly criticized Neil for a while, though he had thought they had finally accepted Neil during the battles with Ackerson's goons. Certainly they had been friendly enough while Natassa taught Neil about their politics leading up to this wedding. Maybe they were having second thoughts.

Or maybe *he* was having second thoughts and seeing things that weren't there. He bit his tongue, furrowing his brow.

Then Electrik noticed them. He waved his hand to his husband Taras and the pair walked over, all smiles. They both hugged Dami tightly.

"After everything Theron took from us, I did not dare to hope that we would see you in a wedding *osaa* one day," Electrik said to Dami. "And yet, here you are, ready to marry a man I would have picked for you myself if given the chance." He smiled at Neil.

Neil took a shaky breath. "I hope I deserve that."

"I would not say it if you did not." Electrik took Neil's hands in his own. "My Basileus. I cannot claim to speak as someone who has faced your past and come to this present, but I can speak as someone who felt unworthy of their position of power. It is a hard road. One where you will question yourself over and over. Did I do the right thing by my people? Am I worthy of my title?"

Neil frowned.

"But know this," Electrik said. "Your people are proof that you belong. Their joy, their peace, their prosperity. And even before you have taken the position, you have worked with Lady Natassa and Damianos to make that happen." He wrapped an arm across Neil's shoulder and pointed out among the crowds. "See your people. See their joy. Look for it when you feel unworthy, and it will lift you back up again."

"And come talk to us if you need advice," Embrik said. "I do not know of an Archon or Basileus in history who ever felt worthy of their position when first taking it. But there is, ah, proof… proof in the…" He turned to Jaden.

Jaden laughed. "The proof is in the pudding, as the mainlanders say."

Matt wrinkled his snout. "Pudding? Bleh." He gripped Neil's shoulder. "We say 'a good Gem bears long life.' I think that's more fitting. You're a good Gem, Neil."

Neil smiled. "Thanks. That means a lot, Matt."

"Now." Electrik waved to the other Archons. They lined up with the rest of the wedding party. "Let us lift the three of you up in marriage and get to the feast, shall we?"

Embrik, being the one Archon married to a royal, stood in front with Melaina at his side and held up his hands. "Athánatos, mainlanders, and Zyearthlings!" Everyone grew silent and looked up from their conversations. Embrik waved a hand at Neil and the wedding party. Neil's face and ears grew hot. "May I present Lady Natassa, Lord Damianos, and Lord Neil. Please join us in welcoming our Lady's chosen husband and his chosen Consort as they lead us into a new, prosperous future."

The crowd clapped, all smiles and cheers. Several Archons and their children and spouses shot sparks of elemental magic into the air. Mistik pressed their lips together, not bothering with their magic, but they clapped just the same.

Ouranos stepped forward and waved a hand. Jústi and Pax, the lightning kestrel and the earth burrowing owl appeared in the air, waving their magic all around.

Natassa, Melaina, and Zeke held their hands forward and their respective Phonar appeared as well – Excelsis, the fire raven, Deo, the fire crane, Lumen, the stone kori bustard, Sémini, the water falcon, and Archángeli, the wind eagle. The birds flew about, sprinkling the air with their elements, filling the grove with smells of forest, ocean, rain, and sand. Then they landed alongside the golden path of tapestries in their zyfaunos forms, each of them bowing on one knee.

Kyrie was, still, the only Phonar missing. Archon Frostrik took her place instead, representing the ice element.

Izzy gripped Neil's shoulder. He turned to her and she smiled. "You got this, Neil."

"She's right," Trecheon said, gripping his other shoulder. Neil turned to him now. He smiled, though it felt somewhat forced. "You deserve this, Neil. We all do. We've finally healed. Let's get you married, huh?"

Neil stared at him a moment, itching to ask him what was wrong. But now wasn't the time. He nodded and took Dami and Natassa's hands again instead. The three of them walked forward, guarded by their escorts at their backs.

Eris waited for them in the grove. Shining crystals lay in a circle at the feet of the four statues, and golden blankets covered the grass, with a variety of plush pillows on the floor.

Neil glanced briefly at the statues. They gave him the creeps if he was honest. Three heavily stylized feminine Athánatos statues, cracked and breaking. One wearing a heavy veil, one wearing a thick cloak, and one poked full of holes, clearly by design. A fourth base for a statue remained, but all that was left of it was a kite shield and a head with a feature-less face. The same empty face all of them had. The Veil, the Cloak, the Purge, and the Seal.

If it had been up to him, he would have had the wedding somewhere else. But as Ouranos said, they gotta honor tradition. At least he didn't have to stare at the statues.

Eris smiled and sat on her knees on one of the big pillows. "Come, Lords, Ladies, Athánatos, Zyearthlings, mainlanders, and Guardians. Rest your bones and hear the tale of the Four Sisters as we know it."

"May the Sisters smile upon us," Neil said with Dami and Natassa, as rehearsed.

Everyone took a pillow. Neil sat cross-legged, careful not to sit on his tail. The Phonar stood guard in their zyfaunos forms all around the grove, and the Archons lined up just outside the entrance to it. Dami wrapped an arm around Neil, and Natassa laid her head on his shoulder. It calmed him.

Eris took out three long sticks, wrapped in colorful fabrics with short, gold and silver chains hanging on the ends of each one. She used two of them to balance the third, then nodded to the Phonar.

Excelsis and Deo lit the ends of the balanced stick with purple and white fire.

"At the start of recorded time," Eris said. "The first Basilea emerged as leader of our people." She used her two sticks to flick the fire stick into the air, shooting sparks about in a colorful display. "The Basilea ruled well, but wanted more power. She sought to take her people's magic and use it to conquer the mainland."

Jústi and Pax added their magic to the stick, spinning lightning and earth between the fire.

Eris caught the stick and flung it up again. Magic whirled around them, making everything bright. "Her people resisted her. So she sought other methods. Dark methods. She used her power to create Shadow Cast."

Someone cleared their throat. Neil turned. Ouranos and Matt wore frowns, glancing between each other. Izzy stiffened next to Neil.

Lumen and Sémini now added stones and water to the stick.

"But her four daughters resisted further," Eris continued, balancing the elements between her sticks. "They found power in the Phonar. Allyship in the Black Cloak. And protection in the Veil. Still, the Basilea fought them. Until she took the ultimate step. She made herself into an immortal summon. She declared Judgement on her people for resisting her."

Archángeli added their wind to the stick, with a little of Frostrik's ice magic.

"But the Sisters fought further. They sacrificed themselves to save their people. In addition to the Veil and the Cloak, they created the Seal, to seal away Judgement, and the Purge, to remove all memories of Judgement's Shadow Cast."

Neil shuddered.

Eris met Neil's gaze. "While this magic is not well understood, and the history full of holes, we see its effects all around us."

And didn't he know it, after the lot of them had faced Judgement head on while searching for Jaden three years ago.

"Basileus," Eris said. Neil sat straight up and met her gaze. She lifted her chin. "While you have been chosen by our Basilea to help lead our people, you must remember – your first priority is to protect your people, your family, and the world from Judgement. By marrying Lady Natassa, you recognize this sacred duty. Do you accept?"

"I do," Neil said, loud and firm.

Eris smiled again. "As expected." She turned to Natassa, spinning the stick in tight circles. "My Lady, do you love this man?"

"With all my heart," Natassa said.

Eris nodded and turned to Dami. "And you, my Lord, do you love this man?"

"With all my heart," Dami said. He squeezed Neil's hand.

Eris turned to Neil. "Neil, do you love these Athánatos who have declared their love for you?"

Neil breathed deeply. "With everything that I am."

Eris smiled. She closed her eyes and spoke a long string of words in the Athánatos language. After five years with Natassa and Dami, Neil prided himself in the fact that he knew most of them. Then Eris switched to English and repeated it.

"A vow of marriage is a vow for eternity," she said. "Every marriage has a purpose, and the purpose for this marriage is love. It is a vow of trust, of love, of commitment, and of joy. It is a vow we take freely, by choice, and one not lightly broken. It is a symbol of love, and of responsibility." She opened her eyes. "Do you accept this?"

Neil glanced between Natassa and Dami, then the three of them turned to Eris, holding each other's hands tight. "We do."

Eris flipped the element stick up into the air and pounded it down, extinguishing the magic. The Phonar raised their feral voices in harmony. "The vow is spoken. Now we must seal it. But first, we seal your soul, your body, and your mind to reality." She turned to Neil. "Your Ei-Ei jewels, my Lord."

Neil took a deep breath. He reached into his pocket.

The shield laying against the Seal's base suddenly shattered to dust.

Dami jumped and Natassa gasped. Everyone stared.

Neil's heart raced. "What--"

Then the Seal's base exploded, along with the rest of her head, flinging dust everywhere. Eris held her arms up, shielding her face.

Neil stood, stepping in front of everyone, arms spread, adrenaline rushing his spine. No, no, no, this couldn't be happening, not here, not *now*. "Everyone--"

"*Defenders, shields up now!*"

Neil turned.

The Black Cloak rushed into the grove, dodging past everyone, his blue eyes wide and hands alight with some kind of magic.

Then the other statues started to crumble.

Dami and Natassa stood too and herded everyone out. Matt called for shields again, and the grove echoed with the high whine of Gems while the air shimmered with green, purple, and rainbow sheens.

Then the Purge cracked apart and collapsed at its base, crumbling to fine dust, leaving two statues fully destroyed. Cracks ripped through the Cloak and the Veil.

"*No!*" The Cloak ran forward and pressed his glowing hands to the two crumbling statues, lighting the area up so bright it blinded Neil. When the light faded, the Cloak statue stood straight and tall, fully restored -- *fully restored* -- but the Veil still looked about ready to fall over.

Ouranos stepped forward, fire and ice swirling around his hands. "Cloak, what is--"

"Well then," a familiar, terrifying voice echoed through the trees. "Good to see the family gathered together."

Neil turned, pulling Dami, Natassa, and Philip behind him, adrenaline ripping through him.

The Mage King himself. The man Neil was replacing.

Theron.

JUDGEMENT RETURNS

Immediately every elemental user there outside of Natassa's family pounded Theron with magic. Fire, ice, water, sand, rocks, lightning, and wind whipped through the grove, crashing through trees, ripping apart the blankets, and making Neil's fur stand on end. Everything smelled of burning, and the crackling sounds hurt Neil's ears.

And here he was with no magic of his own.

Zeke built magic on his hands too, growling.

Ouranos grabbed his shoulder. "Nephew, *no.* If you kill him you will break the Phonar's vow and we will lose them *all.*"

Zeke stared wide eyed. "What?"

"*Shields up, Guardians!*" the Cloak shouted.

"*Defenders, shield!*" Matt repeated, holding out his hands.

The high-pitched whine of shielding returned, and just in time. The swirling mass of magic surrounding Theron rushed back like a tsunami, engulfing the lot of them. Neil pulled Philip close to him and turned his back on the magic, shutting his eyes tight. Even with the shield, heat beat against his back like a hot oven, with quick flashes of ice and water and more than a few stones. Philip might have screamed, but Neil could hardly make it out in the rush of elements flying by his ears.

God, let this end, let everyone be okay, oh god, oh god--

The hurricane of magic ended almost as quickly as it began, leaving Neil bruised and battered, his fur and clothes soaked, frosted, burned, and gritty with sand. By some miracle the chain and arm bands still stuck to him, but the ceremonial body paint had washed off entirely.

But he still clung to Philip. "Don't let go," he said.

Because this wasn't over. And he smelled the problem before he saw it. That sickly, swampy, stench of death. He turned his head and looked up. Steam, smoke, dust, and magic lingered in the air, clouding the ruined grove, and distilling the light, making it hard to see.

And yet, there she was.

Judgement hovered over them, her inky black smile too wide for the size of her face. A gross, simulacra of an Athánatos, with quills, a long tail, and clawed toes, though covered head to toe in an inky, black liquid, with three, glowing blue eyes as if she was a giant Cast. Two massive inky wings stretched out from her back, nearly shapeless. She towered into the sky, standing at least twenty feet tall.

Judgement tilted her head, scattering thick black sludge drops everywhere. One landed on Neil's head, soaking his fur and dripping down his face. He wiped the sludge off, but the words the ink left in his head were unmistakable.

Greetings little Basileus.

Neil roared. Ignoring the pain and the worries for his friends, he whipped about, holding Philip behind him, and pulled out his sword. *"Excelsis, Deo!"*

The two fire Phonar weakly called out from somewhere in the electric fog and lit Neil's sword alight with violet and white fire. Neil lifted the blade toward Judgement, trying to grab her attention.

But Judgement wasn't looking at Neil. She had her gaze elsewhere. Neil glanced frantically around, trying to find where.

His heart seized.

She eyed their Guardians.

Matt and Izzy both lay on the ground, slowly pushing up on their hands and knees. Matt groaned, and Izzy's quills smoked slightly.

Neil ran for them, flames flailing about on his sword. *"Matt, Izzy, move now!"*

Matt and Izzy glanced up just as Judgement reached toward them.

Neil yowled and leapt forward, piercing her hand with his fire sword. She wailed and snatched her hand back, knocking Neil aside. Izzy helped Matt to his feet and they dashed off.

Neil bared his teeth in a feral snarl. This was *not* happening. Not on his wedding day! *Kill the damn summoner, kill the summon.* He could only assume that was Theron, that disgusting bastard.

His mind ran a mile a minute. How did Theron escape? How did he get Judgement?

How was he *awake?*

Judgement screamed like a banshee and raised those inky black wings, spreading Cast all over the ground. The black jelly-like blobs bulged in their centers, revealing three glowing blue eyes. They split their "heads" in wide, dripping smiles, and shrieked, chasing after the wedding guests.

The Athánatos people screamed and scattered into the woods, Cast at their heels, most unable to fight back. Those with elements shot magic at the monsters, but none of the mages were well trained aside from the Archons, and most of the Cast avoided their attacks.

Judgement reached for Izzy and Matt again.

Damnit! Neil waved to Ouranos. "Ouranos, take your family and the Archons and stop those damn Shadow Cast! Everyone else, protect the Guardians!"

Ouranos nodded. "Archons, sisters, to me!" Any Archons who could stand slowly got to their feet and followed Ouranos into the woods with Melaina and Natassa, their fur and hands alight with magic.

Half Neil's heart running off into danger. He prayed they'd be okay.

Philip gripped Neil's arm. "Neil--"

"Come with me," Damianos said, putting his hands on Philip's shoulders. "We will find safety."

"Go with Dami, Philip," Neil said. "We've got this."

Philip frowned, but nodded and the pair of them ran off toward the safety of the palace, taking the other half of Neil's heart with them.

Judgement lunged for Matt and Izzy again. The pair dove in different directions. Judgement reached for Izzy and snatched her up.

"Let her go!" Matt raised his hand up and called hurricane winds to his fingertips, biting sharp gusts against Judgement's inky hands.

But she didn't even react to it. Matt bared fangs. "I said let her *go!"* He slapped his hands together, causing a massive sonic boom with his wind magic, deafening Neil. It shook apart Judgement's hand into deformed puddles and sand, making her drop Izzy. Matt caught her and the pair crashed to the ground.

Judgement shrieked, reformed her inky hand, and grabbed for them again.

Trecheon slid between the Guardians and Judgement, snarling. He blasted hot beams of fire at her, blowing right through her hand, spilling black sandy "blood" through the wound. Roscoe ran up next to Trecheon and slammed his fist into the ground, shooting sharp spikes of earth through Judgement's arms.

Trecheon swirled fire around the spikes, then waved at Matt. "Go, to the palace, get out of here!"

"We've got this!" Roscoe said. "Run!"

Izzy stood and yanked Matt up. The pair ran.

Judgement pulled back again, wailing, gripping at the wounds, though she swatted Trecheon and Roscoe away into the mist, out of view. Sami called out, rushing after them. Neil's heart begged him to go after Trecheon.

But Judgement…

Sacha ran up to Neil. "The hell does she want with Matt and Izzy?"

"I don't know, but this ends *now.*" Neil scanned the area for Theron. Nowhere on the ground.

He looked up.

Theron rode on Judgement's shoulders, gripping the fake inky fur on her neck.

Neil narrowed his gaze. "Eris? You okay?"

Eris stood, coughing, but she nodded. "Yes, I believe…" Sacha ran over to her.

"Did we fully complete the vows?" Neil asked. "Am I Natassa's husband?"

Eris frowned and tilted her head. "No…"

"Then I'm not family yet. I still have time." He turned to Deo and Excelsis. "Take me up!" Excelsis cawed and spread his wings, growing large enough that Neil could ride his back. Neil climbed on.

"I'm coming with you," Zeke said, Archángeli next to him.

Neil frowned. "We can't risk you killing Theron."

"Then I'll go," Leah said. She stumbled forward, but pulled out her collapsible staff and shook it to length. "You need a distraction."

Zeke's tail lashed and he flattened his ears.

But Leah just nodded at him. Zeke sighed, lit both ends of her staff on fire, then waved to Archángeli. She climbed on their back and they took off, trailing fire and waving her staff at Judgement's face.

"I won't let anything happen to her," Neil said, and Excelsis took to the sky. *Kill the summoner, kill the summon.*

Leah pelted Judgement's fur with embers, shouting at her, grabbing her attention. Judgement growled, waving a hand about. Theron still clung to her neck, watching Leah intently, his ears twitching at the sounds of chaos below.

Now was Neil's chance. He lifted the sword and urged Excelsis to dive on Theron. They flew, sword out, aimed at Theron's back.

Judgement flashed her gaze in Neil's direction and snatched him and Excelsis out of the air. Neil yelped, dropping the sword.

"Neil!" Leah and Archángeli flew toward him, but Judgement swatted the pair of them away like a fly, sending them careening into the misty woods.

Neil gasped. *"Leah!"*

Save your breath for yourself, little Basileus, Judgement said, pulling him close to her face. He glared at her, teeth bared, struggling in her grip, though his heart beat so fast he was sure it'd pop through his chest. *You are not who I seek.*

"The hell do you want with Izzy and Matt?" Neil said, though his voice squeaked as she squeezed him.

As if I would reveal that to you. She narrowed her gaze at him. *You are nothing more than a gnat without those jewels, without the Phonar.* She smiled. *Let's see how you splatter like a common insect.* She plucked Excelsis out of her fist and crushed him with a squawk.

Neil glared, baring his teeth and roaring. He chewed at her hand, though she didn't react. He struggled, refusing to give up. *I am not dying today!*

A black alicorn, Angus' stone summon Magna, crashed her horn into Judgement's wrist, ripping her fist off in a wave of black sand and ink. Judgement wailed as the appendage fell, releasing Neil. Neil scrambled out of the loose fingers and jumped.

Deo caught him, thankfully, gripping his shoulders tight in her claws. *My Basileus--*

"Where are Matt and Izzy?" Neil said, out of breath. God, pins and needles *everywhere.*

I am unsure, Deo said. *The magic mist has made it difficult to see--*

"Find them!" Neil said, pushing aside the pain.

Deo called out and dove into the mist, still clutching Neil. He frantically searched through the fog.

The Guardians ran across the mossy lawn toward the palace. He pointed. "There!"

That was a mistake. Judgement glanced where he pointed and turned toward the Guardians.

Neil gritted his teeth. "Damn it!"

But then Darvin appeared in the mist. Neil turned to him. "Deo, drop me and get Darvin to Matt and Izzy. Go!" Deo let Neil go and he rolled on the grass, picking up stones and sticks in his fur. He righted himself just as Deo grabbed Darvin by the shoulders. "Darvin, cloak them!"

"On it!" Darvin waved a hand and Matt and Izzy vanished from view.

But it didn't last.

Judgement lifted a foot and stomped Deo and Darvin. Deo vanished with a squawk and a mess of feathers, and Darvin flattened to his Shadow Cast form, soaking into the grass. The Guardians instantly reappeared.

Neil cursed. He turned back toward the grove. "Chad!"

"He's badly injured!" Sacha lay over him, pressing magic into his body, while Ana held her Gem, enhancing it with her power. Andre gripped his hand, muttering something Neil couldn't make out.

Shit. "Anyone!"

Zeke and Jaden ran out now, their hands and quills frozen with ice magic. Working almost as one, they peppered Judgement's body with ice spikes, spilling hot sand out of every wound.

But she didn't stop moving.

"Damnit!" Neil ran after them, even though he had no way to fight. Every step was agony.

Matt and Izzy had almost made it to the palace. Damianos and Archon Electrik were there, with Philip hiding behind them, blasting Judgement with lightning, waving Matt and Izzy forward.

Judgement flapped her wings, littering the ground with fake Shadow Cast. The Cast formed a barrier around her, Matt, and Izzy, cutting everyone off from them. Izzy shouted, angry. Huge holes blew through the Cast as she slammed them with her destructive healing magic, but they filled in instantly. Matt's wind rippled through the Cast, though the wall wouldn't budge long enough for them to escape.

"No!" Jaden shouted, and he blasted the wall with ice. It did little more than freeze in place. Zeke shot flames at them, but the wall held.

Judgement reached down and scooped Izzy and Matt into her hand.

"Leave them *alone!*" Zeke shouted, and shot ice, fire, and lightning at the massive summon.

But before the magic hit, she vanished. All the Cast, the magic mist, and the sickening smell of death vanished with her.

And so did Matt and Izzy.

They were gone.

CASTING THEORIES

Neil stood in the middle of the atrium, despite the pain, looking over the survivors in this makeshift hospital, picking at loose threads on his worn-out army-green bomber jacket. He needed the "king in the green jacket" as Eris put it. He needed familiarity and strength.

But his mind and body buzzed and his heart had ripped in two.

Yes, he should be here with the Athánatos people.

But he should also be looking for Matt and Izzy. Wherever they were. Assuming they were even alive.

The whole thing had happened so damn fast. Swirling magic, broken Cast, Phonar destruction left and right, injuries all around. And… death. *Death on his wedding day.* Seven of the Archons' guests had fallen. Many more were missing. His heart ached.

God, Izzy and Matt better not be among that number.

It had been hell trying to get everything back under control after Judgement vanished with the Guardians. The wedding guests had scattered about, many of them injured, and finding everyone took all the survivors' attention - an extra hard task while everyone freaked out about their missing Guardians.

It wasn't until Sacha, Jaden, and Ana called for attention and started issuing commands that things moved more smoothly. The Defenders responded well to Jaden and Sacha. Darvin, Roscoe, Sami, and several others were scouring the island now, looking for any trace of Theron and Judgement.

Neil hadn't yet thanked any of them for taking charge like that. He had been so stunned by the whole thing, he couldn't act himself. Thank God for his support systems.

Jaden, Sacha, and Ana stayed as neutral and stoic as possible, their faces like stone masks. But the longer they went without news about Matt and Izzy, the more those masks cracked. Except for Jaden, who seemed to only get more stone-faced and distant. Leah had told Neil privately that this was the hardened attitude he had had when she had first met him. Focused on the outside, broken on the inside.

Neil shook his head. That shouldn't have happened. He should have taken control, damn it. Maybe he wasn't cut out for this leader thing after all. He stuck his hands in his pockets, finger a slim piece of paper. A bucket list. One he had started years ago, when he was sure his assassinhood would kill him. One he had added to later when the Zyearthlings gave him home. One he had finally completed when he got engaged to Dami and Natassa.

A list of things to do before death. Grim at first, then joyful later. Goals he hoped he could finally live out now that life seemed real again. He hadn't shared it with them yet. He planned to bring it up once things got settled after marriage and Athánatos was stable again. But once again, Judgement and the damn Shadow Cast threatened to take that away.

On top of that… Theron.

Theron.

Just seeing him there, casual as could be, and fully aware, was enough to set Neil off. Judgement was bad enough, but she still felt distant and… beatable. At least while Ronan held her as his summon. They had beaten her twice before, at the Desert Wall and in the wilds of Canada.

But Theron… that was something else. Especially when he had somehow bypassed all that Ouranos had done to keep him underfoot.

He should be out *looking* for him!

But Neil was planted here. In the makeshift hospital. Refusing to give up or show weakness.

Especially when he had failed to get everything under control after Judgement vanished.

Zeke and Damianos had left with the Archons to scour the palace for any rips in the Veil, any opening where an enemy could get in and get Theron's jewels out of Ouranos' prison. Neil wasn't hopeful though. Who was left on the mainland who would know how to get through the Veil, let alone who Theron was? Excepting Ackerson, who knew how to get here, but didn't have the means. And it wasn't likely he knew or even cared who Theron was.

The whole thing made no sense.

The Cloak, strangely, stuck around, working some kind of weird magic on the Veil statue, which looked ready to collapse at any time. On top of everything else going on, they definitely couldn't handle that, because as far as Neil knew, if the statue broke, the Veil would fall. Exposing the world to the Vanishing Island, the Athánatos, the Defenders, *magic* - it would be a hell they'd never escape. No one bothered the Cloak while he worked.

Despite the urgency of the missing Guardians, the hospital had a relative calm about it, now that most of the injured had been healed up and sent on their way. Only a few lingered, Chad among them. He had apparently taken an ice spike to the chest and nearly died.

If Ana hadn't been there to enhance Sacha's magic… Neil would have to remind her of that later. Lift her up and remind her that she still had a purpose here.

As it stood, Chadwick wasn't 100%, but he had insisted that Sacha rest and Trecheon and Leah tend to the other injuries. Didn't help that he showed signs of shock and overwhelm while they healed him. Leah said some people reacted that way to healing. Almost like a rejection. They could still heal him, but it would take time and they'd have to be cautious or they could accidentally kill him. He lay on a wicker couch near the back wall, Andre at his side, gripping his hand, while the healers worked on others.

Admittedly, Trecheon wasn't much help as a healer. Whatever had been plaguing him before completely engulfed him now, with the Guardians suddenly missing. He healed a few injuries now and then, utterly silent, following Sacha around like she'd vanish if he didn't.

Damn all of this.

He had help though. Charlotte had no magic, but she had a good understanding of first-aid, and was able to staunch blood and clean wounds while they waited for healers. She wore a remarkable mask. That good stoic Azure outlook, perhaps. She got Philip helping her, which kept him distracted. Neil was grateful.

Leah had done all she could with healing, and when her power gave out, she headed to the Athánatos library with Melaina and Embrik, at Neil's insistence. After all, the Purge had broken. Maybe some of the books with holes in them had been restored. Including the Book of Summons. Could be helpful. She took as many of the summons with her as she could.

Thankfully most of them had recovered quickly, despite Judgement's destruction.

Hopefully she'd find answers.

Sacha walked up to Neil, frowning. Trecheon continued quietly healing some of the Athánatos, but he still stuck close to her. She poked Neil's shoulder. "Hey. You need healing."

"Other people need it more," Neil said, barely able to keep his voice steady. He pulled away.

Sacha flicked her ears back. "Neil, you can't lead when you're injured."

Watch me. "How's Chad?"

Sacha narrowed her gaze. "Neil…"

"Better," Chadwick called from the back wall. He moved to sit up.

Andre held a hand on his shoulder. "Absolutely not. You stay here." Chadwick sighed and lay back down again. Andre carefully wrapped an arm around him, avoiding the injury. "I don't know what kind of backwards-ass place Zyearth is thinking healers are worthless. We could use a hell of a lot more right now."

Sacha cleared her throat and eyed Neil pointedly.

Neil avoided rolling his eyes. "Fine." He carefully slipped off his jacket and let Sacha work on him.

Natassa entered the room, ears flat. Her tail dragged along the ground. "Neil…"

Neil perked his ears. "Any news?"

Natassa took a shuddering breath, then walked to Neil and threw her arms around him as best she could with Sacha healing him. He held her tight with one arm and buried his face in her neck. At least she was safe. He breathed deeply. "Take your time, okay?" he said, as much for himself as for her.

She nodded and stepped back, shoulders slumped. "Unfortunately, we have confirmed it. Father's *féretro* is missing. The box that held his Ei-Ei jewels in stasis, keeping him asleep. Somehow someone got ahold of it and removed the jewels."

"But didn't Ouranos turn him into a Drifter?" Neil said. "The same way Ouranos is."

"He is indeed a Drifter," Natassa said. "I am sure few noticed in the chaos, but a few witnesses mentioned he had no Soul Jewels around his eyes, and was without pupils, just like Ouranos." She swallowed hard. "He was wearing a woven bracelet though. The kind of bracelet he held other Drifters' Soul Jewels on."

"I *fought* Drifters," Neil said, though the memories made his fur stand on end. "They were basically mindless zombies. They didn't speak. They didn't think. Hell, they didn't even react to pain. And now Theron is awake and showing the same mental capacities that Ouranos is? How is that possible?"

"Someone anchored him to his soul."

Neil turned. Ouranos walked into the room with tightly formed fists and a lashing tail.

Neil frowned. "The hell does that mean? I know jack shit about Drifters, aside from the fact that they have no soul."

"They still… own a soul, for lack of a better term," Ouranos said. "But they are temporarily separated from it, either because of injury, or by force. Their bodies remain alive with the Ei-Ei jewels, but their souls no longer possess their bodies."

Sacha flicked her ears. "So when you say he was anchored to his soul…"

"It means someone bridged the gap between his soul and his body," Ouranos said. "When I regained connection to my soul, it was because a stranger built a bridge for me. I recall very little of the event, but the effect is evident."

"A stranger, huh?" Neil asked. "How?"

Ouranos shook his head. "I do not know. I had believed that it was Black Bound elixir that reconnected me to my soul that fateful night. I thought I had remembered that black liquid when I regained consciousness, and it was Matthew's Black Bound elixir that fully broke Theron's hold on me when I was on Zyearth. But seeing how rare Lexi Gems are on this planet, and how much rarer still Black Binding is, I cannot believe that was the cause. Theron has clearly found his own path."

Sacha finished up with Neil and stood. "There. It's not perfect though. Watch that knee for a bit and be careful about sleeping tonight. Still got some bruises and light burns."

"Like I'll sleep tonight," Neil said.

Sacha flattened her ears. "I hear you." She turned to Ouranos, her orange and white striped tail twitching. "I never interacted with you directly when Theron had more control over you, but didn't you say he had like, physical control? Like a puppet?"

"He could essentially insert his essence into my body and use me, yes," Ouranos said slowly.

"So could you do that to him?" Sacha asked. "Get into his head, see his thoughts? You could figure out who took the *féretro* thing, force him to get back here, and put him in his place. Maybe even figure out where he took Matt and Izzy, and stop Judgement if she formed an oath with him."

Ouranos crossed his arms. "I had thought of that but was unsuccessful in trying it. Theron only had access to my thoughts when I was a full Drifter. Once my soul was connected, his access was limited. It seems whatever it was that reconnected Theron to his soul had the same effect, perhaps even amplified since we both have bridges now." He shook his head. "However, one good side effect, I have yet to hear him in my own head. It is likely that our similar states have broken any connection we once had."

"Silver linings," Andre said. "Glad we don't have that shit on top of all this."

"I am as well," Ouranos said.

Neil rubbed his chin. "So where do the souls go? Couldn't you go wherever that is and sever the connection?"

Ouranos flattened an ear and exchanged a glance with Natassa.

Natassa rubbed her arm. Light filtered over her black fur. "Lost souls wander the Aether. A kind of… limbo where a soul awaits its fate. A soul lost to injury would wander it until it is coaxed back or released to Draso's Palace. A stolen soul, however, is chained to the Aether, quite literally. The only way to free it, or break any connection it had to our world, would be to break those chains."

"And that is why we forbid the practice of restoring forced Drifters," Ouranos said, eyeing his sister. "Because the only way to break those chains is with a sacrifice. Either a person living must die and allow their soul to release the bonds of the Drifter, or they must physically enter the Aether as a living body and break the chains that way, which will destroy their physical bodies, killing them."

"We cannot enter the Aether even if we wanted to," Natassa said. "Both the *Fýlakas* in charge of lighting the path and her apprentice died during the war with Theron."

Not that I'd want someone dying for this anyway. Neil's tail thrashed about. "How the hell could anyone have stolen the *féretro* and fixed Theron's screwed up state without us *knowing?*"

"I have not enough evidence to guess," Ouranos said.

Chad coughed. "Hey, Angus, any luck with your scrying?"

Angus sat cross-legged in the corner by a large white pillar, a mirror in his lap, his leather wings slightly unfurled. He stared blankly forward, but then shook his head. "No. Despite having Matt and Izzy's last known location, I can't fixate an anchor point. I don't know if that means their current location is interfering, or if it has something to do with the Black Cloak being so close. His weird time aura has messed with my magic before."

"If the Cloak *really* cared," Jaden said, walking into the atrium, his ears flat against his head. "Then he'd tell us where they are and we could go get them. He's a damn time traveler. He *knows* what's going to happen." Ice crystals frosted over his quills and collected on his fingertips. "I know I said I trusted him, but *fire and ice,* why doesn't he do anything to *stop* all this?"

Angus flicked his ear and his fur fluffed up. "That's the curse, Jaden. You stand here, marinating in anxiety, waiting for what happens next. The Cloak already *knows.* The pain, the heartache, the injuries, the death. And there's nothing he can do about it… except make sure it happens exactly as it's supposed to. He can't stop it. If he does, the end goal crumbles to the ground. His burden as someone tasked with maintaining this damn timeline." He settled back down. "Be grateful you're not wearing the Cloak."

Trecheon flattened his ears and looked away at Angus' words. Jaden frowned and crossed his arms, staring at the floor, muttering about an end goal no one was clear on.

Neil shook his head, torn. He turned to Ouranos. "I don't suppose you've been able to use your bond thing to get to Matt?"

Trecheon paused his healing on one of the Athánatos, glancing over at them, ears perked.

Ouranos rubbed his arm. "No, which is disturbing in itself. It is like I am completely cut off from his presence."

"*Shit,*" Jaden said. He kicked a discarded pillow.

Sacha pasted an ear back, her tail twitching. "That's not a good sign."

"It… is not," Ouranos said. "But I feel as if I would have felt more than just absence if he had died. We felt absence like this before, when the Veil interfered. I cannot be certain though." He paused. "That might be a sign, actually. Perhaps they are no longer on the island. Which would not be ideal, but at least it would give us a place to begin searching." He shook himself. "I regret to say it, but we have another problem as well. Theron's Drifters."

Everyone turned to him.

Shit. The last thing Neil wanted to do was to face down the Athánatos he had grown close to during the last five years. "Where are they? Are they attacking?"

"They are gone," Ouranos said. "No trace of them. While Theron was separated from his soul by the *féretro,* his Drifters had anchors back to their souls. With him free again, I suspect they have lost those anchors and have fallen back under his command."

Neil's body buzzed. "That's *definitely* not good."

Natassa lowered her gaze. "I have a guess as to what Theron will do with them, and it is not one anyone will like to hear. It is likely the reason why we escaped the battle with so few scars. But there is perhaps some hope in it, as it likely means Matt and Izzy are still alive."

Everyone turned to her. Neil flattened his ears.

"He is hoarding victims to create true Shadow Cast again," Natassa said. "And Matt and Izzy's Black Bound elixir is the final key he needs."

THE BLACK BOUND

Izzy woke up to her head pounding and every inch of her body aching. She groaned and turned over on the moss while gritty sand or dirt or who knew what dug into her fur.

Earth and *stone.*

She shook herself free of debris, keeping her eyes tightly shut to avoid dirt getting into them. Everything ached, and several patches on her body burned. "Matt? You there?"

"…I'm here," Matt said coughing. A jangling bell sound echoed between Izzy's ears, but she pushed it aside. "You okay--holy *shit.*"

Izzy rubbed at her eyes and opened them. "What--" She stared, jaw loose. "Holy *shit.*"

They were still on Athánatos island… maybe. There was forest on the left, the palace on the right, and the mossy lawn in between, full of clover and flowers. But everything was… dull. Grayed out almost, like someone had turned the saturation of a picture down to nearly zero. And though light filled the area, a black, cloudless, sunless sky hovered over them. All completely silent and lifeless. No wind. No animals or birds. No residents.

Just emptiness.

Izzy's heart stopped, her mind racing. She blinked several times, but the world around them never changed. She shook her head, pinched herself, held her breath until she couldn't anymore, but the sky remained black and the grass dull and gray.

Not her vision. Not a dream.

So where were they?

Izzy shivered. "What is going on…?"

"Your guess is as good as mine," Matt said. "Maybe some strange magic from Judgement. Definitely nothing good though." He helped Izzy to her feet. "How are you feeling?"

"Sore," Izzy said. "And burnt in some places."

Matt frowned. "Not good…" He looked her over. "We need to get you to a healer."

"If there is one…" Izzy checked the cloth pouch on her belt, grateful she had had the sense to include it in her outfit. Thankfully the Gem seemed fine. She sighed. "Are you injured at all?"

Matt tapped his feet on the ground. "Sore. Tired. Achey. But I've been worse." He frowned. "I'd rather you save your energy."

"For now." Izzy glanced around again. The dull gray world was like some kind of bizzarro, backwards world… Like a mirror or a copy that didn't have all the information to rebuild correctly. And it was cold. Unsettling. Izzy hugged herself, rubbing the fur on her bare arms. What she wouldn't give for her usual Defender uniform right now instead of the fancy Athánatos skirt.

Matt wrapped an arm across her shoulders. "Come on. Let's go into the palace and see if we can figure out what's going on."

Izzy leaned into Matt as they trudged carefully across the clover lawn. She kept her eyes forward. The sky was the most unsettling part of all this, and she didn't want to look at it any more than she had to.

What the hell had happened? She and Matt had been running from Judgement, when she scooped them up and crushed them in her fist.

No, not crushed. She just balled them up in her fist. The suffocating blackness beat against Izzy's ears and drowned out everything but her own frantic breathing. She had blacked out… maybe… then woke up here. Wherever here was.

She chewed her lip. Judgement *could* have crushed them. She could have ended their lives right then and there, and no one would have been able to stop her. Theron would finally have his revenge.

But she didn't. They were left alive. Hell, they had specifically been *targeted,* then kept alive…

Which likely meant only one thing. Theron wanted them for something. "Matt--"

"Hold on," Matt said suddenly. "Is that Baltazar?"

Izzy turned. Baltazar, one of the sentries of Athánatos, stood at the entrance to the palace, sword in hand. His fur was its normal jet black, and he wore bright gold-yellow pants, as was common with the sentries. He wasn't dull colored like the rest of this strange world. Izzy relaxed a bit. "Oh, thank Draso. We--"

Without a word, Baltazar lifted the sword and charged them.

Izzy's fur stood on end.

"Split up!" Matt dashed left. Izzy dove right, rolling on the desaturated moss.

Baltazar rushed Izzy and brought his sword down on her. She threw up her hands, shielding, barely catching the blade. "Baltazar, what are you *doing?* It's me!"

But then she got a good look at his eyes. Pupilless, yes, because he had been one of Theron's Drifters. But now… expressionless. And around his hands and feet, phantom chains, barely visible in the dull, colorless world. Back to the mindless, puppeted Drifter he had been when Theron was active.

Theron had *control again.*

Baltazar beat methodically against her shield, cracking it bit by bit, his face blank.

A wave of panic hit Izzy hard, quickening her heartbeat. Memories of fighting Drifters in a violent attempt to save Ouranos' life on their first visit to the island flashed in her mind - the stink of blood, the desperation, the clash of swords, Ouranos slowly dying, her healing magic refusing to heal, only kill, kill, kill, all those Drifters coming at her, their bodies strewn about, dead by her hand, unaware--

But I had no choice! I had to or they would have killed me! Izzy's whole body buzzed with adrenaline. *But I* know *Baltazar! I can't--*

Matt rushed in and wrapped his arms around Baltazar's waist and lifted him over his head, throwing him to the ground. Baltazar dropped the sword, which Matt stole. He stood in front of Izzy. "Baltazar, don't make me use this--"

"Matt, he can't help it!" Izzy said. "Theron's *back*. He's a mindless Drifter again!"

Matt's ears perked and his quills stood on end.

Baltazar tackled Matt. Izzy leapt out of the way as they rolled around, fighting for the sword, limbs tangled. Matt's magic flew about, but did nothing to push Baltazar off. Baltazar gripped Matt's shoulders and gained the advantage, pushing him hard on his back and snatching the sword out of his hand. He lifted it above Matt's head.

A loud, clear bell rang in Izzy's head, along with Matt's voice, buried between her ears.

Not like this!

"No!" With tears in her eyes, she pressed her hands against Baltazar's back and surged the Black Bound healing magic through them - the destructive healing that had killed Drifters and Shadow Cast alike. The magic ripped through Baltazar's body, turning his fur to ash and his skin gray, shutting down his body.

Baltazar threw his head back, still without expression, and dropped the sword. The blade stuck fast in the ground, just barely missing Matt's head. Baltazar slumped off Matt and lay motionless. Matt scrambled away.

Izzy hugged herself. "Baltazar, I'm sorry, *I'm so sorry.*"

Matt stared, ears flat. But before he could speak, Baltazar moved. His body lifted up by his shoulders like a puppet and pulled him up to his feet. He reached for the sword and turned back on them, the ghost of those chains clanging like bells in Izzy's ears.

Fresh panic ran through her. "What… how?"

Baltazar charged them again. They split up, with Matt whipping up wind around the sentry, trying to distract him. Stones, sticks, and other debris beat against his body and face.

He walked through it like he felt nothing.

"What the hell is going on?" Matt said.

"I don't know!" Izzy dashed to the left as Baltazar stabbed at her. She shielded. "He should have *died.* Why didn't he?"

Matt stared. Bells jingled in Izzy's ears, along with Matt's words. *The chains… chaining him here…*

Izzy's eyes grew wide.

Where the hell did Theron drop them?

"The chains," Matt said. "Maybe if we destroy them?"

Izzy charged her hands with healing magic and reached for the chains around Baltazar's wrists. He leapt back, then stabbed at her with the sword, grazing her hand.

Black blood spilled from the wound. Izzy stared wide-eyed, shock rushing her spine.

Then a jangling bell ran in her head, with Matt's voice again. *Izzy, get back!*

She dove out of the way, feeling the wind of the swinging blade brush her fur. The bell cacophony returned, making her ears ring.

Matt whipped up a powerful tornado in an attempt to lift Baltazar out of the way, moving between him and Izzy. He gritted his teeth. *Get the chains!*

She blinked at him, stuck to the spot. His words... in her head again.

No... it isn't... this can't be REAL.

"Izzy!" Matt said. "You need to get the chains, *now!* I can't hold him!"

Izzy shook herself and refocused. Gotta get those chains. She snatched Baltazar's fallen sword off the ground and lifted it up--

Watch out!

Someone bodied her, knocking her to the ground. She lost the sword in the fall, fighting her attacker.

Stavros. Another of Theron's Drifters... another friend. He pinned her arms with his legs and held out a sharp dagger, his face blank.

"Get off her!" Matt blasted wind at him, knocking him clean off and sending him flying across the meadow. Matt stood there, stunned, his fur on end.

Izzy stared. Matt never used his magic to push anyone. Not after what happened with his high school bully Warren. Shock froze his features in place. His tornadoes vanished in a heartbeat.

A thin film of sticky, goopy Black Bound elixir instantly coated his fingertips.

Baltazar rushed Matt and gripped his hand, squeezing. Collecting elixir.

Collecting elixir.

That's why Theron wanted them alive.

Matt pulled his hand free and stepped back, teeth bared, wind whipping about, more Black Bound elixir building on his hands. The jangles bounced around Izzy's head, with more of Matt's words. *You're not getting this elixir again, Theron, not again, do you hear me?!* Panic. His heart beat in her ears.

She stood. "Matt--"

Footsteps pounded against the thin moss. A lot of them. Izzy turned.

Every Drifter sentry that had survived the war rushed toward them. Each one with a sword. Each one a friend. Each one seeking more elixir.

Each one invincible.

Izzy stared wide-eyed. She gripped Matt's hand, hoping to hide the film of elixir.

"Run."

THE BOOK OF SUMMONS

Leah sat at a large, mahogany table in the high-ceilinged Athánatos library, one of the few buildings in the Athánatos palace fully closed in. She had her snout buried in the Book of Summons, drinking in all the words that the Purge had ripped from its pages so long ago, desperate for answers.

But so far, nothing. Partly because new letters from the Athánatos' ornate alphabet decorated the pages where they were once blank. But they were more archaic and didn't match the modern language Leah was familiar with. Despite years of study of the Athánatos written word, Leah didn't recognize most of them.

Upon closer inspection, many of the words that had been there previously were altered - edits strewn about the page, changing old letters to newer ones, making it easier for modern Athánatos to read. But with the old, once-Purged alphabet skewing the modern edits, trying to read what had been lost was harder than ever. Leah pressed her lips together. That wasn't promising. She'd have to hope one of the older Athánatos would remember the old alphabet and could read it well enough with the new alphabet scrawled on top of it.

Though she wasn't sure any of this would help right now. They didn't need answers about summons.

They needed their Guardians.

But they also needed to get rid of Judgement. Since the Phonar were created to fight Judgement, the Book of Summons had her history, and with the Purged content back on the page, they might find a way to fight back. Both Neil and Ouranos had suggested she look through it, so look she did. It was better than standing around anyway, especially with her magic exhaustion.

Her first visit to this massive, imposing, beautiful library had been filled with anxiety and stress. As the newly-appointed head of the Summon's Department, she hadn't the experience or the confidence to lead a research team here.

A lot had changed in the years she had been away from home. Years that she still struggled to keep track of, considering her weird time travel to the War of Eons with Zeke. Her confidence had improved, she held a somewhat better grip over the Thought Factory, and more than anything, she was surrounded by people who she cared about, and who cared about her.

A shame it had to fall apart like this. She could only hope they'd find something here to stop Judgement. And hope that the others would find Guardians Gildspine and Azure.

Jaden must be devastated. She'd have to check on him as soon as she could.

She scratched the fur on her side, just under the *okaa*, peeling off some of the paint. The Thought Factory focused in on that paint and she slowly peeled it off her fur, giving in to the stim. Paint could be reapplied and this would help her focus, at least for now.

The Phonar surrounded her as they had the last time she had shuffled through this, just before she had met Zeke. They perched on chairs, the table, and ladders running up the big, full shelves of books and scrolls. Though this time, the birds eyed her curiously, anxiously even, their feathers ruffled.

And she couldn't blame them.

She glanced at Archángeli and frowned. "You sure you can't piece together anything from before the Purge?"

Archángeli shook their head, whipping little breezes between Leah's ears. *Unfortunately no. I feel there is some deep knowledge or memory that the breaking of the Purge has unlocked, but I haven't yet figured out how to process it. My mind is a rush of memories that I had forgotten.* They buried their beak in their wing, then fluffed up again, clearly agitated. *It will take time to sift through them. There is so much here and it's all blurred together.*

For you and the rest of us, Excelsis said, dripping harmless purple embers on Leah's snout. *Though I feel the same as Archángeli. There is something to be found. We just cannot process it yet.*

"Keep at it, but take care of your mental health," Leah said. "The Purge had hid a lot at once, and you *lived* it. It's bound to affect you the most." She turned back to the Book of Summons.

"Nothing yet, then?"

Leah lifted her head. Zeke walked in, ears flat. Dirt and sweat clung to his fur, and most of the ceremonial paint had flaked off, though he hadn't changed into normal street clothes yet. His very modern glasses clashed with the old ceremonial dress of the Athánatos. It would have been amusing if the situation wasn't so dang serious. Leah did notice he had put away his *osaa* and silver chain though, wearing only the Athánatos pants and no shirt.

Without another word, Leah dropped her glasses on the table, put the book down, and crossed the distance between them in three big strides. She wrapped her arms around his waist and buried her face in his chest.

Zeke pulled her close to him, resting his head on hers, taking a deep breath.

She snuggled deep into his fur and took everything in - the dirt, the musk of sweat, the faint smell of paint, his arms tight around her, and of course, the social jewel bond that they had so carefully cultivated over the last three years.

Mostly they felt their bond through food smells, though years of refinement expanded that, and now Leah could get full pictures in her head of the scenes their emotions painted for them, scents and all. Right now it produced a gentle, comforting scent. Warm cookies, hot coffee, and the sharp smell of a fireplace.

Her healing magic didn't detect any problems in Zeke, now that Sacha had healed him. Thank Draso he hadn't been badly hurt in that attack. Or… killed. She shuddered thinking about it.

Even before the attack, the wedding had held a mild sense of dread. Because while it was exciting and happy… it also meant the end of her time on Earth. The Master Guardian was calling his Earth-dwelling Defenders home. And despite all the protests from Sacha, he put his foot down. They had jobs to do, and it was time to get back to those jobs.

For Leah especially, considering the strangely unsettling number of new, unregistered summons and summoners popping up all over the settled universe. It had increased exponentially ever since she discovered their old enemy Sharp had somehow strong-armed two summons, Drifa and Kaoru, to take the Summon's Oath against their will.

She still burned at the injustice of it all. It was bad enough that someone as terrible as Sharp had gotten summons, but the fact that he had somehow forced the gryfon and wyvern to become summons was downright despicable. Unheard of.

After Sharp's death, the summons had taken off before Leah could help them. The pair had no one. Nothing. Except a wish for death, which they'd never get as summons. It was a permanent existence. She hoped they were doing well. That they had found a summoner who would take care of them… since she clearly couldn't.

She'd get to the bottom of this.

But despite all her efforts, Leah couldn't do much to research that problem while on Earth. She just didn't have the resources, even with the A.I. Pilot connecting her to the Galactic InterPol databases.

However… the thought of leaving Zeke behind on Earth was too much. Her best friend, her most important companion, her dearest relationship.

It'd only be enhanced by the fact that she had almost no one waiting for her at home. Her Uncle Garnet, sure, but no real friends. Just coworkers she'd occasionally wave to. Most of her friends she'd be leaving behind. Andre, Chadwick, Melaina, Ana and her sisters, Embrik, Angus… even Jaden, who still wasn't bound to come back to Zyearth and insisted on staying until they found Alexina.

And of course, Zeke.

She had been trying to work up the courage for months to ask him to come live on Zyearth with her. But he had Andre here. And he had settled in so well with Athánatos and fallen in love with it. And after he had lost one family with the deaths of his moms and a home on the mainland with his disappearance during the time traveling, she couldn't bring herself to rip him away to a brand-new place all over again. So she had blocked that part of their bond and hid the thought.

She'd be alone again. Back on a planet who looked down on her for being a healer and feared her for being a healer-S.

No one on Earth even gave her healing magic a second thought. There was no fear about touching her. Zeke was very physically affectionate, and even Chad, Angus, and Jaden often expressed their affection with touches, hugs, shoulder bumps, whatever. No qualms about it. Andre especially hugged her with abandon and wanted to learn everything he could about being a healer. He loved it.

If only her fellow Defenders felt the same way.

She hadn't felt it in ages, but the Thought Factory honed in on an old desire of hers - a want to be a summoner. Because summons would be companions she'd always have, who weren't afraid of her magic.

But no luck. And soon she'd go home. Soon everything she had here would be gone.

She'd just have to learn how to live with it. Which is why she used every spare chance to be close to her friends, and especially Zeke, before she lost it.

He stroked the fur on the back of her head, the smell of hot peppers biting her nose. He sighed. "I know." But that's all he offered.

She took a deep breath, taking in the moment one more time, then pulled away. She grabbed his hand and led him to the table, then put her glasses back on. "Haven't found anything yet, unfortunately," she said. "I don't know if the Book of Summons is going to give us much. So far most of what I've found is just about the rules of their unique oath. Nothing we didn't already understand. And a lot of it is an older form of the written language. I'm struggling to read it, especially with the modern alphabet scribbled on top." She sat hard on a chair. "Anything on your end?"

Zeke shook his head. "No. Dami and I couldn't find any rips anywhere. Either whoever did this was damn thorough and already closed the rip up, or this was an inside job… though I doubt that. I can't imagine anyone would want Theron walking about." His tail flailed. "There were a *lot* of footprints in the dust around Theron's little crypt though. Too many to discern one from another. I spoke with Ouranos and apparently Theron's Drifter sentries are all missing. I suspect those footprints belong to them."

Leah twitched her whiskers. Just what they needed.

"Oh, good," Embrik said. "You have returned, Zeke." He and Melaina wandered toward Leah's table, laden with books. Embrik perked his ears. "Any news?"

Zeke shook his head and reiterated what he had told Leah.

Melaina frowned. "The, ah, 'inside job' does not fill me with hope," she said. "Perhaps we should put together a palace census, see who is missing. It would be helpful to keep track of our missing Drifters in any case."

"Good idea," Zeke said. He turned. "Archángeli?"

I shall suggest it to Lady Natassa and return. They opened their wings and left the library.

"I am glad we did not write in any of these books," Embrik said. He put down his pile and passed a particularly ornate book accented in green and gold to Leah. Zeke helped Melaina spread her books out on the table.

"These were fully blank," Melaina said, thumbing through another book. "I had believed them to be empty, waiting to be filled, but it turns out, they have writing that the Purge had completely erased from their pages. We believe these are journals."

"Journals!" Leah flipped through Embrik's book. Sure enough, every page was filled from top to bottom with Athánatos letters and sketches - buildings, trees, even Athánatos quilar.

She twitched one ear. Just like the Book of Summons, most of the alphabet was unfamiliar. Both she and Zeke had studied the Athánatos language with a purpose over the last three years and while fluency was a ways off, she still considered herself relatively proficient. Frustration burned in her chest that she couldn't read it. "These are really old." Zeke pushed his glasses up on his snout and glanced over the book, frowning.

"They are," Melaina said. "Many of the letters have evolved over the centuries. I am afraid even we will have a difficult time deciphering them. I intend to contact some of the older Athánatos and see if they recognize them. Abrax is our current chronicler, so I would hope he would have some knowledge, and Eris is the oldest palace dweller I know. But all the Athánatos from that era are dead. We may not be able to read them."

"Hmm." Leah glanced over at Excelsis. "I have an idea." She brought her book over to the raven. "I don't suppose you can read this? Considering this is your era."

Excelsis clicked his beak and tilted his head. He flicked embers at her. *I am not Athánatos.*

"But you know the language," Leah said. "The Athánatos only picked up English during the last century when Theron's war forced them to the mainland."

Excelsis tapped a talon and ground his beak together, as if thinking. *Speaking yes, though reading and writing is not something I remember doing as a summon. However…"* He lifted a wing. *"With the Purge gone, if I had learned the written language in my mortal life, I may yet be able to read it.*

"It's worth a try," Leah said. "Otherwise, we're in for a long research session." She laid the book on the table in front of Excelsis.

The phoenix preened the crook of his wing, then glanced over the open pages. He squinted, then stood tall, opening his wings and squawking, sending harmless embers into the air. *By the Sisters!*

Zeke leaned over the table. "What did you find?"

This is indeed a journal, Excelsis said. *And I not only recognize the words, I recognize the author's handwriting.*

Leah grinned. "Amazing! Whose is it?" Not that she'd know who it was, but the excitement bubbled in her.

This is a journal of an exalted, Excelsis said. *Of someone with a great destiny.* He met Leah's gaze, his violet eyes shining. *This journal belongs to Archángeli.*

CHAINS OF BURDEN

Matt ran.

Because what else could he do? Fight hundreds of unkillable Drifters in this monochromatic world with a midnight sky?

This had to be a nightmare. It couldn't be *real*.

Though the Black Bound elixir was real. Baltazar squeezing it off his hand with the same clumsy skill Ouranos had had on Zyearth so many years ago was real.

Theron alive and awake was real.

And Izzy… Izzy was real.

Izzy ran ahead and dashed into the forest. She leapt nimbly over a log and headed for the deepest part with the largest trees. Matt followed.

She was real… and he knew it because he had crossed a boundary with her. Without even meaning to.

Using their bond to communicate with her.

He leapt over another fallen log. The sentries followed, right on his tail. He blasted them with wind, hoping they'd fall back, though it didn't seem to affect them much. He'd have to ramp it up if he really wanted to blow them away.

But he couldn't. Memories of his newly-broken magic throwing his high school bully Warren into a wall still haunted him.

Theron using his Black Bound elixir to create Cast even more so.

Gotta keep my powers under control, he thought. *Gotta keep the elixir hidden. I can't give them any more.*

I can't open another path into Izzy's mind.

When he and Izzy had bound themselves to their own Gems as children, they also formed a social Gem bond, like Matt and Ouranos had on Zyearth. Something both he and Izzy had always dismissed until his powers broke through at age twenty, during his senior year of high school.

Matt's magic had been out of control, destroying everything in its path without Matt's input. He couldn't stop it. So the Master Guardian put a Gem suppressor on it. Something to keep his powers safe until he learned how to use them.

Or something to keep on permanently if he couldn't.

Matt ducked under a branch, breathing fast, his heart racing.

Keeping that suppressor on would mean Matt would have lost the magic that let him live beyond a biological life. It would have meant the end of everything - his career goals, his aspirations, his *life*. He'd die before he hit a hundred, body failing and broken, while his family enjoyed the long, comfortable lives of Gem users.

He couldn't handle that.

Another sentry, Lukas, popped up on his left, sword in hand. Taking a chance, he shouldered Lukas, knocking him to the ground, and stole his sword. *Izzy!*

She turned, a loud, angry, jangling bell ringing in his ears. Her eyes widened and her fur puffed up.

Damn it, he had done it again!

He gritted his teeth, kicking himself for letting that slip. He passed her the sword as they ran, his fingers still slick with elixir, despite his efforts. She nodded thanks to him, though panic laced her features. Whether that was because of the Drifter or because he had been in her head, he didn't know.

The damn suppressor hadn't been enough. It failed to keep Matt's powers under control. So he had manipulated it. Made it stronger. Suddenly it was able to keep him in check, enough for him to work through his magic and learn how to use it.

But it had come at a cost.

Izzy was that cost.

The only way the thing could power itself enough to keep Matt under control was to steal energy from Izzy. Whenever he had had it on, Izzy grew tired, lethargic, unable to stay awake or hold a conversation.

That had been proof enough to him that they shared a social jewel bond. Like he had with Ouranos.

And like a selfish ass, he had kept it on during a war game their senior year of high school, trying to prove he could hold it together. That he could learn his magic well enough that he could get rid of the damn thing.

He had almost killed Izzy doing that.

His foot caught on a rock or a root and sent him flying across the forest floor. He landed with a loud crash, catching debris in his fur and quills.

Another sentry, Dorian, caught up to him and raised his sword. Matt panicked and whipped wind through the trees, far stronger than it needed to be, building elixir on his fingers up to his wrists.

Izzy ran her sword through Dorian, spilling strange black blood all over Matt. It knocked Dorian down, however temporary it was. But another sentry, Kit, slid next to Matt, grabbed his hands, and squeezed more elixir off his fur.

"Kit, no!" Matt pulled hard, but couldn't free his hands. "Let me *go!*" He blasted a particularly powerful gust and wrapped it around Kit, then threw him into the woods. He vanished into the underbrush. Matt stared, paralyzed, memories of Warren flying into the cafeteria wall blinding his vision.

Then visions of Theron shoving a Cast charm into Roscoe's eye using a charm made from his Black Bound elixir pushed Warren's memory aside. Roscoe's body turned inside out, spilling ink out of every orifice, drowning him in black while he screamed, high pitched and bloody--*Don't tell me they got more elixir. Fire and ice--!*

Izzy dug her arm under his and pulled him to his feet. "Don't stop, run!" She took off and he followed.

Black Bound elixir from Izzy's grip stuck to his fur as he ran. Izzy's powers were out of her control too. Damn it!

He had tried convincing Izzy they had a bond after the suppressor had been removed for good. Tried apologizing for using it to save himself. After he had almost killed her stealing energy to power the damn thing. But nothing would convince her. She didn't believe they had a bond, so she couldn't believe he had almost killed her.

It wasn't until Ouranos showed up decades later and they formed an accidental social bond that Izzy dared to entertain the idea.

But she was clearly afraid of it. So Matt didn't push.

Until now. Years of instinctual connection with Ouranos made it so easy, so *comfortable,* that without thinking, he had reached for that same bond with Izzy when they needed it most.

She hadn't responded well. And there was no time to talk about it.

But he couldn't seem to help himself, which made the whole thing so much worse. *Violating.*

What was wrong with him?

Why couldn't he make it *stop?*

More loud bell jingles rang between his ears. Izzy pointed.

Another Athánatos stood in the woods just a few meters ahead of them. A feminine one, wearing… jeans and a T-shirt.

And those very faint chains. She had golden yellow eyes and a burnt orange snout.

But Matt didn't recognize her. Who was that?

She lifted her hands. Ice built on their tips.

Ice.

She was a *royal.*

Matt shielded and called out to Izzy, pushing the words through his mouth, trying to ignore their bond. *"Izzy, dive and shield!"*

Izzy dove against a tree and shielded. Matt stood in front of her, covering her with his body, his back turned to the onslaught of Drifters. He added to her shield, though he knew there was little they could do. An elemental on one side and hundreds of enemies on the other.

They were dead.

Matt pressed his forehead to Izzy's. He couldn't get the words out, but the bond conveyed his thoughts anyway. *Whatever you do, hold on to your magic. Don't give them any elixir. Don't give in.*

Izzy wrapped her arms around his waist, a sob escaping her throat. And a single thought, Izzy's thought, floated between Matt's ears with a soft, somber bell sound.

I'm sorry.

The sharp cracking of ice magic ripped past them, clinging to the bark and blasting diamond dust all over Matt's fur. He wrapped an arm around Izzy and closed his eyes, though he kept a tight lock on his magic. No more elixir. Theron wouldn't *win*.

He wouldn't.

But wind whipped about them anyway, no matter how hard Matt pulled back. He tried grasping it, but it only got stronger. So strong it grew hot against his fur. He growled, holding his hands in fists, pulling back on his power. *He can't have me!*

"Release your hold on the magic, Matthew," a familiar voice said.

Matt's eyes flew open. *Ouranos.* He turned.

Ouranos stood next to them, his hands outstretched, wind and fire slowly encircling them, cutting them off from the ice wielder and the Drifters.

Matt sighed relief and reached for Ouranos with his mind, desperate for any bond besides the one he had with Izzy. *Thank Draso you're here.*

But Ouranos didn't respond telepathically. In fact, Matt's mind was devoid of the colorful emotions the pair of them shared. He squinted.

Then he noticed the chains. Ouranos had the same faint chains around his arms and legs that the other Drifters had.

Izzy drew her hands to her snout. "Lightning and air..."

That wasn't Ouranos then. It was that strange, shadow copy, covered in chains, just like the others. Except this one still had his mind.

Matt swallowed hard.

Ouranos moved closer to them, his chains rattling. "Stand close. I will chase them off and get you to safety, however temporary it is. Be ready to run."

Matt and Izzy stepped away from the tree. Matt's body buzzed with anticipation.

Ouranos gritted his teeth and threw his hands forward, blasting fire in all directions, chasing back the Drifters and the other elemental user. He dashed back the way they came. "To the palace. Hurry! They will not stay down for long."

The Drifters lay in piles on the ground, their fur smoldering, many still on fire, though strangely devoid of smell. But they slowly got up, their dead eyes still locked on Matt and Izzy.

"Run!" Ouranos called.

They ran. Again.

With Ouranos pushing the hoard back, they put some distance between themselves and the Drifters and entered the palace. Ouranos zigzagged through the halls, until he came to the library, the only fully closed-in building in the palace. They ran inside and he pulled the door shut. He listened for several minutes in silence, then carefully stepped back away from it, though the chains on his wrists and ankles ground against each other.

Ouranos turned to them, holding his chains in his hands. He flicked his tail, the chains clinking together. "Well then. I am unsure why you two are here but… welcome to hell."

THE AETHER

Ouranos walked around the palace with a book and quill, greeting everyone he found and writing down their names. Melaina's idea of a census was a good one, if anything to make sure they had not missed anyone in the attack.

He shuddered. That should not have happened. Theron should not have been able to escape the prison Ouranos had trapped him in on his own.

Someone would have had to free him.

Who that could be was anyone's guess. Any of Theron's allies on the mainland had no way to access Athánatos. And he could not believe a single Athánatos would want his father awake and able to do harm.

But someone must have. Hopefully the census could say who. Assuming the culprit had left with Theron. Assuming there *was* a culprit. The whole situation baffled the mind.

Ouranos took a deep breath. Perhaps he should have killed the Basileus when he had had the chance, despite the consequences.

He shut his eyes tight, his fur standing on end. But the very thought of it… He shook himself, trying to calm his nerves.

They would get through this. They had survived all other attacks by his father. They would survive this one.

Judgement or not, Theron would not win.

Natassa walked up to him, also holding a book. Her tail dragged along the floor, kicking up dust. "It has been a long day, but I have scoured my half of the palace," she said, slow and quiet. "Shall we compare notes?"

Ouranos patted her shoulder. "Indeed. We should go to the library, see how Melaina and Leah are faring." Natassa nodded, not quite meeting his gaze, and they headed deep into the palace. Ouranos closed his book and tucked it under his arm. "How is Neil?"

Natassa looked away, pressing her lips tight. "Tense. Alert." She shook her head. "But strong. Stubborn too, as always, though perhaps we need that stubbornness right now. Someone to keep us pushing forward. He leads well."

Ouranos managed a smile. "He will make a wonderful partner."

"Mmm." She stared at the ground as they walked, quiet. Like Ouranos, she had taken off the royal chains and much of the paint had already worn off. Even the *okaa* was loose and the hem of her skirt dirty.

He frowned. A terrible start to their marriage. And they had not yet finished the vows. He wrapped an arm across her shoulders. "How are *you* faring?"

Natassa flattened her ears and stopped walking.

Ouranos flicked his tail, his shoulders drooping. "Natassa?"

Her book slipped from her grip and hit the floor. She covered her face with her hands and sobbed quietly.

Ouranos dropped his book as well and drew Natassa into his arms, holding her tight. His mind searched for comfort, for words of healing, but nothing came to him. All he could do was hold her.

She cried in his arms for several minutes before stepping back. "A-Apologies…"

"Do not apologize," Ouranos said, gripping her shoulders. "It is normal to fear. But he will not win."

Natassa hugged herself. "But what if he does…? What if Matt and Izzy are dead? What if I am wrong?" She shook herself. "Or worse, what if I am *right?* What if he is making a new army of Shadow Cast? How can we face that war all over again?"

"We will not face it alone," Ouranos said. "We have allies and tools. Even as we speak, Darvin and Sami are working on making Lexi Charms to combat the Shadow Cast. Sacha and Trecheon are healing the wounded and leading when we cannot. Leah, Embrik, and Melaina are working to rediscover what we lost and find a solution. Jaden, Neil, and Ana will lead powerful warriors to protect us and fight at our side. We have the Cloak, the Phonar, and if we ask for it, the Defenders. We have beaten him and Judgement before, Natassa. This is hard, but it will end the same as before. Better even. We are stronger than we ever have been."

"…So is he, with Judgement at his side."

"Our strength outweighs theirs," Ouranos said. "Theirs is an alliance based around fear and distrust. Ours is based on love and integrity. We will survive."

Natassa looked off. "We should have ended his life when we had the chance."

Ouranos furrowed his brow, though he did not speak.

Natassa met his gaze, tears streaming down her face, her snout scrunched up. "Ouranos… what if he kills Matt and Izzy?"

Violent chills raced down Ouranos' spine to the tip of his tail, but he chewed his lip and kept his worries from showing on his face. "I do not believe he will, Natassa. He sought to capture them, not destroy them. He needs them for his machinations. We will find them and we will bring them home. I stake my life on it."

She stared at him, took a shuttering breath, then leaned into him and held tight. "Be careful with promises like that."

Ouranos frowned.

A twinge of something tingled across his shoulders, setting his fur on end. He perked his ears and glanced around. Then the tingle crossed his back and ran down his tail, puffing up the tuft.

He stood back now, glancing at his tail.

Natassa tilted her head. "Ouranos?"

"I... feel something." The tingle ran from his tail, through his belly, and into his chest. A warmth spread through his body, radiating from his heart, and with it... colors, in his mind. Pinks and yellows against a blue sky, like a sunset.

No. A sunrise.

A rosy-fingered dawn.

Matt.

"Sisters help us," Ouranos said, gripping his chest. "I feel Matthew."

Natassa's eyes grew wide. "Oh, *Ouranos.* Where is he? Is he safe? Does he have Izzy with him?"

Ouranos held up a hand and searched through the colors in his mind. "I am... unsure. I am not getting words, just colors from our bond." He closed his eyes in concentration and sent a response. A solid, silver bird, with jagged white lightning, flying over his rosy-fingered dawn. His summon, Jústi. Hopefully Matthew would understand the message.

The rosy-fingered dawn expanded as a result, growing in size and strength. He had heard him. Ouranos sighed relief. "Oh, thank Draso."

But still no words. Why was Matt not speaking to him? *Matthew? Can you hear me?*

No reply.

Ouranos rubbed his chin. He closed his eyes again and pictured multiple settings in his head - the Athánatos palace, the forest surrounding them, the beach on the mainland. They appeared only as vague colors and shapes when sending them to Matt, but hopefully the message would get through.

Where are you?

Matt repeated the image of the palace, starting on the mossy lawn, then leading Ouranos vaguely through the halls to the library, if he was reading the colors correctly. Then in a violent turn, the colors vanished in favor of a sharp, black and white scene, still set in the library.

Ouranos' ear twitched. There was some... odd connection there, though he could not quite understand it. He responded with a black question mark drawn in the sky, messy and blurred.

Matt took the question mark and reshaped it. Ouranos struggled to make out the shape at first, but slowly it came together.

Him. Matt had made an image of Ouranos.

Except... his shadowy self wore... chains.

Matt had shown him a picture of his stolen soul.

Shock ran from his chest to his extremities and Ouranos eyes shot open. "Sisters alive. *Impossible.*"

Natassa gripped his hands. "What, Ouranos?"

"Our Guardians," Ouranos said. "They are in the *Aether.*"

CHAPTER 10

BONDS

Izzy sat on a chair in front of a big wooden table that would have been a pretty reddish-brown mahogany and smelled of natural polish if they weren't stuck in some weird comic-book desaturated world. The books and scrolls on the shelves around her looked almost threatening in the odd light that had no source. And everything was devoid of smell - incredibly unsettling in the old library, which she had come to associate with the deep, comforting smell of handmade paper, inks, and age-old dust.

She hugged herself, rubbing her bare arms, which only reminded her that she wasn't even in familiar clothing. The little wound on her palm ached, and there were no healers to fix it. Everything about this was terrible.

And she had no idea if they could escape it.

Matt and Ouranos - er, Ouranos' soul, as she now understood it, - stood not far from her, holding hands, their brows furrowed in deep concentration, trying to reach Ouranos mentally through Matt's bond. Such a strange thought. Ouranos was right there in front of them, exactly as the Ouranos they knew and loved, and yet he was so far removed from their good friend.

Izzy could only hope they'd be able to get to Ouranos proper and find a way out of this hell.

Tiny jingle bells echoed in her ears.

She pressed her eyes shut and turned away. Those damn jingles. Matt's damn thoughts in her own head…

It couldn't be real. It *couldn't*. She didn't have a bond with Matt. No matter how much Matt insisted she did.

They. Did. Not.

Matt's eyes flashed open and he let Ouranos' hands go, stepping back. He held his head. "Damn it…"

Izzy stood, pushing aside her worries. "No good?"

"No, it worked," Matt said. "But we can't speak. All we can use are colors. I hope the message came across." He frowned and glanced at the Ouranos in front of him. "I don't suppose you can read his mind."

Ouranos lifted the chains around his wrists. "As long as I have these, our connection is too weak for proper communication. All I can offer as his soul is memory retention, emotional regulation, and empathy."

Matt blinked at him, then smiled slightly. "Well. At least he has a good consolation prize."

"Ouranos…" Izzy said carefully. "Where are we?"

Ouranos lifted a hand, rattling his chains. "We are in the Aether. A limbo where Athánatos souls go to await their fate while the body is still living. A bi-product of using the Ei-Ei jewels and their magic of immortality."

Matt eyed Izzy, then glanced back. "So like… a waiting room for Drifter's souls."

"A fitting description," Ouranos said. "Most Drifter souls are here waiting until their bodies are restored and a *Fýlakas* calls them home." He rubbed the fur under the cuff on his wrist. "Well… that is how it supposed to be. Theron's war changed that when he made Drifters on purpose."

"Which chains your souls here," Izzy said, frowning.

"It does," Ouranos said.

Matt glanced over the chains, frowning. "Those look heavy."

Ouranos lifted one arm, dragging the chains with him. "I suppose they are. Though… it is not a physical weight so much as it is a spiritual one."

Matt lowered his gaze. "You told me that in order to free your soul, someone would have to sacrifice their life. Does that work the same way if we're already in the, um, Aether?"

Ouranos took several big steps back. "Yes, so do not entertain thoughts of breaking the chains. There is a reason it is *forbidden,* Matthew. I can live a normal life chained. You gave me that gift. I would rather keep my soul chained and have you in at my side in the physical world than be freed and lose you."

Matt breathed deeply. "…If you say so."

"Guess it's good we didn't actually break Baltazar's chains then," Izzy said.

Ouranos crossed his arms. "The chains cannot break without *intent.* Specifically, the intent to free the soul. Though I am unsure if your attempt at Baltazar's chains would be considered 'intent' or not, considering you did not understand what it was you were trying to do. The magic is unclear and mostly untested."

Matt crossed his arms, still eyeing Ouranos' chains.

Izzy narrowed her gaze. "Don't you even think about it, Matt."

Matt glanced at her frowning. A bell rang in her ears, off-beat.

"I mean it," she said, baring a fang and pinning her ears back. "Listen to what Ouranos said."

Matt wrinkled his nose, and looked off, but didn't say anything.

Ouranos gripped Matt's shoulder. "My dear friend, for all our sakes, please let this go. You have done more than enough for me. I am content and whole, but I need you in my life to retain that wholeness. You are too important to me."

Matt let out a long breath. "Fine."

Izzy rubbed her arms. "So… you retain Ouranos' memories. I assume that's how you know us."

Ouranos smiled. "It is."

Izzy wrinkled her snout. "So does he have your memories? Does he know what you're experiencing here?"

Ouranos' ears perked up. "I… do not believe so." He rubbed his chin. "This world is maddening. I feel if my actual essence had the memories I have gained as a soul in the Aether, my mental health would be far worse off than it is." He shook himself. "Memories, experiences, the flow of time, even sight, smell, and *sleep,* function strangely here."

Matt twitched his snout. "Sleep. Doubt I'll get any of that here."

"You must endeavor to, if your stay is extensive," Ouranos said. "Your body still has physical needs."

Izzy's quills stood on end. "Then I'm glad I stuffed myself at the wedding. I'm guessing there's nothing edible here. Or drinkable."

Ouranos' shoulders slumped. "You are correct. That is a problem."

Izzy rubbed her arms. "I hope everyone made it out okay. They put themselves in harm's way trying to keep Judgement from us."

Matt walked to Izzy and wrapped an arm across her shoulders. "Me too."

Ouranos adjusted the chains on his wrists. "It is of the utmost importance that we hasten your escape, though there is very little we can do on our end."

"You mentioned ah, a *Fýlakas,*" Izzy said, struggling with the Athánatos word.

"Yes," Ouranos said. "It roughly translates to 'Keeper.'" He flicked his tail. "I have the vague feeling that the *Fýlakas* was killed during Theron's war, though I cannot tell if that is a hunch or a memory telling me so." He crossed his arms. "I am unsure where to go from there. Without the *Fýlakas,* there may not be any other way to access the Aether from the outside."

Izzy snorted. "Well, Theron got us here *somehow*. I'm sure they'll figure it out."

"We can only hope." Ouranos stretched. "It is probably best that you two stay here. The Drifters without bridges to their souls are as mindless as their shells on the outside. They cannot reason or problem-solve and their searching abilities are limited to what they see as they amble about. Since I am also a Drifter, I am mostly invisible to them, so I can search for signs that the *Fýlakas* is calling you home."

Izzy shifted uncomfortably. "Will you even know what to look for?"

Ouranos turned to her. "Yes. Because I have seen it once before. When Natassa entered the Aether in an attempt to release me."

Matt's eyes widened. "She's been here *before?*"

"Yes, though I do not know if my, ah, full self knows this," Ouranos said. "I know it because I saw it when my soul was fully chained. But I was a full Drifter then. I could not communicate or react and most of my memories were lost to the haze." He rubbed one arm. "I am grateful that Natassa chose not to act to free me. I dread losing her."

Izzy's eyes widened and a chill ran down her spine. Matt tightened his grip across her shoulders.

Ouranos nodded to them both. "I will leave you here. Do not answer the door unless I speak, and if this safehouse is compromised, do everything you can to escape. I do not know what would happen if you were to die through physical injury here and there is very little we can do to repair injuries."

"Let's meet in the throne room if we end up having to leave," Matt suggested. "If we can."

"A good plan."

"Ouranos," Izzy said quietly. "I… we saw someone. A Drifter… and an ice wielder."

Ouranos' eyes widened. "A royal."

Izzy nodded. "Any idea who it might be?"

Ouranos folded his hands and pressed them to his nose. "I… cannot speculate," he said. "But I will let you know if I find them." He gave a gentle bow. "I shall return soon, my friends. Please make yourself comfortable however you can." He left, shutting the massive wooden doors behind him.

They didn't make a sound. Izzy shivered. She leaned into Matt.

Matt pulled her close and laid his head on hers. "Did I see someone sliced your hand while we were fighting?"

Izzy lifted her palm. Little pools of black blood ran along the wound. She shuddered. "Yeah. It's not bleeding much, but it sure as hell stings." She grimaced. "Not sure why it's all black like that."

"Let's get it covered," Matt said. He pulled at the *osaa* and ripped a short strip off it. "At least until Leah or Sacha can heal it up." Izzy held her hand out and he carefully wrapped the wound, tying the ends in a little knot. A gentle, distant jingle echoed in her head. "Izzy… we need to talk."

Izzy's fur stood on end and she pulled her hand away. "No, we don't."

Matt frowned deeply, slumping his shoulders. "Izzy--"

"I know what you're going to say," Izzy said. "You're going to push the idea that we have a Gem bond again. You're *insisting* it's real Matt, and it's *not.*" More jangles rang through her ears, louder than before.

Matt twitched an ear. "You can't tell me you don't hear the bells, Izzy. Or my thoughts in your head. I *know* I projected them when we were fighting the Drifters--"

Izzy formed fists. "Figment of my imagination."

"*Izzy--*"

"Just *drop it,* Matt!" Izzy said, stepping back again. "Even… even if we have a bond, even if it's real, *I don't want it.*"

Matt stiffened. "You don't?"

Izzy flexed her fingers, searching her heart. Matt and Ouranos had had their Gem bond for years now and she had seen how close it had made them. Perhaps even closer than she was with Matt, despite their very long history together. There was comfort and joy there.

But also consequences. A lack of privacy. Shared thoughts. Possibly even energy stealing. She wasn't sure. Matt never talked about it.

Images of a war game way back in her senior year of high school flashed through her mind. One right after Matt got his powers. She hardly remembered any details… just one solid feeling. Constant weariness. Particularly when Matt was using his newfound powers. When he had the Gem suppressor turned up all the way to slow his out-of-control magic.

Energy stealing. To power the Gem suppressor.

She couldn't do that again. Her body shook and her ears rang reliving the terror of her energy slipping away, stripping her of everything, threatening to--

"Izzy?"

The jangling bells rang louder than ever in her ears. She shut her eyes tight, gritted her teeth, and pulled her ears down against her head. *"I don't want it!"* She stepped back again, trying to push the bells away. "I don't want it, Matt. *I don't.* For Draso's sake, let it *go.* "

Matt dropped his hands to his sides. The bells faded. "Yeah… Okay… I'll drop it."

Izzy hugged herself, but wouldn't look Matt in the eye. "…Thank you."

Tiny jingles still tickled her brain. Along with Matt's voice. *I'm sorry.* She glanced up at him, but he didn't say anything. He watched her a moment, then walked off, wandering the stacks.

The jingles faded completely. But instead of relief, all she felt was empty.

CHAPTER 11

FAMILY

Zeke leaned against the mahogany table watching Archángeli and Eris intently as they poured over Archángeli's journal together. Both Leah and Zeke had a pen and paper, carefully translating every word Eris said to the best of their abilities. Eris spoke slowly, pausing a lot, and second-guessing words, but at least she had some understanding of it. Embrik and Melaina stood nearby, also taking notes, though Melaina was clearly agitated.

Eris had to translate all on her own. Abrax was missing, which Melaina found troubling. She said she hoped he hadn't died in the attack, but her tone of voice suggested that wasn't what she really worried about. Her nervousness clung to Zeke's fur like dandelion seeds, making him itch.

It was nearly evening and they knew nothing more about what happened to Matt and Izzy. His chest ached. It wasn't quite as intense, but the whole situation made him think strongly of losing his moms. Matt was family after all. Family that he had grown incredibly close to over the last few years, like with Jaden.

Zeke wrinkled his snout. Jaden had to be devastated losing Matt again. He'd have to check in on him.

Despite him growing closer to Jaden, he hadn't really built the courage to call him "dad." Jaden said that was okay, though Zeke could tell something was still missing between them. He compromised and occasionally called Jaden *patéras,* the Athánatos word for father. It left Jaden speechless the first time he had used it and drew a smile every time since.

Matt had struggled calling Jaden "dad" too. He confided in Zeke that after years of calling his adoptive father Dad, using the term for someone else was hard. But he seemed to find it easier after Zeke started using *patéras.* Working through those feelings together helped build their bond. A bond that had only grown stronger with him physically here.

And then Theron tore that to pieces.

Athánatos had become Zeke's safehouse, his haven, his family. A family he finally let himself have after letting his moms go. Aunts, uncle, a sister, a brother… a father. Hell, even the language clung to him and came out in daily speech. Not just *patéras* for Jaden, but *theía* and *theíos* for his aunts and uncle. He even embraced the title of prince. The people of the palace openly called him Prínkipas and he had grown to love it. Athánatos was home.

And Theron was after it. And after losing so much family in his past, he wasn't about to let someone take more of it.

But they had no direction. No idea where to start fighting this. This helpless feeling chewed away at his mind, throwing insults at him.

You're useless.

You let Judgement take them.

You failed.

It was Zeke's first encounter with something akin to Leah's Thought Factory. Anxiety to the max, fighting for control.

Leah reached over and held his hand, rubbing the fur with her thumb. He gripped her back, leaning next to her. This whole thing would be so much harder without her.

He stared at the table, hardly registering Eris reading anymore. Leah… soon she'd be gone. Back to Zyearth where she'd continue the life she was always going to return to. He knew that. But for some reason, it hadn't felt real. Until her Master Guardian gave the order.

She was his whole heart. More so than anyone else. And soon she'd be gone.

She wanted him to go back to Zyearth with her. She had tried so hard to keep that from him, but it bled into his thoughts anyway, particularly when she slept. But that would mean leaving Athánatos behind. His uncle. His aunts. Andre. Trading all those relationships for what he had with Leah.

He shook his head and focused back to Eris' words, trying to keep up with what he missed. It wasn't fair to put the people he loved on a… scale or something. Like a simple weighing of pros and cons. This was far too complicated for that. *All* of them were equally valuable. But he'd be stuck choosing whether he wanted to or not. He didn't… he just didn't know what to do.

Leah clung tighter to his hand, grounding him. He shut his eyes, taking in everything he had with her.

Draso's breath, the hell was he supposed to do?

A gentle, comforting breeze blew through his fur and he turned. Archángeli stood there in his zyfaunos form, their feathers rustling with their own wind magic.

Archángeli was little help with the translation even though they could read it. They had been so shocked about the discovery of the journal that they spent a good half hour sitting on Zeke's lap in their bird form, staring into space, shaking slightly. They let Zeke gently stroke their feathers, but they were clearly disturbed by the whole thing. Even now, though they had transformed into their anthropomorphic form and joined Eris in looking through it, they rarely said anything and mostly corrected words or meanings that Eris got wrong. They wouldn't comment at all on the content.

Zeke pressed his lips tight. Archángeli had been with him his whole life. His first friend, one of his dearest companions. But seeing them like this, he realized he had never really seen Archángeli as a… person. Their dreams, aspirations, feelings, worries, joys, hobbies, whatever. He had just subconsciously assumed that the summon didn't have them.

That was a terrible mistake.

Now his dear friend was opening up a past that they only recently recalled. Memories so far in the distant past that no other living person shared that experience with them. And they didn't know how to navigate it.

It didn't help that most of the journal contained dark, violent descriptions of the events surrounding Judgement and the creation of the Shadow Cast. Scenes of half-Cast wandering the palace. Descriptions of Athánatos who died when the Cast Charms didn't take. Terrible, bloody battles that left limbs and blood and organs strewn across the field. Fear like no one ever knew. Many said it was the end times. No one was safe.

But for Zeke, it was just a history book. For Archángeli, it was one long memory. So while they wrote translations, Archángeli relived every moment in their mind, being forced to clarify when Eris made a mistake.

No wonder they seemed so broken.

They took plenty of breaks. Eris had asked on multiple occasions if Archángeli wanted to leave and let them handle this alone, or if they just needed to stop entirely. But Archángeli, ever dutiful, insisted they continue.

It hurt to watch.

Leah squeezed Zeke's hand. He turned to her, a soft smell of baking apples entering his nose. She frowned at him.

Archángeli's hurting, she said in Zeke's mind. *And so are the other Phonar.* She tilted her head toward the stacks.

Zeke glanced around. All the other Phonar summons had flown to high perches in the library, and many had buried their heads in their wings, cooing, shaking, or just fluffed up, agitated. Zeke flicked his ears back.

We need to stop this, Leah said. *We haven't learned anything new about Judgement, and Archángeli has this mistaken idea that we need to do this to stop her. It's only hurting them.*

Zeke shook his head. Leah once again being his voice of reason. *You're right.* He squeezed her hand and stood.

Eris glanced up. "My prince?"

"I think that's enough for now," Zeke said. "We've gotten through what, two-thirds of the book? And so far we've found nothing useful."

Archángeli lifted their head and clicked their beak, their feathers ruffled. A faint breeze brushed against Zeke's fur. *My Prínkipas, we must continue--*

"No, Archángeli." Zeke walked around the table and did something he had never done for Archángeli before. He pulled them into a hug. "You've been hurt enough. This clearly isn't the right path, and I'm not going to sit here and force you to relive all that, especially if we have nothing to show for it. We're done."

Archángeli didn't move at first, but slowly they wrapped their winged arms around Zeke's waist and laid their head on his shoulder. A gentle breeze tickled Zeke's ear. *Thank you, my prince.*

Zeke held them close.

Eris took a deep breath. "I am with you, Zeke. I see no point in continuing."

"I dare say we all feel the same," Embrik said. "It is a bloody history."

Eris slid the journal away from Archángeli. But then she stopped. "Wait…" She squinted and tilted her head. "One question, Archángeli, if you can."

Archángeli sighed, their hot breath brushing Zeke's fur. They pulled away. *Yes?*

"How many Phonar summons are there?"

Eight, Archángeli said. But the moment they said it, they furrowed their brow. *Actually… no. That's not correct.* They closed their eyes, rubbing their beak with a clawed hand. *Not eight… nine.*

Leah stood now. "Judgement said something about that at the Desert Wall. Remember? She said we only had six of the nine Phonar."

Zeke's ears perked and he turned to Eris. "Eris?"

Eris pointed. "Here. The ninth member of the Phonar." She wrinkled her snout. "The one who started this Order… and proposed they all become summons." She glanced up at the group. "We are missing the ninth Phonar."

Melaina brought her hands to her snout. "Sisters *alive.*"

"But who are they?" Zeke asked.

Eris glanced over the book, shaking her head. "This volume does not say."

The heavy wooden doors of the library burst open and Ouranos and Natassa ran in. Ouranos waved to them. "We have found Matt and Izzy!"

Zeke heaved a sigh. "*Theíos,* thank *god.*"

"Do not embrace relief yet, *anipsiós,*" Ouranos said, tossing the book in his hand on the table. "This problem is bigger than we feared."

Leah pulled her puffy tail into her hands and picked at the guard hairs. "Don't tell me they're dead…"

"Thankfully, no," Ouranos said. "At least that I can tell." His face grew dark. "They are in the Aether."

Melaina gasped and Embrik's quills stood on end. "Sisters save them," he muttered.

Zeke frowned. "What's the Aether?"

"A purgatory for Drifter souls," Eris said. "An… alternate reality, if you will. It is *not* a place for the living…"

"How do you know they are in the Aether?" Embrik asked.

Ouranos explained his vision with Matt. "Matt's rosy dawn still lingers in my head, but it has lost its earlier strength."

"I fear we have no way to get them out…" Natassa said, her eyes shining with tears. "Sagira, our *Fýlakas,* died in the war. There is no one else to light the path."

Eris lowered her gaze and folded her hands in front of her. "That… is not entirely accurate, my Lady."

Everyone turned to her. Natassa perked an ear. "Eris?"

Eris fiddled with her hands. "Historically we have only had one *Fýlakas* and their apprentice because natural Drifters were rare. They only happened by unfortunate accident. But when Theron began his war, we had so many more Drifters wandering the battlefields. Sagira needed help. So she trained and blessed dozens more *Fýlakas.*" She lifted her chin. "Myself among them."

Natassa perked her ears. "Oh Sisters…" She gripped Eris' hands. "Do you remember how to open the Aether?"

Eris glanced aside. "I… am ill-practiced, but give me time to recall the words. But we must make haste. The longer they are there, the slimmer our chance of retrieving them. There is nothing to sustain them there, and sleep will likely evade them." Her expression grew dark and she pinned her ears back. "Worse still, they are not souls. They cannot be coaxed by normal means. Someone must enter the Aether and retrieve them."

Melaina covered her snout with her hands. "Oh, Sisters…"

"Let me go after them," Ouranos said.

"*No,*" Eris and Natassa said together. Ouranos frowned. Eris shook her head. "Apologies, my Lord, but I am serious when I say the Aether is *not* a place for the *living.* It is a dead copy, a place that drains life, energy, and magic. With your soul trapped there, you should not enter the Aether. I can only imagine the damage it could do to you. It is a bad enough place for someone fully intact."

"Then I will go," Natassa said. "I… have navigated it before. I can find them."

Ouranos' eyes grew wide and his jaw dropped. "You have been there *before?*"

Natassa scrunched up her face and pinned her ears back. "Yes, to save you. But I lost the courage needed for the sacrifice and left you behind. It was my greatest failing."

"*No,* Natassa," Ouranos said. "It is not--"

"It is a failure," Natassa said, turning to him with teary eyes and a deep frown. "If I had done my duty, we would have been free of Father far sooner. I will hear no argument."

Melaina frowned. "You cannot mean to go alone."

Natassa stood tall. "I am Basilea. It is my duty to go alone."

Ouranos frowned. "Natassa, it is *dangerous.*"

"I know," Natassa said. "All the more reason to go alone. Especially with Theron free and running the island. You need all the warriors you can have, and I know I am among the weakest. But I can traverse the Aether." She turned to Ouranos, tears staining her face. "I failed you once before. I can make up for that mistake now."

Zeke's tail puffed up. Make up for the mistake. By doing what she failed to do before.

He couldn't allow that.

"You aren't going alone, *theía,*" Zeke said. "Because I'm coming with you."

CHAPTER 12

THE VEIL

Neil trudged up the hill toward the Four Sister's grove, dragging his tail through the clover, careful of his still-injured knee.

At this point, he had done all he could to mitigate the damage from Theron's attack. His people were cared for, his teams worked to find their missing Guardians and find answers about Judgement, and every able-bodied warrior secured the palace.

But one problem still chewed away at him. The Veil.

Even now as he pawed through the flowers, a strange, eerie static clung to his fur, and a sense of dread followed him. He turned to the sky. Subtle, distant "holes" pockmarked the air as shimmers and waves. He hadn't ever noticed the Veil before, but he sure as shit did now.

And no matter what Theron did, no matter what happened with Matt and Izzy, no matter how they fought against Judgement… if the Veil fell, the entire Earth would never be the same and the Athánatos people would lose everything. It'd be a war they'd never win as everyone on Earth would want to study them, conquer them, *use* them. They'd be killed for their Ei-Ei jewels or put to work as slaves, or ripped apart as experiments.

Neil shuddered.

The Defenders would help, sure. But even if the Defenders got them off the planet, a feat in itself, it'd never be home. Neil knew how hard it was losing a home. It was bad enough by himself. He couldn't imagine an *entire population* losing that.

So as much as he wanted to throw aside the mantle of Basileus and search for his friends, right now, he had to check on the health of the Veil and hope to God it could be saved.

Light from the Four Sisters grove pulsed through the trees as he approached, and the air smelled of iron and burning. The Cloak, no doubt, working whatever weird magic saved one of the Sisters.

But then someone ran past him through the trees. Someone dressed head to toe in black.

The Black Cloak.

Neil tilted his head. The hell? Then who was in the clearing? He peeked around a tree.

Two Black Cloaks stood in the clearing, their glowing hands pressed against the crumbling statue of the Veil.

Neil's eyes widened. *Two?* His mind raced. Leah had mentioned her Cloak had green eyes and his had blue, but both of these cloaked figures had those icy blue eyes Neil associated with him. He squinted.

One of the Cloaks' hands sparked and he cursed, pulling away from the statue. *"Damnit!"* He shook his hands, sending motes of light into the air like water droplets. His black gloves smoked.

Then he vanished. Disappeared from view. A loud crack and pop hit Neil's ears as atmosphere filled the sudden void, making the air shimmer.

Neil's tail puffed up.

Then another Black Cloak appeared on the left, his hands also glowing, and he pressed against the statue as well. But then the first Cloak pulled away, shaking his hands and growling. He also vanished with a pop.

Two more Cloaks appeared, this time one with green eyes, and pressed glowing hands against the stone. The statue shone, turning a blinding white, but then the two Cloaks with blue eyes leapt back, hands smoking. The "oldest" one vanished.

The green-eyed Cloak glared at the blue-eyed one. "I'm telling you, it *won't work.*"

"It *has* to," the blue-eyed one said. "It has to, or--" He vanished.

The green-eyed cloak snarled and pulled away, his hands also smoking. He rubbed his wrists. "Damn him for not listening…"

Another blue-eyed Cloak appeared from the right, rushing in with glowing hands again. The green-eyed one turned to him. "Robert--"

Neil lashed his tail about. Robert?

The blue-eyed Cloak - Robert - let out a vicious growl. *"Don't try to stop me."*

The green-eyed Cloak held out a hand. "You can't just--"

"Get back!" Robert pushed harder on the statue, tears pooling in his eyes. The tears ran down his cheeks under his mask, whisking away what looked like black paint or makeup. It left streaky gray or white fur in its path. "I have to do this. I have to, this isn't *right.*"

The Cloak wrapped arms around Robert and tugged at him. "Robert, *let go,* you're *killing* yourself!"

Neil flattened his ears.

"I don't care!" Robert shouted. "Because Jaden was *right.* He's *right,* damn it, we should be fixing all this, not just letting it happen! I can't--" The glow on Robert's hands crackled and fell away, leaving his gloves smoking, and he stepped back. He pulled free of the Cloak and fell to his knees. "Water below…"

The Cloak sat next to Robert. "I know."

"I can't do this…" he muttered. "I can't…"

"You don't have to," the Cloak said. "I will."

Robert stared at the statue for a moment. Dust and pebbles crumbled down the sides, and the whole thing listed to the right. He breathed deeply. "It… it isn't right…"

"I know," the Cloak said. "Trust me, I know better than most. But the alternative is worse. You know that, right?"

Robert was silent for several moments. "I hate this…"

The Cloak wrapped an arm around Robert. "I do too."

Neil!

Neil jumped and turned. But there was no one. Empty. A chill ran down his tail. He pinned an ear back, then turned to the grove again.

Only the green-eyed Cloak remained. He stood in the center of the grove, his hands behind his back. Staring directly into Neil's gaze. "We need to talk."

Neil pressed his lips together and frowned. "You can't fix the Veil."

The Cloak lowered his gaze. "It's complicated--"

"I heard you talking to your counterpart," Neil said. "Robert."

The Cloak's eyes widened a moment, then he held out a hand. "That name stays between us."

"I'm not interested in the name," Neil said. "I want to know what he meant. Can you not fix the Veil? Is it going to fall?"

The Cloak flexed a hand, tiny wisps of smoke flicking off the glove, but didn't speak.

Neil glared, baring his teeth. "Robert is right, you know. You need to be *fixing* this. You have the knowledge to. And if you can't, at least tell me if it's gonna fall so I can *do something about it.*"

The Cloak glared, boring holes into Neil's gaze. "What would you do about it?"

"Anything!" Neil said, throwing his hands out. "We can't risk it falling! It would destroy *everything.*"

The Cloak narrowed his gaze. "Would you become the Veil's new anchor?"

Neil's eyes widened. "What?"

The Cloak pointed to the Veil statue. "The Veil was created by one of the Four Sisters, Prinkípissa Keres. She anchored her life force to the magic of the Veil. Legend says she died for that sacrifice."

Neil's body buzzed.

"But that's not entirely true," the Cloak continued. "She continued to live after it was sealed. It was only after her death that her statue took its place in the Grove and held the Veil for this long. A death she chose many, many years later as an Athánatos. She was stuck on the island while she lived. Leaving the island would have destroyed the Veil. But she saved the island." The Cloak furrowed his brow. "The Veil needs a royal anchor."

Neil pressed his lips tight together. "And you want me to be that royal."

"It has to be you," the Cloak said. "The Veil needs someone who has a strong connection to their own soul. But Ouranos is a Drifter. Melaina was a Shadow Cast for decades and the connection never recovered. And Natassa once entered the Aether. That visit damaged her soul's connection."

Neil lifted a brow. "The hell is the Aether?"

"A purgatory for Drifters' souls," the Cloak said. "Basically a place of death."

Neil's jaw dropped. "Why the hell did Natassa visit *there?*"

"You'll find out soon, but it's not important now," the Cloak said. "The point is, their bonds are weakened. Ordinarily this means nothing, especially with their Soul Jewels binding them, but for the purpose of this ah, spell, it means they aren't candidates for anchors."

Neil flicked his ears back. "What about Zeke? He's more royal than me. Or hell, Jaden's already married to a royal." He rubbed his arm. "I… didn't finish my vows."

"The Phonar recognize you as Basileus," the Cloak said. "That should be enough for the magic to work." He gripped Neil's shoulders and looked him deep in the eye. "It *has* to be you, Neil. Yes, Jaden and Zeke fulfill the basic requirement. Both of them will volunteer. But you can't let them. *It has to be you.*" He crossed his arms and looked at the Sister's statue. "My magic failed. *Robert's* magic failed. You saw only a fraction of the attempts we made to save it. Part of those attempts included letting someone else anchor themselves." He shut his eyes tight, shivering. "It didn't work. *Nothing* has worked." He turned to Neil. "Except you."

Neil pressed his lips together.

The Cloak sighed. "Robert is right. This whole thing is unfair. It's *wrong* on so many levels. But this is one of the very few times that I can say, with certainty, that there's only one path here." His gaze softened slightly. "But I'll warn you, it's a hard process. Hard on your mind. Hard on your body. It will *hurt* while anchoring. And… everything has to go exactly right for this to work. No screw ups."

Neil lifted a brow.

The Cloak looked at him with deeply sad eyes. "I wish we had time to bind you to the Ei- Ei jewels and finish your vows. I wish you had time to think it over and weigh the pros and cons. But this could fall at any time. That's not an exaggeration. We could have *minutes.* And if it fails, there will be no fixing this. The damage will be permanent. *That* much I know as a time traveler." He looked Neil dead in the eye. "So… what will you do?"

Neil narrowed his gaze. "After that whole speech, you're still giving me a choice?"

The Cloak looked away a moment. "When I took this mantle, I… lost my ability to choose. Robert too." He turned to Neil. "I refuse to take that away from anyone else. No matter the consequences."

A breeze brushed Neil's fur, chilling him. Just that morning he had been wondering if he was really worthy to be Basileus. If he really was willing and able to do whatever it took to lead.

And now here he was, faced with a choice that would prove whether he could or not.

He stared at the Veil. "Can I still finish my vows and get my Ei-Ei jewels after I do this anchor thing?"

The Cloak was silent for several seconds, but then quietly said "Yes."

"Then I'd become the new statue in the Grove after I die."

"Yes," the Cloak said. He spoke slowly, deliberately. "When you choose to end your life, you would replace this Veil statue with your own."

Neil flattened an ear. "Will this magic eventually fade too?"

"Not if we finally end Judgement," the Cloak said. "The Four Sisters' magic is temporary because it is the only thing keeping Judgement back and Judgement is constantly draining it. Remove Judgement, and the magic stays forever."

Neil's puffy tail smoothed out and he forced his body to relax. "But… I'd have to stay on Athánatos for the rest of my life."

"You would, yes."

That worried him. He'd miss so much on the mainland. He'd never see the library, the sushi places, the beaches. He'd never shop for himself again or travel the world, or get a chance to see Zyearth.

He'd never complete that bucket list he'd been building for him, Dami, and Natassa.

But… his heart was here. This was his home. This was his purpose. He'd… just have to make a new bucket list.

Theron wouldn't win.

"Okay then," Neil said. "Let's get started."

"Neil!"

Neil turned. Jaden ran up the hill, waving his hands. The panic on his face didn't fill Neil with hope.

CHAPTER 13

PARTING WAYS

Natassa sat on one of the big fluffy floormats in the atrium, stiff, but calm. Or at the very least, keeping an air of calm. Her friends and allies had gathered in their biggest meeting room, the very one they had sat in while discussing how to eliminate Ackerson and his teams just a few years prior. And just like at that time, they had a lot to think about.

Everyone dear to her had scattered around the room. The Archons sat on various wicker chairs, big pillows, and chaise lounges, glancing around and fidgeting. Especially Mistik. Darvin and Sami stood guard by Izzy's husband Roscoe, who, despite losing his wife, remained stoic. Sacha leaned against a pillar, her tail lashing. Trecheon stood at her side, still silent since Matt's disappearance. Embrik, Melaina and Ouranos took their post near the main entrances, ever alert, magic clinging to their fur. Damianos and Charlotte stood near Philip, who fiddled with his hands, his tail constantly moving.

Angus had long given up his attempts to scry into the future, so he stood toward the back of the room with his summons, the stone alicorn Magna, and the zebra-patterned lion centaur Lysander at the ready. Ana stood by him, ears pinned back, fiddling with the deer-shaped Blood Crystal she shared with her sisters. Even Chadwick managed to find his way here, with Andre's help.

Zeke would not leave Natassa's side. And unsurprisingly, Leah would not leave his.

Everyone especially important to Natassa. All at stake with Theron on the loose. People she should be protecting and keeping safe.

People she had failed.

Food from the postponed wedding reception lined tables along the pillars, but no one dared eat. Instead, they stood about in utter silence, rigid and alert. Their combined anxiety choked the very air.

They all waited for Neil. Because Eris would not let Natassa enter the Aether until he knew what she intended to do. And, Natassa knew, until Neil had a chance to convince her to let Zeke come with her. Or stop her entirely.

Now was the time to channel Neil's stubbornness. She refused to put any more of her family in danger. Least of all her *anipsiós* Zeke. Her last connection to Alexina. The precocious, unexpected, brilliant prince that gave new life to Athánatos. She had already failed so many. She would not fail him.

No. She had to enter the Aether alone.

Neil had gone for a walk. To clear his head, he had said. But Natassa knew the real reason. To check on the Veil. The crackling static through her fur reminded her of how fragile their invisible protection had become. Hopefully Neil would have good news.

But when he entered the atrium with Jaden and the Black Cloak, his expression betrayed his worry.

Philip immediately leapt to his feet when Neil appeared and he ran to him, pulling him into a hug. Neil held him tight, then turned to Ouranos. "I hear our Guardians are in the Aether. The Black Cloak told me a little about it, but not how to get them back out."

Natassa stood before anyone else could speak. "I am going after them."

Zeke stood too. "Not alone, you aren't."

"I cannot allow anyone else to put themselves at risk," Natassa said firmly, glaring at Zeke, using all her strength as Basilea. "I am going alone."

Zeke formed fists. "Natassa, it's *dangerous*. I'm not risking two family members. We've lost *enough.*"

Natassa's fur stood on end. But she stood firm still, then pressed a hand to Zeke's chest. "Zeke, Alexina's heart is here. Part of my *own* heart is here. Please, *anipsiós,* you need not endanger yourself."

Zeke paused a moment, then shook his head. "But you need to? *Theía,* you shouldn't have to do this yourself."

Natassa puffed out her chest. "Zeke--"

"We don't have time to argue," Neil said, stepping between the two of them. "The Veil is *failing.*"

The collective gasp from those present sent shocks through Natassa's skin. "Oh, Sisters save us…"

Ouranos flicked his ears back. "That will be catastrophic."

"A silent planet opening their ears…" Sacha muttered quietly.

"We can fix it," Neil said, glancing at the Black Cloak. "Well…. Make a new one, I suppose. Before this one falls. We just need a new royal anchor."

Eris stood now, her tail puffy. "The Sisters sacrificed themselves to create the Veil. Whoever followed in their footsteps would have to do the same."

"In time, yes," the Black Cloak said. "But that's not an immediate requirement. Only the Purge and the Cloak needed immediate sacrifice. Prinkípissa Keres and Prinkípissa Titania lived on and chose their deaths. Neil could do the same." He explained how the Veil's anchor worked. "But the anchor needs a strong connection with their soul."

Natassa's heart sunk deeper and deeper into her stomach as he spoke. "Which means neither I, nor Ouranos or Melaina can do this."

The Black Cloak lifted his head. "I've asked Neil to become the new anchor."

Natassa gasped, covering her snout with her hands. "Neil..."

Jaden stepped forward. "You said any royal could take on this role. If that qualifies Neil by marriage, it qualifies me too because of Alexina. Let me do it."

"Being anchored means I'm stuck here for *life*, Jaden," Neil said. "I literally can't leave this place again or the Veil will fall." He lifted his chin. "You still haven't found Alexina. I know you don't want to be stuck here."

Jaden flicked his ears back... then turned to Zeke.

Zeke frowned. He pushed his glasses up higher on his nose and lifted his head. "I--"

"*Zeke.*"

He turned. Leah's jaw hung loose in shock, her brow furrowed and her eyes glassy. She shook, tense. Zeke bit his lip and immediately went silent.

Embrik stood now. "Then let me. I have no desire to set foot on the mainland again."

"Sorry, but no," the Cloak said. "The Archons are all needed for this spell. They have their own parts to play." He turned. "It has to be Neil."

Natassa frowned. "M-My Heart…"

Neil took her hands. "I can do this, Natassa. It's what I'm supposed to do as Basileus, right? It's the vow I took."

Natassa pressed her lips together. "Yes, but… This is a massive sacrifice. I did not intend to tie you permanently here when we agreed to marriage."

Neil smiled that infuriating calming smile of his. "Yeah, but things change. And it's no big deal, really. It just means I can't leave the island when we're done. This is home anyway."

Natassa's eyes burned. She pulled him close and buried her face in his neck. He held her close and kissed her shoulder. Natassa shuddered. This was another failure. Putting Athánatos' burden on someone else's shoulders.

The Black Cloak cleared his throat.

Neil sighed and pulled away, leaving a cold pocket of air between them. "Alright, I know, we're out of time." He crossed his arms. "Let's focus on the Veil and getting our Guardians back from the Aether." Neil flicked his ears back. "Obviously the first one's on me, but…" He turned to Sacha. "Apparently this is gonna be hard on my body. I need a healer."

Sacha pushed off the pillar, shaking her white and orange tail. "And you have one."

Leah stood up next. "Me too."

Neil shook his head. "Actually, I'm going to ask you to keep looking through the library. Eris said you found something about a ninth Phonar. That might be a big key to taking down Judgement." He turned to Eris. "I hope you'll help her."

Eris bowed gently. "Of course, my Lord."

"I will too," Melaina said.

Archángeli flew down from their perch and landed in their anthropomorphic form next to Leah, as a breeze raced through the room. *I will as well.*

Leah flicked her ears back, glancing at Archángeli, but then furrowed her brow in determination and nodded to Neil. "We'll handle it."

Neil nodded to her, then turned to the group. "And now, our Guardians."

Natassa stood straight, keeping her expression strong. Neil had to know he could count on her. She had to prove she could save *someone.*

But his face softened. "Natassa… please take Zeke with you."

She frowned. "My love…"

"I know you don't want anyone else in danger," Neil said. "But the fact is, we are *all* in danger right now. Nowhere is safe while Theron and Judgement are around." He took her hands in his. "We're stronger when we work together. It's the hardest and most important lesson I've learned since meeting you all." He turned to Zeke. "And I can't think of anyone better to follow you in there."

Zeke stood straight and tall. He nodded.

Neil squeezed her hands. "Don't go in there alone."

She sighed. "I do not like this… but I see your point."

Neil gripped Zeke and Natassa's shoulders. "Take care of each other and bring our Guardians home, okay?"

"Count on it," Zeke said.

Neil nodded, then turned. "And that brings me to Jaden."

Jaden perked his ears.

"I know the Veil and the Guardians are important," Neil said. "But Theron and Judgement are still out there, and someone needs to find them. Especially while the Veil is weakened. For all I know, Theron will try actively destroying it. He needs to be found and stopped before he can damage anything else. That's a Guardian's job. Gather a team and see what you can find."

Jaden lifted his chin, saluted in the normal Defender fashion with a sweeping fist across the chest, and nodded. "We'll get him."

Ouranos' face turned dark. "Jaden. Let me come with you."

Jaden turned to him. "Ouranos?"

Ouranos lowered his gaze, his lips lifted in a slight snarl. "Because when we find him… we kill him."

Natassa's heart leapt into her throat.

But Jaden nodded.

Neil turned to the group. "As for the rest of you all… just sit tight. Protect each other. We're going to leave the Phonar here in case Judgement or Theron or Cast show up, though we'll all have our pendants. If there's a problem, call us. We'll be here."

Ouranos stood now. "We have faced Theron before and won. We will do so again." He raised a fist in the air.

Everyone followed his example. Natassa held hers high, clinging to his words, fighting the fear building in her chest.

Eris moved to Natassa. "My Lady, Prince Zeke, we will need to visit the Aether Spire in the Soul Gardens. Say your goodbyes and let us go."

Natassa breathed deeply, trying to calm her anxiety. She had not entered the Aether in decades, but the sickly, burning, dead feeling of crossing the boundary had stuck with her as clearly as if it had happened yesterday. She did not look forward to doing it again.

And… if she saw Ouranos in chains…

Natassa shook herself of the memories. She turned and threw herself at Neil, holding him close. "Take care, my Heart."

He gripped her tight, his hot breath warming her soul. "Come home to me." She could not find the words, only nodding instead, and kissing him gently. She stepped back.

Damianos hugged her as well, tighter than he ever had before. "Protect yourself, Natassa. We need you home." She frowned, but hugged him back.

Leah wrapped herself around Zeke and buried her face in his chest. They shared no words out loud, but Natassa could see Zeke's expression change as he spoke to Leah through their bond. He held her tight and planted a gentle kiss on the top of her head. She squeezed him once more, then stepped back.

"We're coming home," he said. "I promise. I'll keep up with you through the bond."

Leah pinned her ears back. "If you can. Matt and Ouranos… they…"

"I know." He took a deep breath. "If I can."

Andre walked up. He gripped Zeke tight for a long time, but said nothing. When he finally pulled away, he stood behind Leah, resting his hands on her shoulders. She held his hands tight.

Zeke took a shuddering breath, but nodded.

"Zeke."

Zeke turned. Jaden. He pressed his lips together and pulled Zeke into a hug. "Take care of yourself. I don't…. You can't…"

Zeke hugged him tight. "I get it. I'll be safe. And I'll bring Matt and Izzy home. I fought to get you three reunited and I'm going to fight for that again. Trust me, *patéras*."

Jaden breathed deeply, then stepped back. "Protect each other."

"We will."

Ouranos moved next to Eris. "My vision with Matt suggested they were in the library. Start there."

Natassa nodded.

Ouranos hugged them both. "Come home to us." Then he let them go.

"Come, Lady, Prince." Eris jogged through the palace toward the gardens. Natassa and Zeke followed.

Leaving everyone behind.

Soon they found themselves in the Soul Gardens. The housing of the *féretro*, the resting place of the dead, and home to the Aether Spire – a small, thin building, constructed in white marble, gilded in silver and gold. The gateway to the place of souls, and the only Spire on the island in a Soul Garden. She was grateful they had placed theirs here instead of far on the outskirts like most of the Archon's realms. They did not have time for travel.

Eris held out her hands and muttered in the Athánatos language.

Moonlight, Starlight, Evening, Dawn
Mule Stag, Brown Buck, Doe and Fawn,
The body heals, we know the toll,
We access now, the place of Souls

A wave of heat blew through Natassa's fur, stinging her skin. Slowly a wide portal similar to a rip in the Veil opened up, revealing the dull, lifeless, empty world of the Aether. The portal grew slowly.

Eris strained, but she turned to Natassa. "It is time. When you are ready to come home, my Lady, return to the Spire and recite the returning phrase. I will hear and light the way." She narrowed her gaze. "Be wary. The Aether drains energy, very quickly. It might even get to the point where you can no longer use your magic. Keep yourself rested as much as you can."

"Understood," Natassa said.

Eris met Natassa's eyes. "The Aether has an affect on the mind. You know this. It will tell you lies. Feed on your guilt, your fear, your anxiety.

Amplify your emotions. It will rip you to shreds if you let it. Anchor yourself. Trust each other. Ground yourself in your loved ones here." She frowned. "And be quick. Come home."

"We will," Zeke said. He gripped Natassa's hand.

And the pair of them stepped through the portal.

ELIXIR

Izzy lay down on one of the dull wicker couches in the middle of the library, staring at the black ceiling. Her stomach grumbled and her tongue itched, but she knew it'd be a while before she'd really feel the effects of starvation and thirst. Training had taught her that one.

Then why was she so damn exhausted?

Ouranos had yet to come back, which wasn't great news. It left them little to do but peruse the black and white books, lay about, and attempt sleep. Matt was right though. She'd never sleep here. Even as exhausted as she was.

Matt stood in front of a bookshelf down the way from her, skimming a book, though she could tell by his listless expression that his heart wasn't into it. It was just another failed distraction. He had taken the *osaa* off and most of the body paint with it and pocketed his special ceremonial beads. If Izzy ignored the surroundings, it'd almost be like fall weekends growing up in the apartment suite they had shared with their adoptive father Dr. Fogg.

118

Matt still in pajama bottoms, taking his once-a-week break from early morning runs down the beach, reading a book or laughing with them at breakfast.

Simpler times.

Though removing the paint and *osaa* carried a dark symbolism to it. An unfinished wedding. The end of something before it even started.

She shook her head. It wouldn't be the end. They'd fix this, take down Theron, secure Athánatos, and finish the wedding. Neil, Dami, and Natassa deserved it. Until then they just had to… survive.

She longed to be able to take off the *okaa* but since she didn't have a shirt, she really couldn't. She adjusted the tight fabric as best she could, but it did little to ease her discomfort. The paint had long flaked off though.

Izzy hadn't heard a single bell in her head since her conversation with Matt. But he hadn't said a single word either. He hardly even looked at her.

She frowned. Maybe… she hadn't picked her words carefully enough. She didn't want the bond, that was true, but perhaps she could have been kinder about it.

But then maybe he'd keep pushing it. She covered her face with her arm. There was no right answer here. Maybe she should apologize.

But later. When she wasn't so damn tired. When this whole mess was over. She glanced at Matt. "Hey Matt," she said, hoping to fix what she broke. "How long has Ouranos been gone?"

Silence.

She turned. "Matt?"

Matt plucked a book from the shelf. He shook his head and put the book back, still not looking at her. "I dunno." His hand fell to his side.

Something black stained is white fur. Izzy sat up. "Matt… your hand."

Matt blinked then glanced at his hand. He narrowed his eyes, rubbing his fingers together.

Izzy stood. "Was that from the book?"

"No," Matt said. A very faint bell sound echoed in Izzy's ear, though she pushed it aside. Matt frowned. "It's elixir."

Elixir. Black Bound elixir. Izzy flicked her ears back. "How? You aren't doing anything with your magic."

Matt tilted his head. "I dunno." He turned to Izzy, staring at her hands. "You, uh, you have it too."

Izzy lifted her hand and also found a thin film of the stuff coating the fur. She squinted. What the hell? Her ear twitched. There was a quiet, almost unnoticeable Gem whine hitting her ears. She glanced down.

Her Gem glowed in the cloth hip holster. She looked up. "Matt…"

Matt pulled his out too, and sure enough, it was also glowing and whining. He stared at it, then put it back and held a hand to his head, shaking. "Fire and ice, I feel so *drained.*" He sat on a chair.

Izzy sat too, staring at the elixir on her fingers. She couldn't even feel the magic working. Like Matt, she just felt… weary. Like something had siphoned her energy.

Shock ran through her system. *Energy stealing.* Were they stealing each other's energy? The elixir built on her fur, covering her palms. Panic raced her heart, but then… slowed. She listed to one side, vision slightly blurry. It couldn't be energy stealing. They weren't using their magic. Maybe she just needed some sleep…

Something banged on the door.

Izzy shot up, blinking sleep out of her eyes. Matt shook himself awake too, trying to sit himself up. He reached for his head.

But stopped. Black Bound elixir fully covered his hand and wrist, halfway up to the elbow. He stared, wide-eyed. *"No."*

Izzy glanced at her own hands, also black with elixir. A spike of adrenaline and panic fought off her intense fatigue.

The banging continued.

Matt stood, still shaking his head, as if he struggled to stay awake. More bells filled Izzy's ears, a panicked cacophony. He moved toward her. "Izzy…"

She stood. "That's--"

The door flew open and dozens of Drifter souls flooded the room.

Matt's quills stood on end and he dashed left. "Run!"

Izzy ran. But where to? The room had no other exit.

Baltazar led the charge and chased after Izzy, sans weapons. Izzy dashed between the stacks, trying to lose him, but he was right on her tail.

Then she came to a dead end. She faced him, pulling on her healing magic, hoping she could knock him down just long enough to escape.

But the magic didn't tingle on her fingertips like normal. In fact, it didn't activate at all. Instead, the Black Bound elixir thickened on her hands and ran up past her elbows.

Panic set in now, and her fur and quills stood on end, sending chills and buzzing through her body.

Baltazar tackled her and pinned her to the ground. But rather than attack her, he held her down by her shoulders and another sentry, Lukas, ran up and squeezed her arm, stripping her fur of the elixir and gathering it into a jar.

Her heart beat against her chest. *No, no, no, NO!* She tried to free her arm, but exhaustion weakened her and she couldn't pull away.

It's the bond. The bond is making my magic go haywire!

Lukas finished stripping one arm of the stuff, then reached for the other one.

Izzy kicked, bit, scratched, and screamed at the two Drifters, but nothing moved them. She tried shielding, but the Gem refused to react.

Lukas stripped her other arm, then stepped aside, standing motionless, holding his container of elixir.

And then the elixir began building right back up again on her fur.

"No!" Izzy shouted. "You can't have it! Let me *go!*" Drawing on all her strength and pushing Matt out of her mind, she gripped Baltazar's arms and rolled, throwing them both to the side.

Baltazar clumsily bounced away on the faded floor, crashing into Lukas. The elixir jar fell to the ground, splattering everywhere. Izzy kicked it away and frantically pulled books from the shelves, throwing them at her attackers, hoping to slow them down.

More loud, clanging bells echoed in her mind. And once again, Matt's words.

Get off me! Get away! You can't have it! And finally one desperate call. *Help!*

Izzy threw two more heavy books on Baltazar and Lukas, then ran through the stacks for the entrance. Her heart pounded in her ears at the words in her head.

Not here. Not now! Not when I'm already so weak! This was the *worst* time to be fighting this.

She followed the sounds of scuffling, hoping to find Matt. Hoping she hadn't heard him in her head. Hoping he had just screamed and she had imagined it.

Hoping against hope.

And then she found Matt.

A dozen Drifters had him pinned down while two on each side of him stripped his arms of the ever-building elixir, collecting it in jars. Matt fought, but with so many Drifters, he couldn't push them back. And like with Izzy, it seemed he couldn't call on his magic. Not a single breeze brushed against Izzy's fur. The sight of the calm, emotionless, mindless

Drifters wearing the faces of friends and allies holding her helpless partner ripped her heart in two.

Desperate, Izzy grabbed books off the shelves and hurled them at Matt's attackers. A few hit the Drifters directly in the head, knocking them off, but only temporarily. Soon they got back up and held Matt down once again.

More elixir began building on Izzy's hands. A few Drifters turned toward her.

The jangly bells drowned out her thoughts, replacing them with Matt's. *You can't have it, you can't, you can't, YOU CAN'T* over and over and over, with a desperation so strong it drew tears to her eyes.

Izzy snarled and dove after one of the Drifters, gripping them around the middle as Matt had earlier. She pulled.

But he wouldn't budge. Izzy simply didn't have her normal strength. Instead, the Drifter pushed her aside. Another noticed the elixir on her hands and walked quietly toward her. She scrambled away.

Matt must be stealing her energy. Draso, she was so weak...

Matt's cries in her head grew more mumbled and hopeless, begging the Drifters to stop, begging Draso to help.

Begging Izzy for anything.

Damn it! "Matt, shield, blow them all off you, drop a shelf on them, *anything!*"

But he didn't even react to her voice. Like he couldn't hear her. He didn't even fight anymore.

She shut her eyes, her body shaking. *Damn it, damn it, damn it!* He stole her energy already, so why wasn't he using it?

The bells stopped their cacophony and focused to one clear ring.

And something pulled on her magic.

She pulled back. *You can't have it, you can't!* But guilt ate at her. Matt *needed* that.

But it's MINE. She pulled back, tears streaming down her face.

The elixir on her hands vanished back into her fur and a deep exhaustion struck her instantly, making her collapse to her knees. Fresh panic ripped through her as her body grew weaker. She couldn't hold on, she *couldn't.* Guilt warred with fear, making her stomach churn.

A stiff breeze sailed around the room and books flew off the shelves, ramming the Drifters. It was slow going, but the pile of books grew larger and larger until several Drifters had been knocked out entirely. The pile continued growing, drowning everyone in pages, until everything stopped moving.

Izzy couldn't see Matt anymore. Her heart raced. "…Matt?"

No answer.

She swallowed. *Oh no…*

The books shifted and Matt pulled himself out, coughing. Black Bound elixir covered his fingertips, but nothing more. He rolled off the pile to the floor, breathing heavily. "Fire and *ice.*"

Izzy crawled to him.

Matt carefully stood up, staring at his fingers. "I have never felt more helpless in my life."

Then the pile shifted again. Izzy flattened her ears. "Matt…"

Matt flicked his ears back. "We need to leave. *Now.*" He pulled himself to his feet.

Izzy fought through a wave of vertigo and did the same, gripping her head. She teetered unsteadily.

Matt gripped her hand, offering support. It should have been comforting, but…

Matt pulled. "Let's go!"

They ran. Izzy's legs wobbled under her, and she tripped several times, but they managed to get out. Izzy fought blurry vision. "Throne room…"

"I know," Matt said. He turned a corner.

Dozens more Drifters blocked the way. They slowly turned as one.

Izzy's quills stood on end. She didn't have the strength. She couldn't run. She leaned into Matt's arm.

He turned to her, frowning.

That energy pull again. Strong and immediate and *deep*. Her eyelids fluttered and she collapsed into Matt's arms.

Without another word, Matt lifted her up and dashed away, leaving a powerful breeze behind him. The Drifters followed close behind.

But they'd never get to the throne room now. Not with all those Drifters. No place was safe.

I promise to protect you, Matt's voice echoed, distant and faded. *I'll get us to the throne room. Hold on.* He pounded along, gripping her tight, blasting wind in all directions.

Izzy leaned into him, trying to balance herself, but there was little she could do. She managed one phrase before she passed out.

"Don't die."

CHAPTER 15

RIPPED

Jaden pointed a flashlight and led the way up the hill as they approached the Four Sisters Grove. The sun hadn't quite set yet, leaving the sky purple and indigo, but in the shadow of the forest, everything was already growing dark. He had changed out of the ceremonial wedding clothing and into his more familiar Guardian uniform, one Matt had brought here from Zyearth for him, including his fully repaired golden pendant. The body paint was all gone and the *osaa* packed away.

Right now he needed the façade of the Guardian. Something to hide the fear swirling about his insides, threatening to pull him apart at the seams. Back to the Guardian. Back to the stoic, Azure outlook. He had faced this before. He could do it again.

Mourning could come later.

He glanced back at his chosen team - Darvin, Roscoe, and Sami, all Defenders with experience and discipline, wearing their traditional uniforms as well. Ouranos, who had the most knowledge about Theron's state, still wearing the wedding clothes and flaked paint, aside from his royal chain, which he had packed away. Ana, a familiar companion in desperate times, back to a white blouse and black pants, looking wary.

And Trecheon. Who still hadn't spoken a word to anyone but Neil since Matt's disappearance. He hadn't changed clothes like the rest, except to put on his combat boots and biker jacket. He had wrapped the long diamond shaped loin guard around his waist, but beyond that, he looked like his normal self.

Except for the tense jaw, the furrowed brow, and shaking quills. He stared at the clover as they walked.

Jaden flicked his ears back. He felt Trecheon's pain, intimately. But he lifted his chin and hardened his features. Time to find the Guardian again.

"Do we have a plan, Guardian Azure?" Darvin asked, his deep voice serious and professional. Though it cracked slightly. Like everyone, he was clearly worried about Matt and Izzy. He patted the pouches at his belt, full of Lexi Charms in case of Cast, and even in the thin moonlight, his face betrayed his nervousness.

Jaden fell into the familiar leadership as Guardian. "I think we're forced to admit this is very touch and go," he said. "Theron and Judgement vanished here, but we really have no idea why or even how. Based on what we learned about the Aether, I doubt they went there. Logic says they vanished here, somehow. We just have to find out how. I don't know of any magic that allows you to just *vanish*, especially without any trace."

"Teleporting," Sami said quietly, flicking her white fox tail.

"A dead magic," Darvin said.

"Not entirely," Sami said. She pointed to Jaden.

Jaden frowned. Technically when the Omnir leader Kyo had damaged his Gem decades ago, he had unleashed the dead magic of teleporting. But it was temporary. Uncontrollable. And, because it came from a damaged focus jewel, it left scars.

Roscoe stopped, dropping his hand at his side. "Teleporting can happen if a Gem is damaged." He flicked back his large ears and stared at the ground. "We have proof that Matt is okay, but Izzy…"

Jaden frowned, turning to him. "I see where you're going with this, Roscoe, but I wouldn't worry. When I teleported with a damaged Gem, I left behind a destructive mess. We didn't see any of that when Judgement vanished. I'm sure nothing happened to their Gems."

Roscoe frowned. He crossed his arms, twitching his long, silver ears. "Mmm."

Jaden twisted an ear. Roscoe hadn't completely shut down like Trecheon had, but he also hadn't said much either. After all, he had lost his wife. Jaden patted his back. "We'll get her home, Roscoe," he said. "I refuse to lose her again after I just got her back."

Roscoe shook his head, his bronze antlers catching the light. "I suppose now I have some understanding of how she felt when I vanished during our first encounter with Theron on Zyearth."

Ouranos flicked his ears back.

Roscoe turned to him and managed a smile. "*Theron,* Ouranos, not you. I'm very glad you came into our lives." He frowned, looking away. "Theron I could do without though."

"I question the wisdom of us keeping him alive," Ouranos said. "Though I could not imagine a future where someone would purposefully wake him."

"Did your census find anything?" Darvin asked.

Ouranos frowned. "I am afraid that in the chaos of learning about Matt and Izzy's whereabouts, we forgot to compare notes. We left our books in the library."

"I'll message Leah," Ana said, pulling up her pendant. "She can at least compile notes. Perhaps Eris could help her figure out if anyone's missing."

"A good plan," Ouranos said.

Ana tapped away at the pendant's hologram, but it flickered and stalled, before finally vanishing entirely. "Uh. That's not good. Comms are down."

A twinge of familiar fear zapped through Jaden's brain. He pulled up his own pendant, but found the same problem. "This isn't good."

"What do you think's causing it?" Sami asked.

Ouranos looked up. Jaden followed his gaze. Tiny ripples and shimmers floated in the air above them – the Veil. Ouranos furrowed his brow. "I suspect the Veil may be interfering. It has in the past, and with it on the verge of collapse, it may have a stronger effect than before."

Jaden flattened an ear, but schooled his face. "Then don't get too far from each other today."

Ana folded her arms. "Still, we should do that census. I could run to the library and back pretty quickly here." She turned and gave a half-assed salute. "With your *permission,* of course, Jaden."

Jaden had to smile. Nice to see Ana hadn't changed that much. "Sure. Go find Leah."

Ana nodded, gave a proper Defender salute with a wink, and jogged off back toward the palace.

Jaden got to the center of the clover field and held up a fist, signaling everyone to stop. "Here. Spread out into a wide circle. And buddy up as much as we can. Groups of two or three. No one should be alone, just in case a sentry appears."

"If they should appear," Ouranos said. "Remember they are mindless right now. They cannot think and they do not react to pain. But I implore you, please subdue them if you can, and do not kill them. We have lost enough to senseless death today."

Everyone nodded.

Roscoe frowned. "What are we looking for, exactly?"

Jaden pressed his lips into a thin line. "Honestly, I haven't a clue. That's the problem with this whole thing. Just look for anything off. Magic scarring, summon residue perhaps, even a bad feeling might be a start. We're leaping without a parachute here. But keep your eyes open. We're bound to find something. Magic like that will leave evidence." He turned to Ouranos. "I know the Archons already thoroughly searched this area for rips in the Veil, but it wouldn't hurt to look again."

Ouranos nodded.

"Alright everyone," Jaden said. "Partner up and spread out."

Darvin and Sami took off to the right. Ouranos and Roscoe moved toward the far end of the field.

And Trecheon stood there, watching everything, unmoving. He stared off into space, clearly not fully there.

Jaden pinned an ear back. He gripped Trecheon's shoulder, careful of the biomech. "Hey. Need to talk?"

Trecheon shook himself. He met Jaden's eyes as if he was seeing him for the first time.

Jaden furrowed his brow. He glanced at the rest of his team, waited until they were out of earshot, then turned back to Trecheon. "If you need to talk - vent, mumble, scream, whatever - I'm right here to listen. No judgement. No fear. Okay? Don't try handling this alone. That's what I did and it never works well."

Trecheon stared at him, then blinked and looked away. "Yeah."

Well. A single word was better than silence. Supposedly.

The pair of them investigated near the Four Sisters' Grove, though there wasn't much to look at, especially in the fading light. Jaden searched through the patterns and images on the tapestries, but nothing really stood out. He turned his attention to the footprints on the ground, but that didn't distract him well enough. His mind wandered, filling his head with images.

Matt and Izzy stuck in the Aether, slowly starving to death.

Zeke going in but never coming out.

Theron ripping them all to pieces, tearing down the palace with Judgement at his side.

Alexina… still out there, alone… or dead.

Jaden shook his head and gritted his teeth, then went back to the tapestries. He just had to *focus*.

"If we get Matt and Izzy out safe," Trecheon said slowly. "What happens when you all go back to Zyearth?"

Jaden turned, his body buzzing with adrenaline at Trecheon's "if." He wrinkled his snout. *"When* we get them back."

Trecheon stared at the dusty tapestries, his eyes unfocused, his ears pinned to his skull. "If we get them back," he repeated, setting Jaden's teeth on edge. Trecheon shook his head. "Sorry, I shouldn't be so damn negative… I just thought we were *done* with this shit…" He sat hard on one of the tapestries.

Jaden pressed his mouth into a thin line, processing the rest of Trecheon's question. He stuffed his worries into a corner of his mind. "Have you told Matt how you feel about him?"

Trecheon turned away.

So no, then. "Trecheon--"

"I already know I should tell him," Trecheon snapped. "But what would that matter? It won't change anything. He's still leaving." He tugged at a blade of grass. "…Sacha too."

Jaden's ear flicked. He'd been watching Trecheon slowly close up during the last few months after they all found out Lance was calling them all home. But all this mess had accelerated the problem. And he couldn't let Trecheon break. Not now. He took a deep breath. "Trecheon, I know it feels like everything is falling apart, but--"

Then Trecheon held up a hand and his eyes narrowed. "Hold up…" He leaned down over the tapestry. "Something isn't right here."

Jaden narrowed his gaze, hoping Trecheon had actually found something and wasn't just deflecting. "What'd you find?"

Trecheon poked the air with his finger. And the air around it… rippled. Like he had disturbed the surface of a still pond.

Jaden leaned down and poked it too. More ripples. The dime-sized hole was a strange dark green and didn't match with the rest of the tapestry. It almost looked like a leaf…

Oh Draso. He stood. "Ouranos!"

Ouranos lifted his head and jogged over, the others behind him. "Did you find something?"

"This," Jaden poking the hole again, watching the ripples in the air. "Trecheon found it. I think this is a hole in the Veil."

Ouranos reached down and ran a finger over the strange green patch. "It is indeed… Very small and highly unstable." He frowned. "Normally only the royalty of Athánatos can detect a rip in the Veil. The fact that Trecheon noticed it first is a testament to the state of it…"

Roscoe crossed his arms. "Where does it go?"

"Can you widen it?" Sami asked.

Ouranos held out a hand and tiny red threads appeared in the air around the hole. But they collapsed almost instantly. "I worry about accidentally destroying it and losing our only lead."

"Leave it to me then," Darvin said and he leaned back, falling into the black, inky puddle of a Shadow Cast. He gurgled at them in his Shadow Cast form, then slithered through the hole, slowly vanishing, like water down a drain.

Jaden tapped his foot on the grass impatiently. It felt like hours, but soon Darvin reappeared, slinking his entire body back out onto the tapestry. He stuck his fully formed head out of the puddle. "It's definitely an active portal. And you aren't gonna like where it leads."

Ouranos frowned. "Where?"

"The island of Sol."

CHAPTER 16

ANCHORS

Neil followed the Archons through the open-air hallways of the palace, the Black Cloak on one side and Damianos and Sacha on the other, fighting nervousness that threatened to bring up his dinner. The evening sunset cast long, dark shadows though the palace, reminding Neil strongly of Shadow Cast.

God almighty, this was gonna *suck*.

The Archons still wore their wedding finery, most fighting to keep the paint fully intact. Archon Electrik had even repainted it. As a symbol, he had said. This wedding would happen.

Embrik had let his fade though, and he even took the time to grab a simple T-shirt. "I wore this while surviving on the mainland. I will wear it again to remind me how to survive on home soil."

Dami too had fought to keep his paint and finery intact, though he had put his royal jewelry away. As had Neil. Too delicate.

God, that hurt.

Sacha though, was determined to upkeep her paint like Electrik. Though she had swapped the skirt for uniform pants. Better movement, she had said.

She had also suggested Neil wear his Defender pendant. "The Basileus chain may be too delicate, but the Defender pendant could probably withstand a direct punch from Judgement," she had said. "Wear it as a symbol of strength."

Neil ran a finger over the legless dragon, feeling the outstretched wings, the Gem in its coils, the tucked chin, mentally repeating the meaning of each symbol. *Legless dragon for peace. Outstretched wings for welcome. Gem for power.* He breathed deep. *Tucked chin for defense. For Defender.*

Yes, he was going to be Basileus. But first, he was a Defender. It had taken him a long time to believe he deserved that, but now he clung to it. He needed the strength.

Neil reached over and twisted the paracord bracelet on his wrist. A combined gift from Trecheon and Eris. During the War of Eons, Trecheon had braided paracord as a way to stave off boredom while they traveled from one location to the next. Later, he started braiding bracelets as memorials for their fallen companions.

Now he had braided one for Neil. And he spoke for the first time since Matt's disappearance.

"This was supposed to be a wedding gift," Trecheon had told him. "A bracelet to symbolize new life instead of death, like they used to." He stared at the bracelet. "I haven't tried making one of these since I lost my arms. It was hell relearning how to do it, but I did it." He passed the bracelet to Neil, braided in three colors - teal, purple, and violet. Neil, Dami, and Natassa's eyes colors. "Remember that when you go through this anchoring thing. I'm tired of making memorials." Then he hugged Neil tightly for a long time.

Neil flicked his ears back, lingering in the memory of that hug. A hug of desperation as much as one of friendship. Trecheon's words stuck to him.

He was tired of memorials too.

"If this symbolizes new life," Neil had said slowly. "Then are you making one for yourself too?"

Trecheon bit his lip. He pulled a half-finished bracelet out of his pocket. It had his, Sacha's, and Matt's eye colors.

Neil frowned. "You didn't finish it."

Trecheon shrugged. "Matt…"

They stood in silence for a long time.

"Trecheon," Neil said. "Promise me you'll tell Matt how you feel when you see him next."

Trecheon perked his ears.

"I mean it," Neil said. "Don't wait. You two deserve happiness." Trecheon shut down soon after. Neil wasn't sure how to interpret that.

But he had one more request.

"Trecheon." Trecheon met Neil's gaze. Neil gave him his most serious look. "If something happens to me… Look after Philip for me."

Trecheon's grew wide at that. But he nodded.

Eris then took the bracelet and wove Neil's awaiting Ei-Ei jewels through it so he could carry them with him. "For when we are ready to bind them." She hugged him too, muttering under her breath in the Athánatos language. "A blessing for the future Basileus."

Eris always knew the right thing to say.

Sacha gripped his shoulder, pumping gentle, cooling healing energy into his body, jolting him back to the present. She frowned. "You okay? You look a bit queasy."

He forced a smile. "Better now, thanks."

She smiled and gave him an exaggerated wink. "Got your back, hun."

Neil glanced around. Their little mish-mashed group, ready to attempt something no one had done in thousands of years, with only a cryptid that they didn't quite trust to guide them.

Fun times.

The Cloak walked ahead, leading them to the a room in the back of the palace, which he called the Veilsong room. "We'll start here."

"What are we doing anyway?" Neil asked. "You've been pretty vague about this."

The Cloak pointed to a shape on the floor, a round circle with a wavy border like an exaggerated symbol for the sun. "This looks like a sun, but it's actually the old symbol for Veilsong," the Cloak said. "You'll stand here." He pointed to other circles around the Veilsong. Familiar symbols representing the seven magic elements, plus an eighth one… with a cloak on it. "The Archons and I will invoke the magic of the seven elements, calling for protection. The magic will cling to you, draw energy out of you, and build the first anchor point."

Neil's fur stood on end. "The magic will *cling* to me?"

"Yes," the Cloak said. "Very literally. This is where Sacha comes in."

"So I'm just supposed to stand here while I'm bombarded by mage magic, hope I don't die, and pray Sacha has the energy to save my ass?" He paused. "It's not gonna destroy my clothes and stuff is it? That last thing I need is the family jewels hanging out for all to see. Especially with my future father-in-law here."

"Excelsis assured me it wouldn't," the Cloak said, chuckling slightly. "It clings to *you,* not your effects."

Neil mentally reached for the pendant and paracord again. He adjusted the sword on his belt – his symbol of Athánatos and reminder of why he was doing this. "Good." But he flicked his ears back. "How the hell did the last Athánatos survive it? They don't have healers."

"The first Veil's creation took place over several months," the Cloak said. "Not just because of the need to heal after each anchor, but because of traveling distance. Each of the seven Archon palaces plus this main one has one of these. We have to travel to each one, in order, then back here, to complete the circle. That will erase the old Veil and replace it with the new one."

The heat left Neil's face. "I gotta do this *nine goddamned times?*"

"There's a *reason* we have a healer," the Cloak said.

Sacha crossed her arms now. "I assume we'll be using the Veil portals to get to all the Archon palaces like we did when Ackerson's cronies invaded. Will that weaken it further?"

The Cloak's green eyes darkened. "I hope not."

Neil massaged the fur on his forehead. Building the Veilsong in hours instead of months. This was not a well-laid plan. But what other choice did they have? "Fine. Let's get started."

"One thing first. In private." The Cloak pulled Neil aside, out of earshot of everyone else. Neil scrunched up his face. The Cloak locked his gaze with Neil. "Being the Veil's anchor grants you magic that no other has. The ability to see your subjects in your mind."

Neil lifted a brow. "Wait, what?"

"As we complete the circle, a map will form in your head," the Cloak said. "You'll see the names and location of anyone bound to Athánatos jewels as long as they are in the confines of the island, with one exception - you can't locate Drifters. Or at least the old Veil anchor couldn't."

Neil's tail lashed about. Damn. There goes his idea of looking for Theron with this newfound power. "Okay, great, I guess."

"I'm telling you this for two reasons," the Cloak said. "One, it will be overwhelming at first. But it'll subside quickly and you'll be able to call on it only when you need it." He took a deep breath. "Two... it'll tell you my name."

Neil's eyes widened. "I thought you weren't Athánatos."

"I'm not," the Cloak said. "But I took on Ei-Ei jewels when I picked up the mantle."

Neil pressed his lips tight. "Did Robert?"

"All of us did."

Neil's jaw dropped now. *"All* of you? How many Cloaks are there?"

"Not the time." The Cloak took Neil's hands and gripped them firmly. "No matter what you see in that map, you *must* keep it to yourself. We've kept our identities secret for a reason. Do you understand?"

Neil chewed his lip. "Yeah... sure."

The Cloak narrowed his eyes. "It's for everyone's safety, Neil. Please."

"Yeah, I got it," Neil said, flicking his tail. "Your secret's safe with me."

The Cloak eyed him a moment longer, then nodded. "Good." He led Neil back to the circle and put him in position. He met Neil's gaze. "I'll warn you, Neil. This will *hurt*. And the magic will essentially paralyze you, freezing you to the spot until the anchor is built. You'll have very little autonomy. That being said..." He lowered his voice. "...It's okay to scream."

Neil's whiskers tingled and he tightened his jaw. Yeah, that filled him with a lot of confidence. He zipped up his jacket and stood on the Veil symbol in the middle of the room. *For Athánatos. For Philip. For Dami. For Natassa.*

The Archons stood on their respective symbols, exchanging glances with each other, uneasy. Embrik met Neil's eyes. "I believe this is where most would say that if you need to stop, tell us. But I already know how you will respond if I asked such a question."

"We don't stop," Neil said. "This is bigger than just me. This is keeping all of Athánatos, and all the people I love, safe. Keep going no matter what."

Electrik frowned. "The Cloak speaks truth. If you need to shout, to express pain, do so. There is no shame in it, Basileus."

Neil scrunched his snout. "Sure." But he wouldn't. Because he didn't want an excuse to stop. He couldn't.

Damianos strode up to him and held him tight, though he didn't speak. Neil nuzzled into his fur, breathing in his gentle scent, clinging to his strong hug. Reminding himself why he was doing this.

Then he stepped back.

Dami moved next to Sacha. The golden tiger wore a deep frown on her face.

The Black Cloak stood on his circle too and held out his hands. The Archons followed his example.

So did Neil. He held his body rigid and gritted his teeth.

He would not scream.

The Cloak muttered something in old Athánatos, something so far removed from the modern language that Neil hardly recognized a word. As he spoke, the circles under their feet lit up with a soft hum. Magic of all types formed on the Archons' fingertips, swirling around their hands and wrists. It crackled through the air, making his tongue sting of iron and mist.

Embrik furrowed a brow, frowning deeply.

The Cloak said one more phrase - one even Neil knew.

Sisters. Barrier between life and Judgement. Protect us.

The swirling magic on each Archon froze in place. The Cloak held his left hand toward Neil. "Neil… Brace yourself." The Archons turned their hands toward him as well, their magic traveling over their bodies to their fingertips, then flying through the air.

Pain hit him instantly.

Burning fire! Freezing ice! Wind ripping through the hollows of his ears, deafening him, stones pelting his body, bruising every inch, electricity paralyzing his muscles, sand stinging his skin under his fur… Every muscle locked in place, every organ screamed out in anguish, every fiber of his being begged for this to stop, and in this moment of terrible, blinding agony, he realized he hadn't asked how long each of these would take. The only comfort came from the water element, which swirled around his body, cooling his wounds.

Though not enough.

He pressed his eyes tightly shut and bit his tongue against a scream, though the mental torture manifested internally anyway. His tail shot straight up, all the fur on his body puffed out, and his whiskers burned with mage magic.

I will not scream!

Seconds ticked away into what felt like hours, each moment doubling the pain through his body. Maybe he was dying. Maybe he couldn't do it. Maybe the Veil would just fall.

Maybe this was what he deserved as an assassin.

The Defender in him chased that thought away before it clung.

But as the pain ran through his every cell, something crystal clear and shining ran though his mind. It almost felt like someone… singing. A call, distant and soft, bounding around his mind. The Veilsong.

And… images. The palace, the Four Sisters Grove, the ArchDragon gardens, the clover lawn, the forests. All in a bird's eye view.

An incredible burst of power rushed through him… then left him.

The pounding energy stopped abruptly, taking most of the pain with it. Sharp aches and tingles circulated his body, and he teetered slightly, his vision blurry. His ears rang so loud it gave him a headache, but somewhere Sacha called to him. He leaned in what he hoped was her direction.

Then collapsed completely.

Sacha grabbed him, and pumped familiar, cool, comforting healing through his burning bones. He leaned further into her, focusing everything on her magic, letting it ground him. He blinked tears out of his eyes, trying to make the dull, colorless shapes turn back into the surroundings he knew and loved. Slowly things came back into focus and Dami's face came into view, worried but stoic. Neil's solid support, as he always had been. He licked his teeth.

"Did… I scream?"

Dami blinked, then smiled. "No. You held your position beautifully."

Neil forced a smile. "Good." He frowned. "How… long was that?"

"About two minutes or so," Embrik said, frowning. Hopefully they will all be that quick."

The Cloak coughed.

"Good… good." Neil ignored the Cloak and sat up. "One down… eight to go…" He coughed, his stomach suddenly and violently protesting.

Sacha pressed a hand to his stomach. "Got you." It calmed down. "Wouldn't want you vomiting on top of all this. You need your strength."

Neil frowned. "This must have been bad if you've got your healer voice on…"

Sacha pulled him closer, pumping energy through even harder. "I've seen worse." Slowly she helped him stand. The pain had subsided, but the terrible buzzing in his bones remained. She frowned. "Sorry… Running low. We'll try again before you get the next anchor going."

Neil shook himself, still a little wobbly. "Thanks…" Both Embrik and Electrik ran to Neil's side to support him. Other Archons offered their encouragement, their aid… and condolences. Dami gripped Neil's hand and wouldn't let it go.

"How do you feel?" Embrik asked.

"Like a train hit me," Neil said. But he paused. Something tugged at him, taking threads of energy from his body. But also… welcoming him. He closed his eyes.

And that bird's eye view of their surroundings came back, full force, even clearer than before. Animals scattered between trees and through the gardens. The palace dwellers came into sharp focus as they wandered the area, nervous, but optimistic. He could almost… feel their energy. Tense. Hopeful. Alive. Each one with a name, as the Cloak said. Not overwhelming, but... comforting. He clutched his chest. This had to mean it worked. The Veil's first anchor. It recognized Neil as Basileus. They could do this.

His view of the palace stretched further and deeper, capturing every Athánatos nearby. He desperately searched for Theron, even though the Cloak had said he wouldn't show up, but he didn't find anything.

Though there were two names he wasn't expecting.

Darvin and Sami. In the Four Sisters Grove. But how?

He opened his eyes.

The Black Cloak remained on his circle, his green eyes glassy. He didn't speak. Words from the other Cloak, Robert, ran through his mind. *This isn't right.*

Damn right it wasn't.

And the Cloak knew that intimately. Even if it was clear that they had no other choice.

Neil didn't like the Cloak. He didn't fully trust him. But he also hated the idea of him sitting here wallowing in guilt over something he couldn't help. Neil knew that kind of guilt intimately. That shit ate you up. He lifted his chin. "Cloak."

The Cloak met his gaze.

Neil managed a smile. "We got this."

The Cloak's brow furrowed, a subtle action through the open eye sockets on his mask. He only nodded.

Neil's chest tensed and the queasy stomach returned.

The Veilsong's map rippled through his mind again, and the Black Cloak came into sharp view… along with his name.

Neil's body buzzed and he nearly shouted the name out loud in his shock.

Another supposedly dead Guardian.

Matt's grandfather. Jaden's father.

Tymon Azure.

Welcome to Hell

The moment Zeke's bare feet touched whatever the hell passed as grass in the strange, desaturated comic book world of the Aether, a chill buried itself in his spine and wouldn't go away. He rubbed down the fur on his arms, but it wouldn't lay flat.

His happy, familiar, comfortable home in Athánatos, now a literal hell on Earth.

Eris' warnings about energy draining hit his mind instantly too, as he could feel an intimate pull on his magic as they walked toward the palace. It was… violating. Repugnant. He shivered.

On instinct, he prodded the bond he and Leah shared. *Leah?*

Nothing.

He pressed his lips together and offered a scent instead. Baking apples, their go-to for comfort and assurance.

He got the sharp smell of fresh coffee back. Good. They could communicate a little. Not as good as the visuals Ouranos and Matt had, but better than nothing.

Natassa also seemed quite put off by their surroundings, but at least she didn't appear to be paralyzed like Zeke felt. She pointed toward a weird copy of the palace. "We will try the library first."

Zeke shook himself. "Sure." Natassa jogged toward it, so Zeke pushed aside the discomfort in his stomach and matched her pace. "So, uh, *theía*… what do we do if we meet a Drifter?"

"Run," Natassa said. "This is a place for souls. A soul cannot die. And right now, most if not all of the souls here will be hostile toward us."

Zeke flicked his ears back. "But we can't free them."

"Not without dying ourselves, no," Natassa said. "It is better to avoid them entirely. Prevent yourself from accidentally dying to free a soul." She paused. "Though, this is unlikely to happen. You need to break the chains with intent." She shook herself. "But they can do great harm to you. Perhaps even kill you, though I am unsure. Regardless, we should stay away."

Zeke bit his lip. Not comforting. "And… what do we do if we find Ouranos' soul?"

Natassa stopped. She stared off into space for a moment. Zeke frowned. Eventually she shook herself. "We also run. We… cannot help him." She continued jogging.

Zeke flicked his ears back. He ran after her.

Natassa brought them to one of the side entrances to the palace. They carefully made their way through the palace halls. Zeke kept his ears perked for any sign of movement, but his gaze darted everywhere. The Athánatos palace was normally filled with colorful fresco paintings, beautiful tapestries, and comforting light from the artful holes in the ceiling. It was a place of coziness and joy. But this strange world had stripped it of all that. Now it felt cold, empty.

Dead.

And yet, this was still his home, weird as it was. He couldn't imagine leaving it.

A soft smell of… cloves and cranberries floated under his nose. Something comforting and homely. Leah, trying to give him strength.

It only made his chest ache. If he stayed on Athánatos, he'd lose this with her. But if he went with her to Zyearth, he'd lose Athánatos. He'd lose Andre, Chad, his new family.

He'd lose his mom, Alexina. Assuming they'd find her.

There were no good answers. Damn everything to hell. He gritted his teeth and pushed it aside, focusing on the task at hand.

Hopefully Matt and Izzy had had the sense to shut the library door and just stay there. They could be in and out, super quick, and get back to going after Theron. Before this place ripped Zeke's sanity from his mind.

"Here," Natassa said quietly. Zeke turned into the hall leading to the library.

The library doors were wide open. Zeke's heart fell to his stomach. Not a good sign. Natassa ran ahead and Zeke dashed down the hall to catch up to her.

The library was a mess. Books thrown about, furniture on its side, paper everywhere. None of that familiar library smell though, which made the whole thing extra bad. And not a single sound. The colorless room made him feel queasy. Like it wasn't even real.

Natassa's tail lashed out and she flicked her ears back. "Search the library. Hurry!" She ran for a pile of books and began throwing them aside.

Zeke went for another pile and tore it down in minutes, but didn't find anything. He wandered deeper into the stacks, searching for more signs of a struggle, but there were no more book piles.

Wait.

One small pile of books had shards of broken glass all over the floor. And with it, tiny puddles of something thick and black. Like the Cast, but not nearly enough to be one.

Not good. He turned to get back to Natassa.

A deep scraping of metal on metal echoed through the stacks. Sounded like… chains.

Zeke slipped behind a bookshelf, perking his ears. A Drifter? Ouranos and Natassa had mentioned chains, but Zeke couldn't remember if they meant literally or figuratively.

Gotta get out of here. He dashed for the exit.

A thin black tail vanished behind a bookshelf. The way out.

Shit. There were no more exits. But maybe he could sneak around it… He cautiously walked through the stacks and peered through the bookshelves.

There, wrapped in chains around their arms and legs, was one of the Drifters… but not one of the sentries. It was a feminine quilar, wearing a pair of modern, mainlander pants and a simple T-shirt. She had her back to him, so he couldn't see her face, but then she perked an ear… an orange tipped ear.

Zeke's heart seized. Orange tipped… feminine… *Oh no…* It couldn't be…

Alexina.

He stared, unable to look away. His mom. Alexina. A *Drifter*. Just like Ouranos. Like Theron. No *wonder* they couldn't find her. She wasn't… she wasn't whole.

Oh Draso, she was a *Drifter*.

Zeke racked his brain for all the information Natassa had given him. Some Drifters were here simply because they had lost their souls due to injuries. They could be coaxed back once the body healed. But… did those ones have chains too? Would they also be hostile? He couldn't recall.

But if she was here on purpose… That meant Theron controlled her too. It could mean she wasn't… safe.

Sisters, what should he *do?*

She stopped briefly, standing straight up. Then she turned.

And her gaze met Zeke's.

Everything in his bones pulled him to her. The lost member of their war party. The last missing Athánatos. His mother…

He stood still for several seconds, waiting to see what she'd do. But she just held his gaze. Wouldn't move, wouldn't say a word. The chains rattled with every slight movement, and her face was blank and dead, aside from a furrowed brow.

Zeke bit his lip. Damn it, he had lost two mothers already. He didn't want to lose another. He moved out from behind the bookcase. "Alexina--"

Her eyes grew big and teary. She held out a hand and mouthed something to him.

Help me.

Then she unleashed a barrage of ice and lightning at him.

Zeke yelped and dove out of the way as the magic tore through the shelves and books, ripping everything to pieces. Big, splintered wood rained down on him, catching in his fur and skin. One large piece dug into his back on his left side. He roared in pain and ripped it out, unthinking. Hot blood ran down his back. He twisted his arm and pressed a hand against it as best he could, hobbling away.

Alexina followed him, but he turned and formed an ice wall from floor to ceiling, cutting her off. He immediately fell to the floor, exhaustion overtaking him. He coughed, gasping for air, while Alexina clawed away at the ice. Then she set her hands on fire.

He pressed his magic against the ice wall, hoping it'd hold. A technique Jaden had taught him. But it only worked if he had the damn *energy*.

"Zeke!" Natassa ran up to him, pressing magic into his ice wall. She kneeled down. "Oh Sisters, your *back.*"

"I… don't think it hit anything vital…" He pulled his hand away. Black blood clung to his fur. He stared, his jaw dropping. "Sisters, it's *black.*"

"A side effect of the Aether," Natassa said. She ripped one of the flowing strips of fabric from her skirt and wrapped it around the wound. "It instantly saps the life and energy from your blood." She looked up at the ice wall, then fell back. "Draso's *breath,* is that--?"

"Alexina," Zeke said, his voice cracking. He forced himself to his feet. Alexina continued bombarding the ice wall with fire magic, but it still held.

Tears built in Natassa's eyes. "Oh, heaven help her…"

Zeke's tail lashed. "She's still in there, Natassa. She asked me to help her…"

"You cannot," Natassa said, getting to her feet. "You cannot without giving your life, do you understand? And I *forbid* it, Zeke. I--"

"But didn't Matt do something with Ouranos?" Zeke said. "He *saved him.* He didn't release his soul, but Ouranos is the same as you and me! Can't I do that with Alexina?"

Natassa shook her head violently. *"No,* Zeke, if you even attempt it--"

A fireball broke through the ice wall. It hit a bookshelf near Zeke, blowing books everywhere, though none of them caught fire for long.

"We have to leave *now.*" Natassa grabbed Zeke's hand and rushed out of the library.

Zeke struggled to keep up with his wounded side. "But where do we go? Where would Matt and Izzy hide?"

Alexina blasted fire out of the library entrance. Natassa countered by filling the entrance with another ice wall.

"That will not hold her long," Natassa said, her voice breaking. "We need--"

"Natassa?"

Zeke looked up.

There, in faint chains, eyes wide, jaw slack, stood Ouranos' soul.

CENSUS

Leah sat at the library's big mahogany table and flipped through Archángeli's journal with Eris and Melaina at her side, more determined than ever. The light from the traditional lantern and the bright flashlights and lamps only served to emphasize the falling night, reminding everyone of the many hours their Guardians had been missing.

There had to be something here. There *had* to be.

Athánatos counted on it.

Athánatos is taking Zeke away from you, the Thought Factory spat out. *Lance is taking you away from all your friends and dropping you in a land of loneliness again.*

Leah ground her teeth together, growling quietly. *No.* This was not happening. She was *not* going to let the Thought Monster emerge again. She had better control over her anxiety than that.

Do you?

She didn't respond. Instead, she recognized the intrusive thought. Acknowledged it was there. Gave it the space it needed. Identified why it was wrong.

Then threw off a cliff.

Her breathing calmed. Therapy helped know how to deal with the issues, but it sure as heck didn't make them go away. Especially for the half-truths. Because… in some ways, she would lose Zeke. And she would be alone.

She shook her head. Not the time. She leaned over the table.

With the Phonar's help, they were able to locate all their journals from the past. Well. All but the ninth one. None of the summons could remember if the final member of the team had kept a journal. And actually, none of them could remember anything about that ninth Phonar - gender, species, name, magic, it all evaded them.

Though considering the trauma around them all becoming summons, it was entirely likely they just refused to really *try* to remember. Which Leah didn't blame them for.

Like with Archángeli, none of them were willing to spend too much time sifting through the journals for clues. Leah, Melaina, and Eris were on their own. They had them spread out all over the table, trying to line up the dates and find any correlation between them all, though Leah mostly focused on Archángeli, who seemed to have the least ornate handwriting.

If only this was in the modern alphabet...

To help out, Leah had brought the dragon A.I. Pilot into the room and they started feeding him the letters, old and new. He was able to piece together some of the changes and help build somewhat of a translation machine. Better than nothing.

Pilot gleefully picked away at the letters and words in the journals. "This is *-bzzt-* fascinating! How come you haven't brought this to me before?"

"Because they were blank before," Leah said. "This came out of the Purge breaking."

Pilot's gaze grew dark. "…Ah. Not for a good *-bzzt-* reason then." His little faerie dragon form hovered over Archángeli's journal, flicking his wings and filling the air around him with motes of light. "I hope we can *-bzzt-* find something good then, so this doesn't *-bzzt-* go to waste."

"That's the idea," Leah said. She sighed. "I'm not liking our chances though…"

"Chin up," Pilot said, "brushing" her cheek with a holographic wing. "We're bound to find *-bzzt- something.*"

Heavy hooves thumped through the library and Ana walked into view. "Hey Leah, do you know where Natassa and Ouranos' census books went? They forgot to compare notes."

"I had wondered," Melaina said, looking at the two census books. "I will look through it, if you think you can spare me."

"Pilot and I have this," Leah said. She turned to Ana. "Weren't you with Jaden's team though? You could have called on the pendant."

Ana's crossed her arms and lowered her head. "They aren't working. Ouranos thinks the Veil is interfering somehow."

Leah's tail lashed. "Great. One more problem."

Melaina grabbed one of Leah's pens and a piece of scratch paper and began comparing notes. "Eris, can you help?"

"Certainly my Lady." Eris moved next to Melaina. "Perhaps it would be better to move to one of the study rooms? It would allow us to call out names without disturbing Leah."

"Good idea." Melaina smiled at Leah. "We will return soon and you can report our findings to Jaden's team."

Ana nodded. "I'll be waiting." Melaina nodded back and she and Eris took the books toward one of the study rooms. Ana took a seat and rested her hand on Leah's, rubbing the fur.

Leah's ears flushed. She and Ana had shared some very intimate moments while chasing down Jaden, but while they had grown closer as friends in the last several years, they… struggled to continue with that intimacy. Leah longed to, and Ana clearly did too, but they wanted very different things.

Ana was looking for a romantic relationship. Leah was aromantic and had no desire for romance. They hadn't figured out what that meant for their relationship yet.

And at this point, why even bring it up again? Leah thought bitterly. *Lance is calling me home.*

The whole situation stank on so many levels.

Leah slipped her hand into Ana's and squeezed, wishing she had the right words. At least Ana was perfectly healthy, aside from the excess cortisol flowing through her veins. Small favors.

Leah, Archángeli said in a whiff of wind past her ear. *The journal… it is near to the day when we chose to become summons.* They shrunk away and slowly morphed from their zyfaunos form back to their normal bird form.

The other summons fluffed up and turned as one to Archángeli, eyes wide.

Leah frowned, her heart aching. "Tough memory?"

A… desperate one, Archángeli said. *A last resort that we didn't want to pursue. But it was either that or let the planet fall to Judgement's wrath. We had no choice.*

Leah flattened an ear. "Like the story Eris told."

It is closer to us now, Excelsis said, dropping embers on Leah's nose. *We… feel it intimately. No longer a story, but an experience.*

Leah's tail flicked left and right. She glanced at Ana. The doe smiled sadly and let go of Leah's hand. Leah frowned then glanced back at the book and flipped the pages ahead. "There's still dozens of pages after that incident."

Yes, Archángeli said. *It was a challenge to regain our mental capabilities at first… Learning how to write, to communicate through our elements, to interact with the world when we no longer needed food or rest. But once we were more settled, we continued writing.* They frowned as best they could as a bird, tapping a claw on the table. *I… seem to recall there was one more major event with Daisy before we stopped journaling, though I cannot remember it entirely. I… hope the journal will provide answers.*

Leah's fur stood on end. "Daisy. The first Cloak."

Archángeli nodded. *His line fell when Theron created Shadow Cast.*

"How did the Cloak find its way out of Athánatos?" Ana asked, leaning back in her chair.

"I'm curious too," Leah said. "I remember Melaina saying that the last Cloak died on the island."

Archángeli shook their head. *The Cloak as an entity is a mystery on its own, my Lady. Prinkípissa Olympia cast magic over it that few of us truly understand. I am just glad it found its way out. We had no way of finding a new Cloak as summons.*

Leah chewed on her lip. The Thought Factory churned out intrusive thoughts. Questions she shouldn't ask. How did it feel to become a summon? What was your oath like?

Did it hurt?

But she looked away and imagined herself flipping the Thought Factory sign from "open" to "closed." Those weren't the thoughts to ask someone newly traumatized by a past they hadn't had the chance to explore. Gripping for control, she turned to Archángeli. "Do you want to leave while we explore this? It hurts enough as it is."

Archángeli ground their beak together and fanned their tail feathers, shaking. *I... should be here to help with interpretation--*

"You should be looking after your mental health," Leah said. "Zeke already told you that once. Go rest." She glanced around. "All of you. Spend some time with Charlotte and the others. They could use the company and it'll give you some space to process."

Archángeli lowered their gaze, then hopped over and pressed their forehead to Leah's. *Thank you.*

She smiled and stroked their head. "Of course."

The summons all nodded their thanks and took off, leaving through the front entrance of the library. Leah sighed and pulled the book nearer to her and scanned it with Pilot.

Pilot "landed" on Leah's shoulder, a smile on his tiny face. "That was -*bzzt*- kind of you."

"Something we should have done ages ago," Leah said. "I hope they'll be okay."

"They will be," Ana said. "They're made of tough stuff." She leaned forward, nearly pressing her nose against Leah's cheek. Leah turned, touching noses, her face flushing. But Ana didn't budge. She stared deep into Leah's eyes. "But... are you?"

She frowned. "I'm... fine."

"I know you're not, Leah," Ana said. "You're not yourself. And I don't just mean because of this incident. This isn't new behavior."

Leah flicked an ear back. "What behavior?"

"I see the way you cling to Zeke," Ana said. "More than usual."

"I -*bzzt*- concur," Pilot said.

Leah's hair stood on end. "I don't… I don't cling to him."

"Yes, you do," Ana said. "You've been clinging to everyone in fact. Zeke just stands out. And I know why. You're going home to Zyearth."

Leah closed her eyes a moment and took a deep breath.

Pilot fluttered around her head. "Leah, if you're so -*bzzt*- upset about it, why not ask Lance if you can stay? Be a permanent -*bzzt*- ambassador to Earth."

"Because that's not my *job,*" Leah said. "I'm a historian and summons expert. My job is on Zyearth. And my job just got a lot more complicated with the unregistered summons popping up all over the universe. The Galactic Accord is looking into it, but they don't have a summoner historian right now, let alone a summoner to help. Their last historian retired a while ago and isn't willing to come back and they never bothered replacing her. I'm all they have. They need me and they've been asking for me for the last year. I can't help here."

Ana frowned. She moved closer to Leah and took her hand. "Then why not ask Zeke to come with you?"

Leah shook her head and grabbed Pilot's scanner. "He's felt out of place his whole life. But now he's finally found a home on Athánatos. Family, friends, a place where he belongs. I don't want to take that from him."

Pilot frowned. "I mean, -*bzzt*- I get that, but--"

"Now's not the time," she said, moving Archángeli's book under the scanner. "Let's see what we can do here."

Pilot's wings drooped, but he nodded. Ana sighed and let go of Leah's hand.

Leah frowned. That didn't feel good. But she said nothing.

They spent a good hour or more scanning the page. Pilot carefully translated letters into their more modern equivalents while Leah worked on translating to English. Pilot looked over her work. "Yeah, Archángeli was -*bzzt*- right. This is where they became summons. An entry detailing the time and day that they -*bzzt*- took the oath... then silence for nearly two months." Pilot shook his head, his wings drooping. "Archángeli struggled to -*bzzt*- write after this. Their sentences are broken and not quite -*bzzt*- comprehensible."

Leah glanced over it, frowning. "Yeah, I see that..." She scanned the pages. It contained mostly broken history, detailing attempts to take Judgement down, comments on her immense strength, their various failures and simple suggestions on how to tackle it once again. All things that didn't work.

Then there was the talk of bigger magic. The Veil. The Purge. The Seal. The Cloak. Archángeli didn't give much detail other than it would require a sacrifice for everyone. Even the Veil, eventually. Keres would become the new Basilea if it worked, as she'd be the only one left. Archángeli seemed devastated.

Leah's heart ached. She knew how that battle ended.

Pilot hovered over the book, little light motes dancing on the pages. "Hmm. Seems like they tried -*bzzt*- one more thing before the big Four Sisters event." He pressed his dragon snout to the words. "This... oh. *Oh.*" Pilot leapt back, his body flushing with red, purple and blue colors. "Draso's *mercy.*"

Leah perked her ears. "Pilot?"

Ana leaned forward. "What'd you find?"

"The Phonar..." Pilot said quietly. "They're -*bzzt*- all *Wish Dusters.*"

Leah stood, slamming hands on the table. *"What?"*

Ana covered her snout with her hands. "Oh *god.*"

"Leah!" Melaina rounded a bookshelf with Eris at her side. "We have the results of the census, and it is not good."

Leah's heart plummeted into her stomach. "Why, who's missing?"

"It is as I feared," Eris said. "Abrax is unaccounted for. But so is all of Mistik's family."

Leah's jaw dropped. *"All* of them?"

Eris nodded. "Their three partners and their eight children together," she said. "Including Misty. And I know all of them were here earlier. I saw them enter when Mistik arrived for the ceremony."

Leah's tail lashed out. "Why didn't Mistik tell us their family was missing?"

Eris' bright green eyes grew dark. "Why indeed."

Leah's body buzzed. "We need to get to Neil," she said. *"Now."*

GUILT

Natassa stood frozen, staring at Ouranos' chained soul in that color-drained place of ice and darkness. Chained here for decades, alone, aware, hurting. And she had done nothing to free him. And she had tried... Convinced the *Fýlakas* to let her in the Aether. Hunted down Ouranos' soul. Fought off dozens of other Drifter's souls.

But when she faced him down - when she faced her own mortality - she could not do it. She left in shame and found the *Fýlakas* dead and her apprentice missing. Her one chance, wasted and two more lives lost, for no reason.

And yet, here he stood. Absently, she reached a hand for him.

Ouranos stepped back, his chains rattling against themselves. "Do *not*, Natassa. Not a step further, do you hear me? You should not be here!"

Natassa pulled her hand back, pinning her ears. "Ouranos--"

"*No*, Natassa," Ouranos said, stepping back further. "You should never have come back. I already forbade Matthew, you cannot--"

Zeke stepped between them now. "Stop it *both of you.* This isn't the place for it. Right now we need to get Matt and Izzy and get the hell out of here before--"

A loud crash echoed down the hall, and ice particles slid among their feet. Zeke turned, his eyes wide. "Oh *shit.*"

Natassa turned as well, her hands ablaze and her heart aching with fear and pain.

Ouranos narrowed his gaze. "More Drifters."

"Just one…" Zeke said. He flicked his tail. "Alexina."

Ouranos' eyes grew wide. "Oh, Sisters save us. The royal who attacked Matt and Izzy."

Alexina whipped around the corner, ice swirling around her body.

Zeke countered with his own magic, though it was weak. The bandage around his wound had turned black, soaked with blood. "Tell us you know where Matt and Izzy are."

Ouranos took a step back. "Throne room. *Run.*"

Natassa pushed Zeke toward the Throne Room and held out a hand, trying to rebuild the ice wall.

But she got only flimsy diamond dust instead. She stared, wide-eyed.

Ouranos built an ice wall instead and led the way down the hall. "It will not hold her long."

Natassa choked. "Oh, Ouranos, if Alexina is a chained Drifter…"

"It is likely Theron controls her as well," Ouranos said.

Zeke turned back. Alexina clawed at the wall, smashing it with fire laden hands. "Ouranos, what did Matt do to get you your mental capacities back?"

"He nearly killed us both," Ouranos said. "A risky procedure I dare not repeat."

Zeke flicked his ears back. "You know Matt won't stand for that."

"I know," Ouranos said. "We must make sure he does not see her."

Natassa turned back to her as she ran, guilt eating at her. She had failed Ouranos. Failed Athánatos. Failed everyone.

She slowed. Maybe she could save one. Fix what she failed to before. If she could just get close enough to Ouranos…

Zeke grabbed her arm. "*Theía.*" He pulled her away.

She cursed mentally and they kept running.

Ouranos hesitated at one of the breaks in their path, then went left. Natassa frowned. "Ouranos, this is not the way--"

"We cannot lead Alexina to the throne room," Ouranos said. "If we do, we risk alerting all the Drifters to their location and we cannot possibly hope to best them all. We must lose her first."

Natassa glanced behind her as they ran. Alexina was mere feet behind them. "We cannot--"

"I'll lead her away," Zeke said.

Natassa's jaw dropped. "Zeke, *no--*"

Ouranos pulled them both down a deep, dark hallway, just out of Alexina's sight. She ran past, though it would not fool her long. He turned to Zeke. "Let me lead her."

"Natassa needs someone who can protect her here and not die," Zeke said. "She's Basilea. She's not expendable."

Natassa's ears flattened. "And somehow you *are?*"

"More than you."

"*Zeke.*"

"We don't have time to argue this," Zeke said, gripping her hands. He eyed her. "Meet me at the Four Sister's Grove. You better come back whole. No heroics. Your people are waiting for you. *Neil* is waiting for you. Don't let them down. Got that?"

Natassa flattened her ears. "*Anipsiós…*"

"Promise me, *theía,*" Zeke said. "Don't destroy yourself."

Natassa glanced back at Ouranos, gauging the chains holding him down. He took two steps back, pulling the chains out of reach. "Natassa. Listen to him."

Alexina's footsteps stopped. They were running out of time.

Natassa pressed her lips tight. "Fine… I promise." She shot a glare at Zeke. "But you promise the same. No heroics for Alexina. Because Leah is waiting for you too." She took a deep breath. "We can decide what to do for Alexina when we return. Understood?"

He flicked his ears back. "Fine."

The footsteps approached again, faster and louder with every second.

Zeke squeezed her hands again. "Go get our Guardians." He dashed out of the hallway and waved. "*Mitéra!*"

Natassa choked. The Athánatos word for mother…

The footsteps stopped. Natassa backed farther into the hall, though Ouranos would not let her near him.

Zeke paused a moment, staring down Alexina. For a heartbeat, everything was still. A sliver of hope worked its way into Natassa's heart. Maybe he had gotten through to her. Maybe…

Then a barrage of sharp icicles flew down the path, aimed at Zeke.

Natassa covered her mouth against a gasp.

Zeke blocked a majority of the icicles with a large stone slab, though a few slipped by and sliced his legs and arm, spilling more black blood. He grunted, but did not falter. He held out a hand and another stone slab shot up in front of Natassa and Ouranos, blocking them from Alexina's view. "*Mitéra,* follow me!" Footsteps echoed down the hall. Alexina followed.

Natassa rushed forward. "No, wait, this is--" But Ouranos held gentle hand over her mouth and gripped her shoulder.

"Do not waste his sacrifice," Ouranos whispered, his voice echoing in her ear.

This should not be HIS sacrifice! Natassa screamed in her mind. *This was my job! My burden as Basilea, as the oldest!*

He cannot die!

"Remember you and Neil did this for me and lived," Ouranos said. "Zeke will too. Have faith and trust him."

Natassa shut her eyes tight and leaned back against Ouranos' soul, warm and familiar despite the dead cold of the Aether.

She should have been the one to lead her sister away. She had failed again.

Silence fell through the halls.

"Trust," Ouranos said and he released her. "Come. Let us find Matt and Izzy and get you out of this hell." He pulled Zeke's stone slab back into the earth and rushed for the throne room.

Natassa took in the sight before her. Black blood staining the floor. It left a trail. A trail leading far away from her. From help and safety and family.

She longed to chase it.

"Natassa!" Ouranos called.

She turned her back on it, guilt eating her heart. *Be safe, Anipsiós.* She ran for Ouranos.

THE GREATEST GUARDIAN

Neil lay down on the grass near the Veilsong room in Mistik's palace – the fourth one they had done so far. His mind ran a thousand different directions while Sacha healed him up as best she could. He closed his eyes against the harsh light of the full moon and their many flashlights and lanterns, letting his thoughts wander. Anything to get away from this blinding pain.

Four anchors down. Five to go. That… definitely took longer than the first one.

No word from Jaden, Leah, or Natassa. I should check the comms. Get some peace of mind.

Mistik has been unusually quiet and reserved. Gotta find out what's going on with that.

Darvin and Sami have Ei-Ei jewels.

Tymon Azure is the Black Cloak.

He gritted his teeth.

Good god, how the hell was he supposed to wrap his head around anything else with that thought piercing through? The Veilsong sang in his head with the new anchor, mapping out Mistik's palace and surrounding villages, filling his head with a thousand new names, wandering about, or huddling in their homes. And the only name Neil could focus on was the one right next to him.

Missing Guardian.

The Black Cloak.

Tymon Azure.

He opened his eyes, the pain finally subsiding. Just a little.

Tymon stood next to him, arms crossed, eyes forward, watching the Archons fiddle with a new rip in the Veil to get to Bouldrik's palace. He glanced down at Neil with fierce but tired green eyes, then immediately looked away when he noticed Neil watching him. Neil frowned.

For all they hated about the Cloak, he must be in so much pain. Watching all this fall around him. Being so close to his family and yet incredibly distant at the same time.

Being so powerful, and yet completely powerless.

"There," Sacha said. She shook her hands. "I've… really done all I can." She helped Neil sit up. He groaned, still fighting a ton of aches and pains. "Sorry, hun. I'm starting to push my limits here. We uh… We might want to call Leah to join us. I don't know if I can keep this up."

"Might be a good idea," Neil said, pulling up his pendant. "I swear that last one was longer."

"…They all are," the Cloak said. Tymon said. Neil looked up. Tymon crossed his arms, but didn't look at him. He took a deep breath. "Every new anchor will be longer than the last. I'm sorry."

Neil twisted an ear. Great. "I'll get through it." He pressed his thumb to his pendant. But the hologram appeared glitchy and broken. "Wait, what the hell?"

Sacha's ears perked. "Uh oh." She pulled her pendant's hologram up with the same affect. "Not good."

"I suspect the Veil is interfering," Damianos said, walking up to them. "I have been trying to reach the main palace with updates for a while now, but I have been unsuccessful." He rubbed his arm. "We ah… we are having difficulties opening a rip as well."

"Which means we don't have much time," Neil said. He carefully pulled himself to his feet, keeping his face neutral. Didn't want Dami seeing how much pain he was in. He turned to the Cloak. "Got any way for us to contact the others?"

Tymon closed his eyes a moment, then turned to Neil. "Just trust me."

Neil clicked his tongue, bit his lip to stop his eyes rolling. "Not exactly helpful, Cloak."

The Cloak took a slow breath. "I know."

"Sacha?" Embrik called. "Do you have a little power left? Mistik has hurt their hand trying to open this portal."

"Coming," Sacha said. Dami gave Neil a gentle squeeze and a quick kiss, then jogged over to the Archons as well.

Neil stood next to Tymon, arms crossed, waiting for Dami and Sacha to be out of earshot. He cleared his throat. "Jaden talks about you all the time, you know."

Tymon glanced down at the grass.

Neil glanced at him. "He likes to go on and on as if you're the greatest Guardian that ever lived."

Tymon chuckled darkly. "And Matt speaks as if Jaden fills that role."

Neil managed a smirk. "So who's right?"

Tymon glanced up, staring out into the middle distance. "I abandoned my family and the Defenders because a being inside a cloak started talking to me right before I was set to retire." He shrugged. "I don't deserve the title of Guardian at all."

Neil watched him a moment, then turned and stared off too. "You gave up everything in life to fight the worst enemy the universe had ever seen. For your family." He shrugged. "Matt would call that admirable. I would, too."

Tymon let out a deep sigh. "That's… generous. Not sure if it's right, though." He gripped his head. "I'm not sure if *any* of this is right. Sometimes I wish I could throw the whole plan out the window and save everyone. Stop all of this." He glanced off. "…Though I know intimately that that can't work. So I do what I'm told and hurt as few people as possible."

They stood in silence while the Archons continued working on the rip in the Veil.

"Tell me," Neil said. "Is Alexina alive?"

Tymon stiffened, but he nodded. "Yes."

"And does Jaden get to see her again?"

The Cloak looked at him. "I shouldn't be telling you this."

"You need to tell someone," Neil said. "I kept your name secret. I'll keep this secret too."

Tymon stared at him.

Neil stared back. "To my grave, Tymon."

"Don't say that. And don't say my name out loud." Tymon shook his head. "But… I know you're right."

"And?"

"He does."

A long pause.

"Are they happy?"

Tymon was silent for a long time, staring. "…Yeah. They are."

Neil gripped Tymon's shoulder. "Then you've fulfilled your duty as the Cloak and as his father."

Tymon narrowed his gaze. "Not sure it's worth the cost. You all hate us. Probably with good reason."

Neil pressed his lips tight. "Maybe that needs to change."

Another long pause.

"Will you get to see Jaden again?" Neil asked carefully. "As yourself?"

Tymon's green eyes grew glassy and he stared up at the sky. "Draso willing."

Embrik yelped and stepped back from the portal, shaking his hand. "Sisters *alive,* that stings."

"I *really* don't like that," Sacha said, frowning. "Tell me we have some alternative to get everywhere if things go wrong."

Neil flattened his ears. "Not anything with enough speed, I don't think."

"We will power through it," Embrik said. "Even if it pains us. Our people count on it." He waved a hand at the portal, a strange, faded image in the air, glowing red and blue. "Bouldrik, lead the way. Mistik can you close up?"

Mistik shook their head, clearly distracted. "Ah, yes, um. Of course."

Neil furrowed his brow. He glanced at Tymon. But he couldn't read anything in the Cloak's expression.

Not good.

Bouldrik led the way, followed by Sacha. Dami glanced back at Neil, then followed behind. One by one, the Archons walked through the portal, slowly vanishing into the blurred, glowing image. Tymon nodded to Neil, then also went through.

Neil stared at Mistik, trying to read the Archon. But there was nothing. He stepped toward the portal.

But then Mistik held out their hand and closed the portal, cutting Neil off from the others. Sacha and Dami shouted on the other end, but the portal cut off their words.

Neil's fur stood on end and he backed up, reaching for his sword.

Mistik stood up straight, their face flat and unreadable, chin raised. "Before we go any further," they said. "We need to talk."

Then a dozen drifters and a mess of Shadow Cast appeared through the darkness behind them.

CHƎPTƎR 21

WINGBROTHERS

"Come on, Melaina," Leah said. "You've got this. You gotta get a rip open."

Melaina gritted her teeth, pulling at the flickering red threads in the air. Her shadows made eerie puppets on the walls from the lanterns. "I am *trying,*" she said. "But the threads keep fading away. They are slippery, like clams."

Leah twisted an ear, shifting her weight back and forth as anxiety coursed through her. Ana paced back and forth in front of the table, and even Pilot flickered tensely, unable to stay still.

Mistik was up to something. They had to be, or they would have said something about their family being missing.

Though for all Leah knew, they *weren't* missing. Mistik probably sequestered them away, hiding out while Judgement and Theron tore the island apart. She couldn't even begin to imagine *why* someone would do that, but the why wasn't important. Neil was in danger.

They had to take care of this *fast.*

So the plan had been for Melaina to open up a portal through the Veil and figure out which of the Archons' palaces Neil's team was at. Except, that wasn't working. Melaina had never had a problem opening a rip in the Veil before, but of course when they needed it the most… "Eris?"

Eris lowered her gaze, her face growing dark. "I suspect this is also a side effect of our failing Veil," she said.

Melaina yelped and pulled her hands back suddenly, shaking them as if they were burning. "I… I cannot make the Veil open to us."

Eris stood. "We will need to get to them another way."

"But *how?*" Leah asked. "We don't have any way fast enough, and even if we did, we have no idea where Neil is. We could be looking for *hours.*"

"There is a way," Eris said. She waved a hand. "Follow me."

Leah exchanged glances with Ana and Melaina, then snatched up Pilot's datashard and drone and took off after Eris.

Eris led them to the Veilsong Room. "Here." She pointed to the symbols on the floor. Leah glanced down.

They were *glowing.* Some of them, anyway. The major one in the center that looked like the sun had a slight yellow glow. Two elemental symbols, for fire and lightning, also lit up brightly. Eris waved a hand. "When the Veil's strength is at full capacity, these all glow. Which means that they likely just finished with Mistik's anchor and are recuperating before moving on."

"Slowly, probably," Leah said. "If Melaina can't get the Veil to open up, then the Archons are gonna have even more trouble."

Melaina tapped her chin. "This presents another problem, though. Even with our fastest mule deer, it will take hours to get to Mistik's realm. By the time we got there, they would have moved on, and we will have no idea where."

"Then we need something faster," Leah said. "The Phonar." She dashed for the atrium where Charlotte and hopefully the Phonar waited for them.

But when they got to the atrium, she found two other summons instead. "Rashard! Kjorn!"

The two gryfon brothers turned to her, lifting their heads. Rashard with his white, blue tipped feathers, and Kjorn with his red, black tipped feathers, each staring at her with piercing, solid-colored eyes. Rashard lifted his chin, blowing tiny wisps of icy diamond dust on Leah. *Greetings, Guardian.*

Leah's fur stood on end. "I'm not a Guardian," she said automatically.

Jaden calls you Guardian, Kjorn replied with tiny embers on her forehead. *And so we call you Guardian.*

Now that was a title to live up to. But not the time. "The Black Cloak sent you here."

He did, Rashard said. *You can guess the reason. Make peace with your companions here, then we must leave.*

Ana flattened her ears. "What do you mean by 'make peace'?"

Make peace, Rashard and Kjorn said together.

Charlotte walked forward, her normal stoic mask cracking. Her long white, blue lined quills rustled as she moved. She met Leah's blue-green eyes with her vibrant pink ones. "Leah, what's going on?" Angus stared blankly forward, ears perked, Philip frowned, ears flat and clearly worried, his puma tail swishing anxiously. Even Chadwick looked up from his bed, his long black panther tail lashing about.

Leah paused. It wouldn't do any good to sugar coat it… but she also didn't want to scare them. "Neil might be in trouble. We're going after him." She turned to Melaina. "Melaina, it's probably best if you stay here. You're the strongest mage in the palace."

Melaina frowned, but nodded.

"That goes for you too," Leah said when the Phonar moved as one toward her. "The palace needs protecting."

The Phonar paused, glanced at each other, then bowed, one by one. *Yes, my lady.*

"I'm coming with you."

Leah turned. Andre walked forward, fists at his sides, brow furrowed.

Leah flattened an ear. Andre had become a dear friend in the last few years, just like Zeke. He was a big teddy bear most of the time, all smiles and hugs and laughter, but now he sent shivers down her spine. Sometimes she forgot he was a soldier too.

But this wasn't a normal war. "Andre, you don't have magic."

"Neither does Neil," Andre said, his deep voice echoing in the atrium. "He's military, Leah. We don't leave our own behind. I'm going and you can't stop me."

Leah's tail lashed. "Andre--"

"We ain't got time to argue," Andre said. "'Sides, Zeke would kill me if anything happened to you." He frowned and gently took Leah's hand. "Hell, I'd let him. I'm sick of losing friends."

Leah bit her lip. Andre had never shied away from touching her, despite knowing her magic could see his entire medical history. Though he had always been careful to protect her mental health and not overwhelm her. The first friend she had ever met who took that into consideration with her magic. A precious and vital start to their relationship.

Like Ana, Andre was fine physically, though his stress and worry bled through their touch. But… so did his strength. And she needed strength. She gripped his hand with both of hers. "Fine. Honestly, we could use the help. Grab a sword. Hopefully we won't have to use it, but…."

Andre nodded. "Gotcha. Emergencies only." Angus walked up to him and passed him an Athánatos sword and sheath.

"Andre…"

Leah turned. Chadwick stood from his padded wicker couch. He hobbled toward Andre, but then stopped, leaning against the wall and breathing hard.

Leah twitched her whiskers. Despite all the healing he'd received, he hadn't fully recovered. She had had to stop in their last session before she really repaired much - his body started going into shock, which could sooner kill him than heal him. Just their luck he had to be one of the few that didn't take to healing well. What she wouldn't give for a proper doctor right now.

Andre frowned. He crossed the room, pulled Chadwick into his arms, and gave him a deep, loving kiss. He pulled back. "Sorry Chad, but--"

"I know," Chadwick said. "You have to." He held Andre tight. "Just come back to me, okay?"

"Count on it." Andre kissed the top of his head and helped him back onto the long couch.

"Leah," Charlotte said. "Take this too." She passed her a pouch. "Lexi Charms. In case you run into Cast. We have enough here that we can protect ourselves if we need to."

Leah nodded. "Thanks." She turned to the gryfons.

Rashard bowed his head. *Leah and Ana with me.*

And Andre with me, Kjorn said, also bowing.

Leah and Ana climbed on, carefully positioning themselves between Rashard's wings.

"Leah," Charlotte said. Leah turned. Charlotte frowned deeply, all that stoic Azure nature fading away. "Don't let them die."

Leah's shoulders stiffened, but she nodded to Charlotte. "I won't."

A stiff breeze blew past Leah's ear. Leah turned. Archángeli stood in their anthropomorphic form in front of Rashard and bowed. *Leah, allow me to come as well. I can help you cross the distance to our destination faster. The wind is on our side.*

Leah's ear twitched. "If you think it'll help."

Archángeli nodded, transformed into their feral form, then took to the skies.

Hang on tight, Guardian, Rashard said, bunching down on his haunches. Kjorn took off without warning, with Andre shouting in surprise.

Ana wrapped her arms around Leah's waist and held tight. "How long 'til we get there?"

Rashard spread his wings. *Minutes.* He sprang into the air with such force it felt like Leah's insides dropped to the soles of her feet. She clutched Rashard's neck.

Hang on, Neil, we're coming!

CHAPTER 22

BONDS

Zeke dashed as best he could through the palace toward the clover lawn, gripping the wound in his leg. Black blood stained his fur and pants, wiping away the remaining ceremonial paint.

God, why did it hurt so much?

He continued forward.

Alexina followed close behind, still throwing occasional magic at him, though his zigzagging through the palace he now knew so well made him a difficult target. But he had no real plan here. Alexina knew this place as well as him. There wasn't anywhere for him to hide. Going straight for the Grove was a death wish. And now he had left Natassa alone with Ouranos' chained soul. Promise or not, he didn't trust her not to try and free him at her own expense.

He hadn't thought this through, and now he paid the price.

Sisters, his leg stung.

He slipped down a corridor toward the audience chamber, putting a bit of a gap between him and Alexina. Maybe he could trick her. Make her think he's going for the audience chamber and then head for the outer gardens instead.

A shock ran through his body from the leg wound to the tips of his ears and toes. His vision blurred and he slowed. His energy faded, tugging at his consciousness. The effects of the Aether's energy draining was too much. *No, no, not now, please…*

Eris' voice echoed in his head. *Ground yourself in your loved ones.* He called out for Leah.

But she wasn't there.

Just get to the audience chamber. Just one step at a time.

More footsteps echoed down the hall… in front of him, not behind. He cursed and scooted against the wall, pressing himself up against a pillar. Those had to be Theron's Drifters.

Alexina behind him.

Drifters in front of him.

Blood soaking his hands.

He was going to die.

The footsteps ahead grew louder and four sentries, all Athánatos he knew by name, stared him straight in the face. Blank, emotionless, nothing like the quilar he had come to know at home. They marched forward, swords in hand, singularly focused.

Zeke backed up, gripping his leg. Alexina rushed down the hall behind him, the tell-tale sounds of crackling magic at her fingertips. Zeke pulled on his own magic, but the drain was too much. All he could manage was a few sparks and frosted fingers.

Zeke shut his eyes, slid the wall and curled into a ball, gritting his teeth, hoping it wouldn't hurt much. *I'm sorry, Leah.*

Ice rushed by his face… but it didn't hit him. He opened his eyes.

Diamond dust blew by in waves, crashing into the Drifters, knocking them to the ground. Zeke stared, then turned.

Alexina stood a few feet away, hand outstretched, staring down the hall, her gaze dark and menacing with awareness that hadn't been there before. But she wasn't staring at Zeke. She stared at the Drifters. She bared her teeth.

"Get the hell away from my son."

Zeke stared, wide-eyed.

A dozen more Drifters appeared in the hall, each with a blank face and a sword.

Alexina moved in front of Zeke and threw her hands out, blasting them back with a wave of fire. Her faint chains rattled loudly. "That will not hold them long. Get up, son."

Zeke's jaw dropped. "Alexina? H-How?"

"A mystery we have no time to unravel," Alexina said. "Hurry!"

Zeke gripped the wounds on his side and leg, standing slowly. Black blood had soaked through his clothes and bandage.

Alexina frowned. "You have no chains…"

Zeke shook his head. "I'm… not a soul."

Alexina's eyes widened. "Sisters alive, Zeke, why are you here?"

"Long story…"

"Can you call on Leah?" Alexina looked him over. "You are injured."

Zeke hissed in pain. "We've tried. Can't do much through the Aether."

Alexina called down blasts of lightning, but that did little to push the Drifters back. "Try again, Zeke. She can help you in ways I cannot." She reached out a hand. "And lean on me."

Zeke hobbled toward her. She wrapped her arm around him and pulled him to her. She slowly backed them up, pushing the Drifters' souls back with magic, though it was only a matter of time before they caught up to them. He reached deep into his bond with Leah.

Leah... I need help... I need you... please hear me...

But there was nothing.

Alexina backed up quicker, banging Zeke's leg against hers, black blood staining her own clothes now. "Zeke!"

"I'm trying!" Zeke said. "Can't you call Kyrie?"

"I have been trying since I regained consciousness," Alexina said through gritted teeth. "Either she will not come through the Aether, or something far worse has befallen us all."

Zeke growled. Damn it! He reached for Leah again, blasting the scent of hot peppers across the bond. Danger. *Leah, I need you!*

An overpowering scent of clover, pine, and distant sea breeze assailed his nose and energy rushed his body, cooling his wounds and surging magic at his fingertips.

Leah.

Alexina yelped and stepped back, magic sparking across her hands. The Drifters rushed them.

But they didn't stand a chance this time. Zeke side-stepped, drew on all Leah's spare energy, and filled the hall with thousands of sharp ice spikes. The icicles ripped through the air, tearing through the Drifters souls, pinning them to walls and pillars. Their stoic faces never changed, but with the icicles trapping them, they had a far harder time pulling themselves back up.

Alexina grabbed Zeke's hand. "This is our chance. Run!" She pulled him away, darting down hallways and headed for the nearest exit. Zeke thanked Leah with a scent of warm cookies through their bond. He'd make it out of this after all.

Hopefully.

But… Alexina. She was herself again, but still in chains. Just like Ouranos.

How?

Alexina didn't slow down until they made it to the outer gardens leading to the clover lawn. She hid the pair of them behind a large, gray topiary, and stood silent, ears perked. Zeke listened.

But there was nothing. They escaped. He rested on his knees. "Sisters alive, I'm tired of all this running…"

Alexina's chains rattled. Zeke looked up. She stared at her hands, jaw loose, eyebrows knitted together. Tears pooled at the corner of her eyes. "Draso's holy mercy…"

Zeke stood straight up and pulled Alexina into a deep hug. "Thank Draso you're alive…"

Alexina paused a moment, then wrapped her arms tight around Zeke's waist. "You as well." She pulled back. "Is Jaden…?"

"He's safe," Zeke said. "Embrik too." He paused. "Well, safe as can be, considering…" He gripped Alexina's hands. "Are you aware of what's going on outside the Aether?"

She shook her head. "No, I… the last thing I remember was… Theron taking me… being in labor… the Black Cloak…" She covered her snout and shut her eyes, squeezing out tears. "Sisters help me…"

Zeke pulled her into his arms again. "It's okay, we're all fine now." He bit his lip. "Well, not entirely, but we're getting there. Trust me, okay?"

Alexina leaned into him. "What has happened to me?"

Zeke flattened an ear. "You really don't know?"

"I… do not," Alexina said. She stepped back, staring at her hands. "I remember becoming a Drifter, though I do not know why I have suddenly become aware again. If I have been restored then… then why am I still here?"

Zeke's tail lashed. "You probably haven't been restored."

Alexina shot her head up. "Then… I am like Ouranos. Someone has bridged my soul." She shook her head and hugged herself. "Only I do not know who has done so."

Zeke looked back at the palace, his jaw tense. "I can probably guess who."

CHAPTER 23

RIFTS

Matt dashed through the palace, a dozen Drifter souls still on his tail. He held Izzy close to his chest, praying she was alright.

Her limp body didn't fill him with hope.

He rounded a corner, putting a little distance between them and the Drifters. But not enough. *Never* enough.

He squeezed Izzy, buzzing panic in his chest.

He did this to her. Their bond did this. He was energy stealing. Just like he did all those years ago during the war games.

Footsteps echoed behind him. He dashed around another corner, pressing them against the wall, hoping the Drifters would move on.

It was bad enough he was in her head. It was worse when she didn't even want the damn bond.

But energy stealing… the greatest sin.

Two Drifters rounded the corner and spotted them. He sprinted away, holding Izzy tight, wind rippling behind him.

That familiar pull of energy sapping building in his chest.

No, no, NO! He had taken too much already. And he couldn't even *stop.* This never happened with Ouranos. He never *stole* energy. Why was this happening?

He darted into a series of hallways, weaving around pillars and potted plants. *Get out of their line of sight. Get to safety.*

Protect Izzy.

A tiny, dark, nearly unnoticeable nook in the far corner of a hallway caught Matt's attention. He zigzagged around and slid into it, making the two of them as small as he could, holding his breath. *Protect Izzy.*

The sound of footsteps beat against the walls and pillars. Close. Loud. Fast. Then they slowed. They faded. Soon they were gone entirely. Matt counted heartbeats.

Silence.

Gone.

The throne room. He glanced around, found the place empty, then took the shortest route he knew to the throne room, finally settling behind the massive set of thrones. He leaned against the cool marble. Maybe they were finally safe.

Izzy still didn't move.

Fresh panic buzzed in Matt's bones. He sat her up on his leg, gently shaking her. "Come on, Iz, wake up, wake up…" Nothing. Not even any bell sounds. He pressed his ear against her mouth, listening for breaths, but they were incredibly shallow. *No! This isn't happening, this is NOT HAPPENING.*

She just needed…

Energy…

He closed his eyes, reached for that strange tingling in his chest, and… pushed.

Izzy gasped back to life, her eyes flying open, bells ringing loudly in his ears. She gripped her chest. "Oh, *Draso.*"

Instant relief cooled Matt's bones and he pulled her close. "You're *alive.* I thought you were dying."

Izzy heaved breaths, then pushed Matt, scrambling away on her tail. A loud, angry bell rang in his head. *"Don't--"*

Matt's heart ached. "Iz--"

"Don't, Matt," Izzy said, her breathing frantic now. The bell sounds matched her breathing. "Don't you know what you *did?"*

Matt furrowed his brow and frowned. *"I know,* I know, but Izzy, I promise you, I didn't mean to, I--"

"You think that *matters?"* Izzy said. She stood, backing away. "The fact that you stole energy from me and you *didn't even intend to* is the *whole damn problem."*

Matt stood slowly, holding his hands out. "Keep it down, you'll alert the Drifters again."

Izzy paced back and forth, gripping her head one moment and hugging herself the next. A random cacophony of bells jingled in his ears. "There's gotta be a way to break the bond, to *end* this, there just *has* to be…"

Matt flicked his ears back. That hurt more than it should have, considering he just helped save her. Then again, it was his power draining that caused the problem in the first place. "You… you know we can't, Iz."

"Then how the hell am I supposed to protect myself from you?" Izzy snapped. "How the hell do we *stop this?"*

Matt frowned. He dropped his hands at his sides and slowly slumped to the floor. "…I don't know."

Izzy hugged herself again, staring at him. She blinked several times and took a long, deep breath, curtailing the bell sounds into one clear ring. But a ring that wouldn't go away. "I'm sorry, Matt, I… I'm letting my fear get the better of me and I'm not acting rationally." She smiled, but it was rigid and fake. "We… I… We don't know that this is really the bond, right? This could just be the Aether causing problems or--"

"Izzy," Matt said slowly. "You know that's not right."

Izzy immediately shut her mouth. All bell sounds vanished.

Matt leaned against the throne. "It's energy stealing. I know it and you know it. It's… it's exactly the same thing that happened in the war games last year of high school."

The fur on Izzy's arms puffed up. "Nothing happened at the war games. I was just sick."

Matt lowered his gaze. "Izzy. It's time we stop lying to ourselves about this."

Izzy stared at him. "Matt--"

"I need to come clean about the war games," Matt said, his chest tightening. "Might as well do it while we're waiting to get the hell out of here."

Izzy wrinkled her snout, but slowly sat down, the bell sounds quietly fading.

Matt held out his hands to her, but stopped and pulled back. "I knew that I was sapping energy from you during the war games."

Izzy perked her ears. "What?"

He pulled out his Gem and ran his hands along the cut edges, trying to focus himself. "I messed with the Gem suppression system that Lance had put on me. It wasn't strong enough to hold back my magic when I first broke, so I fiddled with it until it was. I used it to learn how to control my magic. But… whenever I turned it on, you suddenly lost all your energy."

He met her gaze. "It stole energy from you through our bond to power itself and keep my magic at bay."

Izzy covered her snout with her hands, her eyes wide with shock. The bells grew louder and louder.

"And I *knew* it, Izzy," Matt continued, the buzzing in his bones increasing. "I knew it was doing that and I selfishly kept it on anyway." He pressed his eyes shut. "I almost got you killed in that war game because of that."

Izzy's quills stood on end. "Matt, I…"

He held his head in his hands. "I don't deserve Guardianship after doing that to you. When Lance called me into his office after the games, I was fully prepared to leave the Young Defenders and end my bid for Guardianship. But he didn't believe me about the energy stealing. You wouldn't even let me admit I did anything wrong, so I never got to tell you about the energy stealing. And I think over time, I started believing it was all in my head. That I hadn't actually stolen energy from you. And then… Ouranos appeared. Suddenly here was proof that bonds can happen by accident. And I was forced to face what I did again." He rubbed his arm. "I sometimes wonder if the reason your Gem took forever to break was because I stole so much energy from you."

Izzy tucked her knees under her chin, holding her legs and staring at him. Tiny jingling sounds clung to his ears.

"I know there's nothing I can say or do to fix this," Matt said. "I was happy to let our bond fall to the wayside because it's what you wanted and I was so sure I could keep it under control. But I was wrong. I was wrong then and I'm wrong now." He glanced away. "I'm sorry. For whatever that's worth." He folded his hands together. "I don't know how to fix this. If it even can be fixed. But the only way to try is by admitting the problem in the first place and seeing it for what it is."

Izzy stared at him a moment longer, then stood and walked away, saying nothing.

Matt stood too. "Izzy--"

"Don't," Izzy said. Softer this time. Broken. "Don't come near me."

Matt's heart shattered to pieces. And it was no more than he deserved. "…Sure."

An incredibly strong smell of clover hit Matt's nose, making him reel back. He blinked, his eyes watering, though he couldn't tell if it was the strong smell or the broken heart that caused it.

Then something… familiar. But new. A… presence. In his mind. Just like Ouranos or Izzy…

Matt's eyes widened. Just like a jewel bond. A *new* jewel bond.

But how? And more importantly… who?

The strong smell of clover returned. And with it, pine. Oak. The native trees of Athánatos. A striking contrast to the Aether's decidedly scentless environment. It almost formed an image in his head.

Whoever this was, they were calling to him. Urgently. "Izzy--"

"Can we just be quiet until Ouranos gets here?" Izzy said, her voice cracking. "This is a lot to process."

"I know, but--"

"Matt, *please.*"

"Izzy," Matt said. "Someone is calling me through a jewel bond."

Izzy faced him. Eyes red, but no tears. Holding things in. Matt's chest ached even more. She narrowed her gaze and huffed. "You don't have to say 'someone' like you don't know who it is. It's either me or Ouranos, and I sure as hell won't do that."

Matt closed his eyes a moment, letting the clover smell ground him. "It's not either of you. It's--"

"What, you're bonding to people without even knowing who?" Izzy snapped. Tears escaped down her cheeks now, and an angry gong burst between Matt's ears.

Matt winced. "No I… I don't know who it is. It just feels like a bond. And I'm getting a really strong scent of clover."

Izzy scoffed. "Nothing here has a scent."

"Which is why it's really strange I'm smelling clover," Matt said. "I think whoever this is, is calling me to the clover lawn. Maybe even the Four Sisters Grove."

Izzy crossed her arms. "We should stay here and wait for Ouranos, not follow your mysterious scent."

The smell hit him again, tenfold, knocking him back. He waved a hand in front of his nose, but the smell wouldn't fade. "I don't think they're giving me a choice."

Izzy waved a hand. "Then go without me."

Matt's fur puffed up. "Izzy, I'm not leaving you here. It's *dangerous.*"

"So was meddling with that Gem suppressor," Izzy retorted, shattering the remains of Matt's heart to dust. "So go off and do your own thing, like you've always done."

A jolt ran up Matt's spine. That hurt but… it was true. Too often he had run off and done things his way, not even considering his friends and partners. And Izzy… she always got the worst of it. He always hurt her the most.

The clover smell doubled again, beckoning him.

Matt closed his eyes. This couldn't keep happening.

"I'm not leaving without you, Iz."

Izzy turned to him, angry tears running down her face.

Her anger threatened to blow away the dusty remains of his heart. But he mentally swept them up into a tiny pile and drew whatever scraps of strength it had left. "I'm not leaving without you," he repeated. "So if you want to stay… we stay." He sat down on the hard floor. "I don't want to hurt you any more than I already have."

Izzy frowned. "Fine… we'll stay." She sat too, far on the opposite side of their little alcove behind the thrones. "I'm going to sleep. Save… save energy." She leaned against a wall, facing away from him.

Matt watched her. He broke this. Maybe he should have kept quiet...

He shook himself. No, he never should have meddled with the Gem suppressor in the first place. He had broken their relationship a long time ago. And he wasn't sure he could repair it.

A tiny, quiet voice in the back of his mind whispered through the angry bells.

This is why you can't tell Trecheon that you don't have feelings for him, it said. *Because after all the flirting and false hope you've given him, you'd break that too.*

Matt gripped his chest, closing his eyes tight. Damn everything.

He couldn't fix this. But he could keep everyone safe. He huddled in his corner, perking his ears, listening for everything, pushing aside the exhaustion.

The aches in his heart wouldn't let him sleep anyway. He just had to hope everyone else was okay.

CHAPTER 24

BETRAYED

Neil ripped his sword from the sheath and dashed away from the onslaught, his still broken body screaming at him with every step. *This is SO not okay, I'm dead, I'm so dead, there's no way I survive this.* "Mistik, call them off!"

Mistik shouted from somewhere among the Drifters and Cast, but Neil couldn't make out what. They all blended into the darkness.

Three Cast broke free from the pack, identifiable only by their glowing blue eyes, and dashed after Neil with surprising speed.

"Shit!" Neil ran toward what he hoped was the palace gardens. A thin, metal statue of the Veil Sister guarded the entrance, twinkling in the light from Mistik's discarded lantern. He sliced the sword along it, sending sparks up the blade and activating the elemental channeling properties of the weapon. Neil turned and slashed the sword at the Cast, jolting them with lightning. The Cast shrieked and retreated, melting into the darkness.

But that didn't stop the Drifters. Baltazar led the charge, lifting his sword, staring blankly forward.

Neil blocked the attack, grateful for the hours of sword practice with Matt. But his heart ached. *Not Baltazar. Not my FRIENDS.* "There's no scenario where this ends well for you, Mistik!" Neil shouted, holding Baltazar back. *"Call them off!"*

Mistik yelped from somewhere behind the wall of glowing Cast eyes. "I… I cannot!"

Baltazar lifted his sword and began hammering away at Neil's sword. Violent vibrations buzzed through Neil's body with every blow, doubling the aches and pains. Neil snarled, pushing back. "You don't want to do this! Call them *off!*"

"I *cannot!*" Mistik called again. "They are not mine to command!" They gagged and a wave of water splashed through the Drifters, knocking them to the ground. But the Cast swam through the waves and wrapped themselves around Mistik.

Damn it! Neil pushed hard on Baltazar, knocking him to the ground, then sliced the metal statue again, building electricity on his blade. Pushing aside the pain, he dashed for Mistik and stabbed his sword into the Cast holding them down. The Cast wailed and shrieked, but held on.

Neil roared and slashed the blade through the Cast, splitting them. The split closed quickly, but Neil caught a glimpse of Mistik's arm. "Hang on!" He split the Cast again and grabbed Mistik, yanking hard. "Don't hold back, Mistik! Blast 'em with all you've got!"

Mistik's muffled cries turned to snarls and water blasted in all directions, slicing through the Cast and breaking them into droplets. With a hard yank, Neil pulled Mistik free, knocking them both to the ground. Mistik coughed, grabbing their chest. "Sisters *alive.*"

Neil stood, pulling Mistik up. "We need a safe space *now.*"

Mistik's eyes widened and they gasped. "My Lord, *look out!*"

Neil turned just as Baltazar stabbed his sword down, piercing Neil's shoulder. Neil screamed as they both fell hard on the grass. Blinding pain radiated from the wound, and blood splashed his face and ears. Baltazar tugged on the sword, trying to free it, but it had lodged itself too deep and stuck fast.

That terrifying, horrible, blank face.

Neil grabbed Baltazar's arm with his good arm. "Baltazar, *open your eyes.* This isn't you! Don't let him *win!*" It wouldn't do any good, he knew, but the alternative was to kill Baltazar and he *could not do that.* "Hear me, Baltazar!"

A jolt zipped through Neil's head and the Veilsong's map spread through his brain like wildfire, spinning like a bird divebombing, centering on their little spot in the world. Mistik's name appeared, as did the names of the Cast surrounding him, making Neil's stomach churn. All names he knew. Sentries, friends, and--

Oh, god.

Misty! Mistik's oldest daughter, barely of age, recently bound to her Ei-Ei jewels, named the next Archon in line. These Cast were a part of Mistik's family.

But another name flickered in and out of view.

Baltazar.

Neil concentrated all his energy into that name, calling it both mentally and physically. *"Baltazar, hear me!"*

Baltazar froze in place, blinking, then he gasped, his eyes darting about like he had just woken from a nightmare. He locked his gaze with Neil. "Sisters *alive,* my Lord! What have I done?" He stood, gripping the sword's handle.

Neil held out a hand. "No, *don't--*"

Baltazar pulled the sword free.

Neil called out, half screaming, half roaring, gripping his shoulder, as blood soaked his jacket and fur.

Mistik dashed forward and slid up to Neil on their knees. They began ripping the long fabric strips of the *osaa* off their chest. "Baltazar, the diamond fabric on your pants, give it to me, *hurry!*"

Baltazar's eyes widened as realization hit him. "Oh, no, no, *no--*"

"*Baltazar, hurry!*" Mistik started wrapping Neil's wound with the *osaa.* Neil groaned. His eyelids grew heavy.

Baltazar used the sword to rip the diamond fabric off his outfit and passed it to Mistik. "Help him…"

Neil coughed, forcing consciousness to the front of his brain. "Baltazar… this isn't your fault… It's Theron…"

Baltazar flattened both ears. "My Lord, that matters not when--Whoa!" Two Cast snatched Baltazar around the ankles and slammed him to the grass, dragging him away.

Neil sat up, his head spinning. "Baltazar!" But Mistik held him back.

The Cast wrapped themselves around Baltazar, holding him upright, covering every part of him leaving only his face exposed. Baltazar screamed and struggled, but he didn't stand a chance. A third Cast appeared and slammed a long, black tentacle in Baltazar's eye. Loud, popping gurgles drowned out his scream as black liquid poured out of every orifice, melting into the Cast holding him down as Baltazar became a Cast himself.

Neil pounded a fist to the ground. *"Damn it!"* Then the vertigo hit him and he fell back to the grass. His vision blurred. Damn it…

An eagle screech hit his ears.

In a fury of flames and ice, Tymon's gryfon summons, Rashard and Kjorn, hit the ground hard, chasing back Drifters and Cast alike, roaring and screeching. Someone familiar shouted – Andre, perhaps – followed by more shrieking.

Good... someone to protect them... fix the Cast... a shame he wouldn't see it...

A powerful blast of cooling energy hit his shoulder like a rock, blowing him aside. It coursed through his body like ice in the veins, almost too powerful, edging on pain. Then it slowed. His head stopped swimming, his stomach calmed, and the pounding in his shoulder ended.

"I've got you, Neil." Leah's voice. Calm, but not the practiced healer calm. A real calm. He sighed relief. "Just relax for a bit, we've got you."

"Take *that,* you bastard Cast!" Andre shouted. "Ha ha, right in the eye! Git 'em, Kjorn!" Light exploded above him as the fire gryfon blasted Cast with flames.

Neil stirred. "The Drifters--"

"Rashard is herding them somewhere safe," Leah said. "No one will hurt them, I promise."

Ana hovered over them, fists at her side, glaring. "Where's Mistik?"

Neil blinked. "Why?"

"Because Mistik's entire family is missing from the census," Ana said, her voice dark. "And they didn't tell anyone." She snorted. "Abrax too, the bastard."

Shit. Neil's instincts were right after all. Now he questioned whether Mistik was behind this attack or not. Though seeing Misty as one of the Cast... He didn't have all the parts here. He stood. "They were just here. Couldn't have gotten far, especially since the Veil portals aren't working. Though I'm guessing you knew that."

"Little help here, y'all!" Andre called.

"Go help Andre," Neil said. He lifted his sword. "I've got Mistik."

Ana nodded. She picked up a stick and used her Wishing Dust to turn it into an electric cattle prod. She tested it out, then ran into the fray.

Leah frowned, flicking her tail.

Neil smiled. "I've got this, Leah. You gave me a jumpstart, especially since Sacha's been having a hard time keeping up. I'll be fine."

"Just… don't kill them," Leah said. "There's been enough death."

"Not planning to," Neil said. "Go!" He snatched up a lantern and ran for the palace. Mistik couldn't be far.

And they weren't. Neil caught them running into the palace, flashlight in hand, looking around, frantic.

But then they lifted their head. "Misty! Jasper! Julius!" But no one answered. And Neil knew why. Every one of those names were attached to the Cast the others were fighting. Mistik turned, tears in their eyes. "Cora! Theo! Is anyone here?" They ran a hand down their face. "What am I to do…?"

Neil frowned. He sheathed his sword and put the lantern on the floor. "Mistik."

Mistik whipped their head about, eyes wide. "L-Lord Neil…"

Neil crossed his arms. "Ana tells me that your whole family is missing. And so is Abrax. Wanna tell me what happened?"

Mistik wrinkled their snout and furrowed their brow, eyes glassy. They dropped the flashlight and threw themselves at Neil's feet. "M-My lord… I do not deserve your mercy…" They kneeled, staring at the floor. "I… I bear responsibility for Theron's escape."

Neil's jaw dropped. *"What?"*

Mistik shut their eyes tight and lowered their head. "I… did not believe Athánatos was ready for a foreign king." They paused, then shook their head. "No… *I* was not ready for a foreign king. The fault lies with me." They wrung their hands. "I had expressed this worry to Abrax and he promised he could remove you, without violence, if I… If I gave him passage to the mainland. I created a rip that allowed him to traverse off the island."

Neil flicked his ears back. "But why? The hell did he do on the mainland?"

"I… am unsure, but I assume it allowed him to… to restore Theron." They met Neil's eyes. "You must understand, I had no idea his intention was to awaken Theron and Judgement. He only told me when I had approached him before the wedding. When I learned of his plan, I intended to inform Lady Natassa immediately, but it was too late. Theron had already awoken and had used his Drifters to kidnap my family. He threatened them with death should I say anything about his return…" They bowed low. "This was my fault. I deserve nothing short of death for this transgression. No doubt my family has already met this fate, also by my hand…"

"Renna?"

Neil turned. Misty stood in the door with her three other parents and the rest of Mistik's children, staring dumbfounded at the Archon. The Cast all cured. Ana, Leah, Andre, and Baltazar stood off to the side, carrying flashlights and lanterns, all wearing frowns. Ana crossed her arms and glared at Mistik, though the Archon didn't seem to notice.

Mistik stood, eyes wide. "Oh, *thank the Sisters!*" They crossed the room and wrapped their arms around their partners, then pulled their children close. Though Neil noticed Misty stayed put, ears flat.

Andre walked up to Neil. "I knew Theron had turned children into those god-awful monsters before, but seeing it firsthand was…" He shook his head. "That guy's a demon."

"Tell me about it," Neil said.

"We heard Mistik's confession…" Leah said. She pulled her tail into her hands and picked at the guard hairs.

Ana lowered her gaze. "So what are you gonna do now?"

Neil watched Mistik's family crowd around them, and immediately thought of Philip. Watching him get dragged away from Neil after his parents were killed. The instant, palpable relief when he got him back, safe and sound, after the hell Ackerson had put him through.

None of that would have happened if Neil hadn't killed Matron Fawn. If he hadn't made a massive, irreversible mistake.

Like Mistik did.

Neil sighed. "Mistik."

Mistik jolted and turned. They frowned, bowing low. "M-My Lord… I… whatever punishment you have for me, I accept, just please spare my family…"

"Don't… don't call me Lord," Neil said. "I don't want to force that on you." He twitched his whiskers. "We definitely need to address what you did. But with mercy. Something I didn't get when I made the biggest mistakes of my life. But this isn't the time." He held out a hand to Mistik. "Let's finish what we started first."

Mistik flicked an ear. "I… do not deserve such grace."

"Neither do I," Neil said. "But we should take what we get."

Mistik's tail swished slowly side to side. They took Neil's hand. "I… accept."

"Hate to break this up," Andre said. "But we ain't got much time. How're we gettin' to the next palace?"

Mistik reached a hand forward, searching for the Veil. "I… cannot find the threads. The Veil will not open."

Leah twisted an ear. "Melaina couldn't open it either."

"Then we take the summons," Neil said. "Not sure what the hell we'll do with the whole damn ensemble, but we'll cross that bridge when we come to it." He frowned. "That means your family stays here, Mistik."

"We will protect them," Mistik's partner Julius said. "Go. We will have much to talk about later."

"I am coming with you," Misty said, glaring at Mistik.

Mistik flicked an ear. "My child…"

"Hold your tongue," Misty snapped. "You may not feel loyalty to our Basileus, but I do. Lady Natassa chose him for a *reason,* and they represent hope that I have not felt in my lifetime. Your prejudice may be the end of all of us, and still he gives you mercy. Remember that when this is over. If we *survive.* "

Mistik lowered their head. "You speak truth. I shall endeavor to."

"Good." Misty's tail lashed. "But we may yet need another mage to undo what you did." She ran a hand through a puddle near her feet and commanded swirling water around her body. "So I am coming." She turned to Archángeli, who bowed to her. The Phonar mantled their wings and grew in size until Misty could sit comfortably on their back. "Coming, Renna?"

Mistik frowned, but also climbed on Archángeli's back.

"I'll… ride with Andre," Leah said. The pair got on Kjorn's back. Ana climbed on Rashard's.

Then Leah winced. She grew quiet for a moment, then shook herself, almost as if she was coming out of a trance.

Ana frowned. "Leah?"

"It's Zeke," Leah said. "Asking for help. I passed what power I could to him but… he's in trouble too."

Andre cursed. "We need to do this shit fast."

Baltazar walked forward, frowning. "My Lord…"

Neil flicked his tail and gripped Baltazar's shoulder. "Baltazar, I'm gonna make it clear again. None of this is your fault."

Baltazar nodded. "I hope in time I will believe that. But in the meantime, let me protect you. It is my duty to my Basileus."

Neil twisted an ear. He pointed. "You still don't have your Soul Jewels."

Baltazar held his hand up to his face. "I… do not." He flattened his ears. "I still hear Theron's voice in my head. But I find I do not feel compelled to obey. Like… like Lord Ouranos."

Neil turned to Rashard. "Take me to the other Drifters. If I can do that with Baltazar, I bet I can with the others as well. I know we don't have much time, but the more I can strip tools from Theron, the better."

Rashard bowed and led him to a room just off the palace throne room. Ten sentries, all Drifters, walked in slow, disoriented circles, blank-faced.

Neil took a deep breath and mentally reached for the Veil.

Every sentry's name rang clear in his mind. Despite the fact that the Cloak had said he couldn't see Drifters. *Don't look a gift horse in the mouth.* He gritted his teeth and reached for them like he had for Baltazar. *My sentries, my friends, hear me!*

All ten Athánatos jolted, gripping their heads and groaning. They glanced around, blinking. One of the ones closest to Baltazar, Euclid, turned toward Neil. "Lord Neil…"

Neil smiled and took Euclid's hand. "Welcome back, Euclid. I think I like this new power I have."

"Ugh," another sentry muttered. "What happened?"

"I will explain," Julius said. "You must go. Hurry!"

Neil nodded. "Everyone on board. Baltazar, you're with me and Ana." He climbed on Rashard's back. Baltazar climbed on too, and the party took off into the night. Neil clung to Rashard's feathers.

Too much time lost. Too much of *everything* lost. He had to hope they still had time to save it.

And that the return of the Shadow Cast hadn't ruined it for all of them.

CHAPTER 25

SHADOW CAST

Trecheon climbed the steps of the Inner Sanctum on Sol, clutching his mechanic's torch. Jaden and Ouranos on one side, Sami and Roscoe on the other, he wished for the hundredth time that he didn't have to associate every damn trek up and down these steps with death and betrayal.

This was never gonna end. No matter how many years of peace, there'd always be some big war on the horizon. He wasn't sure how much more he could take.

Their sketchy strategy didn't help his anxiety either. Darvin had slipped back through the rip in the Veil, planning to mark whatever location he ended up at, then make a trail to the Inner Sanctum. The rest of the team would meet him there, trek back to the rip, and investigate the area. Not great, especially in the dead of night on the overgrown island, but it was their only lead.

Ana hadn't returned, which suggested they had found something bad in the census. That didn't help Trecheon's mood. But they didn't have time to wait. Ouranos passed a message to her about the situation through one of the palace staff. Hopefully she'd turn up. If anything, just to keep their team together. Couldn't stand it falling apart.

Trecheon squeezed his eyes shut. *But my team is already falling apart.*

The last few years being in a real romantic relationship with Sacha had been amazing. Comforting, sensual, supportive. Sacha was kind, understanding, funny, sexy, and always knew where his boundaries lay and when it was safe to push him out of his comfort zone. He had grown so much with her. Best friend and romantic partner all wrapped into one. His first lasting romantic relationship, he realized. Something war and trauma had stolen from him his whole life.

He couldn't imagine it with a better partner.

But… he could imagine it with a *second* partner.

But he was too chickenshit to do anything about it. Too ashamed, too wary, too *cowardly* to tell Matt about his assassin past. And he couldn't begin to consider a romantic relationship with Matt with that secret still buried away.

He brushed a quill out of his face.

The assassin secret already posed a problem with the relationship they had. Matt openly called Trecheon his best friend and went out of his way to spend time with him. They knew everything about each other… except this. It should never have gone this far. What would he do if he found out *now?* After nearly six years and the layers of hell they'd been through? Matt would feel so betrayed… and he'd have every right to.

Especially considering what Matt already knew. He *knew* Trecheon had feelings for him, but he gave full control of the situation to Trecheon.

Though… Matt's flirting.

Mostly words, lots of looks (good *god* that *sultry smirk)* but during this last visit Matt had ramped it up with touches – a hand on Trecheon's thigh, gentle back rubs, teasing of the ear, even a soft finger down Trecheon's jaw, while looking him straight in the eye.

It sent shivers down Trecheon's spine just thinking about it.

But *why bother*. He was leaving. Sacha was leaving. While he'd never really be fully alone again with the great friends he had here and the friendships he had repaired, it wouldn't be the same.

Assuming they'd even get Matt back.

Assuming the Veil didn't fall.

Assuming Theron didn't destroy everything they had worked so hard to build.

He gritted his teeth. Can't think like that.

"Jaden?" Roscoe's voice brought Trecheon back to reality. He glanced up. Roscoe's long silver ears lay flat against his head and he frowned. "You okay?"

Trecheon turned.

They had made it to the exit, facing the darkness of the Sol village ruins, with only their flashlights illuminating the square. And Jaden stood frozen at the threshold.

Trecheon lit a fist on fire, certain there was something awful waiting for them. But when he jogged up next to Jaden, he saw nothing. The square was just empty darkness with speckles of blue moonlight filtered through the overgrown trees.

Then he realized. This was the first time Jaden had really gotten a good look at the village since coming home. Sure, he had gone through the Sanctum when they first found him and once more when they went looking for his missing X-Zero, but every other trek outside of Athánatos had been through rips leading directly to the mainland.

And suddenly here he was, facing the ruins of his home.

Trecheon chewed his lip. He gently gripped Jaden's shoulder.

Jaden jumped and turned to Trecheon, ears flat.

Trecheon forced a smile. Couldn't let their Guardian fall apart. "We've got you, Jaden. You can do this."

Jaden stared a moment, then that stoic Azure mask covered his face. "You're right." He stood tall and walked forward.

"Ah, good timing," Darvin said, slithering out of the woods. He lifted his head out of the Cast form and slowly transformed back to normal. He jerked a thumb behind him. "I didn't really see anything looking around, but I also didn't have a flashlight, so hopefully when we--"

"Darvin, watch yourself!" Ouranos shouted, stepping back and throwing a fireball toward the center of the square.

The flames lit up a dozen, inky Cast covering the floor of the square. Trecheon's heart leapt in his chest.

Darvin snarled. "Everyone, grab your Lexi Charm pouches! Aim for the eye, pair up with a fire user, keep away from the foliage. Go!" He collapsed back into his Cast form and dove after the monsters. Ouranos rushed after him, hands alight. Roscoe pulled a handful of charms out of his pouch and dashed left with Sami next to him, her hands on fire.

Trecheon called up a pair of fire tornadoes, lighting the area, adrenaline pumping through him, all the muscle memory of fighting Cast coming back to him. "Take point, Jaden!"

But Jaden still stood frozen. He had his sword hilt in one hand and pouch of Lexi Charms in the other, but he didn't move.

Trecheon flattened an ear. "Jaden!"

Jaden shook his head. "Right." He built an ice blade on the sword hilt, then pinched a Charm between his fingers. He rushed forward and tossed a charm at an advancing Cast.

The Cast slipped to the side, avoiding the charm, and rushed Jaden, shrieking. Jaden shouted and slashed at it with the sword, but the Cast snatched it in its black body and ripped it out of Jaden's hands, crushing the ice blade to dust.

Trecheon threw a fire tornado at the Cast, scooping it up in the twister. "Try again!"

Jaden snarled and threw another charm, this time hitting it square in the eye. Trecheon wrapped the fire around the Cast's "face", setting the charm ablaze, then dropped the flames entirely. The inky body of the Cast melted away, leaving an Athánatos behind. He hit the ground, but then stirred and slowly stood. It was hard to tell who it was in the dark, but eventually Trecheon remembered his name. Elias.

Jaden shook himself, then jogged over to his hilt and reactivated the ice blade.

The newly-freed Athánatos stood still in the square, then turned, blank-faced, toward Jaden. He held a sentry's dagger in his hand. Trecheon's heart skipped a beat.

He was a Drifter.

Elias lifted his dagger.

Trecheon dashed for him. "Jaden, watch out!"

Jaden whipped around and slashed his ice sword through the air, ripping open Elias' chest, spilling blood everywhere. Elias fell flat on his face and didn't move.

Jaden stared, horrified. He flipped Elias on his back. "Trecheon, help me!"

Trecheon slid up and fell to his knees next to Elias, but even with his limited healing knowledge, he knew there was nothing he could do. He pressed his hands to the wound, pumping cool energy, but the body refused to respond. Dead. He glanced up at Jaden.

Jaden recoiled. "I didn't--"

Trecheon stood. "The Cast are Drifters!" he shouted at their companions. "Don't let your guard down when you cure them!"

Jaden punched the dirt. "Damn *all of this.*"

Trecheon offered a hand. "Come on, we--"

"Darvin!" Sami called. Trecheon turned.

The orange firelight revealed a mess of Cast dragging a half-transformed Darvin into the woods. Roscoe, Sami, and Ouranos cured Cast as fast as they could, but the Drifters left behind all carried swords and daggers, and immediately turned blank-faced on them, slashing and stabbing, keeping them from Darvin. Ouranos subdued them as best he could, blocking them with stone slabs, pushing them back with wind, anything, but none of them stayed down long.

"They need help." Jaden stood, hilt in hand, though he didn't rebuild the blade. "We--"

A Cast wrapped around Trecheon's ankle and pulled his legs out from under him, slamming him to the ground. Trecheon yelped, his vision blurry and ears ringing from the impact. The Cast pulled him away from the square toward the village, opposite Darvin and the others.

Jaden turned. "Trecheon!" He shot ice spikes at the Cast. They stuck fast in its body, but didn't stop it.

Trecheon snarled, blasting the Cast with fire, but three more took its place, holding him down and dragging him along. "Damn it, let me go!" But they only dragged him deeper in.

"Trecheon, eyes up!" Jaden ran alongside them, charm bag in hand. It took several tries, but he managed to nail all three Cast pulling Trecheon along. The creatures stopped in their tracks, wailing. Trecheon ripped his foot free and Jaden pulled him up.

"The moment I cure them," Trecheon said. "Run." He threw fireballs at all three of them, waited to make sure the cure worked, then took off into the darkness, hoping Jaden would follow. The pair ran headlong through the rotting huts and overgrown trees, until Trecheon hit a gnarly tree root and went sprawling into the underbrush. Something in his ankle snapped, shooting hot fire up his leg.

Jaden stopped and kneeled down. "Oh shit--"

"Down!" Trecheon scooted against a tree and pulled Jaden down next to him. They sat in silence, though the pain in Trecheon's leg blinded him.

Something stomped methodically through the underbrush. The Drifters. Trecheon bit his tongue against the pain and held his breath, hoping they wouldn't find them. Because at this point, their only escape would be to kill them and that wasn't an option.

Jaden tapped Trecheon's side. He put a finger to his mouth in a shushing movement, then formed a series of tiny iceballs in his hand. He stood quietly and threw the iceballs as far to the left as he could, away from them and away from the square.

The footsteps faded into the distance as the Drifters followed the sound. Trecheon leaned against the tree. Drifters gone, yes. Pain in his leg, hell no. And with all their healers far away. Shit. He turned to Jaden. "Thanks... I think I broke my leg. I don't know if we can do some kind of splint or..." He paused.

Jaden stood still, staring at the hut in front of him. And despite the darkness, Trecheon immediately recognized it in the moonlight.

Matt's childhood home.

And Jaden's wife's final resting place.

CHAPTER 26

BROKEN

Izzy stared at the desaturated wall, her back to Matt, and her heart snapped in two. Sleep evaded her still. The cold of the floor seeped through her clothes and fur, stinging her skin like tiny needles.

Her whole world had shattered.

How could Matt do this to her? The energy stealing now was bad enough but… he had done it before? And he *knew?*

She shut her eyes tight, letting tears soak her fur. The greatest betrayal. Her brother, her best friend, her *Guardian partner,* and he *knowingly stole energy from her.* How could she ever trust him again?

He was probably right about the energy stealing being the reason why her Gem refused to break on its own. Hell, it was his fault she got *healing* instead of the elemental magic she was promised. If her Gem had just broken on time, she wouldn't have needed trauma training. Roscoe never would have been so mortally injured. Her Gem wouldn't have activated healing to save him.

She sniffled, her mind swirling with thoughts.

That… that probably… wasn't fair. Even if Matt's energy stealing had delayed her Gem, it had nothing to do with Roscoe's delayed Gem. He'd still need trauma training. But she wouldn't have had to break with healing to save him. They all saw Lance had healers on the ready. He would have been fine.

But…

Izzy glanced at her hand. The Black Bound elixir had built a thin film on her palm again. She rubbed the liquid between her fingers.

Lance's ice spike had hit Roscoe square in the chest during that final battle that caused their Gems to break. He had had only seconds and the healers were hidden too far away. And… Izzy was Black Bound. Though she didn't know what it was at the time, her memories now painted a vivid picture of the black, sticky elixir covering her palms while she healed Roscoe with strength average healers didn't have.

If she hadn't been trauma training with Roscoe… he would have died.

She formed a fist and looked away. That didn't justify Matt stealing energy from her.

She frowned. So… what did?

"Matt?"

She heard Matt shifting, though she didn't face him. He coughed. "…Yeah?" Tiny jingles echoed in her head.

"If you knew the Gem suppressor was stealing energy from me," Izzy said carefully. "Why did you keep it on?"

Matt was silent for several minutes. The jingles faded, but fell into a rhythm. "…My powers were out of control," he said slowly. "Lance told me if I couldn't get my magic under control, I'd be forced to wear the suppressor for life."

A chill ran up Izzy's spine and she turned, her fur puffed up. "For *life?* But that would… it would…"

"It would force me to live by my biology instead of magic," Matt said. He leaned on his knees and stared at the floor. "Die before I hit a hundred, if I even got that old. I couldn't be a Guardian. I'd… die a murderer's death. Because only murderers die by Gem suppression." He looked away. Loud church bells hit her ears. "…No more than I deserve."

"Don't say that," Izzy said automatically.

Matt just shrugged.

Izzy chewed her lip. "I… don't remember you telling us that Lance was planning on keeping the suppressor on for life…"

Matt leaned back. "I didn't tell anyone. Didn't want to be a burden."

Izzy's heart hurt.

Matt met her gaze as tiny jingles rang in her ears.

Izzy sat cross-legged. "So… you kept it on…"

"It wasn't strong enough to hold back my magic," Matt said. "So I fiddled with it. Took off the suppressor's limiter. But it still wasn't enough so it took power from you." He took a deep breath. "I justified it by telling myself it was temporary. That you'd want that for me so I could get my magic under control and we could be Guardians together." He pressed his lips tight. "I should have been straight with you. Fessed up to what I did. I'm not proud of it." He turned his head away.

Izzy hugged her knees. "And… you told Lance that's what happened."

Matt flattened his ears and scrunched his eyes closed. "Yeah. Like I said, Lance called bullshit. Despite the evidence."

Like I did, Izzy thought.

But Matt knew. He should have *told her.*

But didn't he?

Izzy narrowed her gaze, filtering through the memories. Somewhere…
somewhere she had heard that theory about the Gem suppressor before Matt
had confessed to it just now. But where? "You didn't tell me?"

Matt met her eyes. "You wouldn't let me."

Izzy perked both ears. She paused, then waved a hand, trying to laugh
it off. The laugh came out more like a choking sound. "That's not like me.
I like my apologies, especially when it's *you* admitting you're wrong."

Matt narrowed his gaze. "I'm serious, Iz. You shut me down. Told me
that I saved your life. That I beat myself up over things that aren't my fault."
He flexed his hands. "Not sure I agree though."

Izzy frowned. She tensed her shoulders… then poked around their
bond. Felt for a lie. And found none.

Draso, the fact that she had to check him for a lie… that felt so… dirty.

And yet. How had she already known?

Am I going to break what I have with Trecheon too?

Izzy's gaze shot up. But Matt wasn't even looking at her. She flattened
an ear… and opened the bond. Just a tad more.

I've been flirting with Trecheon for years now, Matt thought. *He's
going to hate me when I tell him I don't love him that way. I'm going to
break that relationship too.* He closed his eyes. *Why am I hurting the ones
I love? Why am I doing that to him…?*

Izzy furrowed her brow. She tensed up. *Maybe you actually do love
him.*

Matt whipped his head up and stared at her, loud bells ringing in her
ears. She held his gaze, but didn't speak.

That was how she had already known about Matt meddling with the
Gem suppressor. She had heard it in his head when he had been trying to
tell her. Just like she heard him now.

And she had shut him down.

Izzy's fur puffed up and her ears flushed. A distant ring echoed in her ears. Maybe from the bond. Maybe from her own shame. That didn't change what he did. And yet…

They stared at each other in silence.

Izzy coughed. "So. Are you still smelling clover?"

Matt blinked rapidly and nodded. "Uh. Yeah. I am."

Izzy stood. "Maybe we should go check it out."

Matt watched her, eyebrow raised.

Izzy stretched. "I'm not getting any sleep. Ouranos' soul clearly hasn't found a way out yet or he would have come for us." She eyed him. "And before you start going full hero, I don't think his soul can actually get hurt here, so there's no reason to go looking for him. We should… find our own way out."

Matt furrowed his brow. Jingling bells sounded in her ears. Almost like… pleading for help. Asking her if everything was okay.

Izzy took a casual step back. Because it wasn't. Not yet. But still… "Come on, Guardian. Get your ass up."

Matt took a deep breath and frowned, but he stood up. "This way." He walked slowly toward the clover lawn.

Izzy followed behind. Keeping her distance.

Hoping it would be okay.

.

SUMMONER'S BIRTH

Leah gripped Kjorn's neck feathers, leaning into his body, the loud wind from their rushed flight drowning out everything. Andre leaned in too, one hand around Leah's waist, one gripping Kjorn. He buried his face in the back of her head, trying to shield himself from the harsh winds.

Leah formed a shield around them both, as well as the other two summons, lessening the wind sound. Last thing they needed was something hitting them at this speed.

Andre relaxed a little. "Thanks." His voice was quiet, despite the noise. Distant.

Leah flicked an ear back. "You okay?"

Andre held her a little tighter. "Nervous. Wish I had some magic to help out."

"Try not to worry about it," Leah said. "We've got plenty of mages."

"But not enough healers."

Leah chewed her lip. He wasn't wrong there.

A flash of ice hit Leah's nose. *Hold tight, Guardian.* Archángeli dove ahead of them. Rashard dipped low, flying over the grass and clover, following close behind, Kjorn at his side. Leah stared forward.

They blew past Bouldrik's Aether Spire, situated way on the outskirts of the town, and cut between village huts and buildings, headed for the realm's palace. The village thinned out, leaving a vast, untouched field of wildflowers as the white, open atria appeared in the distance, coming in fast. Archángeli called out and the three summons flapped their wings, slowing. They hit the grass hard, throwing up bits of dust, grass, mud, and rocks, halting at the edge of the marbled pillars leading into the palace. Leah winced, grateful for the shield. Rashard lowered himself and allowed the group to get off. Ana walked up to Leah and gripped her hand. Leah leaned into her.

"Neil!" Damianos called.

Leah glanced up. Sacha and Damianos rushed out of the palace, the Archons on their heels.

Dami threw his arms around Neil's neck, holding him tight. "Thank the Sisters… We have been trying to reopen the collapsed portal with no success… We were losing hope."

Neil hugged him back. "I'm here, it's fine. It worked out, honestly. Brought more help." He waved to Leah and the others.

Sacha strode up to Leah and hugged her. "Thank Draso, because I can't keep up with Neil's healing on my own." She stepped back. "Definitely not complaining, but why are you here anyway?"

Neil cleared his throat, but before he could speak, Mistik slid off Archángeli, and fell to the ground, bowing.

"I have committed a most grievous error against our Basileus…"

Misty grunted, but said nothing. Baltazar narrowed his gaze, gripping the sword at his side.

Embrik growled, stepping forward. "Mistik--"

Neil stopped him. "Later. We don't have time. Is the next anchor ready for me?"

Bouldrik stepped forward. "Unfortunately, no." She crossed her arms. "There are *summons* in the Veilsong room."

Leah's body buzzed. "Summons?"

"Yes," Bouldrik said. "A gryfon and a wyvern. They are… quite violent. I worry for the Cloak's safety, but he insists he has it handled. He has us out here looking for the summoner so we can end this, but we have had no luck so far."

Leah's fur bristled and she turned to Ana. "Drifa and Kaoru."

Ana's eyes widened. "Sharp's summons."

"Sharp?" Andre said. "Ain't he dead?"

"He is," Leah said. "Which means they have a new summoner… and they didn't get a good one like I hoped."

"How did they get here in the first place?" Ana asked.

"I wondered that too," Sacha said. "I think it has something to do with the Veil… It's weaker than we thought. Some things might be able to sneak past it."

"Or someones," Leah said darkly.

A loud boom echoed from the palace, followed by a dragon's roar.

No! Leah took off toward the sound. Several of her companions shouted after her, but she didn't wait. The Cloak needed help *now*.

Flashes of lightning and streams of water flew about to meet her as she rounded the corner to the Veilsong atria. The air filled with shouting, roars, and eagle screams. A sharp smell of a lightning storm hit her nose, along with the briny smell of the sea. She shielded and peered in.

And there they were. Drifa, the violet and gray lightning gryfon and Kaoru, the blue and black water wyvern. They stood their ground in the center of the Veilsong room, planted firmly in their spot, their elements flying about them, shrouding them. Lightning crashed into pillars, breaking off dust and pebbles. Water flew about, splashing everything. Leah reached out for a few drops, hoping to hear him speak and see if she could find any clues as to why they were there.

But there were no words in Kaoru's element. Just screams of pain and anger.

"Holy *shit,*" Andre said, peering at the summons. "How the hell we supposed to fight that?"

"Leah," Ana said, leaning next to her. "Their eyes. They look… strange. All white and glowing."

Leah's eyes widened. Were they? She focused hard on the animals behind the wall of elements. Sure enough, their eyes were pure white. And worse still, little cracks of white covered their bodies, radiating little beams of light, as if lightning magic clung to them.

Leah drew her hands to her snout. "Oh no… they have *reality rot.*"

Ana turned to her, eyebrow raised. "What?"

"Reality rot," Leah repeated. "Summon psychosis. If a summon goes too long without a master, they start to lose their anchor on reality and go feral." She pointed. "See the light lines on their bodies? The worse it gets, the more lines there are. And they have… a lot of lines." She flattened both ears. "If the lines get to their toe tips, then they're beyond saving."

Sacha came up now, with Neil and Dami at her sides. "What then?"

"Then that's the end," Leah said. "Reality rotted summons are notoriously hard to break, far harder than normal summons, and they don't stay down. They'll recover in minutes. And they're nesting… finding one pocket of safety as their last grasp on reality and defending it with all their might, desperately clinging to sanity. We'll never get them out of there."

Leah chewed her lip. "I'm guessing we have minutes, half an hour at most, before they're completely rotted..."

Drifa gave a staccato eagle call, blasting lightning all around her, cracking walls and pillars and damaging the Cloak's shield, forcing him back.

Neil growled. "So how the hell do we fix it?"

Leah frowned. "Give them a safe space. Limit contact. Don't introduce them to anyone new."

"Gussin' that's what the Cloak was doing," Andre muttered.

"Likely," Leah said. "They've seen me and Ana and a little of Andre when we were escaping to Sol, but..."

"That rules us out," Sacha said, tugging on Neil and Dami. "Especially you, Basileus. Back up and don't get involved." She pulled them back. Neil grumbled, but didn't resist.

Leah flicked her tail. "That's all a temporary fix though." She swallowed hard. "They need a summoner. That's the only real cure."

The Cloak, green-eyed and angry, stood on one side of the room, purple shield in front of him, staring down the two summons. He looked exhausted. He was running out of time too.

Andre gripped Leah's shoulder. "You've always wanted to be a summoner, yeah? So let's get you some summons." He stepped out of their hiding spot, moving slow. "Hey dragon, look my way, huh?"

Kaoru whipped about, snorting loudly. He glared at Andre, but didn't attack.

Leah's heart nearly stopped. "Andre, *don't!*"

"I got this." Andre waved her back, then held his hands out, moving closer. "It's Kaoru, right?" He smiled, making himself small, clearly trying to be friendly and approachable. "You're scared. We can help. Let's just--"

Kaoru roared and charged Andre.

"No!" Leah activated her staff and rushed between them, shielding her and Andre, holding out the weapon. Kaoru crashed into her, knocking her down. He chomped on the staff, growling and spitting. Leah held firm, but she struggled against the wyvern's strength. "Kaoru! *Listen!* You're here, you're safe! You need--"

"Leah, watch out!" the Cloak called.

Leah strengthened her shield just as Drifa blasted them with lightning. The shield held, but barely. Cracks formed through it, distorting the air around it. She gritted her teeth. "Andre, *run!"*

"I'm not leaving you to get fried!" Andre shouted.

"I've got you!" Ana called. She dashed up to Leah and ripped her Gem from her belt. "Hold on!"

A rush of fresh energy flashed through Leah's body, practically pouring out of her fur follicles. She pressed it into her shield, repairing cracks and fighting off the lightning. Her whole body buzzed, making her feel sick. This wasn't like Zeke giving her his comfortable, familiar power. It felt foreign, angry. It--

A wave of water burst through Leah's shield, crashing around her, kicking her to the floor and breaking her concentration. The water swept Ana and Andre off their feet, and they collapsed. Ana lost Leah's Gem in the crash, and all the ugly extra energy vanished, taking the shield with it.

Leah pulled herself up on all fours, coughing and shaking water out of her fur. Her vision blurred and she wobbled, dizzy. She turned. *Gotta get my Gem--*

Drifa rushed her, talons out, screeching.

Leah gasped and covered her head with her hands. *"Please, Drifa, don't!"*

Andre dashed between them and wrapped his arms around Leah, shielding her with his body. He pulled her close to him before she ever got a chance to protest.

His screams only barely drowned out the vicious sounds of ripped flesh and clothes.

An eagle cry echoed off the walls, and in a flurry of ice, Rashard blew past them, crashing into Drifa, bashing her away. Andre's grip loosened and he slumped into the puddles, unmoving.

"No!" Leah checked Andre's head, then carefully turned him on his stomach. Deep, angry wounds ripped across his back, staining the puddles and floor red with blood. "Andre, hang on!" She pressed her hands to the wounds.

Nothing happened. She still didn't have her Gem. Panic gripped her chest and she turned frantically, her tail puffed up. *"Ana, where's my Gem?"*

Ana slid to her knees next to them. "Kaoru has it… he knocked me away from it and stole it." Leah turned. Kaoru stood in the center of the room, wings spread, gripping her Gem in his clawed feet.

Leah's eyes widened. *No, no, no!*

Ana ripped off her shirt, tore it to shreds, and used her magic to enhance the strips into bandages. "I've got him. Go get your Gem."

Leah's eyes burned, and she turned back to Andre, torn.

Andre groaned.

Still alive. She gripped his hand. "Don't you dare die on me." She turned to Kaoru.

But the wyvern was no longer attacking. He huddled in the corner of the room, curled into a ball, shaking, staring at Drifa and Rashard.

Despite Drifa's raw strength, she couldn't stand against a veteran summon like Rashard. He beat her down with talons, wings, and beak, blasting her with ice, deflecting her lightning and countering her every physical attack. And even with her pure white eyes, her expression betrayed her terror.

Just like in the woods of Canada when Sharp threatened her.

Every other priority flew from Leah's mind and she ran for the two gryfons, waving her hands. "Rashard, stop, *stop!*"

Ice bit her nose. *They are feral and must be removed! They broke the oath by refusing a master!*

"They were *abused,*" Leah said. "Forced into summonhood against their will! Of course they're afraid of having a master! Please, Rashard, you have to stop!"

Rashard paused and turned to Leah, one feathered ear pinned back. *You cannot force someone into summonhood.*

"I thought so too," Leah said. "But I saw the effects firsthand. They're afraid… Just look at them."

Rashard turned back to the gryfon. She huddled down like a cornered cat, ears back, wings pressed tight to her body, hissing over and over at every tiny sound.

Rashard clicked his beak, his face softening. *I... I see.* He leaned close to Drifa, swirls of ice circling her head in a private conversation. But his ears perked. *She does not speak?*

Tiny droplets landed on Leah's head. *Trauma... stole her voice...* She turned. Kaoru had also regained something of his senses and he hobbled close to Drifa, mantling his wings over her. He met Rashard's gaze with his, sharking. *I... feel my mind... escaping...*

You are feral, Rashard said.

Kaoru's face softened, and the glow from the cracks in his scales and wings lessened a little. His eyes betrayed intense fear. *How... do I fix it?*

Andre groaned again, quiet and fading. Ana cried out, panicked. "Leah, I'm losing him!" Leah turned. The Cloak was there too, pushing healing energy into him, but she knew from experience that the Cloak was a terrible healer.

Kaoru lifted his head and glanced at Andre. Then he turned to Leah and held out his foot. *Take… your Gem…*

Leah gingerly plucked it from between Kaoru's toes. "Thank you…" She rushed for Andre and pressed the Gem into Ana's hands. "Give me everything you've got!" She pushed all she had into her magic. The full weight of Andre's wounds, shallow breathing, and fading heartbeat knocked her back, nearly blinding her, but she refused to back down. "Come on, Andre, come on!"

Slowly the wounds healed. She couldn't see anything with her magic blinding her, but her mind's eye painted her a picture of the flesh coming together, blood replacing itself, and, thankfully, Andre's pain subsiding. The whole ordeal finished in seconds, but it felt like a lifetime. When she finally felt the last wound close up, she collapsed with exhaustion into a bloody puddle.

Still Andre didn't move.

Leah teared up. "Andre, please…"

Then he groaned.

Relief filled Leah's chest and she forced herself to sit up.

Andre pushed himself to a sitting position, holding his head with one hand and shaking. He turned to Leah, wordless.

She wrapped her arms around him. "T-Thank Draso… thank Draso…"

He held her tight, those big strong arms back to their normal strength. "Oh, thank God…"

Gentle snowflakes landed on Leah's nose. *Guardian.* She and Andre turned. Rashard leaned down and tapped his beak to her nose. *These two wish to speak with you.*

Leah's heart raced. She stood, trying and failing to wipe the blood from her clothes and fur. "Kaoru? Drifa?"

Kaoru bowed low, still trembling. He shook himself, flinging little droplets of water off his mane. *This one… he tells me… a summoner will… save us.* He flexed his clawed feet. *You are… summon expert. He speaks truth?*

Leah perked her ears and smiled, hoping she didn't look too eager. "He does. You need a summoner to stay grounded in reality. If you're ready for one."

Hmm… He turned to Drifa. She hunched down, but nodded, tucking her wings close against her back. The light lines glowed worse than ever, traveling down her legs while she huddled to the floor. Kaoru nodded back. *We… are ready…*

Rashard lifted his head. *Introduce yourself to your chosen summoner.*

Leah lifted her chin.

But Kaoru turned away from her… and instead addressed Andre. *Human… we wish for you… to be our summoner…*

Leah's eyes widened and she stared at Andre.

Andre leaned back, his brow furrowed. "Me? The hell you want me for?"

Kaoru lowered his head, spraying water. *You… sacrificed yourself for your companion… A selfless act… we wish for such a summoner…* He nodded to Drifa. *This one… wishes to apologize… for harming you…*

Leah's breath hitched and her eyes burned. Her heart shattered. *Didn't I sacrifice for my friends? Wasn't I harmed too? Why…*

Andre turned to her, his eyebrows knitted together, clearly confused. "I… uh… But Leah…" His voice faded.

Leah breathed deeply and let it out slowly, locking down her emotions. *Don't… don't diminish this. They get to choose. Andre is a good choice. Don't try and take that from him.* She pulled back her tears and forced a smile, hoping he couldn't see her pain through it. "I-It's okay, Andre. They made their choice. I…" She took another deep breath. "They need a good summoner. A good person." She took his hands. "Do you want this? Magic and companions to help?"

Andre pressed his lips together. "I mean, yeah, 'course, but--"

"Let me show you how to complete the oath," Leah said.

Andre squeezed her hands. "You sure?"

"It's okay," Leah said, more firmly this time, fighting back the ache in her chest. "They need a summoner and we're running out of time." She let go of him. "It's okay." She motioned Drifa and Kaoru over. "Place your hands on their heads. They'll say their oath to you, in your head, and if it takes, you'll know exactly what to say back without prompting. Okay?"

Andre frowned at her a moment longer, then did as he was told.

Rashard snorted ice. *Repeat the phrase I gave you, Kaoru. Only to your summoner – no one else. And remember, you speak for you and for Drifa.*

Kaoru nodded. He and Drifa closed their eyes, and a blast of water and lightning surrounded Andre in slow moving swirls. A soft blue-white glow covered Andre's body, and the heavy scent of sea water mixed with the sharp scent of electricity. Andre spoke back the words of the summoner's oath unprompted, a sure sign the oath took.

Ana slipped her hand into Leah's. Leah gripped it tighter than she should have, desperate not to cry. Not to ruin this moment for Andre or the summons.

In a flash, the lightning, water, and summons all vanished, leaving behind that gentle glow on Andre. The glow sunk into his body and everything returned back to normal. Andre turned to Leah with far too deep a frown for someone who just had something so wonderful happen to them. "Leah…"

"I-It's okay…" Leah said, keeping that forced smile, though her voice broke. The tears would follow soon, but she couldn't let him see it. Couldn't hurt him over this. That was selfish. *Selfish.*

Andre's shoulders slumped. Her pain got through anyway.

She breathed deep again, burying the emotions. "Ah… you can um, summon them by just thinking about them and holding y-your hand out. C-Call on them like you would thinking about a… a close friend." She pulled her tail into her hands and picked at the fur. "Don't ah, don't do that here though. The first time summoning is um, usually pretty powerful and uh… yeah, don't wanna hurt anyone or anything. Probably best to go back out to that field. We'll um… we'll need them to get everyone to the next palace, if they're willing."

Andre's expression didn't change. He moved like he was going to hug her.

But she backed up. Couldn't have that or she'd break completely. "Take um, take Rashard and Kjorn and Archángeli and uh, go get that first summon out of the way while Neil… while Neil does this anchor." She moved away from Ana. "I'll ah, I'll stay here and um… clean up with the Cloak. Tell Neil we'll be ready in a second here, okay?"

Ana frowned now too. She and Andre exchanged a glance with each other. Andre turned to Leah. "I appreciate the brave face," he said slowly. "And I get you want a moment alone. But when this is over, I got a shoulder for you to cry on. 'K?"

Tears built up in Leah's eyes. "O-Okay."

"Can I hug you now?"

Leah took a shuddering breath, but she nodded. He gave her a quick sideways hug, which threatened to break her, but she managed to keep a straight face. Ana squeezed her hand and smiled.

And they left.

The Cloak came up next to her. "Leah…"

And that was it. Leah sat hard on the ground and curled in a ball, burying her face in her knees and sobbing. This was so wrong, so *selfish*, how could she be this way? She wasn't allowed to be upset over the summons choosing Andre. They saw something good in him and *they were right* and he *deserved* to have something so wonderful. And she shouldn't be pining after them. They were their own creatures, with their own minds and their own decisions. They weren't pawns to be used, they weren't just a goal to reach for…

And yet…

All she had ever wanted was a pair of summons. Creatures who wouldn't care about her magic or her neurodivergency or her romantic preferences or her weird love of healing. Built-in friends for life…

And she lost her chance. She'd never get another one.

She stared forward, the tears blurring her vision. That was selfish too. Locking a pair of magic beings into a relationship just because she was… she was lonely. That was *wrong*. Her whole motivation was wrong.

Everything was wrong.

She wasn't lonely anymore anyway, right? She had Zeke and Andre and Jaden and Ana and… and…

And she would lose them all when she went back to Zyearth. She squeezed her eyes shut.

But… seeing Kaoru and Drifa so broken… Maybe she felt like she needed them… but they didn't need her. They didn't need a broken summoner. They needed someone strong. Like Andre. This… this was for the best… even if it hurt.

They were better off without her.

"Leah," the Cloak said again.

"I know…" Leah said. "I-It's for the best… You probably k-know better than all of us…"

"No," the Cloak said, his voice dark. Leah glanced up at him. His eyes betrayed worry and he crossed his arms. "This wasn't supposed to happen. Those summons… they were supposed to pick you."

Leah's eyes grew wide, the ache in her chest doubling over. "What…?"

"I don't know what's going on," the Cloak said. "But something has shifted. And I don't like it."

CHAPTER 28

FACE YOUR FATHER

Natassa followed Ouranos through the palace. If she read her fatigue correctly, it should be long into the night, though the light, the sky, the feel of the palace had not changed. This place drained more than just energy. It drained color, sound, light… hope. The constant pull on her body and mind threatened to break her.

It should never have come to this. She should have saved Ouranos years ago. She should have ended her father to prevent further pain. She should not have let Zeke run off on his own.

She should have taken charge, as a Basilea should.

But she failed. And she had no idea how to make it right. She coughed. "You are sure they will be at the throne room?"

"Barring problems with the Drifter souls, yes," Ouranos said. "Once we find them and Zeke, you will all go home, immediately."

"Indeed," Natassa said. "Assuming Zeke is safe."

"He will be."

Natassa took a deep breath. "Ouranos."

"I know what you wish to discuss, Natassa," Ouranos said, widening the gap between them. "And I *forbid it.* You cannot trade your life for my soul. You promised our *anipsiós* that you would not. I expect you to keep that promise."

"No, I…" She paused. "I… am sorry."

Ouranos turned.

Natassa stopped walking and stared at the ground. "I… I failed you when I was unable to stop our father from turning you into a Drifter."

Ouranos flattened his ears. "Natassa…"

"I know you will say I should not blame myself," Natassa said. "But I do. And I have only ever wanted to make it right. And while Matthew bridging your soul is a step toward making it right, it is no more than a bandage – It does not solve the problem as a whole." She frowned. "I know you think the cost to solve that problem is too great and we will need to live with the bandage, but I am sorry nonetheless."

Ouranos furrowed his brow and stepped forward. But then his face contorted and he gripped his head, growling and gritting his teeth.

Natassa perked both ears, her eyes wide. "Ouranos? What--"

"Is the cost too great?"

Natassa turned, and her stomach flopped, making her feel sick. Theron stood a few feet away, his chin lifted, staring at Natassa. Theron's soul, specifically – he carried the same faded chains Ouranos' soul did.

But also like Ouranos, he had his mind again. The spark in his pupilless eye made her quills stand up. He caught her gaze. "Answer the question, *Prinkípissa.* Can you really put a cost on your brother's soul?"

Ouranos strained against Theron's pull. "Natassa, do not--!"

But Theron glared at Ouranos and tugged on his chains, pulling him to the ground, cutting off his words. He turned back to Natassa. "You had a chance to save him, and you *failed,*" he said with a snarl. "Then you had another chance with Matthew and failed there too. You fear the proper cost, and therefore you fail your brother, and Athánatos, over and over."

Natassa took a step back. "I-I…"

"Your failures cost even more lives," Theron continued. "The Keepers died while bringing you back when you failed to save Ouranos. Hundreds more died at Ouranos' hand as he ravaged Athánatos and the mainland. He drove away Alexina who in turn injured your *anipsiós,* who is dying as we speak. This could have been *prevented.*"

"By *you!*" Natassa shouted, hugging herself, tears streaming down her face. *"You* did this when you took Ouranos from us! When you let your grief *ruin you.*"

Theron lifted his chin, his expression unchanged. "I will not deny my actions," he said. "Grief does strange things to us all and I admit, I caused great harm. But that changes nothing. You could have stopped that harm. You could have ended me, saved your brother, and prevented all that pain. But your cowardice stays your hand."

Ouranos snarled, trying and failing to free his chains from Theron's grip. "Natassa, do not listen to this snake! You know *better!*"

"Better than what?" Theron said, tugging on the chains again. "Even you know I speak the truth, Ouranos. You and Natassa both had countless opportunities to end this all. You even admitted you should have killed me when you had the chance. And you had *many* chances, Prínkipas. You squandered them. Now look at you." He turned to Natassa. "But… there is one way to repair the scars." He held Ouranos' chains out toward Natassa.

Natassa's eyes widened.

Ouranos took a sharp breath. "No, Natassa, shut your ears to him, do *not--*"

Theron wrapped one of Ouranos' own chains around his neck, pulling tight. "Silence, Prínkipas. Let the Basilea make her choice." He lowered his gaze, piercing her soul with his stare. "You know the right answer." He held out the chains again. "Do it."

Natassa stared at the chains, her mind at war. Theron spoke the truth, as much as she hated to say so. She could finally right a wrong she should have righted ages ago. The cost was worth it. *Ouranos* was worth it.

And yet.

He lived. He spoke. Formed memories, relationships. His soul may be separate, but it was bridged.

But that left his soul, the essence of his being, trapped in this hopeless, dark, terrifying world. A torture that he would always carry in the back of his mind, until death.

Unless she freed him.

She reached for the chains.

Theron's mouth turned up in a smile, ever so slightly. Ouranos rattled in his chains, but he could not escape.

She could free him.

"Yes, Prinkípissa," Theron whispered. "Come, end his suffering. Rid your soul of guilt. The Athánatos people have Neil as ruler. There is nothing holding you back from fixing this." He held the chains closer. "Absolution is at hand."

Absolution. Absolution. Ouranos deserved freedom. She needed absolution. The Athánatos had Neil.

Neil.

Neil found absolution. He worked hard to undo the damage his assassin past had done. He sacrificed to save the Athánatos people. To save her. He would be proud of her. He would *want* this for her. He…

He would want her with him. And she wanted that too.

Ground yourself in your loved ones.

Neil's gentle scent, his soft hug, his fantastic smile, his musical laugh, his sensual touch… all of it flooded her mind, chasing back the shadows.

She pulled her hand back.

Theron furrowed his brow and bared his teeth. "Will you fail him *again,* Prinkípissa?"

Natassa glared, and blasted Theron back with a wave of water, forcing him to let go of Ouranos' chains. He washed a few feet down the hall, tumbling over his own legs. Natassa stepped forward. "I did not fail him to begin with," she snapped. *"You did.* I should have accepted that long ago."

Theron spat out a mouthful of water and stood. "You are *weak.* "

"You are, Father," Natassa said, lighting her hands on fire, and growling. "You proved that when you used grief as an excuse to *kill*."

Theron snarled, lighting his own hands ablaze.

But a powerful rush of wind knocked him down again, extinguishing the flames. Natassa turned.

Matt and Izzy stood there, their wedding finery in tatters and their stances betraying their weariness. Though Matt held his hand out, covered in Black Bound elixir, glaring at Theron and standing firm. He spoke through clenched teeth.

"Get the hell out of here, Theron," he said, his voice deep and dangerous. "And know that when I find you in the normal world, I'll be the *last thing you see.* "

Theron bared his teeth, but he gathered up his chains and ran, leaving Ouranos behind. Ouranos pulled the phantom chains off his neck and gagged, but otherwise seemed fine.

Natassa sighed relief. "Oh, thank the Sisters…" She threw her arms around Matt and hugged him tight. "I am so sorry we did not find you sooner. Are you hurt? Can you walk okay?"

"…I'm fine," Matt said quietly. "We're… fine." His voice no longer held the anger and strength he had aimed at Theron. It was almost cold… hurt.

She pulled back and looked him in the eyes, frowning. "You are sure?"

"We don't have time," Izzy said, stomping past them. Her hands were also covered in the elixir. Not a good sign. Izzy shook her hand free of it and rubbed her snout. "I suspect the only reason why Theron took off is because he's gonna send his Drifters here to get the elixir. Let's get out of here before he can."

Matt frowned, flicking his ears back.

Ouranos frowned too, twitching his tail. "You did not wait in the throne room."

"No, I…" Matt paused, looking at Izzy. She would not look back at him. A shiver ran up Natassa's spine. Something was very wrong. Matt shook himself. "I… smell something. The clover lawn. It feels like a Gem bond pull."

A heavy silence weighed between them. Something broken. "Izzy… Matt… what happened with you?"

Matt closed his eyes and grimaced. He shook his head slightly. "Later. Right now, I need… I need to go to the clover lawn. Find out why I'm smelling it so strongly."

Natassa's shoulders slumped, heavy with worry. "If you are smelling something through a new bond… whose bond is it?"

"That's what we're hoping to find out," Matt said.

Natassa flattened both ears and furrowed her brow. She took Matt's hand in a sign of solidarity. "Then let us get to it before Theron returns."

And let her escape the constant reminders of her failures.

CHAPTER 29

CONTINGENCY PLAN

Ouranos raced after Darvin and the others as the Shadow Cast dragged him deeper into the black, shapeless woods. Several Athánatos sentries, cured of their affliction as Shadow Cast, but still trapped as Drifters, chased behind them.

The tiny window between each enemy shrank by the second.

Magic gathered at the tip of Ouranos' fingers, dripping into the grass and vanishing in little puffs of smoke and dust. He had the power to end it all. Destroy the Shadow Cast, kill the Drifters, make them safe. But at a great cost. Too great a cost. A cost Theron had been forcing them to pay for decades.

Ouranos would not let him win. He refused to let any more Drifters die at their hands. Even if it meant he faced death himself.

Sami snarled, her hands alight. She rushed to the right. "Ouranos, think you can keep the woods from catching fire?"

Ouranos dipped under a branch, rushing to catch up. "I can try."

"Then follow my lead." She slid to a stop. "Roscoe, put a barrier between us and the Drifters!"

Roscoe slowed too and slammed a fist to the ground, blasting a ten-foot wall of earth out of the dirt. Ouranos reinforced it with stone, hoping it would hold without hurting the sentries.

Sami threw her hands forward, her ears back and her lips curled up, baring her teeth. Fire burst from her fists, surrounding the Cast. They shrieked, flinging themselves into the woods, one by one, embers clinging to their bodies.

The flames licked at the dying underbrush, immediately setting them ablaze.

Ouranos gritted his teeth and shot waves of water after the Cast. He pulled at the embers, extinguishing them where he could.

The Drifters pounded on the stone wall behind them, each strike beating against Ouranos' ears. He winced with every blow.

"Ouranos!" Roscoe shouted. Ouranos turned to find a trail of fire leading deep into the woods, Cast shrieking away, flicking ash and flames into the trees. He snarled and beat the fire back with sand and water, leaving behind a muddy trail. The Cast vanished into the darkness, uncured and silent. The blows against his ears grew ever stronger.

This was not working.

"Sami!" Ouranos called. "Corral the Cast and bring them 'round this stone wall!"

Sami flicked an ear back. "Near the Drifters? Why?"

"Because when we cure them, that is the state they will be in," Ouranos said. He turned and began forming a wall around the Drifters, high and smooth, trapping them. "And they need to be penned. Hurry!"

"I got you, Ouranos," Roscoe said, and he used his magic to pack sand and dirt around the stone walls to reinforce them.

Sami pulled on her magic, forcing the Cast through the underbrush and into Ouranos' stone valley. "Darvin's still in there!"

"I… I'm fine!" Darvin called, his voice bubbling and muffled in the midst of all the shrieking Cast. "Get them safe and I'll escape!"

It was a long process, made longer by the fiery mess Sami's magic left behind, as they had to frequently pause for Ouranos to put it out. But eventually Ouranos' walls grew tall enough that the Drifters could not scale it. He left a small opening. "Sami, Roscoe, cure the Cast one by one and shove them into the opening. Hurry!" They nodded and did so – Roscoe tossing a Lexi Charm, Sami lighting it ablaze, and Roscoe shoving the Cast into the opening as it was cured before it had a chance to escape. Soon they cured enough that Darvin was able to untangle himself from the mess and escape. He helped them get the rest into the little stone valley, then Ouranos sealed it entirely. He crumpled to the charred earth.

Darvin followed suit, collapsing into his Shadow Cast form and spreading out like an exhausted mule deer after a long run, blending into the night. He sighed, bubbling across the surface. "Good *Draso.*"

Sami and Roscoe sat hard as well, heaving breaths. After a moment, Darvin wrapped himself around Sami, cooing quietly. Sami closed her eyes and leaned against a tree, but she muttered thanks and an I love you. Roscoe coughed until he spat, then shook his head.

Ouranos lay on the charred ground and focused on breathing until it became slow and natural again. He stared at the night sky, mostly obscured by the black trees. The Drifters made no noise. Blessed silence.

"Hey," Darvin said, slithering off Sami and poking his normal head out of the black puddle. He wore the hardened mask of a soldier. "Where's Trecheon and Jaden?"

Ouranos' heart quickened again and he sat upright, his tail fluffing up. "Were they not with us?"

Sami's gaze grew dark. "They ran the other way, chased by Cast and Drifters."

"Shit," Roscoe said. He sat up too and pulled up his pendant. "Maybe I can get them on comms. We aren't on Athánatos anymore." But the pendant refused to light up. He beat a finger against it. "Damn it, what now?"

Ouranos tried as well. "Mine also appears broken."

Sami flattened her ears. "Not good…"

"Should we go look for them?" Roscoe asked.

"Hmm." Darvin reformed to his normal self and scratched his chin. "That's a good question. On the one hand, we're very close to where I popped in on the island. It might be hard for me to find it again with the fire damage changing the landscape. On the other…"

"If we are nearby," Ouranos said. "Let us examine the area first, then find our companions. As much as it pains me to say, finding Theron must be our priority if we are to stop this madness. Trecheon and Jaden are powerful warriors. They can handle themselves."

"Good point." Sami stood. "So let's do this quickly. Darvin, lead the way."

Darvin nodded and jogged through the woods, kicking up ash and dust. Ouranos followed.

Several minutes passed, with only the sound of their jogging to accompany them. Worry rippled under Ouranos' fur, but he fought to keep it under control.

"Ouranos," Darvin said suddenly. "We all think that Theron is going after Matt and Izzy to get the Black Bound elixir, right? To make more Shadow Cast?"

"That is the theory," Ouranos said.

Darvin paused a moment, slowing his pace. "Theron had to make his own version of Shadow Cast, yeah?" he asked. "I think I remember you or Natassa saying that once upon a time."

"We believe so," Ouranos said. "I am unfamiliar with how Shadow Cast were originally created, though based on Theron's long experimenting and the Purge erasing all knowledge of the Cast's original creation, it is a logical conclusion."

Darvin flattened his long black ears. "We saw the Purge statue break."

Ouranos turned to him, eyebrow raised. "Yes?"

"Which means that all the knowledge of the Cast has come back," Darvin said, slowing to a walk. "Including the old ways they were created."

Ouranos stopped in his tracks, his fur puffed up.

Darvin wrinkled his snout, frowning. He stopped and turned to the group. "Why hasn't Judgement used the old ways to create Cast?"

Roscoe's gaze grew dark. "Or worse, what if she has and we have no way to restore them?"

But Ouranos' mind flew elsewhere, as his heart raced, and his skin grew clammy. The Phonar had said that they needed time to sift through the flooding memories from before the Purge, though they were there, just waiting.

So what happened when Judgement's memories flooded back? Would she have access to her old methods?

And if so… what would she do with Matt and Izzy if she no longer needed them?

Darvin snorted, feral and angry. "Roscoe, Sami, I hate to say it, but it's time to implement project Black Rock."

Ouranos perked an ear, pulling himself back to reality. "What is project Black Rock?"

Sami and Roscoe exchanged a glance with each other, saying nothing.

Ouranos narrowed his gaze. "One of you answer me, please."

Darvin flattened both ears now, furrowing his brow. "You're not going to like it. But you're going to have to trust me." He pulled a thick, red, leather pouch out of his pocket. He shook it until a tiny black rock rolled out onto his palm.

No… a charm. A familiar charm.

Ouranos' eyes widened. "Tell me you do not have Cast charms in your possession, Darvin."

Darvin turned to him, his furrowed brow and tight lips betraying both worry and determination. "You have to trust me, Ouranos."

Ouranos bared his teeth and stepped forward. "You expect me to stand idly by while you *purposefully create Shadow Cast?* Have you taken leave of your senses? They are *monsters!*"

"When controlled by others, yes," Darvin said. "But we found a loophole." He passed a charm to Roscoe. Roscoe took a deep breath and held it up.

Ouranos' breath hitched. "Roscoe, *wait--*"

"Take care of Izzy for me." Roscoe pressed the Cast charm into his eye.

Ouranos' stomach turned over as black ink poured out of Roscoe's body, bleeding through his nose, his mouth, his eyes, his ears, drowning in the ooze of the Cast and collapsing into a dark puddle in the dirt, strangely silent.

Ouranos fumbled with his Lexi charm pouch. "Sisters alive, you have all gone *mad.* We have limited charms to cure the afflicted and no time to make more! Stand back, before he attacks!"

Darvin put a hand on Ouranos' shoulder. "Look closer, Ouranos. He's not attacking."

The puddle gurgled that familiar, bubbling gurgle, setting Ouranos' teeth on edge. Three eyes blinked on the surface, glancing around. And the eyes were… green. Not the characteristic glowing blue of normal Cast. And more than that… it did not attack.

In fact… it cooed.

Ouranos took a step back, ears flat. "What sorcery is this?"

"We ah, did some experimenting," Sami said. "And we figured out that if you press the Cast charm in your eye yourself, then technically, you control yourself. Meaning Theron can't control him."

"So he's safe," Darvin said. "And more than that, he can't be harmed."

Ouranos glared, forming a fist. "And you think that makes it okay to use the tools of the enemy?"

"I think that makes it okay to protect *against* the tools of the enemy," Darvin said. "Now Roscoe controls his own mind. He can't be hurt, he can't be controlled, but he sure as hell can fight." He crossed his arms. "It's not a good solution. It's not what we *want*. But for now, it's… something." He turned his head. "I don't want to lose any more family."

Ouranos flattened his ears and tensed up, glaring. "And Sami? Will you join him?"

Sami eyed him, lifting her chin. "Will you immediately bring us back if I do?"

Ouranos bared his teeth. "I very well *should.*"

Sami watched him a moment longer, then crossed her arms. "Fine. I won't. For now."

Darvin frowned. "Sami--"

"For now," Sami said. She held out her hand. "Give me a charm. The moment we hit trouble…"

Darvin sighed. He held the charm bag out to her.

A fireball flew through the darkness and lit the bag on fire, burning it to cinders, melting the charms to vapors. Ouranos lit his hands ablaze, glaring into the darkness.

Theron slunk out of the shadows, his Ei-Ei jewels glowing on either side of his head, his chin held high. "Seems like trouble hit you first."

BLUEBIRDS

Jaden stood frozen at the threshold of the beaten, dirty hut. Memories flooded him as he stared. Everything came into clear focus, transforming the rotting room into something familiar.

The kitchen, with its polished wood counters, its fire stove, its collection of wooden spoons, its canned goods.

The dining room with its family table, its highchairs for the kids, its stained wood from the many spills.

The living room with its wicker couches, its inviting candlelight, its… its easel and paints. He gently sniffed the air. It still had a faint scent of linseed oil. The canvas held his last painting, a half-finished, ruined thing, ripped up and rotting beyond recognition, left abandoned after the Omnir attacked.

The Omnir…

A twig snapped behind him. He whipped about, hands iced over, heart beating against his chest.

Trecheon stood there, favoring his leg, hands out. "Jaden… I'm not your enemy."

Jaden stared wide eyed, his breath quickening. "What do you want?"

Trecheon furrowed his brow. "My leg is broken."

Jaden stared a moment longer, blinking stupidly. It's Trecheon. Just Trecheon. He shook his head. "I-I'm sorry, it's just…"

"I get it," Trecheon said. He slid carefully to the floor and leaned against one of the walls of the house. "Matt did the same thing."

Jaden flicked his ears back. "Matt was here?"

"Yeah," Trecheon said. He rubbed his leg, hissing in pain. "Not long after we first met. God, that's *hell*."

"Here." Jaden dug through a drawer in the kitchen and found some metal serving spoons he had brought from Zyearth, thankfully free of rust and debris, and some hemp rope. He jogged back to Trecheon. "We'll use this until we can get you to a healer." He set to work wrapping the leg and reinforcing it with the spoons.

Trecheon grimaced, but nodded. "Thanks." He bit his lip. "Damn, don't I wish for the days I could heal myself."

Jaden lifted a brow. "You could heal yourself?"

"Technically," Trecheon said. "When the Gem was partially bound to me. Izzy called it 'activated' or something."

Jaden pressed his lips into a thin line. He went back to the leg. "That about confirms it then. You have a Sol jewel."

Trecheon flicked an ear back. "Izzy thought so too."

Jaden worked carefully, slowing and readjusting every time Trecheon winced. "I um… I activated those at one point."

Trecheon perked his ears. "You did?"

Jaden nodded. "Lexi Gems are quite powerful, even without a bound user. But it has to be activated first. Just pressing in a little power from a bound Gem does the trick. Machines on Zyearth mimic that, which allows us to activate unused Gems for powering stuff." He tightened one rope. Trecheon winced again, so he loosened it, just slightly. "When I got to Sol, all their Gems were inactive. So I activated them. They hailed me as a hero."

Trecheon pulled his Gem from his belt. "Think you activated this one?"

"Maybe," Jaden said. "Activation lasts longer when they're... when they're not in use." He adjusted another rope. "You got yours from your grandpa, yeah?"

"Yeah," Trecheon said. "Doubt he knew anything about activating it, though after learning all that shit about Theron, he may have known what it was." He splayed his ears. "Sorry."

Jaden tightened one more rope. "For what?"

"For Granddad," Trecheon said. "All this... it's his fault."

Jaden eyed him. "Don't start. You don't know that. And even if he did, you can't be blamed for his actions."

"I'm still sorry," Trecheon said. "I don't have to hold blame to say that."

Jaden furrowed his brow. "Yeah. I guess so." He finished with the last rope. "There. How's that?"

Trecheon tried lifting the leg, just slightly. He flinched a little, but nodded. "Seems sturdy enough. At least it won't break *more.*" He tried to stand, but couldn't put even a little weight on the busted leg. He sat back down. "Man, it's gonna be hell dragging my sorry ass through Drifter and Shadow Cast infested woods. I'd kill for a crutch. It'd at least leave your hands free."

"There's a bunch of trees out back," Jaden said. "I'll see what I can find." He turned toward the back door.

And stopped.

His wife was out there. In the cold ground, under their favorite tree.

His legs refused to move.

Trecheon coughed. "She's buried, just so you know."

Jaden whipped around to him.

Trecheon frowned, pinning his ears back. "Your wife, I mean. Matt and I saw it when we were here last time."

Jaden splayed his ears. "Matt…"

"He talked with her," Trecheon said. "Spent a good half hour or so. Did him a lot of good, I think." He smiled slightly. "Go talk with your wife, Jaden."

Jaden bit his lip. "Theron's out there."

"Yeah well, I'm not going anywhere any time soon," Trecheon said. "And you need your heart lightened. We were after Theron when Matt talked to her too. If he can take a few minutes so can you."

"What if someone finds us?"

Trecheon shrugged. "If I need you, I'll give you a signal."

Jaden raised an eyebrow. "What signal?"

"I'll imitate the scream of a terrified little girl."

Jaden rolled his eyes. "Funny."

"Little gallows humor to lighten the mood," Trecheon said, smirking. "Go see your wife. She's clearly been waiting a long time."

Jaden stared at the door. "You have no idea."

"Then go."

Jaden breathed deeply. He made his way into the garden.

There, at the base of her favorite tree, stood Aurora's grave. A soft mound marked only with a scratched up wooden epitaph.

A wave of agony and grief washed over him as memories of him burying his wife and making that marker hit him like an avalanche. Everything seemed so hopeless then. Only he had survived the attack. The memory was so clear. Pain radiating through his chest to his fingertips, and his eyes burning with tears as he dug the grave. Frustration pounding in his ears like a loud ringing, his fur and skin filled with splinters as he wrote on the cracked wood. The intense, overpowering, violent thoughts about ending himself. He had huddled on the freshly covered grave, staring at the door of his empty, lifeless hut, wishing for death. Begging Draso for it. Contemplating all the ways he'd take care of it himself. If he could just get up.

He lay like that for a whole day and night. It was amazing he hadn't frozen to death. He remembered when the sun rose, smacking him in the face with a beam, confirming he still lived. That made him angry and finally drove him to action.

Just get a knife, the voice inside him said, with the same loud clarity it had that day, sixty years ago. *Get a knife and it'll all be over.*

It was by Draso's graces that Embrik and Alexina had been wandering the island that day. And they happened to be in Jaden's hut when he finally moved.

He shuddered. They still had no idea how close he had been to death at that moment.

But… in all his shame, all the pain, all the anger… he hadn't spoken a word to Aurora.

He sat down next to the grave marker, letting his mind wander. He sighed.

"I remarried." He picked at a loose thread on his shirt. "You… you always encouraged me to, if you died. *When* you died." He snorted. "You refused to Gem share with me. You knew what that meant… you knew I'd far out live you. But you hated the thing. Called it entrapment." He pulled out his jewel. "Maybe it is. Here I am, decades later, still stuck with the pain of losing you, as fresh as if it happened minutes ago. Still hurting." He sighed. "But... I remarried. Someone who'd live even longer. There's irony to that, I suppose."

Wind blew leaves across the garden.

"You'd like her." Jaden leaned against the tree. "So much like you. Fierce and loving and self-sacrificing. She makes a wonderful partner. I think... I think she'd make a great mother. Just like you. If..." He covered his eyes with his arm and scrunched up his face. "If my family wasn't stolen from me left and right. *Draso.*" He choked. Here he was mourning one wife, but it turned into mourning the other.

Was Alexina alive now...?

Was she trying to find her way home?

Did she get any time to be a mother for Zeke?

Did she live to see him born?

Why was his family always *stolen from him?*

Something brushed his cheek. He shot his eyes open.

A feather. A simple blue one, soft and downy.

Aurora loved the blue birds in their yard. She grew seed specifically to feed them.

He picked up the feather and brushed it along his cheek again. Felt like... like her hand. Her soft breath on his fur.

Her forgiveness.

"I'm sorry," he said quietly. "I don't... I shouldn't turn this into a pity party." He paused, then snorted. "No, that's unfair too. I need to mourn. I never let myself after losing everything. I didn't believe I deserved to. That was... wrong. I need to. Just... not now." He turned back to the headstone.

A little bluebird stood on it, tilting its head at Jaden. Jaden reached for it... but it flew off, leaving two more down feathers.

Jaden picked them up. Three feathers. One for each survivor. Matt. Charlotte.

Himself.

A fourth feather floated down and landed in his hand.

He pressed his lips tight. "And… Alexina. I get the message." He stood. The little bluebird looked curiously at him, but didn't fly. He smiled at it. "I clearly have more mourning to do. But later. Once we get through all this." He pocketed the feathers and rested a hand on Aurora's grave marker. "Thanks, Aurora. I needed that."

He turned. A large stick with a crudely curved bit on one end caught his attention. He lifted it. Perfect for Trecheon.

Time to finish this.

Trecheon had managed to stand up and lean against the wall, though sweat beaded on his brow, soaking his fur. "Doing okay?"

"Better," Jaden said. "Though I think I need to come back at some point." He passed Trecheon the stick.

Trecheon situated it under his arm. "Bring Matt next time."

"And Charlotte," Jaden said. "And a proper grave marker." He helped Trecheon get around the debris and headed for the door. "Come on, let's get you some help." They walked out the door.

And found Abrax standing directly in front of them, still wearing the chronicler robes, holding a dagger.

CHAPTER 31

UNMASKING

Leah sat on a stone on the edge of the Veil room. The Black Cloak paced in front of her, rubbing the silver mask's chin, clearly confused. She wiped at her nose. "S-So they were supposed to pick me?"

"*Yes!*" the Cloak said, his voice echoing through the Veilsong room. "That's what was in the…" he shook himself. "They just were."

Leah shrugged, trying to look nonchalant. "I mean… it's not that b-big a deal…"

"But it *is!*" the Cloak said. "You're supposed to… They just… Damn it, they were meant for *you!*"

Leah gathered up all her courage and pushed back the despair and disappointment. Sitting here arguing about what should have happened didn't change what actually did. He needed to know that too. She took a deep breath. They just needed… redirection. "Tymon… let it go."

The Cloak immediately stopped pacing and turned to her, wide-eyed. He stuttered, but couldn't get a word out.

Leah tried smiling, even if it hurt. "It's okay. I know you're Tymon. All the signs point to it. Your summons, your poor healing abilities... especially your eyes. I don't know how you survived the incident on Erdoglyan, but..." She waved a hand. "I suspect the Cloak might have something to do with it."

The Cloak stared a moment longer, then sighed. He slumped across the room and sat next to her. "You always were very observant."

"O-Only sometimes," Leah said. "Usually when I'm not trying. I wish I had more control over it." She sighed. "Curse my brain."

"Don't do that to yourself," the Cloak said.

Leah just shrugged.

The Cloak took a deep breath... and carefully peeled off his mask, pulling back the black hood.

Leah stared.

Sure enough, Tymon Azure sat next to her. Jaden's father, Matt and Zeke's grandfather, summoner extraordinaire, and a Guardian Leah had looked up to her whole life. It was so strange seeing him here after having posters of him and his summons all over her walls for years.

But he looked so... worn. His azure-blue quills were bent and misshapen from the hood, and the fur on his face had black streaks from the black makeup he had around his eyes. He held his ears against the back of his head.

Leah looked at him. "So... how did you escape the Erdoglyan incident?"

Tymon shrugged. "I wonder that myself sometimes. I should have died. And I'd like to say it was the grace of Draso that saved me, but it really was the Cloak, like you said." He gripped the mask tight. "And there's no grace about it."

Leah frowned. "It's gotta be tough... doing what you do..."

Tymon ran his fingers over the mask. "It is. Sometimes it seems impossible." He chewed on his lip, something Leah had seen Zeke and Matt do frequently. "Sometimes I don't even know how I get through it. It hurts." He shook his head. "I agreed to this gig because I was told it was the only way to save my family. To save Jaden. Though so far I've only seen it cause him more hurt."

"Maybe," Leah said. "Though, it also gave us Zeke."

Tymon smiled. "Alright, I'll give you that. But still." He sighed. "I knew being the Cloak would involve hiding my identity, keeping myself from my family, but…" He dropped the mask in the dirt. "I didn't know it'd involve all this pain."

Leah flicked her ears back. "I-It might be better if…"

"If I just fixed everything?" Tymon said. "Just changed the past?" He scoffed. "Can't happen. I've tried. Trust me, I've done this a long time… changing things just… just makes it worse. Hell, this whole summon problem is probably evidence of that." He batted at the cloak's hood. "And every time I attempt it, this thing buzzes in my ear anyway."

Leah lifted a brow. "The Cloak?"

"The entity," Tymon said. "Prinkípissa Olympia."

Leah's eyes grew wide. "Is she… can she see the future then?"

"No, but we have a… plan," Tymon said. "For lack of a better term. We stick to the plan, come cracked or broken Gems. Not that it's done a lot of good. The plan fluctuates so much that half the stuff I expect to happen gets changed." He stared at the mask. "I don't know what to think anymore. I just have to hope it'll all work out…"

Leah stared at the ground. Something didn't add up. Hadn't he known so much more about the events before? What made all of this fluctuate so much? What changed?

"Leah."

Leah looked up.

"Take care of Zeke," Tymon said. "Get him off this planet. Away from all this." He furrowed his brow, his green eyes glassy. "He needs you."

Leah flicked her ears back. "Is that the Cloak speaking, or Tymon?"

Tymon pressed his lips tight. "It's Zeke's grandfather speaking. A quilar who just wants what's best for him, in this world of hellfire and death."

Leah frowned. But she nodded. "I'm going to try my hardest. Because I need him too." She sighed. "But… I don't think he'll leave Athánatos. And even if he does… I don't think he'll leave Andre. And I don't blame him."

"Then you need to convince Andre to go to Zyearth."

Leah sat up, ears perked. "Do… do you think I can?"

"I don't know," Tymon said. "Which is why you should try." He patted her shoulder, then pulled his knees up to his chest, staring out.

Leah said nothing. They could be here for a moment. Just a quiet minute of peace. The calm before the storm. Because she had a feeling they were in for quite a storm. She let her mind wander.

Andre should have been so happy to get those summons. Becoming a summoner should be a joyful moment. And yet, he was so caught up in what she was feeling instead that it ruined everything. Instead of joy, he felt shame and guilt. That wasn't right… and it was all her fault. She needed to fix it immediately.

Andre deserved that.

She looked back at the Cloak. The Cloak said she should have had them, but he also said things changed all the time. They changed here. That was a good thing.

Right?

A chill ran down her spine.

Was it actually okay that Andre got the summons? She gripped her knees and spoke carefully. "If I'm supposed to get those summons, and Andre got them instead… what if I'm still supposed to get them?"

Tymon lifted a brow. "What do you mean? They're with Andre."

"Yes, but not forever," Leah said. "Summons choose their masters. They could… they could still choose me."

Tymon chuckled darkly. "Not these two. Not with their oath issues. Because the only way their oath allows them to leave a summoner is through… death."

Leah's eyes grew wide. "Oh fire, ice, and *stone…* "

Then Andre screamed.

Tymon's eyes widened now. He shoved Leah toward the screaming and pulled the mask on his face. "Go, *go!* "

Leah didn't have to be told twice. She ran toward the clover lawn. *Don't die, don't die, please don't die! I'll never ask for summons again, just please don't die!*

Blasts of water and lightning flashed overhead. Leah's heart stopped. "No, *Andre!* " She dashed out onto the lawn.

Kaoru and Drifa rolled around on the clover, their elements flying about. But they didn't look distressed. They looked almost… happy. She scanned the area for Andre.

Andre was on the ground next to Neil and Sacha, laughing. Sacha rolled her eyes, muttered something, and pressed her hands to his shoulder, clearly healing him. But it couldn't be serious with him laughing like that. Leah sighed relief.

Tymon ran up next to her, the Cloak's mask and hood hiding him again. He blinked a moment, then leaned back. "Good Draso. Bet that was just their first summon. Probably scared the hell out of them."

"I did warn them," Leah said, managing a smile. "But nothing really prepares you, I'm told."

Tymon furrowed his brow. He scanned the area and nodded to Rashard and Kjorn. "Yeah."

Leah pressed her lips tight. "He might be fine now... but that possibility is still there."

Tymon patted Leah's shoulder. "Then you better be there for him so it doesn't happen."

Leah eyed him. "Is *that* the Cloak talking?"

Tymon closed his eyes a moment, then squeezed her shoulder. "That's Tymon talking. Because he's sick of all this pain." He nodded toward Andre. "Go to him."

Leah flicked an ear back. She turned and jogged to Andre. "Hey, we heard screaming, are you okay?"

Andre's smile immediately faded. "Oh, uh, yeah. Fine. Just summoned for the first time. Scared us all. Guess we shoulda listened to you better." He glanced at his arm. "And uh, Drifa nicked me a bit. S'fine though." He stood.

Leah flattened both ears. She walked up to him and threw her arms around his middle, holding him tight. "I'm sorry."

Andre stopped a moment, then wrapped his arms around her. "Don't apologize."

"But I need to," Leah said. She pulled back and met his eyes. "Getting chosen by summons is a great gift. It should be something filled with joy. But you were so worried about my feelings that you didn't get that. My disappointment ruined it, and that's not fair to you. Or Drifa and Kaoru. So... I'm sorry." She gripped his hands. "I want you to love this gift... not worry about me."

Andre slowly smiled. "I appreciate it." He hugged her tight. "Thanks. That means a lot."

Neil grinned and gripped both their shoulders. "Glad everything worked out. But we need to finish this anchor and get our tails moving to the next one. I'll get everyone going here. Andre, can you see what Kaoru and Drifa can do for us when we're ready to move on?"

"Yeah, sure."

Neil nodded and herded the rest of their group toward the Veilsong roomi.

Tymon – no, the Cloak again – walked up to them. He gave Leah a very serious look, piercing her with his green eyes, then walked toward the others.

Leah flattened an ear. She turned to Andre and pulled her tail into her hands, picking at the guard hairs. "Andre… If… I… Zeke…"

Andre frowned. "This about Zeke goin' to Zyearth with you?"

Leah looked down. "Yeah."

"Have you asked him yet?"

She glanced up, eyebrow raised. "Yet."

"S'only a matter of time," Andre said, his brow furrowed.

Leah picked at her tail again. "Yeah…" She met his eyes. "Would you come with us…?"

Andre's eyes grew wide. "What?"

"You and Chadwick, obviously," Leah said. "I don't think Zeke would go without you. And… I don't want to leave you here either. After everything that's happened I… I hate the idea of leaving you here where anything could happen… and we wouldn't be here to help…"

"I…" He looked off. "I get that but… That's a big ask."

"I know."

He rubbed his arm. "I needa think about it."

Leah scrunched her snout and flicked her tail. "Yeah... yeah of course..."

"Cool." He frowned. "It's just a whole new *planet*. And leaving Earth..."

Leah hugged herself. "That's why I'm worried Zeke won't come with me. It's not the same as just moving house. It's leaving everything. But... He's *my* everything. So leaving for Zyearth is also leaving everything for me." Her eyes burned. "I'm scared..."

Andre frowned. He wrapped an arm across her shoulder. "Maybe you could start by talkin' up Zyearth. What's somethin' you love about it?"

Leah leaned into him as they walked toward Kaoru and Drifa playing in the clover. She could talk up the benefits. The great education, the universal basic income, the health care systems, all the things this planet lacked. But Andre needed something... more. She smiled. "Zyearth has the most gorgeous sunsets..."

Chapter 32

Escape Plan

Matt jogged through the palace, headed for the clover lawn, his friends at his heels.

Izzy hung at the back, though Matt could hear a constant, distant ringing in his ear. Jumbled and without rhythm.

Angry, but also sad.

Broken.

He had to hope he could fix it, once this was all over. If they made it through.

As they approached the lawn, the smell grew stronger. And then it… changed. Rather than just clover, the scent of flowers, fresh water, and… and… birds.

The gardens.

He led the group through the outer gardens, following the scent as best he could until-- "Zeke!"

Zeke looked up from the bench he sat on… and so did another quilar next to him. A feminine one with black quills and a burnt orange snout very similar to Zeke's. Matt's eyes widened. That must be--

"Alexina!" Natassa and Ouranos both caught their fists ablaze, but Zeke held out his hands.

"It's okay, it's okay!" he said. "She's fine. Got her mind back and everything."

Natassa extinguished her hands. "I… but how?"

Matt got a strong smell of something burning – definitely outside of the smells he was getting before. He perked his ears and his fur stood up on the back of his neck. "Oh hell… It's *me.*" Everyone looked at him. But Matt looked Alexina directly in the eye. He swallowed… then reached out. *Can you hear me?*

Alexina's eyes widened and her jaw dropped. *Sisters alive… I can.*

Matt held a hand to his head. "Oh, good Draso."

"It is true then," Ouranos said. "You two share a bond."

Matt flattened one ear. "And I bridged her soul the same way I did yours."

"But *how?*" Alexina asked.

"I wonder as well," Natassa said. "We have not even *seen* Alexina outside of the Aether, let alone gotten close enough for Matt to bond with her."

"Time travel," Zeke said suddenly. "It has to be the time travel. Somehow their bond is like… perforating time."

Matt pressed his lips together. "Which means sometime soon, I'm going to meet you as a Drifter. And bridge your soul."

Ouranos lowered his gaze. "My brother--"

"I know it's dangerous," Matt said. "But it clearly works." He held up his hands, still dripping in the elixir from the Aether's pull on his magic. "I just… have to keep an eye open, I guess."

Alexina flattened her ears. She held a hand out to Matt and he took it. A soft smell of warm tea and the sharp scent of a roaring fireplace assailed his nose. Alexina smiled, though it was slightly crooked. "You look remarkably like my Jaden. I take comfort in that."

Matt swallowed hard. *Her* Jaden. Because they were married. He expected it to feel strange - his father married to someone other than his mother – but after all his time with Zeke, with Ouranos, with the Athánatos who he had come to call family, it felt… right. He smiled and squeezed her hand. "Glad to have you in the family, Alexina."

Her smile widened and her eyes twinkled.

Natassa gently gripped Matt's free hand, despite the elixir coating it. She squeezed it. "If you are to bridge Alexina, then we must hurry home." She turned to Alexina. "Because you are Theron's Drifter, just as Ouranos was. If you appear soon for Matt to save you… then Theron must also be using you."

Alexina's smile faded, but she nodded.

Matt squeezed Alexina's hand again. "I'm sure this is really confusing for you, but I think it'd be better to explain it when I see you in the flesh, so to speak."

"Lightning and *air,* Zeke, your *leg!*" Izzy rushed forward, foregoing her normal healer's mask, and ran her hand over Zeke's damaged leg. "What the hell happened?"

"Drifters," Zeke said. "I don't think it's bleeding anymore, but it hurts like hell. Makes it hard to walk on."

Izzy looked over it, but frowned. "I… sorry, but my magic isn't working here… Not much I can do. The bleeding has stopped though, thank Draso. I'll see what I can do for it when we get out of here."

Alexina furrowed her brow. "Will he be okay?"

"Only if we get out of here quick so I can take care of this," Izzy said. She frowned deeply, her ears pinned back. "Something really got your back too."

"It's… not been a good day," Zeke said.

Alexina turned away. She let go of Matt's hand.

"Then let us escape this place while we can," Natassa said. "Before Theron finds us once more."

Alexina rubbed one arm. "Matthew… take care of Jaden and Zeke. I need to see them again."

Matt nodded back. "You will. Trust me, they're in good hands." Zeke smiled.

Alexina flicked her ears back. "I think I shall stay here while you return home. I fear my response when seeing through the Aether's portal while I am unable to cross myself."

"Understandable." Natassa gave Alexina a deep hug. "I will see you soon, sister."

"And I, you," Alexina responded. "I do not know what life I will lead after this bridging of my soul, but I hope it is one with my family in it."

"It is my intent to make it so," Natassa said. She stepped back. "Farewell for now." Alexina smiled, tears in her eyes. She hugged Zeke and Ouranos too, bid them goodbye, and sat on one of the benches, looking at a silent fountain.

Natassa pulled them away, tugging on Matt's elixir-soaked hand again. "Come. Let her rest. We will see her soon."

Matt flicked his ears back, but followed.

Natassa led them to the *féretro* garden. "Once we arrive, we can enter the Spire and I can say the return phrase. Should all go well, the portal will open and Eris can pull us through."

Matt glared. "And then we go after Theron."

"Once Neil is finished rebuilding the Veil, yes."

Matt raised an eyebrow. "Wait, Neil's doing *what?*"

Something black and sticky hit Matt in the eye and words invaded his mind. *Ah. So that's what the rat is doing then.*

Matt's heart stopped. He wiped the sludge from his face.

And standing before them, covering the *féretro* boxes with her inky, slimy body, was Judgement. Blocking the way to the Spire.

Matt immediately shot in front of the group, filling the area with wind magic. Though like before, it wasn't nearly the power he was used to, despite the elixir being out of control. "Everyone scatter! Someone throw me a fireball!"

A fireball rushed by his head and he caught it in a tornado, building it as large as he could before throwing it full force at Judgement. But it moved so slowly. Judgement easily slunk out of its way. She grinned at him, spreading her sloppy wings and flinging sludge at him. *Having trouble there, Guardian?*

Matt roared and built several more tornadoes, picking up fire from the rogue twister. He surrounded her with flames, but once again, she slipped between the funnels and spread all across the *féretro* garden. Sludge smacked Matt's face hard. *You forget that this place drains your magic, Guardian. You are powerless against me.*

"*But I am not!*" Ouranos slid in next to Matt and threw his hands forward, trapping Judgement in a wall of flames. She wailed, but every inky tentacle trying to escape burned away in Ouranos' fire. He turned to Matt. "Go to the Spire. Get to Athánatos and save my sister. Please."

But something glued Matt to the spot. He chewed his lip. "Ouranos--"

"*Absolutely not,*" Ouranos said, stepping away as best he could. "You have already sacrificed too much. I will not have you sacrificing your life, Guardian, do you understand? You help give mine *meaning.* You cannot do that *dead.*"

Matt chewed his lip. "But--"

"Matt, *come on!*" Izzy grabbed his arm and tugged him away. "We need to go *now!*" Matt turned. Natassa was near the Spire, eyes closed, muttering something. Zeke stood by her, his eyes wide staring at Judgement. More and more tentacles of ink escaped Ouranos' flames, slowly breaking it down. Zeke shot fireballs where he could, but like with Matt, his power waned. He waved them over.

"Go, Matthew," Ouranos said. "There is no time. I promise you, I will be waiting on the other side. Do not disappoint me."

Matt furrowed his brow, but he nodded and rushed for the portal.

A tentacle shot out from the firewall, snatching Matt's arm. *You will not escape with my elixir!*

"Let him *go!*" Zeke rushed forward and slashed away at Judgement with a blade of ice. She shrieked and pulled back, knocking the blade away and slicing through Zeke's palm. Zeke screamed, and gripped the wound.

The portal opened. And it wasn't Eris waiting on the other side. It was the Black Cloak.

No time.

Izzy leapt through the portal. Matt grabbed Zeke and Natassa's hands and rushed it. His heart ached for Ouranos.

But only for a second.

Seething, blinding pain rushed his mind the moment he hit the portal's threshold. Hundreds, thousands of images and phrases bombarded his mind, blinding him, shattering his brain. Words chipped away at his skull in multiple voices. *Leah, Alexina, Jaden, Matt, Zyearth, Theron, Judgement, Neil, Veil, Aether, Guardian, Defender, life, death--*

But just when Matt grasped what was happening, everything whited out and went blank.

CHAPTER 33

SHATTERED

Ouranos snarled and blasted hot fire into the woods, hoping to burn his father down. He deserved nothing but *hot death.*

But the glow of Theron's Ei-Ei jewels vanished instantly, dropping them in darkness, Ouranos' flames extinguished.

Ouranos set his hands ablaze again, glancing around, frantic. But he saw nothing in the black woods. His heart ran so fast. How had Theron gotten so close without them knowing? He should not have let his worries about the Cast charms distract him.

Darvin immediately dropped to his Shadow Cast form, and both he and Roscoe dashed between the trees, gurgling and growling with those familiar, haunting Cast noises, trailing blue and teal light from their eyes. Sami pressed her back against Ouranos', also lighting her hands ablaze, darting her gaze around. A twinge of guilt ran down his spine – he should have allowed Sami to become a Cast, before Theron robbed her of the chance. Now she was vulnerable, and it was his fault.

He would protect her with his life. "Sami," Ouranos said. "Stay close to--"

A Cast rushed out from the trees and crashed into Sami, ripping her away from Ouranos. She shouted, dousing it in flames, but the Cast resisted her magic and attempted to drag her away.

"No!" Ouranos gripped her hand, blasting various elements at the Cast, but to no avail. A second Cast slammed into Ouranos and separated them, dragging him through the underbrush.

Ouranos snarled, baring teeth. He pulled on his magic and shot the beast with every element he had. The Cast wailed as fire, lightning, wind, and ice ripped through its inky body, tearing it to shreds, leaving only droplets behind. The creature whimpered as it attempted to pull itself back together. Guilt ate at him. Hopefully the Cast did not remember pain.

Ouranos pushed aside the guilt and scrambled to his feet, looking for Sami in the dark... and immediately froze.

Theron stood before him, holding Sami with an arm across her neck, and her Gem in his hand. He glared at Ouranos with his harsh, silver eyes. "I warned you, Prínkipas. You should have ended me when you had the chance. Now you pay the price." He passed the Gem to a waiting Cast, who held it in its tentacles. It grinned wide, and wrapped itself around the jewel.

Ouranos' eyes widened. "No!"

Another Cast burst forth from the woods and crashed into Theron's Cast, knocking them both aside. They wrestled on the ground, a mess of inky blobs, with only small glances of their glowing eyes and the blinding white of Sami's Gem.

Ouranos drew on his magic and charged Theron, intent on pulling Sami free. But yet another inky blob appeared from the woods and attacked Ouranos, wrapping its hot body around him and holding him down, stripping his mind of all other thoughts. His body screamed as the Cast crushed him, working its way up his legs, toward his neck, blocking any attempts to get the Lexi charm bag from his side. Ouranos set his hands ablaze and forced his fire through the Cast. It broke it apart, lessening its crushing power, but he could not remove it entirely. Pain radiated throughout his limbs, his torso, his chest, and soon he struggled to breathe, his magic grew at his fingertips, every element, ice, water, wind, fire, lightning, but nothing worked, nothing freed him, he was going to--

Another Cast, black and hot, covered them both entirely then peeled back, ripping Ouranos' attacker off him and ending the crushing pressure. He coughed and gagged, desperate for air, and he moved slowly, testing every limb, as the pain shrieked through him.

"Sami!"

Theron screamed. Ouranos looked up.

Sami had his hand in her mouth, biting through the flesh with sharp canines, forcing him to let go. She stumbled away, then rushed for the Cast fighting over her Gem.

Theron roared. "Crush it *now!*"

"No!" Darvin wrestled with the Cast that held her Gem, and Roscoe untangled himself from Ouranos' attacker and rushed in to help. But Theron's Cast slipped away, Gem floating on its body, then curled into a tight ball.

And squeezed.

In a flash of light and defining sounds, the Gem cracked apart, its power ripping through the Cast and tearing down tree branches, stripping the flora of bark and leaves. Ouranos held his hands up as hot, raw magic tore through him, though the pain stopped when one of the stags covered him with their Cast body, blocking it. Somewhere in the chaos, Sami wailed and Theron roared victory. Ouranos' heart broke, his mind thrown into memories of Cix's death by Gem destruction. His eyes burned. *Not Sami...! Please! We have lost enough!*

As quick as it appeared, the magic faded, and Ouranos' protector slithered away, dropping everything in darkness. With a heavy heart and rage at his father, Ouranos reached for his fire.

But someone else beat him to it. Sami stood in the woods, both hands ablaze, and her tail awash with flames. She glared at Theron, her eyes practically glowing.

Theron gawked. "How? Your Gem--"

Sami squeezed her hands into fists, making the fire blaze that much stronger. She pulled her lips back, baring her teeth. Three sets of glowing jewels appeared around her eyes.

Ei-Ei jewels. *Ei-Ei Jewels.*

She snorted. "Good thing I had a backup." She blasted hot flames at Theron.

But the two Cast had gathered themselves up and they wrapped around Theron, protecting him. Before Ouranos could gather his wits, the Cast took off into the woods at full speed, dragging Theron with them.

Pain still ate at Ouranos' limbs, but it faded in favor of shock. He stared at Sami, wide-eyed. "Sami--"

Sami gagged. "My Gem--"

"...Trash," Darvin said. Ouranos turned. Darvin slowly reformed into his stag self, carrying the dusty, sharp remains of Sami's Gem. It no longer glowed, though there was still an air of power about it. But also one of... sadness.

Sami stood straight, her ears back. She carefully took the Gem shards from Darvin and stared at them, her violet eyes glassy. "Well... glad the backup worked..."

Ouranos stepped forward. "Sami... why do you have Ei-Ei jewels?"

She frowned and exchanged a glance with Darvin. Darvin sighed and shook his head. "He was bound to find out sooner or later." He turned to Ouranos and pulled back the fur around his eyes… revealing his own set of jewels. "I have them too."

Shock racked Ouranos' body. "But why? How?"

"The Black Cloak," Sami said. "During the first incident with Theron years ago."

"He asked us to go secure the island after you had created the first Lexi Charms," Darvin said. "But what he was really doing is asking Sami and I to join him. Part of that includes taking on Ei-Ei jewels." He lifted his shirt, revealing faded, burnt-orange streaks across his normally jet-black fur. The tell-tale markings of an Athánatos palace dweller.

Ouranos flattened his ears. "And Sami has fire magic without her Gem…"

Sami pressed her lips together. She pulled her uniform off her shoulder, revealing sharp red streaks through the fur. "I'm bound to the Archon of Embrik. Just in case something like this happened."

Ouranos' eyes widened again. "Embrik was a part of this all along?"

"Not the Embrik you know," Sami said. "A… different one."

Ouranos' fur bristled.

Cast Roscoe rolled into the group, bubbling urgently.

"Roscoe's right," Darvin said. "We don't have time to talk about it. Theron's on the loose. We need to find Trecheon and Jaden *now.*" He dropped to his Cast form and dashed back toward the Sanctum.

Ouranos narrowed his gaze. "When this is over, we will have *much* to discuss."

"Bring it up with the Black Cloak," Sami said, and she chased after Darvin. Roscoe followed.

Ouranos ran after them, his mind torn between anger and confusion. He gritted his teeth. *Trust me… I will.*

Abrax

Trecheon froze in place, staring down Abrax. For a moment, everything stood still. Jaden, Abrax, the rotting hut, the black woods around them, the very air they breathed. Even the throbbing in Trecheon's leg faded, just slightly, as shock ran through his bones. Trecheon's brain both stalled and raced at the same time, desperate for any idea of how to handle this.

Did Abrax know? He had to know they were on to him. Right? There was no way he couldn't. But what was he doing here? Did he--

Jaden snarled. He ripped his sword hilt from his belt, formed an ice blade, and slammed Abrax against the wall, sword at his throat, forcing the quilar to drop his dagger. Abrax squeaked, holding the blade back with his hands, blood dripping down his palms. His eyes and quick breaths betrayed his terror. Jaden bared his teeth. "The hell is wrong with you? You released *Theron? Why in Draso's name would you do that?"*

Abrax shook in fear. "L-Let me go, please, I did not--"

"Don't tell me you didn't release him!" Jaden spat. "From what Neil tells me, you've been kissing up to him during the whole damn war! How did you release him? How'd you restore his mind?"

Abrax cowered. "T-The... the soldier... had his jewels... and the elixir..."

"Which soldier?"

Abrax coughed. "The human they call... Ackerson..."

Trecheon cursed. Damn him! They should have taken him out when they had the chance.

Jaden shook him. "Do you really think Theron cares about you? Or did he promise you some kind of reward? Why did you help him?"

Abrax cowered, his quills puffed up. "I-I did not--"

"*Why did you help him?*"

"P-Please...!"

Trecheon stepped up now, careful of his broken leg. He set his quills ablaze, glaring. "I'd answer him, Abrax, or this won't end well for you."

"It was *Neil!*" Abrax shouted. "That damn mainlander seducing our people, our Prinkípissa! He was breaking traditions and throwing himself where he does not belong!" He growled at Jaden. "We were better without all of you! Theron promised me he would restore us to who we were before!"

Trecheon threw up a hand. "Are you kidding? Theron *enslaved you all* as the worst creatures imaginable, he stripped you of your minds, and used you to *kill!*"

"To end the humans!" Abrax said. "To finally rid us all of the mainlanders, like Basilea Krísi wanted for us. They are *poison*. Destructive, murderous, angry creatures. It was why the Basilea worked so hard to protect us, to give us power!"

Jaden narrowed his gaze. "Who is Krísi?"

"I can guess," Trecheon said bitterly. "Judgement. And I'm guessing the power he's talking about is the Shadow Cast."

Jaden turned to him, his eyes wide. "Oh, earth and stone…"

"Theron will finish what the Basilea started…" Abrax said. "He will tear down the Veil, give us the blessing of the Cast, and save us… he promised…"

Jaden let out an angry, feral growl. "There is something deeply, *deeply* wrong with you if you're willing to let a madman enslave you, turn you into a mindless, helpless, disgusting monster, and use you to murder thousands of innocents just so you can avoid having a mainlander lead your people. A mainlander that everyone else loves on top of that." He pressed the sword closer to Abrax's throat, digging deeper into his palms as they held the blade. *"Where the hell is Theron?"*

A wild, piercing shriek deafened Trecheon and three Cast burst from the hut's entrance and crashed into them all. Trecheon did his best to roll out of the way, though blinding pain ripped through his leg, almost making him sick. He reached for his Lexi charm bag instead, fumbling in the dark, fighting the Cast off the best he could without burning the whole damn hut down.

But then the Cast's battle shrieks turned to painful wails, and the monster shrank away from him, pawing at its eyes with thick tentacles.

"Trecheon, fire!" Jaden shouted.

Blinking back the tears of pain, Trecheon carefully aimed three fireballs at the Cast's eyes, stripping away the black ink and restoring them… to Drifters. Damn it!

"Stand back," Jaden said. Using snow and stinging ice, he herded the Drifters into a tight group, then surrounded them with a thick, tall wall of ice, essentially trapping them. He shook himself, then pulled Trecheon to his feet, passing the crutch to him. "Abrax escaped."

"He won't get far," Trecheon growled. "Go after him. Leave a trail, I'll catch up."

Jaden nodded and tore off into the woods, leaving thick ice spikes in the tree trunks as he ran.

It took several minutes, but soon Trecheon got the hang of pushing through the pain and moving with the crutch. He eventually caught up to Jaden… who had already reached Abrax. He had Abrax pinned to a tree with ice spikes through the chronicler's robes. "I'm only going to ask one more time, Abrax," Jaden said, his voice making Trecheon's fur stand on end. Jaden threw a fist in the air and a dozen sharp ice spikes appeared around him. "Tell me where Theron is *now.*"

Abrax shuddered, his eyes wide. "He… he is going after Neil… He intends to end him in one of the last anchors. The magic release from killing the new Veil's unfinished anchor c-could be enough to destroy both the new and old Veil at once…"

Trecheon growled. *"Shit.* Jaden--"

"I know." He glared at Abrax. "I should kill you right here. But I think it'd be better to decide your fate once Neil is Basileus above you. So for now…" He shot the magic ice spikes through Abrax's robes, pinning him more firmly to the tree. "…Stay put." He turned to Trecheon. "Let's find the others and get to Neil."

Trecheon nodded and hobbled through the woods, back toward the Sanctum.

A loud rip of clothes echoed through the woods.

Abrax got *free.* Trecheon turned.

Abrax charged them both, dagger in hand, shouting, his shredded clothes waving in the breeze.

With a quick wave, Jaden threw his hand forward and pelted Abrax with a dozen sharp ice spikes. Abrax fell back immediately, crashing to the ground. He didn't move again.

Trecheon stared, eyes wide. His stomach churned and he nearly vomited. He had seen a lot of death in his life. Caused a lot of it, in so many disgusting ways. And yet… this one…

"Come on," Jaden said. "Before he attracts the wild animals."

Trecheon glanced back at Jaden, forcing down the nausea. "Are you…?"

"Later." He trudged through the jungle.

Trecheon took one glance back at Abrax. And suddenly he knew why it made him queasy.

That was the same, cold-blooded way he killed as an assassin.

He was looking at himself.

He watched the blood seep into the grass a moment longer, making glimmering puddles in the moonlight, then shuffled toward Jaden.

"…Sorry you had to see that," Jaden said quietly.

Trecheon tightened his jaw. "Don't worry about it. I've been that person myself."

Jaden glanced at him. He gripped Trecheon's shoulder gently.

They walked the rest of the way in silence.

Thankfully, Sami, Ouranos, and Darvin were already out of the woods and headed toward the Sanctum. Darvin sighed relief when he saw them. "Thank Draso. We thought we'd be looking for hours." He frowned. "Damn, Trecheon, the hell happened to your leg?"

"Tripped on a tree root. It's broken." Trecheon flicked his ears back. "Hey, where's Roscoe?"

"Here," Ouranos said, his voice bitter. He pointed to a Shadow Cast with teal eyes, curled around his ankles.

Jaden's eyes grew wide. "Oh *hell*. Did you run out of Charms?" He dug in his bag.

"We did not," Ouranos said, his words dripping with anger. Jaden paused and looked at Ouranos, eyes narrowed. Ouranos huffed. "Apparently these three have decided the safest way to protect against becoming Theron's Cast is to make themselves Cast first."

Trecheon's ears grew cold and he stared at Darvin. "Are you out of your *mind?*"

"We don't have *time,*" Darvin said. "Theron just ran through the Sanctum. I'll explain later."

"You sure as hell better," Trecheon snapped.

Jaden growled. "Theron's going after Neil. We need to get him *now.*"

"Then let's get him," Sami said. But she frowned. "Trecheon--"

"Go without me," Trecheon said. "I'll find a healer and catch up. Go!"

Sami nodded and the group dashed into the Sanctum.

Trecheon gripped Jaden's shoulder. "Don't let him get Neil. Please."

"I won't." And he dashed after them, leaving Trecheon to shuffle behind.

CHAPTER 35

CHAMPION

Charlotte sat on one of the wicker chairs, ears back against her head. It was dark… quiet. A few small lanterns flickered on in the night, and a central hearth warmed the room with glowing coals. Several swords lay bare against the pillars, ready as weapons, but they had already started gathering dust. Many of her allies had fallen asleep on the chairs or the couches. Chadwick still shifted uncomfortably around on the bench, clearly fighting nightmares. Angus slept against the back of one of his summons, Lysander, the lion/zebra centaur. Lysander and his partner, Magna, the stone alicorn, lay in a pile of pillows, snoring quietly. The remaining Phonar took perches around the room, burying their beaks in their wings.

Even Philip slept now, after two of the Phonar, Jústi and Pax, dragged a mattress out of one of the guest rooms. Their only option since the injured wedding guests still needed the cots and spare beds. Philip didn't sleep soundly though, making tiny whimpering sounds in his sleep. Charlotte frowned, grabbed a second blanket, and draped it over Philip, tucking him in. He shifted and settled a little. The sounds stopped. Charlotte managed a smile. She grabbed one of the spare blankets and curled up with it on a wicker couch.

She should sleep too. Be rested.

But… Matt…

Matt had wanted to be a Guardian his whole life. Their father's sacrifice as a Guardian always inspired him. He wanted to save people or die trying, just like Jaden had.

But it was for that same reason that Charlotte had spent most of her life trying to convince Matt not to pursue Guardianship. Guardianship had taken her father away from her. Even now, even after they had discovered him alive and well… nothing really made up for lost time. She lost her childhood with him. And she still blamed the Guardianship.

She had finally given up her campaign after Matt earned Guardianship many years ago while fighting Theron and saving Ouranos and Natassa. Matt clearly deserved the title, much as she didn't want to admit it.

But she never stopped worrying that it would take him from her.

It was a terrible twist of irony that it wasn't Guardianship that stole Matt away. Because now she had no one and nothing to blame. She curled up in the blanket, letting her eyes burn. *Oh Draso, please let Matt be safe…*

"Lady Charlotte?"

Charlotte turned. Eris walked in, her green eyes almost glowing in the gentle light of the lanterns. Charlotte flicked an ear back. "Eris? Any news?"

"No, alas," Eris said quietly. She took a seat next to Charlotte. "I have been waiting at the Spire for quite some time, but have heard nothing. Melaina finally shooed me off to take a break and warm up by the hearth. She is keeping watch now and will alert me if she sees anything." She frowned. "I am surprised to find you awake."

Charlotte shrugged. "Can't sleep."

Eris nodded. "Understandable. Though I dare say Lord Matthew would prefer to see you rested upon his return."

Charlotte pressed her lips into a thin line. "Eris… why do you call him Lord? And me Lady?"

Eris chuckled. "Forgive the habit, my Lady. But this is how we address the royalty of Athánatos. And by your father's marriage to Alexina, Matthew is, by law, a Prínkipas of Athánatos. And by extension, you are a Prinkípissa. I am unsure how far the reach actually goes, considering he married by a mainlander's custom rather than by Athánatos custom, but in my mind, you are Lady Alexina's stepchildren, and therefore belong amongst our royalty." She smiled. "If it pleases you, my Lady. But if you would rather I not address you as such…"

"No, no, it's fine," Charlotte said. "I just… I guess I hadn't thought about things like that." She frowned. Prinkípissa. Something… important.

As much as she loved her life, as much as she was happy where she was, she had never really felt… important.

Absently, she pulled her Gem from her pocket. Well, her Uncle Walt's Gem. He had passed away just before Matt won the Guardianship. Her second father, her pillar of support. She missed him terribly. Made only worse by the fact that he died, leaving her trapped in a Gem sharing bond that left her chained to his focus jewel. She couldn't bond with it – but she was stuck carrying it around, keeping it close, or die herself from power withdrawals. Being Gemless only heightened that sense of unimportance.

Until her last visit with the Dragon Seer… Another futile attempt to get a Gem of her own. But the Seer had had some… interesting news. Something she hadn't shared with anyone. Something that would make her important. *Too* important. She shuddered. "Eris. Do you believe in destiny?"

Eris lifted a brow. "Do you mean, do I believe we have a destined purpose in life?"

Charlotte shrugged. "I guess so."

Eris frowned. She turned to the sky. "I believe all life has purpose. That we all have a role to fill. That could be seen as a destiny." She smiled. "But destiny does not need to be some dramatic end after an epic journey or some role to play that shifts the cosmos. It can be small, personal, intimate. It can be something sought out, or something dropped in one's lap. It could be something chosen or shaped. It could change and evolve. Or it could be static and still as stone. It could lead to one end and open a path to another, different destiny. There is no single answer."

Charlotte frowned, wrinkling her snout.

"But in my experience," Eris continued. "Truly following destiny involves sacrifice. Putting others above oneself. Making a hard choice, or following a difficult path. Embracing pain and struggle while perfecting oneself in pursuit of destiny." She smiled again. "Your brother embodies this. I believe he was destined to be a Guardian. Destined to be the one to pull Ouranos out from his father's clutches. But it took a lot of sacrifice to achieve that destiny. And open his path to a new one, whatever that may be." She gripped Charlotte's shoulder. "I do not believe it is his destiny to be trapped in the Aether. He has too much to prove as a Guardian. And he has another important trait in following one's destiny. Courage."

Charlotte stared at the ground. Courage. She clung to that. And yet… "And what happens if… if you run from destiny?"

Eris frowned. "Many things can happen. I do not recommend it."

Charlotte flattened an ear. "…Do you think Theron ran from his destiny?"

Eris's eyes grew wide a moment, then she frowned, furrowing her brow. "I do. Theron rejected it in pursuit of power… in the name of grief.

But it was name only." She closed her eyes. "May none of us fall into such a trap."

Something crashed loudly down one of the halls.

Everyone was awake in an instant. Philip sat up immediately, his breath quickened, Angus jumped to his feet, and the summons' glanced around, tense, with their eyes aglow. Chadwick sat up, but gripped his leg and laid back down. "Damnit." He whispered harshly up at the Phonar. "Excelsis!"

The raven phoenix glanced down.

"Get these fires out," Chadwick said. Excelsis nodded and with a wave of his wing, the coals and lanterns went dark. Chadwick carefully slid under the couch, hissing in pain, before covering himself with a blanket. "Everyone stay put. *Don't move* and for the love of Draso, don't make a single sound. I'm not great at cloaking noise." Another crash, closer this time. Chadwick tucked his Gem under his body. "Don't move!"

Then everyone vanished in an instant. A power tugged at Charlotte's fur, setting her teeth on edge. She had only been cloaked a few times in her life, and even though you weren't supposed to feel it or notice it, she felt it intimately. She huddled down on the couch, perking her ears, listening for anything out of the ordinary.

A black Athánatos slunk through the room, holding his side. He coughed, muttering angrily. Silently, Charlotte lifted her head to see who it was.

But Eris recognized him first. "Theron…"

Charlotte's heart crashed to her stomach.

Theron rested a hand against Charlotte's couch, dangerously close to her head. She held her breath. Theron snorted. "He… is at Dustrik. The last one." He reached a hand down. A black tentacle wrapped around his wrist. A Shadow Cast. Charlotte stared wide-eyed, covering her mouth, desperate to stay quiet. Theron pulled away. "If I catch him while he anchors at Dustrik… I can finally take down the Veil…"

Eris made a quiet, choked sound. Charlotte huddled down, though Theron didn't seem to notice.

The mage king picked up a sword from the wall. "Just one strike. And then Athánatos is free."

A wave of purple and white flames filled the room and Excelsis and Deo dove down from the ceiling, wings ablaze. Embers washed over Charlotte, filling her head with their voices. *You will not harm the Basileus!*

Theron whipped about, slashing the sword through the sky and cutting cleanly through both Phonar, reducing them to dying embers.

Jústi, Pax, Lumen, and Sémini dove down now, but Shadow Cast rose up and caught each one, dragging them to the ground and holding them down, pressing against the marble floors. The birds fought and squawked, shooting sprays of elemental magic into the air, covering everything with dust, pebbles, and water. Jústi's lightning bolts blasted little divots in the pillars and ceiling, but nothing hit Theron. It was almost as if it couldn't…

Theron hovered over them, glaring, gripping the sword. "Did you forget your place, sparrows? You cannot harm your king. Your oath prevents it."

"But ours doesn't," Angus snarled in the dark. Lysander lit the area with glowing, purple orbs of lighting and threw the magic forward while Magna charged Theron, horn aimed at his heart.

Theron dodged nimbly. He waved his hand and more Shadow Cast engulfed Magna, sticking to her feathers and sinking her into the ground like a tar pit. She whinnied and kicked and bit, but the Cast were too much. Lysander's magic orbs missed their target and circled back, but Theron caught them in his sword and flung them back at the summon, hitting him square in the chest and disintegrating him. Angus still hid behind

Chadwick's cloak, but Theron charged toward him anyway, waving the sword haphazardly.

But he seemingly tripped on nothing and crashed to the ground. He turned back, growling.

Philip, still wrapped in a blanket and only visible in patches from Chadwick's cloaking, had him by the ankle. His eyes widened, clearly realizing he'd been caught, and he scrambled away.

Theron roared. "You little *stain!*" He raised the sword and dashed toward him.

"*Philip!*" Eris gasped.

Charlotte didn't hesitate. Heart pumping, she threw herself toward the swords leaning against a pillar, snatched one up, and ran for Philip.

Theron swung.

And Charlotte blocked. She glared, locking her stance, drawing on years of championship fencing.

Philip scooted back and vanished in Chadwick's cloak once again.

Theron bellowed at her, spitting. He pushed on the sword, pressing his weight into it, threatening to bash her to the ground. It was only her steady stance that kept her from falling. Theron's pupilless eyes were manic. "You are no *Guardian.* No *mage.* You are bound to a useless Gem, bearing false titles and *worthlessness.* You think you can *face me?*"

Charlotte bared fangs, splaying her ears.

That did it.

She pulled on all her strength and thrust herself forward, knocking Theron back. Theron stumbled, wide-eyed, fumbling the sword, but Charlotte was on him instantly, beating him back, throwing everything at him. *Thrust, lunge, attack.* He had no form, no strength, no finesse with the sword, waving it wildly in any attempt to stop her.

Leaving himself open.

She stabbed at his sword hand, making him drop the weapon, then thrust the sword through his shoulder, and leapt on top of him, pinning him to the ground. He gasped, eyes wide.

She snarled, glaring. "I may not be a mage or a Guardian, but I am an *Azure,* and *don't you forget it.*" She pressed her face close to his. "After all you did to us, you deserve nothing but *death.*"

Theron coughed, but he chuckled, strangely. "Ah, but my little Prinkípissa…" Charlotte frowned at the word. He smirked at her. "Playing or not, you carry the title. It makes you *family.*" Charlotte wrinkled her snout in disgust. Theron narrowed his gaze, still smirking. "Which means if you kill me, you lose the Phonar. Are you willing to make that sacrifice? For all of you?"

Charlotte furrowed her brow. He… he had a point. Her shoulders tensed, and her mind raced.

"Hesitation is a real killer, Prinkípissa," Theron spat. Charlotte blinked and pulled her focus back, tightening her grip on the sword, but too late. Theron pulled his knees close to his chest and kicked her square in the stomach, sending her flying across the room. She gasped for air with the wind knocked out of her, tumbling along the floor, finally stopping near the wicker couch, sans sword.

Theron gripped the sword in his shoulder by the guard, ripped it free, and stood, glaring. "You may have qualms about losing the Phonar, but I carry no such burdens. Die!" He charged her, sword out.

A rainbow of elemental magic whipped in front of Charlotte, and the six remaining Phonar stood in between them in their anthropomorphic forms, as swirling magic wrapped around them.

No. Not six.

Seven.

A new Phonar, a barn owl, stood near the center, glaring with bright eyes, surrounded by sharp ice spikes and snow. Charlotte stood, her heart pounding.

Theron paused, glaring. "You cannot harm me."

The barn owl held out a clawed hand, brown and white feathers flicking forward. Snow bit at Charlotte's nose.

Are you sure enough that you wish to test it with your life?

Theron gritted his teeth, gripping his shoulder.

Excelsis stepped forward, his feathers ablaze with violet flames. *You will not harm the summoner.*

Charlotte raised both eyebrows. Summoner?

Theron snorted and waved a hand, calling several Shadow Cast to him. They wrapped around his waist and took off across the clover lawn with incredible speed, vanishing into the night.

Charlotte released a breath, then ran to where Philip was. He appeared as Chadwick dropped the cloak. "You okay, Philip?"

Philip still lay on the ground, covered in the blanket, his fur puffed up like a scared kitten. "He's gone?"

Charlotte frowned. "Yes."

"Holy *shit* I saw my life flash before my eyes..." Philip gripped his head. "That was really freakin' stupid."

"Well, you saved my sorry wings," Angus said, grinning. "So thanks for that. Scrying told me it'd either be you or Eris, and Eris' outcome didn't look as rosy."

Charlotte ran to Chadwick and helped back into his couch. "Damn it, you're bleeding again."

"I'll be fine," Chadwick said, coughing. "Been worse."

"Charlotte!"

Charlotte turned. Jaden, Trecheon, and the others came rushing into the room. Sans Roscoe, she noticed, and with Trecheon in a splint, barely able to keep up. Not good. "Dad? You okay? What happened to Trecheon? Where's Roscoe?"

Ouranos pointed down, his snout wrinkled in disgust. "Here." Charlotte followed his finger. A black Cast with teal eyes wrapped around Ouranos' ankles. "They chose to do this on purpose."

Charlotte gasped, covering her snout with her hands. "Why?"

"Theron," Jaden said. "Have you seen him?"

"Bet they have," Darvin said, pointing to the blood splat on the ground. "Who's hurt?"

Charlotte glared, forming a fist. She lifted the sword. "He is. Shouldn't mess with an Azure."

Jaden grinned. "That's my girl."

Trecheon walked into the room, leaning on a makeshift crutch. He coughed. "Where's he headed? We need to get after him *now.*"

"*We* need to take care of this," Jaden said. "*You* need to stay here."

Trecheon glared. "You need a healer."

"Which is why we have Sacha and Leah," Jaden said. "Look, I know from my years as a Defender that if you screw that leg up too much, they won't be able to heal it right. You need to stay here. Take care of Chadwick and wait for us to come back for you."

Trecheon flattened his ears. "…Fine." He frowned. "Don't let him kill Neil. Promise me."

"He's in good hands," Jaden said.

Charlotte flicked her ears back too. "Apparently they're in Dustrik's realm."

Let us take you there, the barn owl said, spreading tiny white snowflakes. *We know the way and can match the speed of the Cast.*

Jaden stopped and stared wide-eyed at the bird. "Oh Draso... Kyrie."

Kyrie bowed slightly. *Alexina is here, Jaden, but she is trapped and not herself. It was pure willpower that allowed her to send me to you.*

"She's alive then...?"

She is.

Jaden let out a long breath, then kissed his finger and pointed to the sky. "Thank you, Draso..."

Thank him after we free her, Kyrie said. *Let us hurry!*

The other birds nodded and took their feral forms. Each leaned down for someone to climb on their shoulders.

Charlotte stepped forward. "Daddy... Come home. Please."

Jaden smiled and pulled Charlotte into a tight hug. "I will. I promise." He climbed on Kyrie's shoulders.

Charlotte took a step back. The group flew off, melting into the night.

She prayed Draso would keep them safe.

And that Jaden wouldn't do something reckless to get Alexina back.

CHAPTER 36

FAMILY BONDING

Zeke's head swam. He shook his head, trying to make his brain function again. Sharp, almost violent smells assailed his nose – an intense, roaring cooking fire, extra strong coffee, the scent of cookies almost burnt. All of his comfort smells with Leah, but right on the brink of breaking. He couldn't say he blamed her. He was on the edge too. Though at least the scents meant she was safe.

But then the smell bled into his mouth and the taste of burnt... something almost burned his tongue. He rolled his tongue in his mouth, trying to place the taste. Burnt... burnt... custard? Olives? Potatoes? The taste was so different, so distant, so *new,* it didn't even feel like Leah...

Oh no.

His eyes flew open and found himself staring Matt in the face. Matt stared back with the same wide-eyed realization. He blinked.

We didn't... Matt's voice in his head.

Zeke swallowed hard. *We ah... we did.*

They had formed a social focus jewel bond.

Matt pressed his lips together and Zeke furrowed his brow. Their thoughts crossed their new jewel bond at the same time in a chorus of frustration.

Shit.

A sharp, angry tingle shot up Zeke's arms and he leaned back. "Ow!"

"Gah!" Matt did the same thing, shaking his hands. Then a new voice entered Zeke's mind.

Oh Sister's mercy. Natassa. In his *head.* The sharp tingle returned. *Draso's holy mercy, have we…?*

"Matt? Zeke?" Izzy. Thankfully not in his head, though worried just the same. "Natassa? You all alright?"

Matt stood up, holding his head. "I'm… not sure how to answer that."

Zeke glanced around. They clearly weren't in the Aether anymore. It was one of the Spires. Dustrik, if he got the Archon symbol correct, though it was hard to tell with only the glow of fading lamps and focus jewels lighting the area. But if he was right, it was the last anchor before heading back to the palace. Everything was very dark, quite cold, and a little bit misty, but he welcomed it with open arms. Anything but that hell hole.

Izzy walked up to them, frowning. "What do you mean you don't know?"

Zeke stood now, gripping his head. The burnt taste vanished in favor of something rotten. He stuck out his tongue and gagged. "Sisters alive, Matt, be careful with that."

Izzy tilted her head to one side, then her jaw dropped. "You did not."

"It seems like I've bonded with Zeke," Matt said. "And… uh… Natassa."

"You and me both," Zeke said.

Izzy covered her snout with her hands. "All *three of you?* How?"

Matt shrugged. "Fighting Judgement and having way too much elixir on my hands, apparently." He looked off. *Just what I didn't need. Especially when Izzy already hates the bonds we have...*

Zeke frowned, flicking an ear back. *Be careful where you aim those thoughts, Matt.*

Matt perked both ears, then frowned. "Oh, uh… right."

Izzy frowned. "Oh hell, Zeke, your leg's bleeding again. Hold still." She ran her fingers up and down the wound, then moved to his back. Zeke sighed. His wedding clothes were ruined, but at least the pain stopped.

Natassa frowned. Zeke's arms suddenly grew cold. Fear. She hugged herself. "Why did we not time travel?"

Matt looked around. "Maybe we did."

"The Aether absorbed most of your time travel," a new, feminine voice said. Zeke turned. A smallish figure walked into the Spire, covered head to toe in black, with a black hood and silver mask.

The Black Cloak. But their eyes… Not blue. Not green.

Bright magenta.

A new Cloak.

A sharp taste of something spicy hit the back of Zeke's throat and Matt threw himself between them and the new Cloak. He glared. "What do you want?"

The Cloak's magenta eyes softened. "Your help."

Matt flicked his ears back.

"You did time travel," the Cloak said. "Forward. With just enough time, if you hurry."

Zeke lifted his chin. "Enough time to do what?"

"Stop Theron," the Cloak said. She wrung her hands together. "I'm not supposed to say this or even be here, but I'm with Robert, I can't just stand idly by while--"

"Wait, wait," Zeke said, holding out a hand. "Who the hell is Robert?"

The Cloak's eyes widened and she covered the metal snout with her hands. "Oh Draso's wings, I wasn't-- oh god…"

Matt stood to his full height. Wind whipped around their ankles and the harsh, bitter taste of extra strong coffee filled Zeke's mouth, almost making him gag. Matt glared. "We don't have time for this. Stop Theron doing what?"

The Cloak furrowed her brow. "Killing Neil."

Zeke's eyes widened and every fiber of fur stood on end. "The Veilsong room. Now!" He dashed for the palace. The others followed behind.

Someone crashed to the ground with a yelp. Zeke slowed and turned.

A Shadow Cast had snatched the Cloak, dragging her into the darkness. "Wait, *stop!*"

"*Zeke, Natassa, fire!*" Matt shouted and threw a Lexi charm at the Cast. But three more Cast appeared out of the darkness – the Lexi charm vanished into one of their bodies, now useless.

Zeke snarled. Damn it! He lit his hands on fire anyway and shot long ribbons of flame at their attackers. The flames lit up the area beyond the Spire.

And revealed at least a dozen more Cast.

The Black Cloak vanished among them.

Matt bared his teeth. *Zeke, Natassa!* He threw his hands up, forming massive tornadoes, tearing up the clover around them.

They responded instantly, filling the tornado with flames and ice. He threw the magic forward, cutting through the waves of Cast like a knife through butter.

"On it!" Izzy rushed through the break in Cast, nipping them back with her overactive healing magic, vanishing into the dark. But a moment later, she jogged back out, the Black Cloak draped over her shoulders. She made it back to the Spire, dropped the Cloak on the clover, and immediately began healing her.

Zeke glanced over his shoulder at them. Three blue eyes stared back from the dark. "Izzy, watch out!" He dropped the magic in Matt's tornado and turned it on the eyes in the dark. Izzy ducked, barely avoiding the flames. He dashed next to her, forming a wall of fire, protecting them from the Cast onslaught. He turned to Izzy. "She good?"

The Cloak coughed and sat up. "Ow…"

Izzy nodded. "She's fine." She helped the Cloak to her feet.

The Cloak gripped Izzy's hand. "Izzy, listen to me. No matter what happens, you *cannot* let Natassa go after Neil while he's at Dustrik's Veilsong room. Do you understand?"

Izzy blinked, but nodded. "I'll do my best."

"*You can't,*" the Cloak said. "This is the last chance we have to fix this."

Izzy frowned. "Okay… okay, I won't."

"Good," the Cloak said. "Because if you do, she'll--"

A red and black gryfon flew through the air and snatched her up in his claws, vanishing into the night sky.

Izzy gasped. "Wait, don't!" She threw her fist down. "Damn it!"

"That was Kjorn," Zeke said. "The Cloak's summons."

"Clearly trying to stop her speaking," Izzy grumbled. "The Cloaks are at war with each other."

Zeke flattened his ears. "All three of them, apparently. Not good."

"Zeke, Izzy, a little help!" Matt called. Cast surrounded him and Natassa in a massive high wall, barely held back by blasts of fire.

Zeke ran. But a rush of wind and water shot down in front of them, dousing everyone and washing them away, scattering them across the lawn in the dark. He scrambled to his feet as quickly as he could, hands ablaze, expecting to face down Theron.

But it wasn't Theron standing by the Spire in a blazing ring.

It was Alexina.

Trust Me

Jaden clung to Kyrie's feathers, ice clinging to his quills, his heart threatening to leapt out his throat.

Kyrie. His wife's summon. Proof she lived.

Proof Theron controlled her.

But hope. Hope that he could save her.

He could *save her.*

He just had to get to her.

"Look!" Ouranos pointed down.

The ground was slick with Shadow Cast, visible only by the bright reflections from the moon and the Phonar's flickering elements. Occasional glimpses of the Cast's glowing blue eyes rippled on the surface of the mass, as if the Cast were taking turns leaping out of the mess like dolphins in a pod.

Jaden's heart nearly stopped. How'd Theron get so many?

Sami moved closer to Jaden, riding on Deo's back. "Should we cure them?"

"No time," Jaden said. "We have to get to Neil, *now*. Darvin!"

Darvin looked up.

"See if you and Roscoe can redirect the Cast," Jaden said. "Give us a chance to get to Theron first!"

Darvin saluted. "Yes sir, Guardian Azure!" He dipped backwards off Excelsis and splashed into the Cast in his Cast form. Roscoe slithered off Excelsis after him. Jaden watched, his heart pounding, but slowly, the Cast began to split and a majority turned away from Dustrik. Not all of them, but enough to make a difference.

Hopefully.

"There!" Sami pointed. "That must be them!"

Jaden looked up. It was dark, but flashes of magic burst into the sky, lighting up what he took to be one of the Spires of the Aether. Hopefully Dustrik's Spire.

He growled. "Hurry, Kyrie!" Kyrie let out a harsh raspy call and dove down low, picking up speed.

He started making out shapes in the flashes of light. Mobs of Cast, hovering over them like oiled waves. But, slowly the figures came into view. Zeke. Natassa.

Matt and Izzy.

All fighting back Cast. All well, so it seemed. Despite the urgency of the problem, instant relief cooled his chest. His family, home. The Aether hadn't claimed them after all.

Now it was time to make sure they were safe.

But then one more figure appeared, just barely visible in the wake of elemental magic and the moonlight.

But it was a figure Jaden recognized instantly. And his heart seized.

"Alexina!"

Matt stood there, shock gluing him to the ground, taking in the sight around him.

Cast all around. His friends… his family, by his side, fighting as best they can.

Then… Alexina.

And, somewhere distant, his father screaming her name.

He formed a fist and furrowed his brow. He was *done with this.*

Zeke moved next to Matt, bringing the sharp, sour taste of lime with the bond, making Matt pucker. Zeke's eyes widened. "Alexina!"

Alexina stared, her face as blank as the Drifters he'd fought before, and blasted them all with ice and lightning.

Matt shielded his group from the onslaught. He snarled. Black Bound elixir built on his fingertips, and magic flowed wildly through his body, rippling through the fur on his bare chest, finally freed from the shackles of the Aether.

The Aether. Alexina waited for him.

He just had to *get to her.*

"Matthew!" Matt turned. Ouranos alighted next to him, Jústi at his side. He squeezed Matt's shoulder. "Thank the Sisters you and Izzy are all right."

"Matt, watch out!" Izzy called. Alexina shot lighting at the pair of them. Jústi screeched and bolted into the air, trying to gather Alexina's lightning, though the kestrel struggled to contain it. Ouranos threw out his hand and fought back the Cast with waves of fire, but he kept his eyes on Matt. "There is something different about you. What did the Aether do to you?"

"Not the Aether," Matt said. "But we don't have time. Is Darvin with you?"

"Alexina!"

Matt turned. Jaden and a summon Matt didn't recognize flew toward Alexina, snow and ice trailing behind them.

But Alexina turned on them and fought them back with a barrage of fireballs. Jaden avoided the first few, but several more caught the pair and grounded them instantly, throwing them among dust, clover, and Cast.

"Jaden!" Zeke ran for him, with Natassa at his heels. Powerful aches in Matt's shoulders accompanied Zeke's sharp lime taste, and if Zeke's faltering was any indication, he felt the aches too. Matt hissed in pain. Izzy ran up next to him, gripping his shoulder, though the cool healing energy did nothing for him.

Darvin suddenly appeared next to him, his body half falling apart in its inky Cast form. He gripped his arm as it fell apart. "I'm sorry, Ouranos, we couldn't deter them for long." Another Cast wrapped around Darvin's feet, and whined. Had to be Roscoe. Matt bit his lip.

"Well then," a voice from the dark said. Matt growled. *Theron.* Theron's silver-blue eyes glowed in the light of the Cast's eyes. He narrowed his gaze, lifting his chin. "I had not intended to reveal Alexina just yet, but you forced my hand." He moved behind her and met Matt's gaze. "Because we all know you would not dare harm her. Would you, Guardian?"

Matt formed fists. Elixir blackened his fur to the wrists.

Enough.

"Darvin, cloak me."

Darvin frowned. "What?"

Ouranos' eyes grew wide. "Matthew, my friend, you *cannot--*"

"Trust me, Ouranos," Matt said, looking him square in the eye. "Trust me as you did on Zyearth all those years ago."

Ouranos flicked an ear back.

Matt gripped his shoulder, elixir dripping through his fur. *"Trust me."*

Ouranos furrowed his brow. But he nodded, and Matt's mind filled to the brim with his familiar rosy dawn. *I trust you.*

"Darvin, cloak, now!" Matt charged Alexina.

Darvin gasped, but he did as he was asked. Matt vanished from view.

Jaden turned his head, his hands frozen over as he fought back Cast. "Matt, *don't!*"

Theron's eyes widened and he stepped back. "Alexina, *go--*"

But too late. Darvin's cloak dropped, revealing Matt just as he faced Alexina. He took his elixir soaked hands and pressed them against Alexina's Ei-Ei jewels.

And with that familiar pull on his belly, along with the bombardment of thoughts and feelings, he vanished again, taking Alexina with him.

The boom deafened Jaden.

Everything seemed to move in slow motion. The loud boom. The flash of light that turned the night to day. The vast, overpowering tang of wild magic on his tongue and in his nose. The wail of the Cast and the shocked screams from his allies.

The dread in his chest threatening to burst through his rib cage.

But it was all over in a second, drowning the world in darkness once more. He blinked rapidly, desperate to make his eyes work again.

But all he could see was a crater. Deep. Smoking. Smelling of rotten magic.

Lifeless.

He gripped his chest. No. *No.* She had been *right there.* And Matt… oh, Matt… He choked.

A hand gripped his shoulder. He looked up.

Ouranos.

"Trust him, Jaden."

Theron groaned from somewhere in the dark and stood, wobbling among shredded Cast bodies as the monsters slowly worked to rebuild themselves. He held his head and glanced at the crater, blinked stupidly. Then his eyes widened. "Oh Sisters--"

Rapid footsteps echoed in the dark and someone crashed into Theron, knocking them both to the ground. Jaden stared.

Matt.

Theron fought him back, shooting elements left and right, but Matt blocked them all with a shield, eventually slamming Theron into a pillar of the Spire. He dug his arm under Theron's chin and glared at him, teeth bared.

"I was willing to give my life for Ouranos as a Drifter when I didn't even know him," Matt snarled, spitting his words. "How much more willing do you think I'd be with my own *family?* "

Someone wrapped their arms around Jaden. He turned his head.

Alexina. Aware, and awake, with pupilless eyes glowing in the moonlight. Soulless, but bridged.

Like Ouranos.

Jaden held her tight, but kept his eyes on Matt.

Theron roared. "She is *my* family, you--"

"*Wrong answer.* " Matt slammed Theron against the pillar as hurricane winds whipped about them, tearing up the clover and snatching the Cast into twisters. "I'm tired of giving you *warnings.* This ends *now!* "

But before Matt could act, Theron pushed him back and dashed off to the side, surrounded by Cast. He threw his hands in the air, filling the space with his elemental magic. Matt stumbled, but steadied himself. He snarled, calling the twisters to him.

Zeke, Ouranos, Natassa, and Alexina moved behind Matt, each one filling a tornado with a different magic – ice, lighting, fire, and earth. Matt's Gem glowed brightly, its whine piercing Jaden's ears. Elixir built on Matt's hands.

"You have no family, Theron," Matt spat. "You lost that right when you chose Judgement over them." He glared. "This is *my* family. And I'll protect them with my *life*."

Jaden's jaw dropped as it hit him. Jewel bonds. All of them shared a social jewel bond with Matt.

Alexina included.

Matt and his bonds thrust their hands forward, blasting Matt's colorful tornadoes at Theron and his Cast. The magic ripped through the inky monsters, tearing them to shreds with wails and shrieks, losing Theron in a hurricane of magic, dust, and Cast remnants.

But from the wreckage, waves of elemental magic flew back at them, chasing away Matt's magic.

Matt immediately dropped the tornadoes and shielded. The shield glowed bright rainbow before vanishing from view, and blocked every attack, though the magical clash blinded them all.

When the magic fell, Theron was gone.

Natassa gasped. *"No.* He has escaped! *Neil!"* She rushed for Dustrik's palace.

"Natassa, *wait!"* Zeke called and rushed after her. But a wall of Cast separated them. Zeke leapt back. "Damnit!"

"We have to get her back!" Izzy said. "The Cloak said-- Gah!" A Cast shot itself at her. She swatted it away with destructive healing magic.

"Then let's get these guys down and go!" Matt said. "Get your Charms ready!"

"Into the fray, love," Alexina said, pressing her back against Jaden's. "Like we always have."

Jaden dropped a handful of charms into her hand. "Let's do this."

OATHBREAKER

Neil slumped through Dustrik's palace, headed for the Veilsong room. The moonlight supplemented their ever-increasing supply of lanterns, flashlights, and torches. His whole body ached. Even places he didn't know he had ached.

Two more. Just two more. And the last one was at the Palace. Home. God, he needed sleep. Leave Theron for everyone else to find.

He shut his eyes. Not that he'd ever let himself do that.

Dami gripped Neil's shoulder with a smile. "We are almost there, love," he said. "You have done so well. Athánatos is better for it."

Neil managed a smile, but didn't try talking.

Sacha walked next to them, wearing a thick glove on her natural hand while she stripped the cover off her biomech one. She made a face, then shoved the glove and cover in an extra thick bag, tying it tight, leaving her biomech exposed.

Neil flicked his ears back. "Sorry, Sacha, I—"

"Shut it right now, Basileus," Sacha said, waving a mocking finger. "You can't help it that my Gem overloaded and blasted Lexi acid. I'm just glad it was on the fake hand and not the real one." She smiled. "And I'm grateful we had Leah and Ana. You'd be boned without them."

"I'd say you owe me, but uh…" Ana's voice trailed. Neil chuckled. Despite everything, it was nice to make fun of their checkered past. Made everything feel whole again.

Andre huffed. "Wish we had more healers. Hey, Leah, there any way to force a healer Gem if I got one?"

"If there are, I promise you no one knows how," Leah said. "Zyearth hates healers, remember? Why waste our time producing more of them? You'd be more likely to find homegrown rituals or potions trying to give you elemental magic. Not that any of them would work."

"Such bullshit," Andre said.

Ana tapped her chin. "I wonder if I could use my magic to change a Gem's power to healing?"

"Let's not test that," Neil said. "What if you couldn't change it back?"

"Good point," Ana said. "Damn."

"I'll be fine." Neil entered the Veilsong room. The last Veilsong room before home. He sighed and climbed on the platform with the Veil and Archon symbols, every bone screaming at him, then stood in the center. He ran his finger over the Defender pendant and adjusted the Ei-Ei jewels on his wrist.

I am a Defender, he thought to himself. *I am Basileus. And this is to protect the ones I love.*

The Archons took their places around him. The rest of his allies surrounded the room with lanterns and torches, bathing the whole platform in flickering light.

Neil rolled his eyes. Because he needed this to be more ominous and dramatic. God.

The Cloak approached Neil, his green eyes piercing him. Neil fought hard not to glare at him. "The last one took about fifteen minutes," he said. "So how long does this one take?"

"You don't want to know," the Cloak said.

Neil sighed. "...Great."

"Almost done." The Cloak gripped Neil's shoulder. But he paused, staring at him.

Neil raised an eyebrow. "Something wrong?"

The Cloak stared a moment longer then took a deep breath. "Whatever happens here… don't leave the circle."

An unpleasant buzz ran down Neil's spine. "What does that mean? What's going to happen?"

"Don't leave the circle." He moved toward the platform.

Neil gripped his arm and pulled him close. "Cloak… Tymon… Why do Darvin and Sami have Ei-Ei jewels?"

Tymon glared. "We don't have *time.*"

"You're telling me to stay put with a vague warning about what's going to happen next," Neil growled under his breath. "For all I know, this is the *only* time. Tell me."

Tymon closed his eyes. "The Cloak was created to fight back Judgement and the Shadow Cast," he said. He lifted a finger. "A single Cloak. Just one person fighting back against an otherworldly entity. Unsurprisingly, it didn't work." He folded his arms. "So I made a team of Cloaks. Darvin and Sami are a part of that team."

"Since when?"

"Since I asked them on Sol back when you first met them," Tymon said.

Neil narrowed his gaze. "So you made them your *pawns*."

Tymon snorted. "No. Pawns suggest you're replaceable. Cannon fodder until the next pawn comes along. But they aren't pawns. They're allies in this war against Judgement. I need them if we're going to win."

Neil took a heavy breath. "If you know everything that's going to happen, why the hell aren't you just fixing everything?"

Tymon looked at him sadly. "Trust me… I've tried. But it doesn't work. All we can do is follow the path laid out for us." He gave Neil a pointed look, then took his place with the Archons. "Everyone, ready your elements!"

Neil's heart raced. *Don't leave the circle.*

Leah gasped and gripped her chest. "Wait, *wait,* I feel Zeke, he's *back,* but he's--"

Then the elements hit him full force.

Neil closed his eyes and gritted his teeth against the pain, though his mind screamed at him. You'd think after multiple hits of this he'd get used to it--

"Andre, *look out!*" Leah shouted.

Neil's eyes flashed open.

A blast of lightning and ice shot at Andre, though Leah leapt in front of him, shielding him. The force of the magic shoved them both back.

Immediately, Kaoru and Drifa shot forward, leaving a sharp tang of lightning and the sting of ocean water in Neil's nostrils, completely overpowering the elemental magic coursing through him. They flew at something in the dark… but several large, black tentacles reached up, snatching their legs and wings, dragging them into the darkness.

Cast.

A *lot* of Cast.

Don't leave the circle.

Leah stood, baring her teeth. She activated her staff and swung it around, gathering leftover elements from the summons, then she slammed it to the ground, shooting lightning and water at their attacker in the dark.

A figure swatted it away. A familiar figure.

Theron.

He glared with his harsh, silver-blue eyes. "It is time I rid our home of outsiders." He charged forward, hands alight with elemental magic, his gaze on Neil.

But Leah wasn't done yet. She tackled Theron, knocking them both to the ground, scratching with foot and hand claws. But Theron gripped her arms and with a will threw her aside, sending her flying. Andre caught her and the pair skidded along the floor, crashing into Ana and sliding toward a mess of Cast. Leah got her pouch of Lexi Charms out, though the Charms were their only defense against the monsters.

Theron turned back to Neil… and got a swift punch in the jaw from Sacha. He fell back, smashing against the ground. Sacha leapt on him, her biomech fist high in the air.

He kicked her in the stomach, stopping her in her tracks and flung her aside. She gasped for air, gripping her middle. Theron stood and adjusted his jaw. He turned.

Baltazar stood there, sword in hand. The weapon flickered with various elements it had picked up from the fight. "Death to *traitors.*" He charged Theron.

Theron shot a bolt of lightning at him, though Baltazar deftly dodged and caught the lightning with his sword. He whipped about and flung the lightning back at Theron. Theron caught it, sparks flying, and Baltazar swung the sword while he was distracted. Theron leapt back, but the sword still bit his side, spilling steaming blood. Theron roared at him, waved a hand, and tossed Baltazar away with a barrage of rocks and sand. Baltazar managed to escape most of it, but two large rocks pinned his tail, allowing the sand to bury him and stop him. He slumped on the sand and didn't move.

Neil called out, but the vicious magic drowned his voice.

Theron growled, turning back to Neil.

And faced Dami.

Dami pulled on lightning from Electrik, forming dozens of electric cages all around him. He glared at Theron.

"You are *done.*" He threw the electric cages forward with incredible speed.

But the Cast were faster. One by one, Cast absorbed each cage of lightning, zapping it from the air, killing the attack. And Theron walked free, unharmed. He glared, then waved Dami away in a wash of water.

"Dami!" Neil shouted. Dami vanished into the darkness as the water doused every lantern and torch in its wake. Neil turned back to Theron. Marching to him. Unopposed.

Don't leave the circle.

"Archons!" Tymon called, holding his hands out. "Hold!"

Electrik met Tymon's gaze. "But--"

"*Hold!*" Tymon shouted. "Just a minute longer!"

Theron lifted his fist and sharp ice spikes appeared over his head, aimed at Neil. "A minute too late." He held his hand forward.

And the Black Cloak slid in between Neil and Theron. The blue-eyed Cloak.

Robert.

Neil's eyes widened.

"Robert!" Tymon shouted. *"Don't!"*

"I'm tired of sitting here and doing *nothing!*" Robert shouted. He held up his hand. Tymon cried out as Rashard and Kjorn burst from the air, dragging the scent of hot coals and deep winter with them. They landed on either side of Robert, almost robotically, and bombarded Theron with elemental magic.

Theron held up his hands and a dozen Cast came to his rescue, shielding him from the elements. Robert roared, yanked out a pouch, and pelted the Cast with Lexi Charms. Each one fell to Kjorn's fire, leaving a Drifter behind. Though each one collapsed to the ground and didn't move.

Neil's heart broke. *No...*

Theron held his hands up. "You will not stop me!" He threw a fist to the ground, and everything shook like an earthquake. Sharp spikes of earth and stone burst from the earth, piercing Rashard and Kjorn, breaking them apart to their base elements. The punishing magic stopped. Theron dashed forward and punched Robert hard, knocking him aside. Robert tumbled away, groaning.

Theron hovered over him. "I am *Basileus!"* he shouted. "None shall take my place, and none shall oppose me and win!" He turned once more to Neil.

But one more stood between them.

Natassa.

Neil's heart stopped. "Natassa, *no!"* With a will, he pulled against the elements pinning him. But the Cloak's words echoed in his mind.

Don't leave the circle.

Damnit! He didn't care, he had to save her. He pulled hard... but the magic held fast. He could do nothing.

Theron laughed. "You do this *now?* After all this time?" He crossed his arms. "You lack the strength, Prinkípissa."

Natassa growled. She formed fists, sending sparks of electricity, blasts of flames, and angry ice spikes into the air. "Not this time, *Theron.* All my life I have made excuses for you, feared you, believed you could once again be the father I remembered growing up. All this time I believed I had failed you. But it was *you* who failed *me*, time and time again, hurting and killing in the name of grief, when really it was in the name of *power*." She bared her teeth. "I am finished making excuses. I need to do what I should have done decades ago." She hunkered down, magic clinging to her fur and circling around her. *"No more failure."*

Theron raised an eyebrow. "Well then. Let us see, shall we?" He charged her.

And she charged him.

Neil's heart pounded so hard, he couldn't even feel the pain from the magic.

Elements encircled the pair as they connected in a flurry of magic and light. Lightning, ice, fire, rocks, and wind flew about, crashing into the floor, the pillars, the nearby trees, escaping to the sky in a colorful display.

Then the light faded. Neil blinked rapidly, trying to adjust his eyes.

Theron had his fist in Natassa's belly. A dozen thick, sharp ice and stone spikes stuck out of her back, bathed in red. She coughed.

Blood splattered on the ground.

Neil's fur stood on end and the pain concentrated on his heart. *"NATASSA!"*

Theron twisted his arm, letting Natassa slump to the floor, blood pooling under her. Several ice spikes melted away in an instant.

The relentless Archon magic stopped. Neil's mind flooded with the new point on the Athánatos map. One more anchor done. Names bombarded him. Except Natassa's name.

It was gone.

Despite the pain and damage his body suffered, he dashed off the platform, stumbling and slipping, and slid to his knees beside Natassa. "Sacha, Leah, healing, *now!*" But reaching for her, he knew it was already too late. He turned her over. She stared blankly into the sky, blood leaking down the side of her mouth.

Her body lay limp in his arms.

And everything stopped.

All the pain… all the agony, the aches, the screams he held inside, the war he survived, the friends he lost, the desire for death, the compassion and empathy the war stole from him, the cold, dark, lonely life of an assassin… Nothing, not one thing, prepared him for the pain of holding his dead fiance in his arms.

He didn't even move when he heard Theron's footsteps behind him, coming in for the final kill.

But someone slammed into Theron, knocking him aside. He turned.

Mistik. The Archon stood between Theron and Neil, waving their arms, calling on their water magic. "You killed our Basilea!" The other Archons called on their own magic, though after the Veil anchor, no one was at full strength.

"She chose that path," Theron spat. "As did you." He shot ice shards at Mistik.

But they gathered them up in the raging waters of their magic and flung them away. "You will not harm the Basileus."

Theron glared, baring his teeth and flicking his ears back, his fur bristling. "You will die with those words on your lips." He hurled lightning at Mistik, shocking their body. Mistik cried out, then collapsed, foam building in their mouth, their eyes wide and dead. Misty screamed in the dark.

Neil sat on the ground, vulnerable.

A bird's screech hung overhead. Neil absently looked up.

All seven Phonar -- no, all eight -- dove from the sky below, aimed at Theron. Free from all summoners. And… angry.

Theron growled. He leapt on a mess of Cast. The blobs wrapped themselves around his legs and took off into the night, the Phonar chasing after him. The remaining Archons unleashed their building magic as well, sending it flying after Theron, then most collapsed to the floor.

The Veilsong room went totally silent.

Sacha scrambled over, dragging a foot, barely able to move. "Step back, Neil, let me--"

"She's gone."

Sacha stopped. She shook her head. "No, just let me try, *please--*"

"She's gone, she..." Neil looked down at Natassa's perfect face. The light cream around her eyes and snout, those beautiful violet eyes, her soft lips... marred by dirt and blood and death.

He blinked, staring, his mind blank. He gently closed her eyes and mouth, then pressed his forehead to hers, his eyes still open, shock racking his body. Only then did the tears start.

"She's gone."

CHAPTER 39

BONDBREAKER

Matt caught three Cast in a tornado and threw them aside, huffing. With all the magic draining from his time in the Aether, this was harder than normal.

Didn't help that his senses were overloaded from all the bonds he now carried. The sharp taste of lime still lingered in his mouth from Zeke. Ouranos' rosy dawn filled him with hope, though it was almost overpowering at this point. And Izzy's cacophony of bells nearly deafened him. Scents hit him hard, bombarding his nose with the smell of hot fire, burning sulfur, and ash. Alexina. Angry, fighting, and letting Matt know it through their new bond, finally made manifest in the present. His arms and legs tingled with anxiety and adrenaline, which he took to be his bond with Natassa. At least he knew she was--

"Gah!" Pain exploded through Matt's ribs and he fell to his knees, gripping his chest, gasping. His heart instantly felt empty and cold and… dead. What the hell was that…?

"Ahh!" Zeke also fell. Also gripping his chest and shouting.

Then the pain vanished. And so did the tingling in his limbs.

Matt met Zeke's eyes. *Oh, no...*

The Phonar cried out as one, letting loose raw, feral sounds, then tore off into the sky toward Dustrik's palace. Zeke gripped his head. "No... Archángeli..."

Then Ouranos gripped his head, calling out. Matt's mind exploded with vibrant colors and a thousand emotions at once. Ouranos closed his eyes tight... then opened them. He glanced at Matt, lowering his hands.

Ouranos... had pupils. His Soul Jewels fit snuggly on his head among the other Ei-Ei jewels.

Ouranos had his soul back.

Matt's fur stood on end and his eyes widened. Only one thing came to mind.

"Natassa."

Ouranos leapt to his feet and dashed for the palace. Zeke followed, running like Matt had never seen him run before. Darvin, Sami, and Cast Roscoe rushed after them like bats out of hell.

Izzy fought back two remaining Cast, then turned to Matt. "Matt, what's going on?"

"It's Natassa," Matt said, his voice breathy.

And he ran.

The palace was a blur. No sound except for everyone's empty footsteps and frantic breathing. Ouranos led the way, though he faltered as he ran. He filled Matt's head with heart-wrenching blues, blacks, and grays.

Ouranos stopped abruptly, almost skidding to a halt. Right at the threshold of a large room with symbols all over the floor. Zeke stopped with him. Neither moved.

The colors in Matt's mind went dark.

Matt slowed. He peered around them.

The room was a mess. Smashed marble, magic scarring, shattered lanterns, overturned torches… and blood.

So much blood.

Neil sat in front of the platform. Holding Natassa. Covered in blood. He rocked slightly, his eyes staring blankly forward. Leah, Dami, Sacha, and Andre surrounded him. The Archons sat in a semicircle, their limbs sprawled out, elements crackling at their fingertips. A dozen or more sentries lay still on the floor.

Misty hovered over Archon Mistik, soaking wet and bloody. She sobbed quietly.

The Black Cloak leaned against a pillar, hand pressed against the mask, covering his eyes. His shoulders shook.

"…It wasn't supposed to happen like this."

Matt turned. Another Black Cloak, the blue-eyed one, on his knees on the floor. Tears flooded his eyes. A third Black Cloak, the new one with the violet eyes, kneeled beside the blue-eyed one and hugged him.

Darvin and Sami stared at the two Cloaks. They exchanged glances. Darvin wrinkled his snout and pulled Sami close.

"She's gone."

Neil. Matt turned back.

Neil stopped rocking. He held Natassa's lifeless body close to him. "She's gone… she's gone…"

Izzy ran up to Matt now. "Matt?"

Her voice made Neil look up. He blinked, as if trying to make sense of the scene. Finally he turned to Ouranos. "I… What… Where do I take her, Ouranos?"

A wave of dark sadness hit Matt like a truck, making his knees buckle.

Ouranos stepped forward. "Oh, my dear friend…" He reached down. Neil pulled back, leaning away, but Ouranos shook his head. "I have no intention of taking her, brother. Come. We will bring her home…" He gripped Neil's arms and helped him stand, still holding Natassa. Blood dripped from the wounds in her back and her arm fell lifeless at her side. Two small ice spikes slid out of her body and crashed to the floor in a drippy, bloody mess.

Izzy drew her hands to her snout. Tiny, distant, unsure bells rang in his ears. Izzy's eyes grew glassy. "O-oh… oh no, not Natassa, no… no…" Roscoe curled around her feet, cooing in that strange, gurgling Cast voice.

Matt wrapped an arm across her shoulders since Roscoe couldn't yet.

A strange… absence of taste washed over his tongue. A deliberate, conscious lack of flavor, as if nothing would ever have taste again. Zeke stared at Natassa, jaw loose, tears streaking through his fur.

"…Oh Draso." Harsh, bitter smells of vinegar and salt hit Matt's nose. Alexina. She stood at the threshold, covering her face with her hands. Jaden held her tight, rubbing her back.

Neil still stood in the middle of the room, unmoving, glancing around. "How do I get… home?"

The room filled with the sounds of wing flaps and the Phonar descended on them all. They bowed as one. Excelsis then lifted his head, waving tiny purple embers around the room. *Come… we shall take you home.* He lifted his wings and grew until he was close to Rashard's size. Ouranos helped Neil settle on Excelsis' back. He tucked Natassa's arm on her belly. Like she was just sleeping.

"We will be right behind you, brother," Ouranos said. "Fly her home."

Neil nodded, his face still dull and expressionless. He held her close and nodded to Excelsis. The black raven took to the sky.

Ouranos turned to Jústi. The kestrel bowed low, then waved her wings, grew in size, and invited Ouranos onto her back. Ouranos briefly glanced at Matt. Tears streamed down his face. He nodded, wiped at his nose, then patted Jústi and followed Neil in the sky.

And everything fell silent again.

Matt watched them vanish into the dark. He should say something. Do something. Get the group moving. Get them all to the palace. Neil needed support. The group needed direction.

Someone sobbed. Leah.

Zeke rushed to her, throwing his arms around her. Andre pulled them both close, gripping them tight. Ana stood there, dumbfounded, her expression blank.

Izzy sobbed now. She slid from Matt's grip to the floor. Roscoe curled around her, and she leaned into his black form. Sacha walked dully to Matt. She opened her mouth to speak, but nothing came out. Tears filled her eyes. Matt hugged her and she buried her face in his chest.

Dami continued staring where Neil had taken off to. Archon Electrik wrapped an arm across his shoulders, but Dami didn't even seem to notice.

All three Black Cloaks stayed glued to their positions. If Matt really listened, he could hear them sniffling.

Matt watched everything, his mind refusing to latch on to any one thing. He counted his breaths. One… two… three… four…

On his tenth breath he forced himself back to reality. "Eyes up, Defenders."

Everyone turned to him.

He drew on every scrap of training Guardianship had given him. *Give orders. Give them something to do. Let them find purpose in that. For now.* "Everyone. Find a summon or get a mule deer, or whatever we need to do to get back. We don't have much time."

Izzy stared up at him. "Time for what…?"

"For Neil," Matt said. "Because he's going home, holding someone dear to him, and he'll need all the support he can get." He cleared his throat. "Plus we'll need to triage healing… most of us need it now."

Izzy blinked, trying to process his words, but she nodded. "Aye, Guardian." She started helping everyone pair up. Sacha pulled back from Matt's hug, wiped her tears free, and followed Izzy's example. Darvin and Sami soon followed too. Leah stood as well, wiping her face, and spoke with one of the summons. The green-eyed Cloak waved his hand and Rashard and Kjorn appeared. Andre took a deep, shuddering breath and waved his hand. Two new summons, a gryfon and a wyvern, appeared from the air. Jaden pressed his lips together, lifted his chin, and began pairing everyone up, directing them to the various summons.

Matt allowed himself one moment of fear, anger, sadness, and pain. One moment.

Then it was time to get to work.

REST

Neil followed Excelsis dully through the palace. He had a vague idea that they were going to the *féretro* garden, but he wasn't sure why or if that was even what they were doing. He just followed the bird, holding Natassa close.

She lay snuggled in his arms. Like she was sleeping. Safe, and warm, and calm. Finally, no more pain.

No more pain.

He fought back the rising aches in his chest and lungs.

Ouranos walked next to him. Stoic, calm, quiet. Neil caught a glimpse of him as they walked.

The Athánatos prince had his Soul Jewels again. His pupils. His soul. Neil couldn't stop staring.

"You have your soul back," Neil said quietly.

Ouranos slowed. He stared up at the sky, his neck and face stiff, clearly trying to fight back tears. "Yes… I do."

"How?"

Ouranos fiddled with his hands. "The only way to retrieve a soul stolen and bring it back to its living body is through a sacrifice. A soul for a soul…"

Neil blinked. His eyes widened. "Natassa."

Ouranos nodded. "Natassa." He ran a finger down the jewels on his face. "She once told me that her biggest failure was not retrieving my soul from the Aether when Theron first stole it. I suppose, in death, she… she set out to correct that." He took a shuddering breath. "I wish… she believed me when I told her I never once saw her as a failure."

Neil's chest ached.

"Neil?"

Neil shook his head, looking for the voice.

A red and black face popped up from behind a pillar. Trecheon. "Hey, I didn't think that-- oh *god.*"

Neil frowned. "She's gone."

"Who's gone?" Charlotte peered around the corner. She gasped. "No, no, Natassa!"

Trecheon hobbled forward. He had a makeshift splint on his leg. "Let me see, Neil. Let me heal her."

"My friend," Ouranos said. "You cannot."

Trecheon glanced up. "Oh… You… your soul…"

"Natassa's final gift," Ouranos said, his voice cracking.

Charlotte choked.

Eris rounded the corner now. She froze, eyes wide. "Oh no… Oh, my Lady… my Basileus…"

"Eris," Neil said. "Can you make sure Philip doesn't see Natassa like this? He doesn't… he's seen enough in his life. He doesn't need more."

"I…" She paused, then bowed. "Of course, my Lord." She hurried off.

Excelsis turned to Neil. *He will need closure, my Basileus.*

Neil took a deep breath. Such a weighted word now. Basileus. He shook his head. "Natassa… she needs rest." Neil pulled her closer. "Give her a moment. Take care of her first. Then he can have closure. Okay, Excelsis?"

As you wish, my Lord, the phoenix said with gentle embers on their heads. *Come, friends.*

Trecheon and Charlotte joined their procession.

Neil counted footsteps. It was all he could do to stay grounded.

They finally made their way to the *féretro* garden.

Neil took it all in. So peaceful. So calming and beautiful, even at night. Moonlight filtered through the trees and got caught in the crystals hanging from the branches. The Ei-Ei jewel boxes scattered about like fall leaves.

Excelsis flew to a large blank patch of clover. *Let the Lady rest here.*

Neil crossed the clover lawn, weaving around the boxes, and placed her gently on the ground. He stepped back. The harsh iron scent of blood still lingered.

Excelsis hovered over her and let out a gentle breath. The blood dried and faded into her fur. Ouranos walked up and placed a white shroud over her. He gripped Neil's shoulder.

"She is resting now, brother," he said. "We should let her…"

Neil allowed Ouranos to pull him away. But he never turned his gaze from her.

Trecheon stood next to him. "I… I'm so sorry, Neil…"

Neil stared forward. "Why is my life like this?" he said, his voice cracked and broken. "Why is it that the moment everything looks like I can have a decent life, it gets stripped away from me?" He formed fists. "Is this my punishment for being an assassin?"

Trecheon looked at him. He opened his mouth like he wanted to speak, but then closed it and hugged him instead.

"Neil."

Neil turned.

Jaden stood a few feet away, with Matt and Izzy and Zeke and all the rest of their friends. Neil stared at Jaden, numb and empty, his whole body buzzing like it was ready to explode.

And Jaden stared back. Brow furrowed, eyes focused, ears pasted back, his jaw loose.

Silence.

Then in four big strides, Jaden crossed the space between them and drew Neil into the biggest bear hug he had ever felt. A strong grip. The grip of a soldier.

The grip of a father.

"It's not fair," Jaden said. Quietly, just for Neil. His voice was surprisingly steady. "It's not fair, and nothing will make it so. But it's survivable. It's *survivable*, Neil. Cling to that." He gave him a squeeze. "Someday you'll be okay. But you don't have to be today. Or tomorrow. Or any time soon. And that's acceptable."

Neil blinked, staring off into the middle distance, absorbing Jaden's words. Until it clicked.

Jaden was him.

Both snails under Ackerson's boot. Both soldiers the war refused to release. Both sons who lost a father.

Both zyfaunos who lost a family.

But Jaden survived, a tiny voice in Neil's brain said. *He's alive. He's even happy.*

Not that he could ever see himself happy again. Not now.

And yet.

This is your future. Don't let it go.

Neil's vision blurred and tears stained his fur. He gripped Jaden tight, shut his eyes and sobbed.

He had to hope this would be right again. But until then, he had to feel this, full throttle. He couldn't be the soldier, shaking and pained, alone in the cold hospital tent in DC. He couldn't be Theron, bottling it up until he exploded and destroyed everything he loved.

He had to feel it. Here, and now.

But not alone.

A hand rested on his back. Metal.

Trecheon.

Then another hand. A flash of white and blue. Matt. Then another. Golden brown. Izzy.

And then another. And another. And another. Darvin, Sami, Sacha, Leah, Zeke, Ouranos, Charlotte, Eris, Ana.

Dami…

Oh, Dami…

Sobs and sniffles in the air. Hands pressed against him. A shield.

"Feel it with your whole heart, Neil," Jaden said quietly. "For as long as you need."

So he let himself drown. With all his friends' hands ready to pull him back up again.

When he was ready.

It had been a long time since he had felt so drained. Drained of everything – energy, willpower, tears, emotion… life.

But not hope. Somehow that still lingered. Like a diseased rat biting his ass. He'd probably be grateful for it later. He'd get a white dove, sitting on his shoulder, cooing gently, reminding him it was okay to hope. But for now, it was a rat. Biting his ass.

He sat on a wicker couch in one of the audience rooms, hands folded. Staring.

"Eris," he said, his voice cracked and hoarse. "What happens now?"

Eris lifted her head from the table, her green eyes puffy and wet. "I… beg your pardon?"

"Natassa… she's…" He couldn't quite say it. "Am I… Do I still become Basileus?"

Eris stared forward, ears twitching as if thinking. "I… am unsure. I… this has never happened before. There are no protocols."

Neil took in a breath, feeling every atom of air enter his lungs.

Eris stood, her normal stoic, quiet expression slowly returning. "What do you wish to do, my Lord?"

He glanced up and met her eyes. And a terrible thought ripped through his mind.

I want to die.

He tested the thought. Released it into his brain and let it flow through his body, down to his tail tip. Poked it, prodded it, checked to see if there was action behind the words. The world around him faded, pulling him deep into his mind, into the familiar, dark, yet welcoming world promising escape through death, as it had in DC.

But the outside world called him. The birds chirping, the wind through his fur, the mild scent of pine.

Eris's gentle expression. The affection, empathy, and sadness in her eyes. But also that tiny sliver of hope.

Dami's soft hug, his comforting scent, his deep, deep love resonating through Neil's bones.

No… no, he really didn't want to die. He had felt that before, and this wasn't the same. This wasn't the war where he had lost everything. He still had people to protect. To love.

But.

"I don't know."

A rush of purple fire swirled about them and Excelsis appeared before Neil, in his full anthropomorphic form. He took a deep bow, falling to one knee, mantling his wings. Then the other Phonar, one by one flew in, standing by Excelsis, elements rippling around them. Each one taking a knee and bowing. All eight. Finally together.

They had no reason to stay. Theron's… actions released their oath. And yet, here they were.

Excelsis lifted his head. Embers spread everywhere. *Lord Neil. The Phonar still recognize you as Basileus. We still bless you as leader. However…* He stood, folding his wings together in front of his chest. The other Phonar followed his example. *Your life is your own. This is your choice.*

"Basileus."

Neil turned. Embrik walked into the room with the other Archons trailing behind. He paused, then rested a fist on his chest and bowed his head. "The Archons also recognize you as Basileus. We look to you to lead." One by one, each Archon pressed a fist to their chest and bowed. Including Misty, who immediately filled the role her renna left behind. She had tears in her eyes, but she stood strong, water rippling around her feet with her newfound magic, showing her support like the others.

Except Electrik.

Neil stood. "Electrik?"

But Electrik frowned instead, his brow furrowed. He stepped forward and took Neil's hands. "Dami's love and joy. My dear son." He shook. "I speak to you now not as an Archon but as your father-in-law. You have already sacrificed so much for us. When you had first come here, it was because of your love for Natassa, and later your love for my son Damianos. And yet, you chose to offer so much more, by confining yourself here as the new Veil. Over and over again."

Neil flicked an ear back.

Electrik squeezed Neil's hands. "But these sacrifices are hard." He locked his gaze with Neil. "You have the right to refuse. Athánatos will survive, as we always have, and you will always be welcome here. Damianos will follow you to the ends of the Earth if you ask him, even… even if it means leaving here. But you agreed to be Basileus alongside Natassa, not by yourself. That was the condition. That… is not an option anymore. You are no longer obligated." He let go of Neil's hands. "And we will understand if you choose to leave that responsibility."

Neil stared at his hands, Electrik's warmth still lingering. There was some truth to that. Originally he had continued coming here for Natassa and Dami. But… that changed. Everything else had grown on him, called to him. The gardens, the palace, the smiling faces of the people, the children… He relived hours walking through the gardens with Dami. Playing soccer with the children or practicing reading. Working in the kitchens with the cooks, teaching them new things. Helping the Defenders and Athánatos alike restore all of Theron's damage.

That wasn't all for Natassa.

That was for the people he had come to love.

When Ouranos had been getting him ready for their wedding, Neil questioned everything. Did he belong? Was it really okay for him to be Basileus?

Was any of this right?

But… standing here now… It was never more clear. This was where he belonged.

This was home.

He closed his hands, trying to hold on to that warmth just a little longer. "I… I chose to renew the Veilsong. I didn't choose that just because of Natassa. It's… it's for everyone. I don't want to see it fall." He looked up at the Archons. "Athánatos… it's home."

Electrik slowly smiled.

Neil took a deep, shuddering breath. "I want to finish what I started. So… if you'll have me… I'll stay."

Electrik's smile widened now. *"Eímaste mazí sas,* Basileus."

Neil stood tall. This is what Natassa would want. This would honor her memory. It would hurt for a long time… a very long time… but… if Jaden could get through it, so could he. He could be happy again. In time. He drew on all the strength he could. Not his own damaged strength, but the strength of his friends. The Archons. The Veil itself. The Veilsong's mental map floated in his mind, feeding him the names of the Athánatos – his subjects. He drew on that strength too. And of course Dami, his ever present love.

He would need it… when they went after Natassa's killer.

Something shiny caught his eye. The Basileus chain. *His* Basileus chain, sitting on the table next to Eris. He walked up to it and ran a hand down it.

Eris gently threw it around his neck and together they laid it over his shoulders. It was… heavy. But strong. He'd need that to go after Theron.

But first, they needed to finish the Veilsong. He settled his body, wrapped himself in his borrowed strength and looked Electrik in the eye. *"As to teleiósoume aftó.* Let's finish this."

VEILSONG

"Everything's just about in place," Matt said. "You ready, Neil?"

Neil stood in the center of the Veilsong room in the Athánatos palace. Every Archon symbol glowed brightly enough that they didn't even need the lanterns. The Archons took their places around the center.

Melaina stood just off the platform behind Embrik. She hadn't taken her sister's death well… she had sobbed loudly in Embrik's arms, then fell silent and hadn't spoken since. She wouldn't leave his side. Even Alexina's return didn't help much.

Alexina. She was back, she was safe, but… she wasn't whole. She was a Drifter, like Ouranos had been. Bridged, aware, and bound to Matt in a social bond, but she was without pupils, and she had lost memories and time. Even though Ouranos had his soul back, having Alexina as a Drifter… It was almost like starting all over again.

Like Natassa's sacrifice for Ouranos didn't mean anything. It stung more than it should.

Misty stood on the Mistik Archon symbol where her renna once did. Soon she'd take on the formal name of her title and become the new Mistik. But the grief was too close now.

Neil knew the feeling well.

And so did Philip. He shut down entirely hearing about Natassa's death. Probably reliving the deaths of their parents. Neil wished more than once that he could take that from him. Carry that burden for him. But he couldn't.

Eris took Philip to the *féretro* garden. For his closure. He hoped they wouldn't stay too long.

The Black Cloak stood on his symbol. The green-eyed Cloak. Tymon. His eyes hadn't lost their glassy look.

Part of Neil wanted to scream at him. Demand he fix this. Bring Natassa back. But he kept coming back to Tymon's insistence that they had tried that. Over and over. And it never worked. Even with the blue-eyed cloak Robert jumping in… Nothing changed.

What must it be like…? Knowing everything that's going to happen… all the pain and loss and trauma… and being unable to fix it?

Better to cut him some slack. They didn't need more shit on top of all this.

Matt turned his head. "Neil?"

Neil frowned. The rest of his friends and allies surrounded the Veil room. Tymon's, Angus' and Andre's summons faced every entrance, with the Phonar scattered among them. Alexina, Ouranos, Dami, and Melaina stood around the stage, magic wisping through their fur. All four healers, Leah, Trecheon, Izzy, and Sacha, stood close to the platform, each of their Gems charged by Ana's Wishing Dust after all the healing they had to do to fix everyone. And every Gem user surrounded them all, ready to form a domed shield over the whole group. Matt, Jaden, Darvin, Roscoe, Sami, and Chadwick, who finally felt well enough to stand. Even Charlotte and Baltazar stood by, carrying swords, ready to fight.

Matt's doing. They weren't going to lose anyone else.

All they needed was Neil's go ahead.

Dami turned to Neil, ears back, frowning. "My love… are you ready?"

Neil took a deep breath. Dami… his solid rock. Thank the Sisters he still had Dami.

He ran a hand over the Defender pendant once more. Twisted the bracelet with his Ei-Ei jewels. *Defender. Basileus. Home.* "Yeah… I'm ready."

Matt raised a hand. "Defenders, eyes up!"

"Aye, Guardian!" everyone cried.

"Summons, elements active!"

The summons – Drifa, Kaoru, Magna, Lysander, Rashard, Kjorn, and all eight unbound Phonar, let out loud, feral cries and lit themselves up with their magic.

"Healers, at the ready!"

"Aye, Guardian!" Izzy called. She, Sacha, Leah, and Trecheon stood as close to the stage as they could, their Gems already whining.

"Elementals!" Matt cried. "Magic ready!"

Ouranos, Alexina, Dami, and Melaina lit the air around them ablaze with elemental magic. "Aye, Guardian," Ouranos said quietly.

"Swords!" Matt called. "Weapons up!"

Baltazar and Charlotte raised their swords. "Aye, Guardian!"

"Defenders!" Matt called again. "Shield!"

Each Defender raised their hands and formed a large, unbroken shield around the whole group. It turned green, then purple, then it vanished.

Matt turned his head back. "When you're ready, Basileus."

Neil took a deep breath. He ran his hand over the royal chain around his neck. The Defender pendant hanging next to it. Then he glanced over his jacket.

Still stained with Natassa's blood.

Ana had offered to repair it with her magic, but he refused. For now. He needed the reminder for why he was doing this. Cleaning could come later.

"Basileus," Embrik said. Neil turned. Embrik furrowed his brow. "Neil. My friend." He frowned. "...It is okay to scream."

Neil flicked his ears back. He nodded, then turned. "Cloak. I'm ready."

Tymon nodded. He spoke a long string of the Athánatos language. The Archons repeated it.

Then the elements hit.

And this time, Neil screamed.

He screamed for the pain. He screamed for Natassa's death. He screamed for the dark emotions building in his brain, for the desire for death that he refused to give in to, for the anger, the despair, and the hate that threatened to eat him up and spit him out like it had for Theron.

He screamed to let it go, release it all, remove it from his mind, and purge its poison before it did permanent damage.

He screamed for all the people they had lost with these stupid battles. For the people who didn't have a voice anymore.

He screamed... because the alternative was silence. And that wouldn't do.

Eventually the punishing elements stopped and Neil collapsed to the ground. The healers were on him in an instant and washed the pain away like a hot shower. But still Neil screamed, deep in his mind.

Why Natassa? Why now, before they even got married? Why didn't anyone *do* anything?

Why did he lose all the good things in his life…?

A pair of hands rested on his shoulders. "Love…"

Neil sniffled. Dami.

Not all the good things, his brain reminded him.

Damianos carefully pulled Neil into his lap. He rested his head on Neil's, holding him close. "It is finished, my love… The Veil is complete." He kissed the top of Neil's head. "Your people are whole."

Neil closed his eyes and dove inside his mind, looking for the Veilsong map. And there it was – a complete map of all of Athánatos, where he could find all its inhabitants with pinpoint accuracy. Ouranos, Melaina, all the Archons, Dami… and the Cloaks. Tymon. Robert. Darvin and Sami. And… a new one.

Arden Azure.

His eyes flashed open. And he locked eyes with Baltazar.

The Drifters.

With Dami's help, he scrambled to his feet and mentally dove back into the Veil, searching for all the affected Drifters. And… he saw them. All of them. He formed fists. There were *dozens.* Sentries and citizens alike. Damn Theron. He called for them.

Friends, Athánatos, my people! The Drifters froze on his internal map. He called out once more. *Hear your Basileus and be free!*

He paused. Slowly, each of those Drifters turned to the main Athánatos palace and started toward it. There was… a strange peace with it. He could only assume it worked.

But no matter how hard he looked through the growing hoard, he couldn't find Theron's name anywhere. That damn bastard. With a sigh, he opened his eyes.

Dami hugged him tight. He held Dami close, trying to compose himself.

Jaden marched up the platform. "We have a Veil. Now we need to get Theron."

"No," Matt said. He stood tall, his Golden Guardian pendant glowing in the light of the symbols. "We need rest."

Ouranos frowned. "Matthew--"

"We need it, Ouranos," Matt said. "Rest and food and just a little time to think." He tapped his wrist. "We've hardly slept or rested in days. We need to be as good as we can be to go after Theron."

Andre crossed his arms. "And what happens when he escapes the island?"

"He doesn't want that," Neil said. "He wants *me*. He wants more Drifters and Shadow Cast. We've stripped him of that. For now." He flicked his tail. "I hate to admit it, Matt, but you're right. We need to regroup, now that we have a second to catch our breath." He brushed off his sleeves… then noticed Natassa's blood. He flattened both ears, then took the jacket off. Just for a little bit. "I'll go see if Stefanos can whip something up."

"And let's get the cots someplace safe," Izzy said. "Take shifts sleeping, even if it's only for a few hours."

"Good idea," Matt said. "Let's get to work, everyone."

Neil sat on a clover hill, overlooking one of the large atria in the palace. Close enough that the ring of summons holding guard kept him safe, but far enough that he could see the stars and sit in relative solitude. Half of the team slept in cots, the other half munched on food Stefanos and his cooks managed to scramble up. His bucket list sat on the grass next to him. He wasn't quite ready to look at it.

Both Dami and Neil agreed that it'd be in bad taste to try and force a wedding now. Wait til the dust settled… and their hearts healed. As much as they could anyway.

Eris said she'd be happy to confirm Neil as Basileus in the meantime. Get him his Ei-Ei jewels. After Theron though. Nothing felt safe until Theron lay in the dirt. Even with everyone protecting him, they couldn't risk Theron interrupting the bonding ceremony.

He sighed and lay back on the clover, staring at the sky. A tiny tinge of blue barely lined the far horizon, though it was enough to dim the stars. Clouds slowly worked their way in, covering the rest. A common occurrence on Athánatos.

Maybe it'd rain. Natassa loved the rain.

"Basileus."

Neil sat up. The Black Cloak, Tymon, stood next to him, holding two plates. He eyed him, his green eyes shining.

Neil sighed and laid back down. "What?"

"You shouldn't be alone."

Neil kept his gaze on the sky a little bit longer. "Archángeli and Deo are right over there."

"You know what I mean."

Neil sighed. "...I know."

Tymon sat next to him. "Eat something."

Neil pressed his lips together. He sat up and took Tymon's plate.

Quiche. Because of course it is. With sausage and peppers and three types of cheese. Natassa's favorite. He took a delicate bite. Chewed it slowly. Let the spices and flavors mix in his mouth. Let it remind him of slow mornings with Natassa, with coffee and laughter and peace and intimacy.

He let himself drown. Just for a little.

"What's this?" Tymon took the piece of paper at Neil's side.

Neil swallowed hard. He fattened his ears. "A bucket list."

Tymon eyed him.

Neil raised an eyebrow, then chuckled a little. "Oh, right. Alien. It's a list of all the places I wanna go and things I wanna do before I kick the bucket." He waved vaguely at the paper. "Most of it included travel. The only travel I ever did was as a scared and beaten soldier. Wanted to see places that were healed. Hoping to take Natassa, Dami, and Philip with me." He shook his head. "That was already out the window when I agreed to become the Veil, but… seems even more pointless without Natassa."

Tymon lowered his head. "…I am so sorry."

Neil looked at him, tears pooling in his eyes. "You really tried everything to save her?"

Tymon nodded slowly. "Every attempt… every attempt made things worse. Sometimes half the Archons died, cutting off our attempts at fixing the Veil. Sometimes Dami *and* Natassa died. Sometimes she beat him… and his magic exploded with sharp rocks and ice, killing her and you anyway, destroying the Veil and leaving Athánatos vulnerable and ruined. Sometimes…" He fiddled with his hands. "Most times… most times just you died. The Veil vanished. This silent planet opened its ears and you can imagine the chaos that ensues. Philip… didn't take it well. Natassa goes mad with grief. Dami shuts down entirely, and never speaks again. All hope lost." He shook his head. "This was… the best outcome. And it kills me to say that." He shut his eyes tight, the black makeup making his face look like a skull. "And I realize that no matter what I say or what I do, you're still in pain. You still hate me. And you have every right to."

Neil sighed. "I don't hate you, Tymon."

Tymon opened his eyes, but wouldn't look at Neil. "…Thank you. Because I sure as hell hate myself."

"I know the feeling," Neil said. "Which is why I don't hate you. You have enough of that already." He pulled himself back up before he dove too deep into despair. "So," he said, taking a big bite this time. "Who's Arden?"

Tymon sat up in shock. "How'd you know that name?"

"Saw it in the Veil," Neil said. "Do all your Cloaks have Ei-Ei jewels? And how many of you are there? More than five?"

Tymon stared at the clover. He adjusted the mask a little and took a bite of the quiche. "Not important."

"Probably is," Neil said. "Might as well tell me. I'm gonna find out eventually."

Tymon paused mid-bite. He put the quiche on the plate and readjusted the mask. "Arden is another Azure."

"I got that," Neil said. "So who is she? Matt's grandma? His great aunt? A long-lost sister?"

"...His daughter."

Neil nearly dropped the plate. *"What?"*

Tymon took a long, slow breath. "I know everything seems bleak and hopeless now. But if anything can bring you hope, let it be Arden. Because she's proof that someday, eventually, everything will be okay."

Neil blinked. "Yeah... okay. I'll take your word for it." He paused, staring at his food. "So uh... who's her other parent?"

"Not Trecheon, if that's what you're hoping for," Tymon said. "But don't give up on them either."

They ate for a minute in silence. Neil stared at the grass. "She looked so... sad."

"The curse of a Cloak," Tymon said. "Though she chose that curse. All of us did. Except me." He turned to the stars. "But not everything is pain. She'll have loving parents who raise her, friends and family to grow up with, wonderful partners later in life, and… and once all this is over, she can be happy again."

Neil frowned. "Can you?"

Tymon stood. "Eat your food, then come down and rest. We've got a hell of a lot to do."

Neil flicked his tail. "Tymon."

Tymon looked at him.

"You told me taking this job meant you gave up your ability to choose."

Tymon nodded.

"You told me about Arden without hesitation," Neil said. "You're literally giving away the future like it means nothing."

"Yes," Tymon said. *"That* was a choice."

Neil narrowed his gaze. "Why?"

Tymon turned to him. He stared, his eyes glassy.

Then he walked down the hill to the palace.

The End of an Empire

Ouranos stared up as evening fell, painting the sky with purples and blues and dark rain clouds. Everyone who would not fight was safe in the palace. The rest of them waited on the clover lawn, itching for the moment when Archángeli returned with the order to strike. They no longer wore their wedding finery, instead trading it for fresh Defender uniforms. The royal chains they traded for Defender pendants. Not as a sign of defeat, but a sign of strength, and solidarity with each other.

It had taken far too long to find Theron after his bitter defeat, but finally, they had a location. They just had to get to him. Ouranos longed to get to him. Because Natassa's death had one positive among all the grief and despair.

He was no longer shackled. The Phonar had been released of their oath. He had his Soul Jewels back and his magic at full strength.

Nothing could keep him from ending his father's life. However he pleased.

A streak of soft blues cut through the angry red in his mind. Matt. He glanced at Ouranos, frowning.

Ouranos flattened his ears. This was a side of himself he did not know existed. Something rageful and… cruel.

Something his father was.

That did not sit well with him.

But… for now, just one time, he gave fully into it. Because he needed to. The only way to end his father was to match his rage.

Just be careful, Ouranos, Matt said in his head. *I don't want to lose you too.*

Ouranos could not bring himself to respond.

Neil walked up to them, sword in hand and knife on his belt. He wore his green jacket again, cleaned and free of blood. His royal chains lay draped across his shoulders. He glared, narrowing his gaze. "I want to fight with you."

Ouranos flicked an ear. "My brother, we have discussed this."

"I know and I don't friggin' care," Neil said. "That bastard *killed* Natassa. I deserve a chance to face him."

Trecheon gripped Neil's shoulder and looked him deep in the eye. "Neil. We need you here. Your people need you."

Neil glared. "I need *revenge.*"

"*Neil.*" Trecheon snapped. Neil flattened his ears. Trecheon narrowed his gaze and spoke quietly. "That's the assassin talking."

Neil frowned. His tail flicked.

"That's the war talking," Trecheon said in his normal voice. "That is years of pain and suffering and anger. That's not the Basileus who plays games with children and cooks with his subjects and loves so fiercely." He pulled Neil close. "That's not the Defender, Neil."

Neil's shoulders slumped.

"I know it's hard," Trecheon said. "It's really easy to give in to that revenge mindset. But that's how you make mistakes and get yourself killed. And we're not going to have any more death." He turned. "You got that, Matt?"

Matt paused, ears perked.

Trecheon walked up to him, pressing his face close to Matt's, their noses nearly touching. "You're a soldier. A Guardian. This is an act of war. Not an act of revenge." He hugged Matt tight. "Don't get yourself killed."

Matt stood still a moment, then pulled Trecheon close. Waves of reds, golds, and whites ran through Ouranos' mind. They felt like… love.

Ouranos wrinkled his snout. He should tell Matt as such. If they survived this.

Matt patted Trecheon's back then broke the hug. He stood tall, drawing up little tornadoes at his feet. "Alright. We have our tasks. Healers?" Trecheon, Sacha, and Leah stood close by. Sacha held Trecheon's hand, even though neither of them could feel it with their biomech. Matt turned. "Summoners?" Angus and Andre stood now, with the Phonar still at their heels. Ouranos was grateful for their continued support, however much longer it would last. "Mages?" Jaden stepped forward now, leading the remaining mages. Defenders, Athánatos Archons, Ana, Melaina, Dami, and Chadwick. He nodded to Matt. Matt took a deep breath. "And finally… us." He turned.

Ouranos stood next to Zeke, Alexina, and Izzy. Matt's bonded partners. Matt had separated them into their own group, intending to draw out their strength as one. They were a good mix. Four elemental mages and a healer with a death hammer. Izzy was still… hesitant, Ouranos could tell. Uncomfortable with the bond. But her rage at Theron outweighed the discomfort.

Despite the pain, the longing, the ache, Ouranos finally felt confident.

Theron's death was inevitable.

Baltazar came rushing up to the group. "My lord, Theron approaches!"

Neil stood straight up, ears perked.

Ouranos' blood ran cold. "He is here?"

Baltazar nodded. "With Judgement and an army of Cast, though it is unclear if they are true Cast or Judgement's Cast."

Neil closed his eyes a moment. "Judgement's Cast," he said. "They don't have names attached to them. Easy pickings."

"Let him come," Matt said. "We're ready for him."

"Almost," Dami said. He walked up to Neil. "My love… give me your sword."

Neil frowned. "Dami--"

"It is not a request," Dami said. "It is to ensure you do not attempt to enter the battlefield looking for revenge." His face softened. "Please, my love. I have already lost my closest friend. I cannot bear to lose my husband as well."

Neil splayed his ears. He stepped forward, drew Dami close, and kissed him. Then he pulled back and passed the sword to him. "This applies to you too, Dami. Don't get killed."

"I won't let him," Matt said. "Trust me."

The distant, mad cackling shrieks of the Shadow Cast filled the air, sending chills down Ouranos' spine.

Matt formed fists. "Eyes up, Defenders." He pounded his fist into his hand. "Let's get the bastard."

They charged into battle.

The setting sun outlined their enemies in sharp contrast. Judgement and her Cast. Theron and his elemental magic.

Ouranos' fingers itched to strip Theron's life away.

"Stick to the plan!" Matt said. "Everyone has their roles. *Do not deviate*. Let's go!" Trecheon, Sacha, and Leah rushed for the nearby woods near the Four Sisters' Grove, to wait and heal when necessary. Jaden pulled his team and the summoners toward Judgement, shouting battle cries and holding their attention.

Matt turned his team toward their true target. Theron.

Theron turned on them, teeth bared, and shot a barrage of elemental magic at them – lightning, ice, fire and stones. But Matt had predicted this.

Formation one! he called out mentally. *Element deflection!*

Ouranos dashed right, headed for the stones. He called on his own magic and batted each one away, returning a barrage of his own.

His pack did the same. Zeke collected ice and flung it at their enemy. Matt caught the fire in tornadoes, sending them zooming back. Izzy followed behind Ouranos, smashing the rocks with her hammer, and shooting them at Theron, holding a shield around them as best she could.

Alexina carried the most rage. She gathered his lightning in her fists and charged, electricity rippling through her fur.

Theron stepped back, hesitant, his magic flying wildly above his head.

A dozen Cast emerged from the ground catching the elements meant for Theron. But they were false Cast. Each one fell to the magic they stopped.

Second wave! Matt called. *Ouranos, Zeke, stage 3! Fire and ice!*

Zeke threw a beam of ice Matt's way and Ouranos followed with a fire flare. Matt caught each in tornadoes, spinning them through the emerging Cast and bearing down on Theron.

Four more Cast appeared and wrapped around Theron, dragging him to the left, leaving half a dozen more behind to rip through Matt's magic.

"Damnit!" Matt called. "Alexina!"

Alexina stopped and drew her hands up, forming a lightning storm like Ouranos had never seen. Matt held his hands up and using his wind magic, he and Alexina whipped the lightning storm into a massive phoenix and threw it at him. The Cast surrounded him, weakening the phoenix, but eventually it broke through, crashing hard into Theron, sending him flying. He tumbled on the clover, landing on his belly, then stirred, shaking his head. Steam wafted off his fur and a rotting smell of flesh filled the air.

Now! Matt called and the group charged as one, magic flying.

Theron stood, fire in his eyes. He shot his hands forward, blasting them with magic. And this time he had learned.

He hit Izzy first, smashing her with an ice spike. She deflected the spiked end, but the inertia knocked her down anyway, leaving her bloody and coughing on the grass. A fireball whizzed toward Zeke, which he dodged, but Theron followed it with a wave of water and wind, washing Zeke away toward Judgement, effectively removing him from the battlefield. Lightning fell from the sky, chasing Alexina, and while she dodged the first few, one finally hit… though it hit a shield. Matt had shielded her. The bolt did not directly hit, but the shockwave from the shield destruction knocked her down anyway, leaving her stunned on the clover.

Ouranos snarled. He refused to go down like this. *Matthew, shield me!* Matt did in a quick burst of purple and green just as Ouranos slammed into Theron, knocking them to the ground. Ouranos hovered over him, formed a sharp ice spike in his hand and stabbed at his father.

Theron barely dodged, pushing hard on Ouranos' shoulders, magic flying everywhere. "You will never win, Prínkipas!"

"That is *your* delusion!" Ouranos called and stabbed again. Theron blocked with a stone slab, but Ouranos pushed it aside and stabbed again, grazing Theron's shoulder. Theron roared. He blasted Ouranos with fire, but Matt's shield held. "I tire of this!" He stabbed again, barely missing Theron's head. "Lay still and *die!*"

This time the ice spear connected, digging deep into Theron's upper chest. Theron roared… not in pain, but in anger. He pulled the spear free and smashed Ouranos' head with it, finally forcing him off. Ouranos rolled a few feet away.

Theron stood, covering the wound with his hand. "Look at you, Prínkipas. Anger and grief control you. Look at the destruction your grief causes." He spat blood on the clover. "You truly are my son."

Ouranos stopped, his eyes widening. "I…" He shook his head. "I am not you. This is to be used once, to rid the world of your *evil*."

Theron scoffed, wiping blood from his mouth. "I told myself the same thing when I turned Melaina."

Rage burst from Ouranos' chest and he charged Theron, roaring.

Theron threw a hand forward, blasting twin beams of fire and ice at Ouranos. Ouranos skidded to a halt, holding up his hands. The shield held.

Soon Matt was at his side, pressing magic into the shield. "He's too strong," Matt said. "I think he's drawing power from Judgement. I can't fight him and hold the shield up at the same time."

Ouranos coughed, his limbs aching. "My magic is… draining."

Matt frowned. "Then hold here. I'll get help." He closed his eyes, filling Ouranos' mind with bright blue, like the sky, clearly calling his other allies.

But even now, Ouranos felt his strength waning through the bond. The Aether had done its damage and Matt was not yet at full strength.

He prayed to the Sisters for help he knew would not come.

Neil crossed the clover lawn on the outskirts of the battle, relying on darkness to hide him.

He couldn't stand it. He couldn't sit buried in the throne room while his friends, his *family,* risked everything to take down Theron. He had to do something. This was why he was Basileus.

Though what the hell he was supposed to do with no magic, no summons, and no sword was anyone's guess. All he had was a hunting dagger, which he pilfered when no one was looking. Mostly for skinning, not for combat. Fat lot of good it'd do against an eldritch demon.

But he had to try. Or at the very least… watch.

He wanted to see Natassa's killer fall.

Jaden and his team clearly struggled with the Cast onslaught. Magic flew everywhere, though admittedly it was hard to tell what was going on in the dark, especially with the flashes of plasma ruining his night vision.

Trecheon and the other healers were in a clump of trees near the Four Sister's Grove, waiting for orders. Well, they were supposed to be. Neil watched Theron fry several of Matt's team, and both Sacha and Leah had taken to the field, going after Zeke and Alexina. Izzy was already at Alexina's side, helping Sacha lift her and take her to the Grove. Alexina growled and waved her arm, trying to get back to Theron, though she was clearly injured and needed healing. But at least she was alive.

"Neil!" Trecheon hissed. Neil turned toward the grove. Trecheon snarled. "What the hell are you doing here? Go back!"

Neil pointed to the battle. "With all that mess? Hell no."

Trecheon glared. "Fine. But no heroics." He glanced over the field. Sacha and Izzy had nearly made it back with Alexina. Leah had Zeke sitting up, but he was clearly disoriented, so she also helped him toward the Grove.

Neil frowned. This wasn't supposed to happen. How'd this go so wrong, so fast?

And where were Matt and Ouranos?

A quick survey of the battlefield gave him his answer. Theron stood in the clover field, blasting twin beams of magic at them. The magic flew in all directions, held back by Matt's shield, but they were pinned. There was no way they'd get free.

"Neil!" Sacha shouted. "What the hell are you doing here?"

Neil glared. "Don't tell me to go back."

Izzy glared back. "Don't do anything stupid. We--"

Someone screamed. Everyone turned back to Matt and Ouranos.

The shield had finally given way and smashed into the pair, sending them flying.

Izzy gasped. "Matt!" She moved toward them, dragging her leg.

"Izzy, no!" Sacha pulled her back. "You need healing first!"

"Someone's got to go after them!" Leah said. "He'll *kill them!*"

"*It's suicide,*" Sacha said. "I don't know what the hell he's got going for him, but he's twice the mage he was before. None of us here have the strength."

Neil watched helpless. But then Black Cloak's words came back to him. "When you choose your death, your power will complete the spell and make the Veil permanent again." One phrase stood out. *When you choose your death.* He pressed his lips together. The Cloak didn't mean when he chose to release his Ei-Ei jewels.

He meant now.

His body buzzed. He meant *now*.

"Trecheon…" Neil licked his lips, trying to calm his mind. "Look after Philip for me."

Trecheon stared at him. "What?"

Neil didn't answer. *For Athánatos.* He stood, pulling the knife from his belt. Trecheon's eyes widened. *For Dami. For Philip. For Trecheon.* Neil ran forward, knife in hand.

Trecheon called out to him.

He almost stopped. It would have been easy to stop. Remember that he still had Dami, Philip, Trecheon, his friends, his family, and Athánatos. He still had all of them to live for. But that voice pounded in his ears again. *For Natassa.*

This was why he was here.

This is where he belonged.

He ran faster, pushing his legs, closing his ears to the world around him. He couldn't stop. The moment you do is the moment you falter. The moment you hesitate. The moment you *think.*

And if you actually think about what you're doing, you can't do it.

As far as magic hits went, he couldn't imagine one better.

Theron had his back turned, unaware. And Neil had the element of surprise. He pulled on all his experience as a soldier, a swordsman, and an assassin, then leaped, knife over his head, holding it tight in both hands. He stabbed it down into Theron's spine at the base of the neck with all his might.

Theron threw his head back.

The knife wailed as it dug into flesh and bone, shooting blood and spinal fluid into the air and all over Neil's jacket. Theron let out a shocked, high-pitched gasp, curling his back in, eyes wide with fear and pain.

Tymon's words beat around Neil's head. *His magic exploded with sharp rocks and ice.*

Neil leapt back. For a split, fleeting, perfect second, everything was fine. *I did it! I—*

Not fast enough.

Ice spikes and stones ripped out of Theron's back in a final burst of magic as he fell to the ground. The sharp tips pierced through Neil's body like a thousand arrows. Arms, legs, torso, even an eye, spilling blood everywhere, making everything red, overwhelming his mind. Every inch was pain, blinding him, making his ears ring, his heart stop, his breathing hitch, chasing away every thought in his mind but intense, overpowering pain a thousand times worse than the Veil spell.

But for an instant, he remembered Ouranos' words. A soul for a soul. His thoughts crystalized. One last thought.

For... Alexina.

Then the pain stopped.

THE MAGIC HIT

"NEIL!"

Trecheon's mind exploded with discordant color, blurring his eyesight, deafening his ears, locking his legs in place. He stared at the bloody sight before him, a mess of images he couldn't quite interpret, trying to piece it together.

Blood.

Ice.

Rain.

Death.

Judgement howled, throwing her hands and wings up, her voice growing louder and higher pitched until she finally popped in a rain of black sludge and dust. All her Cast vanished instantly. Jaden and his team stood looking around, dumbfounded. The summon's voice faded.

She was gone.

That meant… Theron…

But the scene wouldn't align. It just floated in Trecheon's vision as… broken fragments… Who screamed Neil's name? Did he? Or--

Alexina wailed next to him, gripping her face. He turned to her just as she pulled her hands back. She stared at her palms. All three Ei-Ei jewel sets lined her face. She shot a glance at Trecheon, her pupils restored, tears streaming down her face. Like Ouranos.

The loud grind of stone on stone pelted his ears and he turned back to the Four Sisters statues. Only two Sisters remained.

But a third statue, the Veil, reformed before his eyes. Pebbles and stones melted together into a stylized puma, shirtless, wearing the traditional Athánatos pants. A thin Veil covered his face down to his feet. He held a sword aloft, and a thin, but distinct chain had been carved along his neck. The rain affected tears on his face.

Lightning ripped through Trecheon's heart, shocking him to reality.

"NEIL, NO!" Izzy. She rushed from the safety of the grove to the disaster before them, her hands and wrists already black with elixir, her Gem alight and whining.

A burst of energy shot through Trecheon's legs and he ran for Neil, his heart pounding in his deafened ears. His Gem glowed brightly, magic licking at his fingertips. He passed Izzy and slid on his knees next to Neil, pressing his metal fingers deep in the wounds.

But nothing reacted.

Come on, come on, don't you dare die on me, you idiot, don't you dare! He pressed harder, magic burning through the tips of his quills. *You can't leave me here! You can't--*

"Out of the way!" Izzy slid next to Trecheon, pushed him aside, and dug her elixir-soaked fingers into Neil's flesh. Her whole body glowed

green as the magic worked through her. "This isn't happening, Neil, do you hear me? It's not!" Her Gem's whine pierced Trecheon's ears.

Trecheon sat back on his knees, numb. His eyes burned, but for whatever reason he couldn't cry. He could only stare as Izzy's attempts proved as futile as his own. "Izzy--"

"*NO!*" Izzy screamed. "We've lost too much, damn it! We've lost *too much, we're not losing Neil too!*"

Trecheon blinked, his vision clouded. He shook himself and opened his mouth to speak.

One of the smaller ice spikes popped out of Neil's body, leaving fresh, pink flesh and tan fur behind.

Trecheon's eyes widened.

Izzy laughed, almost in hysterics. "See? See? Can't leave us that easy, puma!" She pressed harder, the elixir rushing up to her elbows.

Slowly, bit by bit, the ice and rock spikes popped out of Neil's body, landing on the clover with sharp hisses and dull thuds, leaving healthy flesh behind.

Hope welled up in Trecheon's chest. "Izzy, you're doing it, *you're doing it!*" Others rushed up next to them – Roscoe, Darvin, Sami, Ouranos, Alexina, Matt, everyone. They hovered around them, eyes wide with hope.

All but Alexina. She threw herself in Jaden's arms, sobbing on his shoulder.

Trecheon almost snapped at her. Why the hell was she crying? Did she *want* to destroy everyone's hope? Izzy was saving him!

But Izzy grinded her teeth, tears rolling down her cheeks. "It's *not enough!*" The green glow around her exploded outward and she yelled, pushing harder. The ice spikes spit out quicker and more violently, vanishing in the air in a hiss of steam before ever hitting the ground. The wounds healed instantly – she even gave him his eye back. She had restored everything.

But he wasn't breathing. He wouldn't move.

Despair fought against hope in Trecheon's heart. He pressed his hands to Neil's fully repaired body again, desperate to help.

But there was nothing. No signs of life. His body wouldn't respond to Trecheon's magic. Trecheon's breathing grew frantic. "Izzy--"

"It's *NOT ENOUGH!*" Izzy pushed again, but with no wounds to heal, her magic glow spread through the clover lawn, and the plants responded instead. The clover expanded exponentially, flowers popped out of the dirt, vines of unknown origin grew instantly in intricate patterns all around the body.

Then Matt collapsed next to them, gripping his chest and gasping, his Gem's colors fading in its holster. He coughed loudly, violently shaking. *"Izzy--"*

Izzy shot her head up at Matt, and the glow stopped instantly. The elixir vanished into Izzy's fur and she covered her snout with her hands. Tears streamed down her face. "M-Matt, I am so *sorry*, I d-didn't… I didn't…" She dissolved into sobs and curled up in a ball. Roscoe was at her side in an instant, holding her close, quiet, crying, shaking. She buried her face in Roscoe's neck. "I-I'm a healer… I-I'm a healer… why am I even h-here if I c-can't…" She melted into Roscoe's arms.

Leah rushed up and slid next to Neil next, pressing her hands against him. She stared blankly, holding her breath, eyes glistening. "I… he… There's just…" She looked up and met Trecheon's gaze. "…Nothing." Zeke knelt next to her, holding her tight, though all she could do was stare.

Ana rushed forward now, her face dripping with tears. "No, no, this wasn't supposed to happen…" She laid a shaking hand on his chest. "You were supposed to beat this…"

A flash of black caught Trecheon's eye. He turned.

The Black Cloak. Standing there, solemn, his green eyes shining.

Trecheon stared up at him. He should be screaming. *This is your fault. You knew this was coming and you didn't stop it. What is wrong with you?* But his mouth wouldn't move.

But Jaden's did.

Jaden marched up to the Black Cloak, glaring, standing so close that he almost touched his nose to the silver mask. *"Fix this."*

The Cloak blinked tears out of his eyes. "I can't."

"You're a Draso-damned time traveler," Jaden spat. *"Fix this!"*

"I *can't,"* the Cloak said. "I can't, I…" He held his head and turned away. "I can't…"

Trecheon sat back, still kneeling, staring at Neil. His brain refused to connect things properly. His body was healed, but he… still died? He and Izzy had healed him, but he wouldn't breathe?

Why was he laying here staring at the sky when the only sign of violence left was ripped and blood-stained clothing?

…Why did Neil sacrifice himself?

The magic hit. That big hit that'll change the world. That one kill that will save thousands of lives. That old assassin lie.

But Neil got it. He finally got that magic hit. The biggest hit he could have ever gotten.

Real, physical, excruciating pain burst from Trecheon's chest and tore through all his extremities, even pulsing through his phantom limbs. His fur stood on end, his arms and legs ached, his body buzzed.

This couldn't be *real.*

Someone wrapped their arms around him. Then a second someone. Four arms folded tightly around him, anchoring him to reality. His brain searched for more anchors. Their soft, warm breath against his face. Their poorly controlled sobs in his ears. The warm, wet, tear-stained fur on his neck. The gentle, familiar scents wafting past his nose, drowning the sharp scents of blood and magic.

Sacha.

Matt.

His brain searched for meaning. Why didn't they say anything? Someone should say something. Anything. Anything to drown the sobbing all around him.

Neil moved.

For a wild, elated second, hope gripped him again. But when he looked up, all he saw was Ouranos carefully pulling Neil into his arms. Leaves, clover, and flowers clung to Neil's body and floated down in a colorful display, mixing with the fading rain around them.

Absently, Trecheon blinked at him. "What are you doing?"

Ouranos stood to his full height, his Soul Jewels shining, and his pupils clouded with tears. "He was a Basileus of Athánatos," he said. "And he will be treated as such. And… Natassa… she needs company while they rest…"

Trecheon stared. He briefly glanced at Theron's mangled body. Neil's knife stuck straight up out of his neck, the fur soaked through with blood. Blood pooled under him and ran up like veins through the melting ice spikes.

Ouranos glanced down too. He pressed his lips together, furrowing his brow and flicking back his ears with building anger. Lightning and fire rippled through his fur. But a second later his face softened and he shook his head, pushing back the wild magic.

"He never…" Trecheon's mind stalled. "He never… He and Natassa didn't get to marry…He didn't get the jewels…"

"And yet he was a better Basileus than Theron ever was," Ouranos said, his voice cracking. "Because he belonged here." He paused, as if trying to compose himself. "He will receive his jewels in death. They will marry in Draso's Palace. We will honor that marriage here." He took a long, shuddering breath. "And our people will mourn." He turned toward the palace.

Damianos stood in front of him.

Ouranos paused, frowning. "Dami…"

"Let me take him," Damianos said. His quiet voice was surprisingly steady, though he held himself stiff and took obviously deliberate, slow breaths.

Ouranos' shoulders slumped. "My friend… are you sure?"

"He has carried me for many years now," Dami said, his voice breaking. He reached over and gently closed Neil's eyes. "I… should be willing to carry him one last time."

Ouranos furrowed his brow. He bowed his head, then leaned forward for Dami to take Neil.

Dami gently pulled Neil's lifeless body into his arms and pulled him close, resting Neil's head on his shoulder. He pressed their foreheads together.

Trecheon stood, his legs shaking. Sacha and Matt stood with him, supporting him.

Dami closed his eyes and tears streamed down his face, his eyebrows knitted together and his chin quivering. He pressed a long, loving kiss to Neil's forehead. "Rest now, my Emerald Prince. The Veil is strong. Your people are safe." He took a shuddering breath, struggling to finish the last sentence. "And we will see each other again." Then he turned toward the palace and started the slow march through the clover lawn.

Dully, Trecheon followed, dragging his feet.

Matt took one glance at Theron, then met Ouranos' eyes. Ouranos glared, only for a second. Some secret message between the two of them.

They left Theron's body on the grass.

REMEMBER YOUR NAME

"Our Basilea and Basileus are gone."

Ouranos stood on an elevated stage in the crystal gardens, near the Ruler's Walkway, the path of statues featuring Athánatos rulers of their past and present. The gardens glistened in the early morning light, making the Ei-Ei jewels on the statues glow and sparkle. Athánatos surrounded the stage – Archons, their families, sentries, citizens. Everyone here to celebrate the wedding, plus more. Sniffles, quiet sobbing, and the occasional wail filled the air. No one spoke, but no one was silent either. The pain was too great.

Despite the days since the unfinished marriage, many still wore their wedding finery. Some, particularly the Archons, even repainted and repaired their outfits. Misty took her place as the newly christened Archon Mistik, wearing a grand and beautiful wedding outfit, her body paint sparkling in the afternoon sunbeams, filtering through the parting clouds. A gesture Ouranos would have to thank them all for later, once he had the strength.

It took every scrap of strength he had left just to stand.

He took a deep breath, trying to gather his thoughts. Briefly, he glanced at the marble stand on the end of the path of statues. The base where Natassa and Neil's statues would rest. These statues would normally be erected to celebrate their rise in royal status. A mark of their marriage.

Now it was for a funeral. Their last testament.

He flexed his fingers, then turned back to his people. "Our people have long been without a stable leader. But then we had Natassa." He waved a hand to the base.

Archon Bouldrik stepped forward. She waved her hands, and a bright, shining boulder appeared on the stand. With intricate finger movements, she chipped away at the boulder with her magic, forming Natassa's likeness. Standing tall, chin up, determined smile on her face.

Ouranos sucked in a breath, fighting back tears. "Natassa valued life. She believed in justice. She led with kindness and joy, and she went to great lengths to serve the ones she loved. Even so far as sacrificing herself for two great loves – for Neil, who she believed represented a new hope for our people. And for me… In her death, she restored my soul." Ouranos ran a finger down his face, tapping the Soul Jewels. "Though I would rather have my sister than my soul."

Bouldrik finished the statue, chipping away the final details, and boring tiny holes around her eyes for the Ei-Ei jewels.

Ouranos turned to Izzy and Zeke. Izzy nodded back, tears flowing, as Melaina instructed her in setting Natassa's Ei-Ei jewels into the statue. Zeke followed her example, stoic and calm, though his eyes glistened. Like the Archons, Zeke had refreshed his wedding finery, and held his head high as he honored his *theía*. His royal chain draped across his drooping shoulders.

It made Ouranos' heart ache to watch, and he instead turned to the Ei-Ei jewels.

Yellow, for the mind.

Red, for the body.

And… crystal clear, for the soul. Representing death. The Soul Jewels would no longer carry the color of their master's eyes.

Tradition dictated that the deceased's closest friend or family put the Ei-Ei jewels to rest. For Natassa, that decision was… hard. So many fit that role. Ouranos took comfort in this. He could only hope all of them would bear such a burden at death. Thankfully, Izzy and Zeke made the decision easier by stepping up.

Izzy leaned into Zeke when they finished. He wrapped an arm around her and together they walked back toward Leah and Roscoe.

Archon Bouldrik walked forward again, forming a new boulder next to Natassa. Ouranos braced himself.

Dami moved next to Ouranos. "Neil was selfless. Sometimes to his detriment," Dami said. "He also valued life, though he struggled to find the value in his own. But he proved over and over that he intended to use his life to protect the innocent. Without any knowledge of Athánatos or its people, he flung himself at the enemy, time and time again. He… he loved fiercely and unconditionally. A love not only for myself and Natassa, but also for the Athánatos people. Particularly for its children."

Ouranos glanced behind him. Dozens of children crowded near the front of the masses, many of them clinging to books. *Tiger and Phoenix Learn to Dance.* One of Neil's favorites to read to them.

Philip let out a dark, choked sound. He wiped at his nose and moved closer to Trecheon. Trecheon rested a hand on his shoulder.

Bouldrik finished Neil's statue. Standing tall, as an equal, with Natassa, his hands on her shoulders, his familiar, welcoming grin on his face. As it should be.

Dami waved Trecheon and Philip over. Trecheon tilted his head, but he followed. Ouranos held Neil's woven bracelet with the Ei-Ei jewels in place. "Neil never received the Ei-Ei jewels he was entitled to. But we will honor him with them anyway." He carefully plucked the jewels from the bracelet. "If you two would do the honors. I will show you how to place them."

Trecheon flattened his ears, but he nodded. With Damianos' help, he and Philip placed the jewels around Neil's eyes. Bouldrik took the bracelet from Trecheon and situated it on Neil's wrist, a permanent adornment. Philip stared numbly at the statue when they finished.

Ouranos stared too. He looked… whole. It fit him well. A shame… a shame he never got the full strength of the jewels. Like everything he had, he would have wielded them for good.

Eris moved through the crowd now, holding Neil and Natassa's jewel chains. She carefully placed them over the statues' heads, letting them rest on their shoulders as if they were alive and ready to lead.

"One more," Matt said, stepping forward. He held two Defender pendants. Not black like was standard, but gold and shining. He placed them around the statues' necks. They hung just above the royal chains. "Neil and Natassa were as good as any Guardian I've known. I… I'm granting them each the title of Golden Guardian. A title well earned."

Ouranos breathed slowly, then turned back to the crowd. "The first job of any Basilea or Basileus is to protect their people. Neil and Natassa lived that to the very end." He took a deep breath, drawing on the sadly familiar final poem of the funeral liturgy. "We honor them here."

"*Tous timoúme edó,*" the Athánatos replied as one, shaking voice.

Ouranos continued. "Draso honor them in his Palace."

"O Drásos tous timáei sto Paláti tou."

"Sisters, grant us peace."

"Adelfés, dóste mas eiríni."

Everyone fell silent for several seconds. But then Damianos lifted his voice and sang. Ouranos recognized the song instantly, though Dami sang it in English. An Athánatos lullaby, for peace. As he sang it, Athánatos voices joined him, in English and their native tongue, lifting up to the skies.

"Lay still, my joy
The night is cool
Lay still, my heart
The sun returns 'ere the morrow.

"The Veil holds us
Lay still, lay still
The Veil remains,
Lay still, lay still.

"Lay still, my sweet
The Sisters protect us
Lay still, my heart
We shall dance another day
Together."

Ouranos wept unapologetically during the song, though he did not dare to try to sing along, lest his voice break with his heart. When the song finished, he wiped his face clean and turned to the crowd.

"I have heard the rumors among you, so let me confirm," he said. "Natassa died facing down the mad king and saving Neil so he could complete our Veil. Neil later died fighting Theron, taking a mighty risk to save myself and Matthew when Theron worked to overpower us. They did what we could not – end the mad king's reign."

Angry murmurs rippled through the crowd and more than one called out *katharízo!* A purge. Something Ouranos secretly hoped would be called for. The crowd grew louder, more insistent, until Ouranos held up his hands.

"A purge of a Basileus is a grave decision," he said. "We do not do this lightly. But after all Theron hurt, a purge feels not only right, but indeed necessary." He turned to Theron's statue, old and chipped, and lacking the Ei-Ei jewels that a deceased Basileus should be blessed with.

He would not get such an honor.

Holding tight to his emotions lest he explode the statue's head completely, Ouranos called on his stone magic and beat back the features on Theron's face. He smoothed out the nose, gouged out the eyes, pressed the lips into the snout, and even compressed the quills into nothingness, leaving only a blank, shapeless head behind. With a will, he dug an angry cross into the stone where the face once was. The ultimate shame for one purged. No face. No likeness to remember him.

Ouranos stepped back from his handiwork, wiping sweat off his brow and taking slow, steady breaths to cool his anger. He stared into the shapeless face.

"*Na min thymátai kaneís to ónomá sou,*" he said quietly. "May no one remember your name."

THE MAGE KING'S WAKE

Trecheon stood still and quiet, still stuck in that deep dissociation after Neil's funeral.

Theron's body lay outstretched on a marble table, cleaned and peaceful, soaked in some awful smelling liquid, matting his fur and quills. Trecheon's blood boiled. He looked far too peaceful considering everything he had done. All he had hurt.

Sacha curled up against Trecheon's side, an arm wrapped across his waist. She lay her head on his shoulder, sniffling quietly. He rubbed her arm, pressed a kiss to her forehead, then glanced around the room for a distraction before he started crying himself.

Ouranos had gathered quite a group here. All the Defenders, Ouranos' entire family, all the Archons and several sentries, most of their mainland allies…

Philip…

The poor kit flopped back and forth between loud, angry grief, quiet sobbing, and full dissociation. At first, he wanted nothing to do with anyone, but eventually he gravitated toward Trecheon, of all people.

Trecheon welcomed it with open arms. Philip had lost too much. The last of his family.

The moment Philip noticed Trecheon in the room, he slumped toward him and stood next to him, their shoulders touching. Trecheon wrapped an arm around him too. Neither of them spoke, but Neil's words ran through his mind. *If something happens to me, look after Philip for me.*

Trecheon didn't fully know what that looked like yet. But he planned to step up no matter what.

Ouranos walked into the room pushing an ornate cart with a bowl of dust and a lit torch. He stood between the crowd and Theron's body, then took a deep breath.

"I know the Athánatos understand why we are here," Ouranos said. "But for our friends and allies, let me explain an Athánatos wake." He positioned the bowl and picked up the torch. "A wake is different from a funeral. Funerals are formal affairs, open to the public, and a chance for everyone to mourn publicly. A wake is more intimate. It is open only to the people who the deceased touched the most… for good or for ill."

Philip choked, crossing his arms and turning away, his ears flat against his head.

"Wakes are private," Ouranos said. "Nothing you say here will ever be repeated outside these walls." He turned and lay the torch on Theron's chest, instantly catching the body on fire. Philip winced and turned away. Ouranos turned back to them. "When a body is burned, it is a sign that the deceased had a powerful impact. When they are burned exposed, without a sheet to cover them, this signifies that that impact did great harm. Though we call for his name to be forgotten, those he hurt the most wish to remember his face and the harm he caused, to honor those harmed, and to make an effort to never let that harm happen again. Burning uncovered is a consequence of that harm. It is the ultimate shame in death."

Philip let out a tiny sob. Trecheon rubbed his back, fighting tears again.

Ouranos adjusted the bowl of dust on the rolling table. "This is *kátharsi* – catharsis. Anyone who wishes to speak their mind about the deceased may take a handful of the dust, say whatever they wish to say, then toss the dust in the flames. This signifies the ending of a relationship, good or bad." He dipped a finger in the dust and rubbed it into his fingers. "There is a reason why *kátharsi* and *katharízo* – catharsis and purge – originate from the same word. It is sometimes cathartic to purge someone from our minds." He lifted his head. "There is no putting on airs here, nor will you be judged for your words. If you wish to scream, to cry, to curse, or to condemn, you are welcome to. No one's voice holds more value than any other's. In the same stroke, no one is obligated to speak either, nor are you obligated to stay and watch."

Trecheon raised a hand. "...Are we having one of these for Neil and Natassa?"

Ouranos smiled sadly. "We are, yes. They shall be burned together. Archon Electrik and his partner have offered to host that one. He said... he said he wanted it to be more like a party, based on something Neil once told him. Neil and Natassa will be covered and blessed with *chrónos* – an accelerant that speeds up the burning process, as a sign of dignity. It will make the flames burn violet."

Trecheon sniffled but nodded.

"That wake will be tomorrow," Ouranos said. "Today... I thought we needed *kátharsi*. Dispel our anger before a celebration. However sad that celebration may be." He took a deep breath. "The pyre today will likely last at least three hours. No one is expected to stay here that long, though you may if you wish." He bowed to all of them. *"Ston eléfthero chróno sas, me tin epilogí sas.* At your leisure, by your choice." He took a spot among the crowd next to his family.

Trecheon patted Philip's shoulder and gave Sacha a squeeze, his mind working overtime. All his thoughts, his feelings, his anger could barely catch footing as it roiled around in his brain, trying to find the exact phrase, the exact wording that would fix this.

Not that anything would ever fix this. Nothing he said would bring Neil back.

Maybe he shouldn't even bother.

But then Matt stepped forward. He took a handful of sand and stared at the flames. Trecheon bit his lip, bracing himself for the righteous anger he knew Matt so well for. Matt took a deep breath.

"Thank you."

Trecheon's ears shot up and everyone in the room, even Philip, turned and faced Matt.

Matt didn't flinch. He rubbed the dust between his fingers. "Thank you for bringing Ouranos and Natassa into our lives. Thank you for giving Izzy and me a chance to prove we can be Guardians. Thank you for humbling me through your son." He turned to Ouranos. "My life would be considerably bleaker without him."

Ouranos smiled, wiping at a tear.

Matt turned back to the fire. "Thank you for bringing me Trecheon and Zeke." He glanced back at them both. "I don't even know if we'd have them if it wasn't for you. And I can't imagine life without them."

Trecheon's heart skipped a beat. Sacha gave him a tight squeeze and kissed the side of his head.

Matt sighed and turned back again. "I wish all these wonderful things didn't have to come with so much pain and death. I wish you hadn't fallen so deep into grief that you caused so much destruction. I wish… that I could have met Ouranos, Natassa, Zeke, Neil, and Trecheon and all the friends and allies we've found here, naturally, with joy. Even though I don't see how I could have." He took the dust and threw it into the fire. It flared up in a thousand tiny embers. "I hope you've found peace now." He dusted off his hands, then walked over and gave Ouranos a long, deep hug. Then he found Zeke and did the same.

Finally he turned to Trecheon. Trecheon hugged him first, burying his face in Matt's chest, wishing he had any words as powerful as Matt's.

Matt snuggled against Trecheon. "I meant that," he said quietly, just for the two of them. "You're the universe to me… I hope you know that."

Trecheon gripped him tight, his chest swelling and his eyes burning with tears. He tried speaking, but the words stuck. He had to hope Matt got the message without a Gem bond. He took Matt's squeeze to mean he did.

Ouranos stepped forward now. He took a handful of dust. "I wish… I wish you had been the father I had imagined as a child. I wish I never would have seen the true quilar you turned out to be." He pressed his dust-filled fist to his forehead. "But I am grateful you have unwittingly brought me friends, family, and support to work through the pain you caused. Something you sorely needed. Now… now I do not have to worry I will become you as I face the same grief you once did." He tossed the dust into the pyre.

One by one, they stepped forward. Baltazar spoke long and loudly about all the pain Theron caused Athánatos. Melaina quietly wept, speaking in broken sentences, wishing for a father she never had. Damianos only whispered in his native tongue, which Trecheon took to be quiet grief at first, until he caught Zeke and Leah discussing his angry, violent curses. Andre viciously grabbed a handful and threw it in haphazardly with a "Good riddance, you damn bastard."

Izzy was quiet, speaking only of her grief about losing Neil. She sobbed unapologetically, pausing briefly to talk about how Neil had become her best friend, something that made Trecheon's heart ache. Leah, surprisingly, loudly cursed him in Japanese, taking a page out of Dami's book. She ended her tirade by throwing herself at Zeke and Andre. Sacha, for her part, said nothing, but she held the handful of dust for a good five minutes before tossing it in, little bit by little bit, watching the flames reach for the ceiling, entirely and utterly silent. She slumped back to Trecheon, wrapped her arms around him, and hugged him tight for a very long time. He held her close, feeling her shake as she fought back sobs.

Alexina's hurt the most. She scooped up a handful of dust and ground it in her palm, glaring. Her own quills caught fire with her magic, sending little embers into the air around her.

"I hate you," she said with such vicious poison that Trecheon could practically taste it. "I hate all you took from us. I hate that you let your grief over Mother's death rule you so poorly that you destroyed countless lives as a result. I hate that despite your death, there is no justice for the damage you caused. It is a permanent scar on Athánatos and the world. I hate… I hate that you know peace while the rest of us lay here, broken and hurting."

She threw the dust into the flames… then burst into tears. She slowly made her way to Matt. "I-I am sorry… my outburst undoes all your g-good will… I…"

Matt shook his head and pulled her into a hug. "Not at all, Alexina. Not at all. We all mourn differently." She sobbed with him for several minutes before thanking him quietly and wandering toward Jaden. Jaden held her tight, kissing her forehead and rubbing her back.

Five minutes passed in utter silence. Philip looked up at Trecheon. "Are you gonna say anything?"

Trecheon frowned at him. "Do you want me to?"

Philip flicked his ears back. "…What would Neil say?"

Trecheon pressed his lips tight.

Sacha squeezed him. "Anything you say will be good, hun. Neil would say so himself."

Trecheon sighed. He knew she was right. He patted Philip's back. "Alright, I get it." He stepped up and grabbed a handful of dust.

God, he could say so much. Just unload. Theron had taken *so goddamned much* from him. His parents, his grandparents.

His brother.

He shut his eyes. Neil. His solid rock throughout all his life, even when Trecheon didn't want him.

Grief hit him like a truck at full speed.

Draso's holy mercy… he'd never hear Neil's voice again. Never hear his laugh. Never listen to him argue with Izzy about Arizona ice teas, or tease Trecheon about stealing his bacon, or enthusiastically read a book to Athánatos kids. He'd never watch him outrageously flirt with Matt just to get on Trecheon's nerves, or ice skate with skills he had no right to have, or cry after a long bout with the therapist, or… or remind Ana that she deserved happiness, despite their difficult history.

Never feel that solid hug again. A practice they'd only just started.

Never bask in his unwarranted optimism. Something Trecheon needed so desperately these days. All his days, really.

His eyes stung and his throat ached.

He lost too much. Theron took too much…

He stared at the dust again, his vision blurry.

What would Neil say?

He took a deep breath, and turned to Theron's smoldering remains. "Rest in peace. I hope the demons that plagued you are finally gone."

And he tossed the dust into the flames.

My Sacrifice

Jaden sat quietly on the bed in Alexina's chambers. The bed had been freshly made, the room cleared of dust, the bathtub in the adjacent room filled and steaming. Lanterns, far more than needed, lit the room brightly, as if to chase away the demons plaguing them all. The gentle smell of quiche, a Neil specialty, wafted about from the two plates on their little table. But none of that mattered.

All Jaden could do was watch his wife, the love of his life, the quilar he had lost for so many years and finally found again, slowly pull herself apart. Elements rippled through her fur and quills in a cycle – first fire, then wind, then water, lightning, sand… ice. She paced the room, throwing her hands about, switching rapidly from English to Athánatos and back again, with no care for syntax or grammar, muttering about all the pain Theron had caused. Every now and then she paused, running her fingers over the full set of Ei-Ei jewels she possessed, all thanks to Neil.

Jaden would never get to thank him. His throat burned.

He folded his hands in his lap and just… watched Alexina. He knew better than to try and stop her. She needed to get it out of her system, and when she was ready, they could talk and find a solution. Or… closure, in this case.

"Everything about this is *wrong, filtatos,*" she said, once again throwing her hand in the air. She spun off a string of her native language, something about the injustice of leaving her father alive. "He should have been killed years ago." She glanced at him.

Jaden waited a moment to see if she expected a response, then nodded his head. "I know, love."

"So why was he not?"

Jaden waited again. She stared at him intensely. He lifted a brow. "Do you want an actual answer?"

"Yes!" Alexina said. She shook herself. "No… I am unsure." She hugged herself, the elements slowly fading away. "I am sure the answer is complex and multifaceted, but it does not change the outcome. It just-- This--" She picked up a small pot and threw it against the wall, shattering it. "This should not have happened!"

"I know," Jaden said. He stood, his hands itched to hold her, to cling to her, to comfort her in any way, but… "Alexina."

She waved a hand. "Sorry, I am not…" She looked off, her ears pinned back. "I am not ready."

Jaden bit his lip. He sat back on the bed. "I'm here when you need me."

Alexina crossed her arms and looked away. The elements faded entirely now. She took a deep breath. "…The Black Cloak saved me."

Jaden perked his ears.

She rubbed her shoulders. "The night Ackerson came for us. While you and Embrik led Angel away… Theron appeared."

Jaden stood again, his body buzzing.

Alexina fiddled with her hands. "I… had been feeling contractions sporadically throughout the day. I was unsure if they were real or more false ones. Our stress ruled us in those days and caused complications."

Jaden stepped toward her. She met his eyes, then gently took his hand. He pressed a kiss to it. "In your own time, love."

She took a deep breath. "Not long after you left, my water broke." She stared at the floor. "I sat on our bed, pushing, fighting, writhing in pain, trying so hard to keep quiet lest I attract Angel… and another appeared instead."

"Theron."

She shook her head. "The Black Cloak. Ty… the one we knew so well. With green eyes." She shook her head. "The healer."

Jaden narrowed his gaze. "The terrible healer."

"Do not speak ill of him," Alexina said. "He brought me home to you. He saved Zeke when none of us could. Please, my love."

Jaden frowned, but nodded.

Alexina sighed. "He helped me deliver. Cleaned up my baby." She smiled sadly. "I got to hold Zeke in my arms. I even fed him. For just a little while." She frowned. "But the pain from the afterbirth lingered. Ty… The Cloak did his best to heal me, but the blood would not stop. I felt weak. The Cloak could not keep up, and we were too far from any hospital. And then… the sounds of Shadow Cast echoed in the woods."

Jaden took both her hands and squeezed.

"It was too much," Alexina said. "Too much for me, too much for Zeke. All I wanted was to see him safe… and so I gave him to the Black Cloak. I begged him to save Zeke. Get him away even if that cost me my life." She flicked her ears back. "And then… he proposed that I let Theron take me."

Jaden's eyes widened. *"What?"*

"The Cloak could not save me," Alexina said. "I was soon destined to become a Drifter. My soul would leave me before my body expired. And if Theron found me in such a state, I would be useless to him. He would kill me. Cost us the Phonar. Further weaken the Veil, the Cloak, and the Seal. Or… the Cloak could lead Theron to me. Heal me up as best he could. And… let Theron take me as his Drifter. If Theron could control me, use me, then he would do everything in his power to heal me. So… that was what we did." She glanced off, furrowing her brow and baring one tooth. "I understand the logic. But that does not undo the pain." She ripped her hands free of Jaden's. "The pain!"

Jaden flattened his ear. "I know."

"But you do *not,*" Alexina said. "How could he, my own father, do this to me? Use me like a tool? Save me not because I am worth saving, but because I am more use to him as a puppet?" Her quills caught fire again. "What was *wrong with him?*"

Jaden pressed his mouth shut.

Alexina sighed. "You are lucky. To have a father who loves and cares for you."

"Loved," Jaden said, with more bitterness than he intended. "He's dead. Died as a Guardian. As Matt thought I had." He crossed his arms. "…But you're right. I had a good father who loved me. He sacrificed everything for me." He flattened his ears. "After everything that's happened… I really wish he was here right now."

Alexina furrowed her brow. "Who was he?"

Jaden frowned. "My father?"

Alexina shook her head. "The puma. The one who…" She ran her hands over her Ei-Ei jewels.

Jaden flicked an ear back. "Neil Black. One of the members of Ackerson's team, Outlander. Leah mentioned him, along with Trecheon when we were going after one of our targets."

"I know his name," Alexina said. "I lost much because of Theron, but I remember his name. However, I do not know who he was." She wrung her hands together. "The man who won my sister's heart. The mainlander who my own people called Basileus. The stranger who took on pain and suffering a hundred times over to build us a new Veil." She turned to Jaden, tears welling in her eyes. "The sacrifice who gave his soul for mine." She took a deep breath. "I do not know him." Her voice broke. "A-And I very much want to."

Jaden's shoulders slumped. He opened his arms and Alexina carefully made her way to them. He gripped her tight as she lay her head on his. So grateful she was here. So grateful for Neil's sacrifice. So angry that Neil had to sacrifice in the first place.

Alexina was right. Everything about this was wrong.

"He was a Defender," Jaden said, his voice catching in his throat. "A Guardian, just as Matt named him. And it was a title well deserved."

Alexina sobbed quietly. "Please tell me more…"

Jaden stroked her back. "Of course. We have all night."

TOMBS

Zeke wandered the palace, his head swimming. He should be getting to bed, but every time he closed his eyes, all he saw was Neil's body stuck through with ice spikes. His magic responded, icing the tips of his quills, making him shiver. He quietly sang to himself, as Ouranos taught him years ago, calming the magic.

It'd be a while before he'd sleep peacefully again.

Leah clearly felt it too. After the wake, despite the late hour, she vanished into the library, her nose deep in the Book of Summons, lanterns and flashlights all around. Archángeli and Pilot stood by her side, quietly helping her translate runes, though she rarely looked up from the book.

Zeke had frowned at her. "Leah… it's done. We don't need that anymore."

"We might," Leah said, her voice tense and scratchy.

"For what?"

Leah paused. "I don't know yet." She flipped through the book. "But we're missing something. I can feel it."

Zeke splayed an ear. "You're not thinking something in there will bring Neil and Natassa back, are you?"

She winced. "No. As much as I wish we could… That's… perverted."

"Then what are you even looking for?"

Leah paused on a page and wrote something down. She stared blankly for a moment, brow furrowed. "Answers."

"To what?"

She paused again, then shook her head. She never responded.

He watched her for several moments, poking at the bond. It smelled of a roaring, intense fire, chewing through wood and burning everything in its wake. Seeking something, with so much reckless abandon it destroyed everything it touched. He tried calming her with the scent of the sea, slow the burning, but nothing even touched it. Instead he wrapped her in a tight hug.

"Don't burn yourself out, Leah."

"I won't," she said, though it was so automatic, he wasn't sure she even really heard him. He gave her another squeeze, holding on to the fact that she still lived despite everything. He just had to hope he wouldn't lose her to this.

"Trust us -*bzzt*- Zeke," Pilot said, his voice forcefully cheery. "Leah's in good hands!"

Take heart, my Prince, Archángeli said with their familiar gusts of wind around Zeke's ears. *I will watch out for her.*

Zeke took a deep breath. The Phonar could leave at any time now. They had promised to stick around after Natassa's death to fight Theron and Judgement. But now Theron was dead. Judgement was gone. Why they stuck around, he had no idea. But he was grateful for it. Something normal, at least for a little while, even if Archángeli wasn't a constant presence anymore. He gently hugged the summon bird. "Thanks." He'd have to check on Leah later.

But for now, a walk. Something to cool his head.

He automatically headed toward the gardens. That late at night, it should be empty. The last thing he wanted was the pity of palace staff.

This needed privacy.

He dragged his feet along through the black gardens, following the marble path, lit only by moonlight. Past the crystal trees, around the fountains, beyond the bird perches, until he got to the ArchDragon gardens.

He made his way to a single, familiar bench, where Neil had once told him it was okay to let his moms go and embrace the life of the Athánatos. It'd… it'd be good to sit there and think about what Neil had said. Remember that it'll be okay to let him go someday too. Just… wallow in solitude for a while.

But to his surprise, the bench was occupied.

Eris.

He stopped there, debating whether he should talk to her or just find another spot. But then he heard her sniffling. He sighed and took a seat next to her, searching for the right words. But before he could, Eris spoke first.

"I am the oldest living Athánatos, to my knowledge," she said, her voice raspy and quiet. "I have lived for thousands of years. I have seen kings rise and fall. Witnessed war and death. Experienced peace and prosperity." She shook her head. "I helped clean your grandmother at her birth, presided over her wedding, and placed her Ei-Ei jewels in her statue at her death. I watched your grandfather fall deeper and deeper into madness and grief." She looked up at the stars. "I have always told myself to be patient. Be steadfast. Because this too, shall pass, as it has for so many centuries." She folded her hands in her lap and closed her eyes. Tiny tear tracks ran down her cheeks.

Zeke gently rubbed her shoulder.

"And yet," she continued. "This tragedy hits harder than others. I was watching a new era emerge, with new friends, new ideas. A new shift in our very long history – a history that rarely changes. And now…" she sniffled. "That is gone."

Zeke flattened his ears. He leaned back, looking up at the sky. The stars sparkled brightly through the new and steady Veil Neil had left behind. He recognized the constellations the Athánatos named – the Mule Stag to the east, the Great Tamer to the west, and the ArchDragon Sov hovering overhead, protecting them all. Names and stories Natassa taught him. He flexed his fingers against the cold, marble bench, Neil's words about finding his place in Athánatos and letting go of his mothers' ghosts clinging to his memories. Tears pricked at his eyes.

"It's not gone," Zeke said, trying to keep his voice stable. "I can still hear everything Neil and Natassa taught me. And I'm still here. The Defenders are still here. Athánatos will rebuild." He steadied his breath. "It hurts now, but… We'll push through. We have to."

Eris glanced at him, her lime-green eyes practically glowing in the moonlight. She didn't look convinced. Not that he blamed her. He wasn't convinced himself. *Yet,* he thought. In time, he would be. Hopefully. They just needed time.

"You should go with Lady Leah to Zyearth," Eris said suddenly.

Zeke jerked so hard in shock that he almost fell off the bench. "What?"

"She has been contemplating asking you for months," Eris said. "I am sure you are aware, though I assume you two have not discussed it since I have heard of no concrete plans. But you should go with her."

Zeke rubbed his neck, wincing. "Eris, this is my *home.*"

"No," Eris said. "This is your *origin*. It is your heritage and your blood. But it is not your home. Right now, it is a tomb." She took his hand. "Your home is with your heart, and your heart is with Leah."

Zeke flicked his ears. "It's with Andre too, and Jaden, and--"

"You have told me on multiple occasions that Leah fills your heart like no other," Eris said. "After all you have lost, you need that right now. You *need* a full heart if you ever hope to make this place more than a tomb."

Zeke furrowed his brow. "Eris…"

Eris locked eyes with him. "If you feel like you cannot leave Andre and the others, then convince them to go with you. But there is nothing for you here." She squeezed his hand. "Athánatos has a lot to rebuild. And rebuild we shall, as we have throughout our long centuries. But you are young to have faced as many tragedies as you have. You need peace and good company and healing. You will not find that here for some time, my Prince." She patted his hand. "Please… go with Leah and find these things. You can always come back once you have. And by all means, please come back. You can share your peace with us then. But I worry if you stay, this place will steal any hope of healing." She met his eyes. "Your *Theía* would not want this for you."

Zeke pressed his lips tight and frowned.

"Think on it," Eris said. "I know it is a big ask, but I would not ask it if I did not think it best for you. I want to see you thrive. It is what Natassa would want for you."

"I…" Zeke tensed up. "I'll think about it. It's all I can promise right now."

Eris frowned, but she nodded. "Think on it," she repeated. "And remember my words." She let go of his hand. "It is late, my Prince. You should attempt sleep." She turned back to the stars.

Zeke let out a long breath. "You should too."

Eris bit her lip. "If sleep visits me tonight, it will be here, under the great constellations of Athánatos. For now, I will let them speak to me. Go to sleep, my Prince."

Zeke followed her gaze, her words swirling about in his head. He pointed. "First, can you tell me about a constellation?"

Eris glanced at him, then chuckled lightly. "If my Prince needs a bedtime story, then I shall deliver it." She pointed. "Let me tell you of the new ones – the Lion of the Mountain and the Violet Princess, and their rage against the Mad King."

GUARDIANSHIP

Trecheon trudged toward the guest dwellings of the palace, feeling absolutely drained. That wake was far harder than it should have been. Far more than Neil and Natassa's funeral. He sighed. Their wake tomorrow was supposed to be a party. During the last few years, Neil frequently joked about having a party for his funeral.

Though it was a stark reminder of Neil's favorite topic during the war. The Dead Funeral. He always believed no one would care when he died. He joked his funeral would be as dead as he would. Funeral jokes faded during their assassin days, while they both fought self-hate and didn't need the additional reminders, though it still came up occasionally. When he started bringing up the idea of a funeral as a party, Trecheon took that as a sign of healing.

But not as a sign of it actually coming to pass.

God.

There would be joy in that party. It's what Neil would want. But not for Trecheon. It'd take time for him to find joy again. For now, all he wanted was sleep. Just some time to shut everything off.

"Trecheon?"

Trecheon turned. Damianos and Philip stood in the doorway of one of the guest sleepers. Trecheon pressed his lips together. Philip looked every bit like Neil. All his best features. He'd have to tell him that one day, when things settled. "What's up?"

Damianos furrowed his brow, his eyes shining with unshed tears. But he managed a smile as he gripped Philip's shoulder. "We… have something we need to discuss."

Trecheon raised an eyebrow. "Oh?"

"Come inside," Dami said, and turned back into the room.

Philip flicked his ears back, frowning. "Please?"

Trecheon nodded. "Always, kiddo."

Kiddo. Philip was fifteen, complete with adult coat and teenage rebellion. Definitely not a kiddo anymore. And yet, the kit standing there shook with fear, clung to Trecheon's side during Theron's wake, and had now lost four parental figures. He still needed… guidance.

Damianos sat on Philip's bed. "We wish to discuss the topic of, ah, guardianship."

Trecheon raised an eyebrow. "Guardianship?"

"Of Philip."

Trecheon's thoughts immediately flew to his conversation with Neil before he started the Veil anchors. *If something happens to me, look after Philip for me.* That meant… guardianship. Right? He sat down on a chair. "Okay, what about it?"

Dami put a hand on Philip's back. "When Neil, Natassa, and I officially announced our engagement, we endeavored to, ah, define parental roles. In the last few years, Natassa and Neil filled those roles well. I, however… Philip and I worked better as friends than in any authority figure relationship."

"Dami lost a lot in the war, when he was still young like me," Philip said. "Family, a home, our childhood." He rubbed his hands together. "We bonded over that."

Trecheon nodded. "I remember."

"That being said," Dami said. "I asked Philip if he wanted me to try again. To… to adopt him. Athánatos has become his home."

Shock ran through Trecheon's system. Adopt Philip? Keep him here? With all that horrid grief still chewing away at him, he hadn't thought far ahead enough to consider what Philip might do. But the idea that he'd just stay on Athánatos hadn't even crossed his mind.

"Uncle Trecheon?"

Trecheon shook his head. "Sorry, sorry." He cleared his throat. *Gotta stay neutral. Gotta let Philip do what makes him comfortable, no matter what that means for us.* "So, you're staying here?"

Philip pinned his ears back. "Actually… I was hoping I could move in with… you."

Trecheon's ears and quills shot straight up. "Really?"

Philip nodded. "I love Dami and I love Athánatos but…" He rubbed his arms. "It just reminds me of Theron. And Neil. I don't… I can't do that. At least not now."

Trecheon flattened his ears. He looked back at Dami. The Archon prince had his ears splayed and tears built in his eyes, but he managed a smile. He nodded to Trecheon. Trecheon turned back to Philip.

The very last thing Neil told him flashed through his head.

Look after Philip for me.

Trecheon's chest ached, but he nodded. "Of course, Philip. Once we get everything settled, you can live with me."

He expected a smile, or a nod, or something. Instead, tears built in Philip's eyes and he frowned deeply. He slowly walked to Trecheon and hugged him. Trecheon held him close. He wanted to say so much. He wanted it to stop hurting. But right now, he just needed to feel.

Eventually he and Dami tucked Philip into bed.

"I don't think I'm gonna sleep tonight…" Philip said.

Trecheon nodded. "Me either, kid." He sighed. "You remember which room is mine?"

"Yeah."

"And Dami's?"

"Of course."

"Then if you need anything, come and find one of us," Dami said. "I dare say none of us will sleep well for the foreseeable future. But we can support each other."

Philip snuggled under the covers. "Thanks. Can you… leave the lantern lit?"

"Of course," Dami said. He set up the lantern and the pair of them left. Dami leaned against the wall and shut his eyes. "That was far harder than I anticipated."

Trecheon flicked his ears back. "You were really hoping Philip would stay here, huh?" Dami nodded. Trecheon forced a smile. "I know everything's really bleak right now, but we'll visit all the time. You won't lose him completely." He gripped Dami's shoulder. "We're not going anywhere."

Dami turned to him, frowning. He furrowed his brow, shook his head, then slowly walked to his room.

Trecheon tilted his head. That was… ominous.

Philip's quiet sobs and sniffles echoed behind the door. Trecheon listened for a few minutes, trying to hold it together. Philip was going to need him tonight. So he'd better get his own emotions under control.

Time to visit Matt.

Chapter 49

Excuses

Matt entered his guest room in the ambassador wing of the Athánatos palace absolutely exhausted. Steam rose from a hot bath in the corner, a plate of piping hot food sat on the table and someone had put fresh, clean blankets on the bed.

He stood in the doorway, staring at it all. So… normal. So cared for. As if they were just supposed to carry on like nothing happened.

Like Neil and Natassa weren't dead.

Like Theron hadn't killed them.

He covered his face with one hand, shutting his eyes, fighting back the emotions. He had to be strong. That was his job.

Mourning could come later.

He stripped off his clothes and hopped in the tub. Just a quick bath before dinner and sleep. He'd need both if he was going to keep up his strength. He settled into the tub, watching the candles around him flicker.

The soft orange light reminded him of trips to the beach. Surfing with Trecheon, walks on the sand. On one trip, Neil had declared himself the grill master, then proceeded to burn everything he touched. Sami took over after that, and when time came to eat, the first burger she passed to Neil was one of his burnt ones. His look of disgust garnered more than a few laughs.

"Guess I'll drop the title of grill master," he had said, and everyone agreed. He declared himself "beer master" later and he and Matt shared a cold one, watching the sun set and feeding bits of fish to the seagulls.

He shook his head of the memory. *Later.* He grabbed the soap and got out as quick as he could. Didn't want dinner getting cold. He glanced over the plate as he dried off.

Quiche. Filled with sausage, bell peppers, and mushrooms. A Neil specialty.

Something caught in his throat and he choked. He turned away. He wasn't hungry anyway. Better just get right to sleep. He finished drying off and got dressed.

Someone had rested his sword in the corner of the room. Matt sat on the bed, staring at it. A dozen spars with Neil flooded his brain. One of the few zyfaunos who could keep up with him. He had such form too… Always right in-step with Matt. Or even ahead of him. When Matt and the others had come here for the wedding, Neil had asked Matt to teach him some advanced techniques, and they threw themselves full strength into training. Two weeks ago, Neil finally bested Matt, knocked him to the sand, and pinned him down. Matt would never forget his cheers of joy. Neil told anyone who would listen about the match for days.

He would have made a great Defender sword partner.

Would have made.

But he was gone.

The ache in Matt's throat came back, dragging up fresh aches in his chest. Matt leaned on his knees, unable to take his eyes off the sword.

No more spars. Neil was gone. He was *gone.* He--

Someone knocked on the door.

Matt jolted. He shook his head, blinking back tears and searching for strength. Whoever was there needed that. It was Matt's job to help. He breathed deeply then opened the door.

Trecheon stood on the other side.

The aches doubled now. Without a word, he pulled Trecheon into a deep hug, holding him close. He rested his head on Trecheon's. *Thank Draso you're okay... you're here, you're safe, you're alive...* He closed his eyes. *I don't know what I would have done if...* He couldn't bring himself to finish the sentence.

Trecheon held him tight, gripping his shirt. It seemed like a lifetime before Trecheon slowly pulled away. "...Can I come in?"

"Of course," Matt said. "Always." He waved Trecheon in and shut the door.

Trecheon walked in slowly. "You handling things okay?"

Matt shrugged, hoping Trecheon didn't notice him shaking. "I mean... as good as I could be." He glanced at the sword in the corner again. "Feels like everything reminds me of Neil. Hard to fight back the emotional waves." He rubbed his arm.

Trecheon turned to him. "You still have that shitty smartphone?"

"Yeah, why?"

"Download a puzzle game," Trecheon said. "Block breakers or bubble poppers or something. A game that's pretty mindless to play but needs your focus. Supposedly that helps to stave off the PTSD. Helps your mind compartmentalize."

Matt managed a smile. "Sure, I'll give it a shot." He crossed his arms. "I doubt you came here to talk about Tetris though. So what's up?"

Trecheon sat on the bed. "Philip… he asked if he could move in with me. If I could be his new guardian. Er, parent, I guess."

Matt sat next to him. "You nervous?"

"No," Trecheon said. "I mean, yeah, I guess I worry that this ol' war veteran isn't what he needs now, though I don't really have the headspace to give it proper thought. I'm just… surprised. That he picked me so fast."

Matt leaned back. "He's lost so much. Probably looking for any kind of stability."

Trecheon scoffed. "As if I'm stable enough for this."

"You are to him," Matt said. "You've always been there for him."

Trecheon didn't say anything.

Matt leaned closer to him. "Are you afraid you can't do it?"

Trecheon shrugged. "I dunno. Maybe." He smacked his forehead. "God, I didn't even bring this up with Sacha…"

Matt managed a chuckle. "You won't have to worry about that. She'll be fully onboard, and she'll help you navigate everything."

"I guess."

"She will be," Matt said. "All of us will. You won't be raising him alone."

Trecheon's ears flattened against his head. He looked away. "You're going home to Zyearth."

Matt's eyes widened. Oh shit. He was right. Lance had called them all home…

But with the circumstances…

"Lance won't call Sacha home," Matt said. "Not after all this. Not when you and Philip need her."

Trecheon sighed. He shifted his body weight and leaned against Matt. Matt, surprised, wrapped an arm around Trecheon. Trecheon nestled against him. "But what about you?"

Matt's body buzzed. Lance wasn't going to let him stay just to help with Philip. Trecheon and Philip had a whole village to help out. Matt staying wouldn't be a priority, and rightly so.

But leaving him here, alone, and so far away… The very thought threatened to break him. But he'd never convince Lance to let him stay.

Unless… there was something more here…

Trecheon had obviously had romantic feelings for Matt for quite some time. Even though Trecheon tried to pretend he didn't, everyone knew he was lying to himself. But Matt… he had been so sure he had no romantic feelings for Trecheon.

And yet…

Matt rubbed Trecheon's side, sifting through his feelings. Their closeness, physically and emotionally. The way Trecheon melted into him, and the way Matt fit so snuggly around him. The teasing, the flirting, the jokes from their friends about them being romantic.

Could Matt see himself in a relationship with Trecheon?

He closed his eyes and imagined, hoping for that rising blossom of joy in his chest that romantic love supposedly brought on. What would it be like to hold hands, cuddle on the couch watching a movie, going on a date… kissing?

Or… more than just kissing?

But there was nothing. The mental images didn't feel right. Aside from kissing, it was no different than the deep friendship he already celebrated with Trecheon. That couldn't be romantic love.

But if exploring a romantic relationship kept him closer to Trecheon for longer…

But it had to be on Trecheon's terms. Matt had always said that. He wasn't going to lie to Trecheon and confess feelings he didn't have, even if that meant having a chance at staying here. He didn't want to hurt him. Trecheon needed to start this. And in order for that to happen… Trecheon had to confess.

Matt pulled Trecheon closer, wrapping both arms around him now. "Under normal circumstances, I don't think he'd let me. But… in the right instance…" He rested his chin on Trecheon's head, careful of the quills.

Trecheon stiffened next to him. But he still wouldn't speak.

Matt sighed. He lay his head on Trecheon's now. "Trecheon, you know you can tell me anything, right? Anything you've got on your mind. I'm here to listen. Anything at all."

Trecheon leaned closer to Matt. They were silent for several minutes. Matt willed the confession out of Trecheon. *Come on, Trecheon… give me the excuse to stay… to… to try this with you. To see where my heart really lies.* He gripped tighter. *Give me an excuse to hold you together. Hold us together…*

Trecheon stirred a little, lifting Matt's heart. He braced for a confession.

But Trecheon just loosened up and pulled back. "Thanks Matt. I mean that…" He looked away, wiping at his face. He turned back, wearing a fake, broken smile. "I'll let you know if I need to talk." He stood. "But for now, I think I should get to bed in case Philip gets up and needs me. And I need to check on Sacha. I just wanted to check on your first. Get some sleep, okay?" He headed for the door.

Damn it! Matt stood too. "Trecheon."

Trecheon turned back to him.

Matt frowned. One more push. His heart quickened. He closed the distance between them and pulled Trecheon into one more hug. "Take care of yourself, okay? Don't do this alone." And, with his face flushing, he pressed a kiss to the top of Trecheon's head.

Trecheon froze up again.

Matt pulled back a bit and looked Trecheon in the eye. *Come on, Trech... you need this... WE need this...* He smiled, hoping it was inviting. *Let me be this for you.*

Trecheon held his gaze for a long time, his brow furrowed. He smiled... but it was that bland, fake smile that he used to hide his true emotions. "Thanks. Truly." He patted Matt's shoulder. "I'll... see you in the morning."

And he stepped back.

Matt's heart ached. Even now, even after all they lost, even with Matt throwing the door wide open, Trecheon kept his feelings locked away.

The question was... why?

"Yeah... see you in the morning, Trech."

Trecheon gave Matt's hand a final squeeze and left, shutting the door behind him.

Matt stared at the door, numb. That... hurt. Why did that hurt? Was Trecheon pushing him away? ...Did Matt actually have feelings for him?

Draso's mercy.

Move. But he didn't. *Move, Azure. Do something. Anything!*

Puzzle games.

Matt dully wandered back to his bed. Maybe he can try that puzzle game idea. He had a few preinstalled on the phone. Any would do. He picked up the phone from the side table and unlocked it.

Trecheon's picture smiled at him. Trecheon, Ouranos, Izzy, himself... Natassa.

And Neil.

Their beach picture from several years ago. Happy and safe and joyful. Matt had spent the day surfing. He and Neil shared a beer and good food. He watched the sunset with Trecheon at his side.

Darvin had teased them about being romantic at each other.

At the time, Matt took it for playful joshing. But looking back…

His gaze kept wandering to Neil's grin. Natassa's gentle smile. Faces he'd never see again.

He put the phone down, sat hard on the bed, then buried his face in his hands and sobbed.

CHAPTER 50

BUILDING BONDS

Izzy walked slowly through the halls of the palace. Everything still felt numb. Her feet dragged along like lead weights. All she wanted to do was sleep. She was long past the denial stage of grief, but she still wallowed in the experience, the aching. But sleep… sleep might provide an escape, at least for a little while.

But she had to talk to Matt. She had to make this right.

Matt was on his bed in one of the guest rooms, messing with something on his cheap smartphone from the mainland. Based on the little beeps and upbeat music, it was some kind of game, though he clearly struggled to concentrate. He stared at the phone, but he had that dull, thousand-yard stare… as Neil used to call it. He held his ears pinned close to his head, and he hunched over, almost like curling himself into a ball. And his eyes looked red and puffy.

Izzy bit her lip. She took a deep breath, then poked at their bond. Just to see. Or hear, really. But all she got was a dark, constant church bell. A funeral bell. Deep, resonating… painful. She gripped her chest, fighting tears. *Damn it…*

Matt looked up and they locked eyes. Instantly he sat up straight, perked his ears, and put on a smile that Izzy knew intimately. Matt's comfort smile. Making himself a safe space, taking on the sadness and burden of others. The brave face. Always effective. Though Izzy knew all too well that this was also the sacrifice smile. Matt putting others' feelings first in times of crisis. Admirable at times. Detrimental at others.

He blinked several times, readjusting the smile. "Hey Iz. Sorry, I was distracted by this game. Trecheon says that playing a mindless game after a traumatic event might lessen the PTSR effect, so I thought I'd try it. You doing okay?"

Normally Izzy would be the first one to shake Matt out of his comfort smile and demand he take some time for himself and stop trying to repair everyone's brokenness. That it wasn't his job to fix everyone's pain. But now…

"Izzy?"

Izzy's eyes burned. "I-I'm sorry…"

Matt's smile faded and the friend, the brother that Izzy knew so well immediately took over. He threw the phone aside, crossed the room, and pulled her into his arms.

Izzy held him tight, sobbing into his chest. This wasn't fair, this wasn't right, this shouldn't be *real*. Neil didn't deserve that. Natassa didn't deserve that. They shouldn't have had to sacrifice themselves. Her brain fed her a thousand scenarios where she could have stopped this, could have fixed it, could have sacrificed herself instead so they could live…

They didn't deserve this…

Earth and stone, when did she get so weepy? She was a *soldier,* damn it. She lost people all the time. She'd lose more in the future. She was a *Guardian,* she should be *strong,* she--

You should be allowed to feel. Matt's voice, deep and comforting, floated through her mind. Gentle, melodic bells accompanied him, reminding her of... of Earth Christmases, of ice skating, of opening presents, of... of Neil's grin while he snatched a mug of her homemade hot cocoa and a cookie. Of Natassa singing and laughing at mealtimes.

Draso's mercy, she'd never see that grin again... hear that musical laugh.

You're allowed to feel, Matt said again. *Soldier or Guardian or whatever, you are allowed to feel...* Then he jolted and loosened the hug. "Oh Draso, Izzy, I'm sorry, I'm doing the telepathic thing again--"

"No, no, it's okay..." Izzy said. She pulled back and wiped at her face. "I... actually came to talk to you about that."

Matt pressed his lips tight. "Izzy, the energy stealing thing after Neil died wasn't your fault. You just don't have any *practice,* and--"

"And that's the problem, isn't it?" Izzy said, sniffling. "I don't have any practice. I've always shunned the bond. And... I shouldn't." She hugged Matt again. "Neil was one of my best friends. I hadn't connected to anyone like that in a long, long time. Something about Neil just made me feel... safe." She shook her head. "Of course Roscoe does too, and all my other friends, but there was something... unique about Neil. And I've been trying to think of who else makes me feel like that and... that's you." She squeezed her eyes tight. "But I've been pushing that aside. I think it's been a slow, slow trickle since the incident with the war games, but it got ramped up after your bond with Ouranos, because suddenly *my* bond with you felt real again. But then I found that friendship in Neil, without the bond baggage, and that just made my relationship with you worse."

Matt didn't respond. He gently rubbed her back, but said nothing. She felt it all though. A cacophony of bells with a cascade of emotions, centering around fear and worry. And in the noise, Matt's thoughts floated about. Izzy grasped one.

I am so sorry I did that to you...

Izzy took a step back and met Matt's gaze. "Matt... I should never have pushed it aside." Matt furrowed his brow and opened his mouth to speak, but Izzy pressed a finger to his lips. "I don't want to hear it," she said. "We can make excuses all we want, but it changes nothing. When I saw what the bond did for you and Ouranos, I should have immediately tried cultivating ours. We should have been learning about it together. I... I let fear control me." She took a deep breath. "I can't do that anymore. I've already lost Neil. I don't want to lose what I have with you too." She smiled, hoping she looked sincere. "I want to cultivate the bond."

Matt's eyes widened. "Really?"

"Really."

Matt smiled. His real and true genuine smile. "I'd love nothing more." He hugged her again.

She hugged him back, closing her eyes and letting the bond between them flow naturally. Rhythmic jingle bells echoed in her mind. She sniffled. She'd probably always associate that with Neil.

Neil would want that, Matt said. *He'd want you to remember him for Christmas and family and good times together. It'll hurt for a while, but we'll get through it together.*

Izzy slowed her breathing. She snuggled into Matt. *Yeah... we will.* She pulled back. "So... can I play your puzzle game for a bit?"

Matt laughed. Musical bells echoed the laugh in Izzy's head. "Yeah, sure. We'll take turns."

They played back and forth for nearly an hour. Izzy wasn't sure if it really helped all that much, but it was a good distraction, and it was a way to start building the bond, talking to each other and sharing each other's emotions through their minds. Izzy expected it to be unpleasant, but it was immensely comforting. Like a greater, deeper extension of the love they already shared, with beautiful, symbolic bells to ring in that joy. At the end of the hour, Izzy's heart was considerably lighter. Not... healed. She wasn't sure she'd ever fully heal. But it was better.

"So," Izzy said, passing the game to Matt. "What's it feel like to have four bonded partners now?"

Matt took the game and ran his fingers over the phone. "It's... crowded," he said, a slight smile on his face. "Comforting too, knowing you all are safe around me. But crowded. It helps that Ouranos and Zeke already have a lot of experience with bonds and they know how to avoid overwhelming it."

Izzy flicked her ears back. The bell sounds trickled to a tiny jingle. "Am I overwhelming it?"

Matt eyed her, smirking. "More like underwhelming it. You're still scared to open it up. But it's okay," he added. "Give it time. Neither of us need emotional floodgates opening right now." He poked at the game until he got a game over. "Damn." He passed it to Izzy. "Alexina though... she's a lot like her siblings where she keeps her emotions off her face, but she feels them very passionately in her mind and... and I feel all of it, intimately."

"Is it bothering you?"

"Only a little," Matt said. "I can build the barriers myself okay most of the time. It'll be something to work on, just like it was for Ouranos and me."

Izzy started up a new game. "Did… did you two time travel when you bonded? Like with Ouranos?"

Matt stared at the floor. "...Yeah. About a day in the past, like with Ouranos. I think that's why she regained herself in the Aether before we had actually met."

Izzy frowned. "I'm surprised you didn't do something to try and… alter the outcome."

Matt shrugged. "Wasn't far enough in the past."

Izzy eyed him. "Horse spit. That's not like you, Guardian."

Matt closed his eyes and formed fists with his hands. "...The Black Cloak was there. The one with purple eyes."

Izzy's eyes grew wide. "Did she stop you?"

Matt looked away. Dull, distant bells echoed in her mind.

She didn't push it after that.

They played for another thirty minutes, making small talk until Matt yawned. "I know we're enjoying this, Iz, but it's late and we've got a lot to do tomorrow. Let's get some sleep."

"Yeah…" Izzy gave him a squeeze. "Thanks, Matt."

Matt squeezed her too. "Always. Let me know if you need anything in the night, okay?"

"Will do." Izzy stood and headed for the door.

"Hey Iz?"

Izzy turned back.

Matt's ears pinned back. He opened and closed his mouth, clearly searching for words, but nothing came out.

It came through the bond, though.

Why won't Trecheon admit he's in love with me?

Izzy frowned. She walked back over and gave Matt a long hug. She fumbled for words.

Matt sighed and hugged her back. "I'm going to ask something, but you only have to answer if you can without… betraying anyone."

Izzy leaned back, frowning.

Matt took her hands. "Is Trecheon hiding something from me?"

Izzy's eyes grew wide and her ears perked. Then she frowned again. "I'm guessing you don't need the bond to know the answer to that one."

Matt splayed his ears. "Definitely not." He pressed his lips tight. "I won't ask you what he's hiding. That's between you and Trecheon. Though I admit… I'm curious." He furrowed his brow and glanced off. "I can't begin to imagine a secret so dark that Trecheon would be afraid to tell me. Or that it'd keep him from admitting his feelings for me." He shuddered, but then squeezed her hands. "But if you talk to him again about it, whatever it is… tell him it's okay to tell me. Nothing is going to chase me away."

"You mean that," Izzy said, more firmly than she intended. "You can promise that, whole heartedly, that there's nothing, *ever,* that would keep you from Trecheon."

Matt raised a brow, but nodded. A tiny, distant bell echoed between them. Felt almost like… fear. But a stronger, louder, more confident bell followed, chasing it away. Izzy got the message. Matt was scared… but he was serious. Nothing would keep him away.

"Izzy," Matt said. "Trecheon is the universe to me. I meant what I said at the wake. I can't imagine life without him. I won't ever leave him. That's a promise."

Izzy squeezed Matt's hands. "Okay… good. Then I'll tell him tomorrow," she said. She chewed her lip. "So… does that mean your feelings for him have changed? Are you in love with him?"

Matt furrowed his brow and looked off. "I… don't know. If I knew, I'd just tell him first, but I don't want to accidentally lie to him. I'm… still leaning toward no, but…" his voice trailed.

The bond finished it. *If we're exploring a relationship, I can stay here. I can make sure he's safe.*

Izzy flattened one ear. *So you don't have to live in fear that something will happen to him when we're gone.*

Matt looked away. "It's… hard, admitting that."

Izzy hugged him. "I know." She stood. "I'll talk to him tomorrow. I promise."

Matt smiled. "Thanks."

She left. It was a start. No matter where it went.

CHAPTER 51

NEW MASTER

Matt dreamed.

He was quite aware of it being a dream, which was unusual for him.

He stood on the clover lawn outside the Athánatos palace, soaked in rain, a good distance from the battle with Theron and Judgement. Ouranos faced them with some facsimile of Matt at his side. Magic flew everywhere. Their allies were down.

And Neil stood ready.

"Neil, *no!*" Matt called to him. But his legs wouldn't move. He looked down. His feet had melted into the clover. His legs were literal stone.

He shot his head up, waving his arms. "No, Neil, don't do it, Neil, *don't!*"

But Neil ran in anyway. Sunk his knife into Theron's neck. Died by ice spikes. Izzy's wail echoed across the lawn so loudly it made Matt's ears ring.

Matt held his head. "No, no, *no!*"

Then the scene reset. Theron and Judgement. Ouranos with the Matt doppelgänger. Magic flying everywhere.

But this time, Cix took Neil's place, knife in hand. Matt's old sword partner. Theron's victim on Zyearth.

Matt's eyes grew wide.

The black and white wolf glowed with fire magic, gripping the knife tight, snarling and gnashing his teeth. He rushed Theron.

Matt shouted. But no sound came out.

Knife in neck.

Ice spikes through Cix's brain.

Death and blood and screams.

Then it reset.

No, no, please, Draso, make this stop.

Judgement, Theron, Ouranos, fake Matt. Magic, fear, blood, death.

Christian appeared this time, backwards hat and all, holding the knife aloft. He rushed Theron. "See you in hell!" He stabbed the mage king.

A Cast wrapped around him and shoved a Charm in his eye, exploding his body into blood and flesh and dust.

Then it reset.

And Natassa stood there, protecting Neil. She rushed Theron. But he whipped about, punching ice spikes through her stomach, spilling blood everywhere in a violent rain. The iron smell permeated everything, almost blinding him.

Then it reset. Neil stood there again.

Matt tugged at his legs. "Come on, come on, let me do something, let me save them!" But they wouldn't budge.

Judgement, Theron, Ouranos, himself, magic, Neil, death.

Then Cix.

Then Christian.

Then Natassa.

Then Neil again.

Over and over and over and over and over and--

Tears streamed down his face. It didn't matter that this was a dream. He was locked in it. The pain, the burning eyes, the smell of death, the screams, the taste of blood on his tongue, it was all too real. "Let me help… please… Let me stop this…"

A never-ending cycle. Like time traveling over and over, desperate to stop it, failing each time.

Then the Black Cloak appeared on Matt's left. His eyes faded from blue to green to magenta and back again in rapid succession. Red tears ran down the silver mask.

Matt turned to him. "Why can't you stop this?"

The Cloak fixed his gaze on the scene before them. "I can't." They spoke with three voices as one chorus.

Then the Cloak vanished in a puff of ice dust.

Matt sobbed. He glanced back up, locked in place, desperately wishing to wake up, tired of seeing Neil, and Natassa, and Cix, and Christian die over and over again.

But it wasn't any of them this time.

It was Izzy.

Matt's eyes grew wide. "No, no, not Izzy, not her! She's fine, she's alive, you can't take her from me!"

Izzy faced Theron, glowing bright green, her hammer in hand. She lifted it up and rushed him.

Judgement cackled, a haunting, gurgling sound.

Matt threw a hand out. "Izzy, *no!*"

She brought the hammer down.

A violent pounding beat against Matt's ears, and he leapt out of bed, snatched his sword out of the corner, and glanced around the dark room, lit only by the fading lantern light. Tears stuck to his fur and sweat to his quills, despite him being shirtless.

The pounding continued, this time with a loud jangling bell in his ear, coming from the door. "Matt, open up now, please!"

Izzy.

Matt rushed for the door and threw it open. "Izzy? What's going on?"

Izzy stood at the door, Charlotte next to her, fear gripping their features, ears back, quills puffed up. "Come quick, it's Jaden!"

Matt's body buzzed, all the fears from his dream rushing back. "Dad?"

Charlotte pulled on his hand. "Judgement has him!"

Matt's eyes widened. *"What?"*

Tears ran down Charlotte's face. "Hurry, *please!*" She pulled him into the hall. A dozen others ran past them, friends and Athánatos, with screams and shouts. Zeke, Leah, Dami, Ana, Melaina.

With cold night air biting through the fur on his bare chest, Matt rushed down the hall after them, clutching his sword, as wisps of wind followed behind.

Ouranos was at the edge of the clover lawn already, with Trecheon, Alexina, and Neil. No… Philip. Sacha stood by too, as did Roscoe, Sami, and Darvin. Even the Phonar summons had scattered around the lawn, their elements lighting up their feathers, though they stood frozen.

Matt pushed past them all and followed their gaze.

Judgement.

She spread through the clover lawn like a damn oil spill, cackling loudly, highlighted in blue moonlight. She held something in her hand. A flash of white.

Jaden.

Unmoving.

Judgement grinned, turning to Matt. *I had hoped you would come for him, little Guardian,* she said, dripping black on Matt's head. *Just so you could see how useless your friend's death was.* She touched an inky finger to her snout, waving her globby wings. *Should have removed Theron's Ei-Ei jewels first. This one would have been far harder to claim otherwise. Not as strong as your mad king. That will have to be remedied. But strong enough for now.*

Matt gritted his teeth, wind bursting around him, the Black Bound elixir spreading over his fingers. "Let him *go!*"

Catch me first.

And she vanished.

With Jaden.

BEST LAID PLANS

Everyone immediately exploded into panic. Leah shouted something about summons and ran into the palace, with Zeke chasing after her, Alexina ran out into the grass after Jaden while Melaina and Embrik ran after her, Trecheon shouted a string of curse words, while Sacha tried calming him down, and everyone was screaming.

And Jaden was gone.

With a will, Matt calmed his wind magic, pushed aside the chaos, and reached for his training as a Guardian. "Defenders, *at attention!*"

Immediately every Defender there paused, exchanged glances, then stood at attention with a salute. *"Aye, sir!"* Their voices in unison made the rest of the group pause, finally calming everything.

Matt stood tall, trying to stop the shaking. *Don't panic. Panic is how we lose Jaden. We need control. Because losing control is how we lost Neil and Natassa.* "Excelsis."

The black raven flew up and landed in front of Matt. He mantled his wings, bowing low, spitting tongues of purple fire. *Guardian.*

"I know you're not technically bound to any master, but we need your help," Matt said. "Scour the island for Judgement and report back if you find anything. We're going after her."

Excelsis bowed his head. *We shall, Guardian.* He cawed loudly at the other Phonar and as one, the eight birds took to the sky and spread out.

"Angus, Andre," Matt said. The pair turned to him. "Have your summons do the same. They're faster than us and they can't be killed if Judgement finds them. They're our best hope. And if anyone sees the damn Cloak, tell him we need his summons too."

Angus sighed. "Aye, Guardian." He called on Magna and Lysander and sent them off. Magna whinnied loudly and leapt into the air, spreading her black, stone wings, while Lysander dug all four lion paws into the grass and sped off, vanishing into the darkness.

Andre raised an eyebrow. He called on Drifa and Kaoru, gave both their heads a friendly pat, and explained what they needed to do. They nodded to him and flew off. He watched them go, but he frowned. "You know Judgement likely ain't on the island anymore. Her whole purpose is to destroy the damn planet."

"Oh *hell,*" Trecheon muttered.

"I don't think that's the case," Matt said, holding up his palm. "I don't think she can get off at all. Neil *just* replaced the Veil. He didn't *repair* it, he *replaced* it. Meaning it's a whole new Veil. It doesn't have any rips in it. Even the ones placed there on purpose with the old Veil."

Ouranos perked his ears. "Sisters *alive.* Which means the rip in the throne room is no longer there."

Matt nodded. "Right now, the only people who can make rips in the Veil are Athánatos royalty, and Dad doesn't have Ei-Ei jewels, so he doesn't count. She's stuck here. Which gives us an advantage." *I think.*

Sacha crossed her arms. "Then why didn't she possess an Athánatos royal?"

Everyone grew silent.

"Because she can't," Leah said. She jogged up to the group with Zeke at her side and the Book of Summons in her hands. "I knew we had forgotten something. Glad I looked through this." She flipped through pages of the book. "There are conditions to Judgement finding a summon master. Safeguards the Sisters put in place when they Sealed her. Any attempt to make it really hard for her to anchor herself to reality again, even if the Seal broke." She pointed to a page, but wrinkled her snout. "Well, there's only two conditions… not great, but it's better than nothing."

Eris glanced over the book. "What are they?"

Leah tapped the page. "One, Judgement can't attach to any Athánatos without express permission."

"So Theron gave her *permission*," Sacha said, growling. "Damn bastard."

"Two," Leah continued. "Judgement can only possess those with a broken or weakened focus jewel bond. That's how she got Theron. He was a Drifter, so he was missing a jewel set. And Jaden's Gem was damaged during the Sol Genocide. It's how he went teleporting away in the first place." She shifted, her tail flailing about. "I suspect that's what she did now. Somehow called on Jaden's dormant teleporting power from his Gem."

Izzy raised an eyebrow. "She can do that?"

"I can't think of any other way she could just vanish like that," Leah said. "With no Ei-Ei jewels, she has no way of entering the Aether."

Angus twitched a large ear. "If your book is right, that might explain Ronan's time skipping. Time healing, even when healing massive wounds, should eventually resolve itself, but Ronan has never been able to fix his time glitching. Not even when we were kids and he fixed minor wounds. He must have damaged his jewel bond at some point."

"So," Matt said. "We may have some hope here. She can't escape the island. She can only go after people with damaged focus jewels. She won't kill Dad because then she's really got nowhere to go and he's her only anchor to reality." Matt's fur stood on end with that last one. Draso's wings, he had to hope that was true.

"The question then becomes," Ouranos said. "What is it that she wants?"

Silence again.

"Escape," Charlotte said quietly. She sniffled, wiping at her nose, but she furrowed her brow in determination. "She wants to escape. Which means she needs an Athánatos royal with a weakened jewel bond and the motivation to bond with her."

"Power," Trecheon said. He crossed his arms. "She specifically said Jaden wasn't strong enough. She needs someone stronger."

Matt wrinkled his snout. "She clearly doesn't understand power when she sees it."

"Well, we have power in spades," Darvin said. "All she needs to do is find a way to break someone's Ei-Ei jewels and convince them to become her summon master."

Ouranos shook his head. "Which may be a wall to climb… or it may not, depending on her wiles. She will hold on to Jaden until she finds what she wants, but will remove him the moment he is no longer useful."

Ana stepped forward. "If that's the case, then we need to move *fast.* " She flicked her wrist. "So let's give her what she wants."

"Absolutely *not,* " Matt snarled, crossing his arms. "Unacceptable."

The group had gathered in the main audience chamber again, and had spent the last half hour discussing what to do. It was the longest half hour of Matt's life. He wanted nothing more than to blindly run through the island until he found Jaden – only his training and wits kept him glued to the spot.

They hadn't heard anything from the summons.

Didn't help that the discussion hadn't really led anywhere. Their conclusions hadn't changed. Judgement wanted off the island, and she needed a willing Athánatos with broken Ei-Ei jewels to get there, and if they wanted her to show up with Jaden, they'd have to bait her with one.

Ouranos immediately volunteered to be bait. Matt shut it down instantly.

Ouranos lowered his gaze. "Matthew, you need proper bait. I can be that."

"That would mean severing your soul jewels again," Matt said, growling between words. "Undoing everything Natassa did for you. Unacceptable."

Ouranos lifted his chin, glaring. "And is this situation not also undoing Natassa's sacrifice? And Neil's? They *died* to protect us and Athánatos. Judgement running free threatens all of that. As it stands, you cannot even escape the island without leaving a path behind for Judgement to follow and begin her quest to end the world anew." He pressed a hand to his chest. "I can become a Drifter again and attract her here."

"But to what end?" Matt said. "We get her here, and then what? The only way I know how to end a summon is by *killing the summoner.*"

"…Or severing their focus jewels," Trecheon muttered.

Matt turned to him.

Trecheon flattened an ear. "That's how we got her away from Ronan. We severed him from his Continuum Stones. Archángeli told me that if we just killed him, she'd be able to jump to a new summoner immediately. But if we sever the focus jewel, it severs her grasp on reality and she'd have a hard time coming back." He looked off. "Wish I would have thought about that with Theron."

Matt ran a hand down his face. "Don't we all." He shook his head. "That doesn't fix it though. We can't sever Dad from his Gem. He'd die just the same."

"The same would be true with Ei-Ei jewels, Brother," Alexina said, glaring at Ouranos. "Volunteering would cost you *your* life instead of Jaden's. Neither he nor I find that acceptable."

Ouranos lifted his head. "A price I am willing to pay."

"*No,*" Matt said. "We are *not* trading one life for another. We've done that *enough.* We're not letting her *win.*"

Izzy shifted her weight, flattening an ear. "Then what do we do?"

Matt paced. "I don't know." He turned to Leah. "You got anything, Leah?"

Leah continued flipping through the Book of Summons, but she shook her head. "S-Summon magic is tricky… just the idea that there's a malevolent summon is unheard of. They're supposed to be neutral, just doing what their masters tell them. But Judgement and the Phonar bend a lot of rules." She flipped to a page. "But Trecheon's right. Breaking the focus jewel bond of her summoner is the most effective way to sever her from reality."

Matt pinched the bridge of his snout. "So the only option we have is convincing her to attach to a master, then severing that master's jewel bond, and killing them. All for a temporary reprieve."

Leah wrinkled her snout. "Summons are forever, Guardian Azure. I… I don't know if there's any way to fully eliminate her." She turned back to the book. "Though again, Judgement defies normal summon rules. Maybe the book has something. But I doubt it. Even the Seal from the Sisters eventually broke."

Everyone grew silent.

"What if we recreated the Seal?" Charlotte asked.

Matt turned to her, eyebrow raised. "What do you mean?"

"The Seal held her for centuries, apparently," Charlotte said. "Millennia even. What if we Sealed her again?"

Eris stood. "The Seal still requires a sacrifice."

"But not immediately," Leah said. "The Black Cloak said Prinkípissa Titania lived on after creating the Seal. Like…"

"…Like Neil was supposed to," Trecheon finished for her.

A twinge of pain shot through Matt's chest, but he pushed it aside. "Then this might be our only option. How do we create the Seal?"

"…I can help with that."

Matt turned. The Black Cloak stood off to the side, his icy blue eyes shining and vibrant against the silver mask.

Matt growled, baring his teeth, his hackles standing on end. "You have *some nerve.*"

"I know," The Cloak said, his gaze sympathetic. "It's a requirement of this hell job. But I can still help."

Trecheon clenched his hands into fists and marched up next to Matt, snarling like a feral beast, his quills alight with flames. He pointed at the Cloak. "Neil and Natassa are *dead* and you did *nothing* to stop it. How the hell can we trust you again? How do we know whoever you choose to do this isn't *also going to be a sacrificial lamb?"*

"I didn't want them to die," the Cloak shouted, making Matt jump. The Cloak threw a hand in the air. "I was *actively trying to stop it,* but everything I did just made things *worse.* I tried saving the Veil we had, but somehow that changed the timeline and made it so Drifa and Kaoru joined Andre instead of Leah."

Andre's eyes widened and he turned to Leah. She pasted her ears back and frowned.

The Cloak waved his other hand. "I stopped Theron killing Neil while he was building a Veil anchor, and *that got Natassa killed.* And I tried *so* many times to fix that and every attempt made it even worse." He gripped his head, hunching over. "But the timeline where Natassa dies is what we got stuck with and that made everything *even worse* because it meant Natassa and Neil gave their souls for Ouranos and Alexina, and now we don't even an Athánatos royal with a weakened jewel bond!" He threw his hands down.

Matt frowned, furrowing his brow.

"I have no idea what's supposed to happen after all that," the Cloak said, looking away. "I don't even know if we *can* Seal Judgement because the two Athánatos who fit the criteria to trap Judgement are whole again. This is in your hands now." He breathed deeply. "But if we can find someone to Seal her, then I'll show you how."

Everyone grew quiet. Matt splayed his ears, his brain working overtime, unable to focus on a single thought. This was slipping from his grasp. Time was running out. He--

"I'll do it." Charlotte stood up.

Matt's whole body buzzed and his eyes widened. He waved his hands. "No. Absolutely not, Char, you can't-- You don't even fit the criteria, I mean--"

"Yes, I do," Charlotte said. "I'm the only one here with a weakened Gem bond." She tapped the Gem at her side. "Shared Gem binding with a dead primary partner. This thing gets too far away from me and I die. Couldn't get weaker than that."

Matt frowned. "You don't have Ei-Ei jewels. And we can't give you real ones because then you don't have a weakened bond she can use anymore."

"I can fix that," Ana said. "Gimmie a couple of fake ones and I can enhance them so they look and feel real. Hell, that'd probably be safer, since there'd be no chance that Judgement can actually use them to escape the island."

Sacha flicked her ears back. "But Judgement wants someone with a weakened bond, not a fully bound Ei-Ei jewel user."

"Then we only give her two sets," Alexina said. "Make her look like a Drifter."

Matt glared. "Do you really think we're going to convince Judgement we created a Drifter on purpose? It'd never work anyway, she'll still have her pupils."

"She need not pose as a Drifter," Eris said quietly. "Instead, should Judgement question it, Charlotte can claim she was in the middle of binding and was interrupted. Sisters know we have had our fair share of interruptions."

Shock ran through Matt's system. *No, this isn't happening!* "Charlotte, no offense, but you're just not *strong* enough. Judgement wants someone with power. And what's going to protect you when you go after her? If we all go in as your bodyguards, she won't go after you, and if you show up alone, she'll know something's up."

Everyone grew quiet.

Charlotte furrowed her brow. "Then I need to become the next Phonar summoner."

Matt's fur puffed up. "What?"

"Oh," Eris said. "Yes, I see what you mean! Ask two of them to join her as their new master. Judgement would not be able to resist a summoner who controls her greatest enemies, and they can protect her without suspicion because that is their jobs."

Charlotte lifted her chin. "There, see? I can do it. And I can save Dad."

Matt's heart sank, and his mind raced. "But…" He turned. "Cloak, would Charlotte have to stay on Athánatos as the Seal?"

The Cloak blinked, but shook his head. "No. While the Veil is attached to Athánatos, the Seal is everywhere. She could… go home."

Matt glared at him. That hesitation…

"There's no reason for me not to do this, Matt," Charlotte said. "You've always done everything for me. Let me do something for our family now."

Shit. *Shit.* This was not going right. "But Charlotte--"

"We don't have time for you to find every excuse to stop this," Charlotte said, glaring. "You always throw yourself headfirst into every problem. It's time I step up and do the same. Not just for Dad, but for everyone. We can't risk Judgement getting out." She lifted her chin, her face locked in the determined, intimidating look she gave her opponents before a fencing match – hard gaze, mouth in a thin line, defiance in her eyes. "This isn't me *asking.* You aren't going to stop me."

Matt's body buzzed and his heart raced. But he knew when not to fight her. He'd never win. And… he hated it, but she had a lot of good points.

There was no one else to do this. "Fine… I… fine. It's fine." He turned to Ana. "Let's… how do we get those fake Ei-Ei jewels?"

Ana grinned. "Gimmie some glass and I'll get right on it."

At that moment, Archángeli landed in the audience chamber, blowing wind around everyone's ears. *I am afraid we were unable to find Judgment…* The rest of the Phonar landed behind them, one at a time.

Zeke frowned. He glanced between Charlotte and Matt, then smiled at Archángeli. "That's fine. We've got a new thing we wanna try anyway."

Charlotte stood tall, though Matt recognized the stiffness in her actions. But she brushed her shirt free of dust, held her head high, and let out a shuddering breath. "Let's do this."

...OFTEN GO AWRY

Matt stood off to the side, watching the team prepare. Normally he'd be in the thick of things, making sure everything worked perfectly, leading where he could, helping out as much as possible. But now… it was all he could do not to scream.

No matter how you looked at it, this wasn't right.

Ana had gotten a hold of an old glass bottle and smashed it to bits, looking for the perfect sized glass shards to turn into fake Ei-Ei jewels. Charlotte would put them on, then claim her place as a royal being Alexina's step-daughter. Assuming Judgement was willing to talk.

Ouranos squirmed uncomfortably at the idea, but he went along with it anyway. Matt hadn't talked about it with Ouranos yet, but their bond had amplified ten-fold now that Ouranos had his soul back. Every feeling, every thought, every bright color in the bond echoed through Matt's mind like the saturation had been turned up to eleven. In time, Matt would probably find that comforting, but considering the dark cloud that covered them both, right now it was just painful. Matt endeavored to keep his emotions under control as much as he could. If he felt that with Ouranos, surely Ouranos felt it with him, and they both needed to be clearheaded.

It probably didn't help that he had three other bonds to wrestle with now. Izzy's was a little easier, since it wasn't *new,* though it might as well have been new since they had suppressed it for so long. The constant sound of church bells beat against the back of his mind, and little, disjointed, worried phrases rumbled around his head like a pinball.

A distant taste of iron and blood hit the back of his throat. He smacked his tongue against the roof of his mouth, trying to dispel it, though he already knew it wouldn't work. That was Zeke's bond, working overtime, while he spoke with the Phonar about their plans for Charlotte. He couldn't hear them, but he caught snippets through the bond of them discussing who would be the best phoenixes to attract Judgement. The blood and iron taste stuck fast. Apparently Zeke didn't like this plan either.

Soft scents of clover and pine hit his nose, slightly masking the blood and iron taste. He turned. Alexina. The Prinkípissa oversaw everything, directing Archons, locking down saferooms for the palace staff, and drawing plans for the best places to host Charlotte while they tried attracting Judgement. The scents between their bond read like comfort. Safety. She was finally home and ready to defend it no matter what. She was a born leader. Ouranos was next in line to be Basileus, but Matt wondered if he'd pass on that.

Based on the dull, lifeless colors and empty thoughts between their bond, Ouranos was in no shape to lead. At least not now.

Matt breathed deeply. Four bonds. Three of them were Athánatos. All of them family, in multiple ways. And he was going to go back to Zyearth, leaving three of them behind. Why couldn't Trecheon have confessed his feelings and given him an excuse to stay here?

He chewed his lip, his body tense. Because he had a secret. Something so bad that Trecheon felt he couldn't share it. And somehow that meant they couldn't have a relationship. His heart ached, and his body buzzed with shock, making his stomach roil.

After all they meant to each other… what could be so bad that Trecheon couldn't share with him?

Charlotte stood still while Eris and Ana worked to place the newly minted fake Ei-Ei jewels on her face.

Images of Neil's final moments, stuffed full of sharp ice spikes, hit his mind's eye, temporarily blinding him.

That could be Charlotte… He gripped his head, trying to stuff the memory away, but it stuck fast. *Oh, Draso's mercy, that could be Charlotte!*

A rustle of fabric whisked past his ear. He turned.

The Black Cloak.

The blue-eyed one again. The familiar one. But also the murderous one. He flattened his ears. Murderer probably wasn't right. But it wasn't entirely wrong either. Not when he knew so much and didn't do anything to fix it. It was as bad as if he had killed Neil himself.

He frowned. No… that wasn't fair either. He had tried. Too bad he had failed so spectacularly. He eyed the Cloak.

"Is Dad alive?"

The Cloak eyed him back.

Matt glared. "You owe me that at least."

The Cloak sighed and looked up at the sky. "Yes. For now."

"For now."

"There's a small window, like Ouranos said." He turned his gaze to the floor. "It's shrinking every second. But for now, yes, he's alive."

"And we're going to save him."

The Cloak stared forward, his eyes unfocused. He only shrugged.

Matt moved in front of him. "Tell me we're going to save my dad," he said. "Tell me Charlotte is going to live. We've all survived far too much to let that all fail now."

The Cloak met his eyes. "I already told you, I don't know anything at this point."

"I don't believe you," Matt said. "You're a damn time traveler. You know what's going to happen. *Tell me she's going to live.*"

The Cloak shook his head, his eyes sad. "I wish I could tell you everything is going to be okay. I wish I could go fix all of this and save everyone. You'd think being a time traveler would give me that power, but it doesn't. All it does is give me a front row seat to everyone's pain, over and over again. Pain only made worse when I try to save people." He glanced back at Charlotte. "…You'll understand one day."

Matt narrowed his gaze. "The hell does that mean?"

"You'll see," the Cloak said. "Don't be in a rush."

Matt huffed. Some help he was. He turned back to Charlotte.

His sister. His brave, fierce, intelligent, determined sister, facing down their greatest enemy, without magic, without *hope,* when no one else could.

What good was it to be a Guardian if he couldn't guard his own sister…?

"I've lost too much," Matt said, his voice shaking. "We all have. I can't do this again. I can't lose anyone else. Any more family. Please." He reached for the Cloak, then stopped and dropped his hands instead. "Please tell me they'll be okay."

The Cloak looked away. "I can't promise anything. I'm sorry."

Matt stood there, staring at him. He rubbed one arm and looked back at Charlotte. "What will I do if she dies?"

The Cloak breathed deeply. "You'll grieve."

Matt turned to him.

"You'll grieve," the Cloak said again. "You'll cry on a friend's shoulder. You'll reminisce about your life with her. You'll write songs and remember stories and share them with loved ones. You'll mourn… and move on. Because that's the only way to handle death. But you'll survive. You'll find happiness again. Because that's what she'd want for you."

Matt turned back to Charlotte. Damn it, he wasn't ready to let her go. Not like this. His heart ached and his eyes burned. "…I'm so tired of having to walk that path."

The Cloak's eyes narrowed. He turned away and crossed his arms. "Convince the Phonar that all of them need to attach themselves to Charlotte."

Matt's ears perked. "All of them? Can a summoner do that?"

"Usually, no," the Cloak said. "But like Leah said… the Phonar break rules."

Matt narrowed his gaze. "And that'll save her."

The Cloak went quiet for a moment. "…That'll give her the best chance to survive."

Matt bared his teeth. "That's *not good enough--*"

"That's all I can promise," the Cloak said. "It's her best chance."

Matt flattened his ears back. Then he turned and ran for the Phonar.

DESTINY'S PAWN

Charlotte sat in her guest room on her bed. A tiny bit of privacy before starting all this. Just a little. Time to gather her composure and prepare to follow through with all those big promises she made. She glanced at herself in the mirror, her heart pounding against her chest.

The false Ei-Ei jewels gazed back at her. The yellow Mind jewel. The red Body jewel. And no Soul Jewels. Just like Ouranos. Like Alexina.

Before Neil and Natassa gave their lives for them.

Her eyes burned thinking of Natassa. Of all their times cooking together and playing chess and talking about what it's like to lead. She loved Natassa's laugh the most. Soft and musical and always brought a smile to her face.

And Theron stole it away.

She rubbed her eyes. This wasn't fair. But so much of her life wasn't fair. Even what she was doing now wasn't fair.

But… it was necessary. No matter the cost.

The sound of beating wings entered the room, followed by a gentle gust in her ear. *My Lady, if we may speak before the summon ceremony?*

She turned. Archángeli. Zeke's summon. His old summon. Despite everything, Archángeli felt the most like a friend. She smiled. "Sure, we can talk. What do you need?"

Archángeli perched on the back of a chair. *Zeke tells us that you wish to take all the Phonar on as summons.*

"I'm gonna try to, yeah," Charlotte said. "I can't rely on anyone else to help me, and apparently Judgement will be able to tell if you're not actually attached to me as summons. We can't risk her realizing this is a trap." She rubbed her arm. "Leah's not happy about it. Apparently that'll be hard. There's a reason summons typically only work in pairs. But the Cloak seems to think I can take all of you on. If that's okay with you."

If that is your wish, my Lady. Archángeli fluffed up their feathers. *Though I worry that your weak bond to your Gem may make that difficult, since you have little magic of your own. I wish to know more about the nature of your Gem bond, to make sure we fulfill all the requirements. In my time speaking with Pilot, I learned that your relationship with your Gem is highly unusual. Can you explain?*

Charlotte took a deep breath. "Usually Zyearthlings get their Gems at age 20, when we come of age. There weren't any family Gems to pass down when I came of age, so we went to a Dragon Seer to see if she could find a Gem for me. But there weren't any compatible Gems, so I started Gem-sharing with my Uncle Walt. That means I got long life, but not magic. When he died, we tried to see if his Gem could be bound to me as the primary user, but it can't."

Archángeli tilted their head. *And it is unusual to have no Gem to bind to?*

"Very," Charlotte said. "We used to go back every year to the Dragon Seer to see if she had a Gem for me, but ah… I stopped doing that about five years ago." She looked Archángeli dead in the eye. "You can't tell anyone what I'm about to say."

You have my word, my Lady.

"During my last trip, the Dragon Seer told me Draso chose me to be without a full Gem bond," Charlotte said. "She said it was my 'destiny,' if I chose to follow it." She shrugged. "I didn't know what she meant, but… I think I do now."

Archángeli perked their head. *You believe this is your destiny. To become the new Seal.*

Charlotte nodded. "It sounds so… pretentious." She waved her hands in the air. "Oh, look at me, I'm the chosen one!" She sighed and looked away. "I think the Seer wanted this destiny thing to give me confidence, but it just makes me feel small and stupid. Like… like a pawn or a tool instead of a sentient being."

Archángeli flew to the bed and sat next to her. *And yet, you chose this path anyway.*

"Of course," Charlotte said. "Because I want my dad back. I don't want to run from destiny, like Theron did. I want Judgement gone for good, especially after everyone she and Theron took from us. I'm so sick of losing everyone…"

Archángeli got quiet. Charlotte turned to them. The bird shifted back and forth on their feet. *My Lady… There may yet be more loss on the horizon.*

A tiny shock ran up Charlotte's spine. But just a tiny one. She anticipated this. "I'm going to die, aren't I?"

Archángeli bowed their head. *I… cannot predict that. But… my memories of the days of the first Seal have been slowly returning to me. And while the Black Cloak technically spoke true that Prinkípissa Titania lived after creating the Seal, she did not live long, nor did she live comfortably. The Seal ate away at her, body and mind, physically and magically, and after a year, she gave up her Ei-Ei jewels and died, taking her place in the Grove.*

Charlotte splayed her ears. "And that will happen to me."

Again, I cannot predict what will happen, Archángeli said. *Titania had sealed Judgement at her full strength, as a new summon. Judgement's long centuries may have weakened her. Or perhaps your Gem will Seal her better than Titania's Ei-Ei jewels. …Or perhaps it will make things harder since you have a weak bond and a cabal of eight summons draining your power. It is all unpredictable now. However…* Archángeli lowered their gaze. *Death is possible.*

"Death is likely," Charlotte said.

Archángeli said nothing.

"Archángeli," Charlotte said. "What do the Athánatos do for Drifters who can't coax their souls back to their bodies?"

Archángeli turned to her. *Do you mean… how do they lay them to rest?*

She nodded. "Ouranos has mentioned something about a ritual, but I never heard what that ritual was."

Mmm, Archángeli stretched a wing. *They will freeze the brain of the afflicted.*

Cold ice ran down Charlotte's spine. "And… is it… quick?"

It is quick and quiet and painless, Archángeli said. *It is like going to sleep. The afflicted loses consciousness, then the brain shuts down and they pass on. There is a reason they chose that method. They call it* telikós ýpnos *– final sleep.*

Charlotte churned Archángeli's words in her mind. "Archángeli… if this proves to be too much… if I can't handle this without being in constant, writing pain… Tell Zeke I want *telikós ýpnos*. I want him to do it, if he's willing. I want family." She met his gaze. "Can you do that for me?"

Archángeli's gaze grew dark. *Matthew will not stand for that.*

"It's not his choice," Charlotte said. "Can you tell Zeke?"

Archángeli bowed, spreading their wings. *Of course, my Lady.*

Charlotte sighed. "Come on, let's get this over with." Archángeli nodded and took off out the door. She followed slowly behind, taking in the world around her. The gentle night air. The moonlight on her face. The feel of marble under her feet, and the echo of her footsteps in her ears.

I just hope Dad survives this.

CHAPTER 55

DECEPTION

Everything hurt.

Jaden had been here before. Countless times. He knew the feeling intimately. Pain was a rite of passage for Guardians.

So why did this one feel so different? He tried to move… then stopped.

Someone was nearby. And if they weren't calling out to him, it was probably an enemy. He let his body go ragdoll, hoping they'd leave him alone.

Something wet and sticky smacked him in the face. And there were… words. *There is no use pretending, Guardian. I can tell when you are awake.*

Shock ran through every atom of his body. Oh, *shit.*

Judgement.

Another splat of sludge. *You are remarkably perceptive. A shame that appears to be your only good quality, as it is useless to me.*

Jaden opened his eyes. They were in the woods somewhere, which explained the roots and stones poking into his back. Swatches of moonlight highlighted the rocky ground.

And Judgement stood above him, twice his size, grinning at him, her blue Cast eyes, blank and lifeless.

Fear gripped his heart, but he stood and faced her anyway. Pain radiated up his leg. His foot was broken or twisted. No chance to run. He shoved the fear away and glared. "What do you want?"

She chuckled, a dark, gurgling thing. *I already have what I want, little Guardian, at least for now.* She poked his shirt, leaving a black stain, her finger at least as thick as his arm. *A host.*

Jaden raised an eyebrow, but then his eyes widened. "Oh, *hell.*"

Ah, you see it now. She leaned down, pressing her face close to his. *You are not an ideal host, but I suppose beggars cannot be choosers, as your mainland saying goes.*

Jaden's mind raced, a thousand questions popping up at once. Why him? If he wasn't ideal, who was? Could he control her like his dad did with the gryfon brothers?

Could she hear his thoughts? He remembered Alexina talking to Kyrie telepathically, but that was a conscious decision. That didn't mean Kyrie heard *everything.* Did it?

This was *not good.*

If you are contemplating how you can try and control me, Judgement said. *The answer is you can't. I do not conform to the typical rules of summons. In this relationship, I reign.*

Jaden narrowed his gaze. *But can you hear my thoughts if I'm not talking to you?*

Judgement grinned again. *Quiet one, aren't you? Good. A nice change of pace from Theron's constant prattle.*

Jaden smirked internally. Apparently not. Good. That gave him an advantage. "So I suppose Theron wasn't an ideal host either then, was he?"

Judgement waved a hand. *Far from it. Strong willed and bent on revenge against invisible enemies long dead. No understanding of true power or its purpose.*

Jaden lifted a brow. He hadn't expected an actual response. If she was willing to talk, he needed to give her something to talk about. Find answers. "For all Theron was, I wouldn't have pegged him as someone who didn't understand power."

TRUE power, little Guardian, Judgement said. She slunk a few meters away, trailing black sludge over the forest floor. *Theron believed power's only purpose was to harm, no matter the means. But true power is to exert one's will on others, for one's purposes, to one's ends.*

Jaden rolled his eyes. "The Cast are an embodiment of exerting your will on others. Clearly he understood *that.*"

Judgement roared, throwing her hands in the air, spewing black sludge everywhere. Tiny blue eyes floated on the surface of the sludge bombs. Her false Shadow Cast. She turned to Jaden, glaring. *He failed to see their art!* she snapped. *To him they were only tools – weapons of destruction. But they are the ultimate expression of LOVE.*

Jaden raised an eyebrow. *And I thought Theron was deluded.* Judgement huffed, and began petting one of the Cast. Jaden pressed his lips together.

Abrax had said the same thing. They were expressions of love. He could use that. "Oh… oh, I see! Because they're our purest form, right? The soul exposed, eternal life given, freedom from pain and mental anguish?"

Judgement pointed, her eyes lighting up. *Yes, yes! You understand.* She paused, rubbing her inky chin. *You were quick to make that connection. None of your kind has ever seen them as anything but monsters.*

"My apologies, my Lady," Jaden said, taking a short bow. "When one is introduced to beauty as a beast, influence takes over and it's hard to see the truth through the lies." He took slow, steady breaths, drawing on a lifetime of diplomacy and deception necessary to succeed as a Golden Guardian. *Just get her to trust me. Get me back to my team. Get me to a position where I can break free of her.*

Judgement eyed him up and down. *Hmm. So you do recognize royalty.*

"And greatness," Jaden said, laying it on thick. "A product of many years as a Golden Guardian. It was a necessary skill, especially while traveling intergalactically. A shame I didn't recognize it with the Cast. I've clearly been on Earth too long."

Judgement lifted her chin and narrowed her gaze. *If you are well traveled, then you must know of other planets where my Cast would be loved and accepted.*

A shock ran down Jaden's spine, but he didn't let it show on his face. "Indeed I do, my Lady."

She paused. *Lady. Indeed. I see.* She shrunk down to his size and slithered up to him like an octopus, long black tentacles gripping the ground and pulling her along. She lifted his chin and looked him in the eye. *Perhaps you have more worth than I previously thought.* She tilted his head left and right like someone examining a horse for sale. Jaden's belly roiled in disgust, but he stood calm and let her. Then she stepped back. *Kneel, slave.*

He did as he was told, pain shooting up his damaged foot.

Guardian, she said. *Are you willing to spread the truth of the Cast through the heavens to all those willing to hear it?*

Jaden swallowed hard. "I am, my Lady."

Good. Stand, my servant.

Jaden stood, hoping she didn't notice his shaking legs. "What is my Lady's wish?"

To escape this hell planet, Judgement said. *That has always been my desire, ever since Ronan spoke of the worlds outside this one. It was why I had enticed him to seek you out in the first place. I imagined it would grant me passage off this planet. A shame he was so useless in that endeavor. To think I had wasted so much time with him.* She lifted her head. *But first, we must escape the island. Which means we need a willing royal to create a rip in this new Veil and allow us passage off.* She grinned wildly, her dripping, inky teeth taking over her entire face. *Your wife, perhaps?*

The fur on the back of Jaden's neck stood straight up, but he nodded. "But we need to convince them I'm alone first. No one will let me off if they think I still have you in tow."

Then fabricate something, Judgement said. *You're clever enough.* She pointed an inky finger at him. *But do not think to deceive me. Yours will be a painful and violent end if you do.*

Jaden bowed again. "Yes, my Lady. Which way to the palace?"

Behind you, she said. *My Cast will take you most of the way until you can walk on foot. We are at least an hour away. Do not mess this up, or it will be your life, Guardian. You are not my only potential host.* She slunk into the earth and vanished, leaving only two of her false Cast behind. A voice echoed in his head. *And remember… I am always at your side…*

Jaden let out a long breath, trying to slow his heart. A reprieve. A small one, but a reprieve nonetheless. The two Cast slunk around Jaden's legs and carried him across the bumpy forest ground toward the palace. He struggled to balance at first, but eventually found his stride, despite the ache in his damaged leg.

One hour. One hour to figure out how to fool Judgement into thinking he was on her side and work with his kids to get her out of his life.

He prayed to Draso it was enough time.

CHAPTER 56

A NEW SUMMONER

Charlotte stood in the audience chamber of the throne room, surrounded by family, friends, and Athánatos.

And the Phonar as well. Eight phoenixes, all in their anthropomorphic forms, elements swirling about their bodies. They all held themselves stiff, their gazes fixated on Charlotte.

It made her shiver.

"So the plan then," Alexina said, her voice calm and collected. "Is to have the whole Phonar Order attach to Charlotte. She will then engage Judgement however we can, and if Judgement leaves Jaden and joins her, we initiate the Seal."

The Black Cloak stood off to the side, shifting back and forth. "That's the plan, yes."

Alexina narrowed her gaze at him. "And you know the magic of the Seal."

"I do, my Lady."

She crossed her arms. "So what does it entail?"

The Cloak lifted his head and spoke a string of what sounded like an old form of the Athánatos language. As he spoke, a deep rumble ripped through Charlotte's belly. She rubbed her arms, her fur on end. Everyone around her looked equally disturbed, glancing around for the source of the thing. The Cloak narrowed his gaze. "Trust me. I know the magic well."

Alexina glared right back.

The Cloak's gaze softened. "Trust me, my Lady. As you trusted me with Zeke."

Alexina flicked her ears back. She turned to Zeke, her brow furrowed. "Fine. For now, I trust you." Alexina took Charlotte's hands. "Trust him too, for whatever worth it has."

Charlotte nodded. Alexina hugged her, then stepped back.

"Charlotte," the Cloak said. She turned to him. He nodded. "Remember your lies. You have only two jewels because your binding ceremony was interrupted. You have the eight summons because you intend to force Judgment to let Jaden go. Speak as little as possible to avoid falling into traps that'll give you away." He took a deep breath. "I have faith in you."

Charlotte bit her lip and nodded, but she said nothing.

Leah moved next to Charlotte. "We'll start with just two and see how you handle things," she said. "Two summons are normal, and they can attach themselves to anyone, regardless whether they have magic or not." She wrinkled her snout. "It's adding more than two that's the unknown."

Matt frowned. "There really hasn't been a summoner with more than two summons?"

"Not that I know of," Leah said. "Which could mean either our bodies can't handle it well or summons just don't want to share. Either way, we have absolutely no frame of reference here." She rubbed her arm. "I have no idea what will happen."

"We'll take it as we go," Charlotte said. "Who are we starting with?"

Archángeli and Kyrie walked forward in their anthropomorphic form and bowed.

Leah met Charlotte's gaze. "Remember what I said. They'll start the oath, and you'll know if it works if the response words come to you immediately. Every oath is a little different, so you can't just make it up. It's to ensure the oath is legit." She smiled, though her eyes betrayed her sadness. Whether that was worry for Charlotte or something else, Charlotte couldn't tell. She gently squeezed Charlotte's hand. "Good luck." She stepped back.

The summons stood in front of Charlotte, their pupilless eyes staring deep. They swirled ice and wind around her as distant words spun through her mind.

Charlotte Azure of Zyearth, their voice said in unison. *We call on you to be master of our Power. Grant us safe passage and fulfill this oath.*

As if someone else had taken control of her body, Charlotte walked up to them and gently placed her hands on their heads. "I accept your oath and take responsibility for your power," she said, her mouth moving automatically. "May we complete this oath together."

Aleiha basorim, the summons said, their voices melding together. *We are one soul.*

"We are one soul," Charlotte whispered.

Archángeli and Kyrie vanished into dust and ripped around her body in a violent wind. Power filled her body and her heart beat fast and hard against her chest. But instantly she felt their presence in her mind.

We are with you, my Lady, Archángeli said. *Call on us when you need us.*

She breathed a sigh of relief. At least one worked. Thank Draso.

Leah clapped. "Good, good," she said. But then she flicked her ears back. "I… wish we could have you summon each pair before attaching you to new ones. New summon bonds explode pretty violently on the first summon. But they can take anywhere from five to twenty minutes to cool down and I-I don't think we have that kind of time…"

"It'll be fine," Charlotte said. "I feel great. Let's keep going."

"Charlotte?"

Charlotte looked up.

Zeke frowned. "Take care of Archángeli for me? They've been my friend for a very long time…"

She smiled. "Of course, brother."

Zeke smiled at that. "Thanks, *adelfi*."

"Let us try Excelsis and Deo next," Ouranos said. "In Natassa's honor."

Charlotte nodded. The fire phoenixes stepped forward and bowed, their white and purple fire wrapping around them. And they began anew. The summons offered themselves. Charlotte accepted freely.

But the wave of power hit far harder this time, knocking her to the ground, and crushing her soul. She barely held in a scream.

Matt and Izzy were at her side in an instant. Izzy's cooling healing energy flowed through her, but it did nothing to ease the crushing power. She couldn't breathe, her ribs ached, and she gagged.

But suddenly the weight lightened. She turned. Ana kneeled next to her, resting a hand on her Gem. "I can't do much, but I can give your Gem a little boost to take on the extra summons." She rested a hand on the false Ei-Ei jewels. "These too. I don't know if I can fix it enough so you can take on all of them, but this'll help."

Charlotte sighed relief. The crushing pain vanished. "Thank you."

Leah flicked her ears back. "Are you sure you want to keep going?"

Charlotte's ear twitched. She eyed Matt, then turned back to Leah. "…Will it kill me if I do? I don't… if I die before we get Dad, then this whole thing is a waste."

Matt covered his mouth with his hand and looked away.

"It… shouldn't," Leah said. "I-If you can't handle it, I think the oath just won't take. That's typically what happens with normal pairs…"

Charlotte took a deep breath. "Then let's keep going."

Ouranos frowned, but he waved over Jústi and Pax. Charlotte's spine tingled, remembering the pair of them years ago on Zyearth begging her for help for their master, all while fighting a battle themselves. Both of them had sought her out and apologized not long after Ouranos had been freed from his father's clutches, and while they weren't friends, per se, they were at least… familiar. She reached out to them.

They swirled their elements around her, reciting their oath. The return oath instantly manifested in Charlotte's head, ready to complete it, though the pressure and pain from the last oath already left her sore and tired.

This oath was… hesitant. The previous two she felt compelled to fulfill. This one she was given an… option. Only if she wanted. She could let it go.

Her body screamed at her to let it go.

But she had to do this. She pushed through and spoke the return oath, placing her hands on their heads.

The pain hit again, knocking her down. Izzy was there again, and Leah joined her. Ana was there too, her magic pulsing through Charlotte's Gem, but the pain didn't fully subside this time. She clutched her chest and threw up.

Izzy pumped her full of cooling energy. "I don't think we can try for the last pair."

"We *have* to," Matt said, desperation in his voice. He helped her sit up, but she still struggled with her breathing. Matt rubbed her shoulder. "She needs this."

Izzy glared. "Matt, we *just* reconciled over you forcing things on me. Don't start doing the same thing to your sister."

Matt gripped Charlotte's shoulder, almost too tight, chewing his lip. "I'm not… This isn't for me, it's… The Black Cloak told me that having all the Phonar gave her the best chance to survive."

Charlotte's ears perked.

Izzy bared her teeth. "Matt, we can't *trust him.*"

"No, he's right…" Charlotte said. "I need all of them. I trust the Cloak. I can do this." She forced herself to stand, though she wobbled.

Ouranos caught her. "Charlotte, there is no need to push yourself so. You have enough to hold back Judgement and entice her to join you."

She pushed away from Ouranos. "Leah, you said this is magic build up, right? Getting ready for the first summoning?"

Leah flicked her tail and nodded.

"So once I summon for the first time, I'll be okay?"

"In theory…"

Alexina stepped forward. "Are we truly unable to let her summon the ones she has and release that energy? I know we are short on time, but this could give her the best chance to take on Lumen and Sémini."

One of the sentries ran into the room, huffing. Baltazar. "Lord Ouranos, Lady Alexina… Scouts have spotted Jaden headed for the palace."

Matt perked his ears. "Headed *here? Alone?*"

"Not alone," Baltazar said. "He was riding a pair of Shadow Cast at incredible speed, but when he got closer, he stepped off and continued on foot. One of our scouts said he made eye contact with him, but he made no attempt to speak. He said he almost seems… possessed.”

“Then we don’t have time.” Charlotte held her hands out to the last two summons. They reached for her with their elements, filling her mind with the oath and her chest with crushing pain. But the return phrases manifested anyway, and she completed the oath.

And then the pain just… stopped. For a frightening moment, she wondered if she was dead. But no. Power replaced the pain. Immense, shocking, terrifying power… but also comforting. The eight birds spoke to her in her mind, filling her heart with a strange joy.

We are with you, Lady Charlotte.

“Charlotte…” Matt frowned. “Your eyes are… glowing.”

Charlotte blinked. “Well. Better to attract Judgement then.” She lifted her chin. “Let’s go find Dad.”

THE SEAL

Jaden's whole body buzzed with adrenaline as he walked toward the palace, limping on his bum leg. The early morning just barely pushed aside the dark of night, painting the sky indigo.

One whole hour and he had nothing. Every time he had an idea he thought would work, it crashed and burned the moment he thought of his family. If he rushed in and explained as quick as he could before Judgement escaped, Matt would do something to try and save him and get killed. If he tried using code words from the war with Zeke, Judgement would pick it up and kill them both. If he tried convincing them that Judgement let him go, Leah or Izzy would try healing him and immediately know something was off and Judgement would kill them. If he tried getting a message to Alexina to pretend to open a rip in the Veil and escape, Alexina would recognize the deception instantly and Judgement would kill them both.

There was no outcome here where everyone lived.

He couldn't even bring himself to reach out to the sentry when he spotted him in the woods. Saying or doing anything would put whoever he interacted with in danger. He was a ticking time bomb.

The palace came into view over the hill. The thinnest rays of sunshine peaked through the trees. Dawn's rosy fingers.

Jaden stopped.

This… wouldn't do. He couldn't go through with it. He couldn't condemn his family to death. He was better off ending his own life instead and leaving Judgement an orphan.

A lump grew in his throat. After all this. All he had survived. He finally had his wife, his kids, his home in sight. And then… this. Death for his family… or death for himself.

Draso, why did you do this to me?

He took a deep breath and lifted his Gem out of its holster. If he didn't do this now… he'd never do it. He'd leave everything open for Judgement to ravage them all. He eyed the Gem, shaking, his throat closing up. *Just end it, Azure… Be the Guardian.*

All he had to do was destroy the Gem…

An inky tentacle snatched it out of his hand and the Cast slithered off into the woods. Jaden's eyes grew wide. "Wait, *stop!*" He dashed after it, but his broken foot collapsed under his weight and he crashed to the ground. Before he could try again, another Cast scooped him up and rushed for the palace, dragging him away from the Gem. He fought in its grip. "No, no! Give me back my Gem! Judgement, make them give it back! No one will believe me if I don't have it!"

This is the punishment for betrayal, slave, Judgement echoed in his head.

Jaden's fur stood on end. How did she…?

I admit you are clever, Judgement said. *But if you will allow the play on words, your fear clouds your judgement. A shame for you that you recognized it too late.*

Jaden's body buzzed. Oh, *hell.* When he was testing if she could hear his thoughts, he had only thought of her name… and she recognized it. She played him.

A strange, amused feeling rushed through his body. *Well, well, what is this I see waiting for us?*

Jaden turned. And his heart stopped.

Because it wasn't Matt or Zeke or Leah or Izzy or Alexina standing on the clover lawn.

It was Charlotte.

Charlotte stood on the clover lawn, the power of the summons coursing through her, their presence comforting. She had insisted everyone else stay behind. Hide in the palace, just in case this didn't work. Just in case releasing all eight summons at once was too much for any of them. Matt was right about one thing. She wasn't going to sacrifice any more lives to Judgement. She held her chin high, holding her body steady.

And yet, fear gripped her heart.

Draso has a great destiny for you.

A great destiny. To face down Judgement. To recreate her Seal and save the universe. To save her father – a father she had long thought dead. It was a great destiny.

A great destiny. That ended in death.

We will help take on the burden of the Seal as much as we can, my Lady. You are not alone. Archángeli's comforting voice, like a cooling breeze on her brow.

But she had no interest in entertaining false hope. So she said nothing.

The early morning sun lightened the sky, painting everything in a gentle, faded blue, barely outlining the trees, the hills, the palace, the Four Sisters grove. Neil's Veil statue, fresh and clean next to the aged Cloak… and the empty Purge and Seal.

She choked. Neil… Natassa… they deserved so much more…

The light crept across the lawn until it caught something new – and black. Judgement. She crawled along the ground, leaving inky residue and crushed clover behind her. Her sloppy wings and too-wide, fanged grin shocked Charlotte's pained heart. Those three, glowing, expressionless eyes left little blue highlights over her blobby skin.

And wrapped in her side, held down by inky tentacles, was Jaden.

Jaden stared at her wide-eyed, struggling in the summon's grip. "Charlotte, what are you doing? *Run!*" But Judgement wrapped a tentacle around his mouth, cutting off his words.

Not that she'd obey them anyway. She stood her ground.

A splat of Judgement's sludge hit her snout. *Well then. We have a fighter here.*

Charlotte wiped her snout clean and threw the ink aside. She formed fists. "Let my father go, Judgement."

Or what? Judgement said. *I see your bonds, little Prinkípissa.* Charlotte's fur stood on end. Judgement chuckled. *Yes, little one. I know how the bonds of marriage works. Your father married a royal. That, by extension, makes you one. You even have the Ei-Ei jewels to prove it.* She tilted her head. *Though not all of them, it seems.*

Charlotte narrowed her gaze. "We were *interrupted.*"

Ah, Judgement said. *A shame. I know Theron's children had access to their magic after losing the Soul Jewels, but the same rules do not apply if you never completed the bond. No elements for you to play with.* She rubbed her chin. *Pity. A broken Gem bond, and incomplete Ei-Ei jewels. Your only hope to push me back is with your fists.* She grinned wider.

Jaden struggled more, pulling a hand free, though Judgement immediately pulled him back.

Charlotte's heart raced, and she snarled. *"Wrong."* The summons' magic ripped through her, pressing against her mind, filling her with strength and hope. Hope she dared to cling to. She threw her hand out and called on the Phonar.

As one, the phoenixes burst forth, filling the air with vibrant scents of thunderstorms, forest fires, ocean breezes, and deep winter, as their elements flew about her.

The pain in her bones started the moment they appeared. She held on and refused to give in. Jaden counted on it.

Judgement's grin vanished instantly and she shrieked, flying back… and leaving Jaden on the clover lawn. The phoenixes chased her down, screeching and calling, divebombing her, shocking her with magic. She swatted at them, but their new-summon magic ripped apart her limbs. Jústi's lightning tore through her hand, Archángeli's wind tattered her wings, Lumen's rocks and stone exploded her shoulder. Each wound rained down sand and blood and inky flesh, leaving them hissing on the lawn. Any Cast she formed fell instantly to Excelsis and Deo's fire, and Kyrie and Pax combined snow and earth into a muddy, slippery mess, halting her escape.

For a wild moment, Charlotte dared to hope. Though the pain of the summon's power crashed through those hopes, beating against her brain.

Jaden shook himself and hobbled toward her, his foot at an odd angle. Clearly broken. He waved a hand at her. "Charlotte, go, *go!* Before--"

Judgement screamed, loud and violent. She rebuilt her arms with inky black and raised them high, blasting back the Phonar. Before the phoenixes could recover, she rushed across the lawn, leaving trails of blood and dust.

She swatted Jaden away, and snatched Charlotte in her massive hands. Charlotte cried out, but didn't make much effort to fight back. This was what they wanted. Hopefully.

Judgement shook her. *You FOOL. You have only eight Phonar. You do not have the necessary components. You cannot hope to best me!* She pressed her enormous face close to Charlotte's, snorting black sludge all over her. Judgement grinned, crooked and sloppy, her body dripping away through the wounds, even as they healed. *In your efforts to save your father, you have made yourself my perfect companion. I relinquish my hold on him… but I trade a life for a life.*

Charlotte growled. "So be it."

"No!" Jaden shouted. Matt, Izzy, Zeke, Ouranos, and the Cloak came running out of the palace toward them. The Phonar recovered and rushed Judgement in a colorful display of elements, though even Charlotte could tell they moved slowly.

Charlotte held her tongue and closed her eyes.

Then Judgement claimed Charlotte as her summoner.

A fresh wave of pain shocked her, and Judgement's greasy, rotten presence filled her mind to the brim, darkening her vision and making her ears bleed. The summon's body sank into her, and Charlotte collapsed to the clover, her senses blinded with pain.

I claim you as my own, Summoner, Judgement said. *Face the wrath of Judgement.*

She coughed, then threw up. "Cloak…!"

"I'm here." Calm. Collected. Good. Someone needed to be. He gripped her shoulders, massaging them gently, and helped her sit up. "Sit still. Don't try to move. Judgement is in your mind, so I'm going to create the Seal."

Charlotte coughed, tasting copper. "…Matt."

"I'm here." Matt held her hand. "We all are, Char." More hands gripped her. Zeke. Ouranos. Izzy.

The pain threatened to steal her consciousness now. Judgement beating against her skull, begging to be let out. She held her back as best she could, pulling on the Phonar's power. "…Hurry."

The Cloak wrapped arms across her shoulders and held her close to him. He mumbled in some form of the Athánatos language, making her body rumble as before, though far deeper and stronger. Almost like she was purring. It strangely soothed her pain, just a little.

Judgement retreated, but not of her own volition. The Seal chased her back. Fresh panic, Judgement's panic, roiled through Charlotte's belly and she threw up again.

"What are you *doing?*" Jaden shouted. "You're killing her! Stop!"

"My love, do not interfere." Alexina. "Trust her."

Judgement screamed so loudly in Charlotte's ears, her head threatened to burst, but she pushed back, relying on the growing seal and the deep purrs from the magic.

"NO!" Jaden shouted. Charlotte picked up sounds of a struggle. "No, you can't do this, Charlotte, you can't! You can't let her *win!*"

"*Let me do this!*" Charlotte shouted. "Let me do this, because I'm sick of losing *everything!*" She forced her eyes open, forced them to focus. Jaden's face came into view through unshed tears.

"Then let me take it," Jaden said. "Give it to me—"

"Dad, please…" Charlotte met his eyes. "Let me do this… I can't lose you again… I can't--Gah!" Judgement screamed once more and vanished deep inside her body… and the Seal took her place. The purring rumble vanished and a thorny, violent, screeching thing buried in her mind. Every movement ached, every breath made her head swim. She coughed – blood again. "Oh Draso, tell me it's done…"

"Hold on." Izzy. Her healer's voice. Her quiet voice.

The voice for the dying.

The healing started… but it did nothing. The cooling power rushed her body, but it didn't touch her pain. Not even Izzy's power. The spiked Seal continued bouncing around her brain, ripping apart her neurons. Tears streamed down her face.

She couldn't hold it, couldn't hold it, *couldn't hold it.* "…T-Tell me the Seal is done…"

"…There." The Cloak said. "It's done."

Matt tightened his grip on Charlotte's hand. "Char?"

She blinked tears out of her eyes and glanced at the Cloak. "Is this… tell me this goes away… tell me this isn't what the last Seal lived with every day…"

The Cloak closed his eyes a moment, then shook his head. "I wish I could tell you different."

Oh, fire and ice and *flame*… She couldn't live with this. Not for a moment longer. She tried to stand, but her legs gave out instantly.

Jaden reached forward and caught her. "I'm here…"

This was it. She leaned into Jaden. "…Where's Archángeli?"

A cooling wind brushed her fur. *Here, my Lady.*

She tried reaching for him, but the pain was too much, and her arm fell to her side. She coughed, blood pooling on her lips. *"Telikós ýpnos…"*

Zeke's eyes widened. "What?"

Ouranos pressed his lips together. "Charlotte, that is… are you sure?"

She nodded as best she could.

Jaden held a hand to his snout. "Charlotte, *please.*"

Matt's grip on her hand tightened further, to the point of pain. "What? What's that? What's she talking about?"

"I want it to be… Zeke…" Charlotte said.

Zeke frowned, flattening his ears, but he nodded. "If… you're sure…"

Matt turned to him. "What is going on? Someone *tell me.*"

Ouranos rested a hand on Matt's shoulder. "It is the final sleep, brother. What… what we did for Cix when his Gem bond broke and we could not save him."

Matt's eyes widened. "Wait. Brain freezing?" He turned to Charlotte. "Charlotte--"

"I can't *live* with this," Charlotte said, tears staining her fur. "If this doesn't kill me, the pain will. Please, Matt."

Matt opened his mouth to speak, but he stopped. Tears filled his eyes. He moved his jaw, clearly searching for words, but remained silent.

She took his hand. "Please…"

"Brother," Ouranos said. "Comfort your sister…"

Charlotte reached out for him.

He scrunched his nose and wiped at his eyes, but he reached back for her, pulling her into his arms and resting his chin on her head. He held her, gently. "I'm here… I'll always be here…"

Jaden moved close to her too, holding her hand to his forehead. "I… I'm here too. We're all here, Charlotte."

She leaned into his hug. "Thank you…"

Ouranos took her hand. "My sister… a loved Princess…" He smiled at her. "Draw on the strength from your brothers, your father, your friends." He nodded to Zeke. Zeke blinked tears out of his eyes, but he leaned forward, cupped her head in his hands and pressed his thumbs to her temples. She closed her eyes, trying desperately to push aside the pain and listen to those around her.

"Soon you will enter Draso's Palace," Ouranos said. "To the open arms of your mother, your lost family and friends, your uncle, and all those who went before you. Neil and Natassa will welcome you with hugs and bright smiles."

Charlotte choked, sobbing.

"Rest, sister," Ouranos said. "Draw on that love now… and rest."

"…I-I'm so sorry, Charlotte," Zeke said, his voice breaking.

Matt held her tight. "…Love you, sis."

Jaden kissed her hand. "…Thank you."

She couldn't speak. She hoped leaning into them got her message across.

A cold snap jolted between her ears.

And the light vanished.

HOME...

Matt sat cross-legged on the wedding rugs in the Four Sisters Grove, still here despite the fact that there wouldn't be any wedding. Dusty. Muddy. Covered in leaves. A symbol of what they lost.

~~The dawn had long passed, and the light of midday filtered through the~~ trees, catching the crystals still hanging in the branches, and painting rainbows on the three remaining guardians around him. The Cloak, fully restored, more mysterious than ever. Neil, the Veil, fulfilling his duty as Basileus and protecting his people.

Only a patch of dead grass and dirt remained where the Purge had been.

Matt stared up at the final statue. A tall, determined, feminine quilar, holding a vast kite shield that protected her body from her neck to her toes. She held a fencing sword at her side, because of course she did. Unlike the royal statues at the palace, this one's features were vague and stylized, but the resemblance was uncanny regardless.

Charlotte. Standing as the new Seal, as she wanted.

Finally Judgement was in her place.

Matt's chest ached and burned staring up at the statues. Charlotte, holding Judgment back with the Seal. Neil, protecting Athánatos with the Veil. The Cloak, watching everyone burn around them as they fought to keep the timeline steady. Neither Charlotte nor Neil deserved to die for that. The Cloaks didn't deserve the pain that came with their roles, as much as Matt didn't like or trust them.

Fire and ice…

How was he supposed to move on after they had lost so much?

He'd always been told this was the fate of a soldier. You make friends, you lose them. But this wasn't the same. That wasn't supposed to include Natassa. It wasn't supposed to include his sister.

It wasn't supposed to include Neil, who had finally escaped the life of a soldier.

This wasn't supposed to happen.

He held himself and shut his eyes tight, bowing his head and letting the tears flow.

Just one moment. One moment of mourning. One moment of full tears and crying and then he'd go back and help everyone else. They deserved that much. But he needed this before he broke entirely.

A gentle rosy dawn lit up his mind. He lifted his head.

Ouranos walked into the grove. Slow, dragging his feet. His tail scraped along through the clovers and caught on the strings of the wedding rugs.

For a quick moment, Matt pulled on his mask, ready to hang it on his face and hide away the tears so he could be strong for Ouranos. But there really wasn't a point with his Gem-bonded brother. He'd see right through it. And maybe Matt needed him to.

We need not wear masks with each other, brother, Ouranos said, filling Matt's mind and heart with an array of bright colors. *We need to see each other without it, if we wish to help our loved ones through this time.*

Matt sighed. *Yeah, you're right.*

Ouranos sat on the rug next to Matt. He took Matt's hand and together, they stared at their lost loved ones in the form of the Seal and Veil.

"Charlotte will receive an Athánatos wake," Ouranos said. "With a covered burning, and a statue alongside Neil and Natassa, if you wish it. She was just as much an Athánatos as Neil was. Our people will honor her."

"I'm sure that'd bring some comfort to Dad," Matt said. "He's taking this really hard."

"We all are," Ouranos said. "It was a death too soon after the losses we already faced."

"Mmm." Matt stared at the statues. His gaze wandered to Neil. He and Natassa's wake had been put off again, with everything going on. They had wanted a celebration of their lives. That felt impossible after everything with Judgement. Just… a few days. A few days without disaster.

Draso, just give us a few days…

"I have asked Embrik and Melaina to rule Athánatos as Basileus and Basilea," Ouranos said.

Matt turned. "I ah, had wondered if you would pass the mantle or not."

"I will never be Basileus," Ouranos said. "I cannot carry the title when it reminds me so strongly of the father who hurt and neglected us all. I cannot carry it when Neil had done so much good in its name without ever being officially awarded the title. Nor can I carry it when it holds the weight of my sister's death in its very syllables. I had so believed that we could take Theron down once and for all. We had the strength." He sighed. "I did not realize the sacrifice it would take."

Matt took a deep breath. He gave Ouranos' hand a squeeze.

"Melaina and Embrik have agreed to take the roles. Embrik will retake his given name – Kyros – and find someone from the palace to take the Embrik title. Athánatos is in good hands." He let go of Matt's hand and stared at his palms. "I am not the hands Athánatos needs. I…"

"Stop, Ouranos," Matt said, taking his hand again. "Don't start convincing yourself why you aren't good for that role. This has nothing to do with that."

Ouranos looked at him, his eyes glassy. "Then what is it? Why do I feel this shame?"

"You feel a burden, Ouranos," Matt said. "A burden to take care of your subjects. But you've done that already. You fought your father. You helped trap Judgement. You gave them the Seal and the Veil."

Ouranos stared at the ground. "Only through death."

"Through sacrifice," Matt said. He looked up at the statues. "…I miss them. I'll miss them for the rest of my life. But… they chose this. They chose to sacrifice themselves for a chance at peace. And we have peace now." Matt took a shaking breath. "It hurts. It'll hurt for a long time. But we have the peace to explore that hurt and come to terms with it." He wrapped an arm across Ouranos' shoulders in a sideways hug. "You've done enough, Ouranos. You've saved your subjects. You don't need to carry that burden anymore." He squeezed him. "You deserve peace."

Ouranos stared at Neil, his eyes shining with tears. His pupiled eyes, something Matt was still getting used to. He took a deep, shuddering breath. "I want to come to Zyearth with you."

Matt's eyes widened. "What?"

"I can no longer live on Athánatos," Ouranos said. "I have lost too much here. My parents, my sister, my brother in Neil, even Charlotte… and myself. The memories carry burdens I can no longer shoulder, and every clover, every birdsong, and every vein of gray in the marble walls are a constant reminder. I need an escape." He turned to Matt. "So I wish to move to Zyearth with you, and make it my… home."

Matt blinked, but he gripped Ouranos' hand. "Of course. Absolutely."

Ouranos let out a long breath, relaxing his shoulders. He pressed his forehead to Matt's. "Thank you, my brother."

Matt rubbed his shoulder. "Always." He stared up at Charlotte. She came to Earth for a wedding. She'd stay here now, forever, as the Seal. Earth had taken so much from them.

He couldn't stand the idea of it taking even more. He knew what he needed to do now.

He patted Ouranos' back. "We'll work out the details later. But right now, I have to talk to Trecheon." He moved to stand.

"I am glad you did not confess love to Trecheon," Ouranos said.

Matt froze instantly. He sat back down, filtering through the colors in Ouranos' bond. Gentle blues and greens and whites. Like waves on the beach. Nothing malicious. So why did that hurt? "Why?"

"I know you were trying to open a space for Trecheon to confess his feelings for you," Ouranos said. "I felt it strongly in the bond that night. But I am glad you did not force a confession yourself."

Matt frowned. "What do you mean?"

"You are still uncertain about your feelings for him," Ouranos said. "There is no shame in that. But I worry that if you had confessed those uncertain feelings in certain terms that you would feel compelled to follow through, regardless of how you actually felt. You have a tendency to put other's needs before your own. Often admirable, but sometimes it is to your own detriment in an attempt to please. I would hate to see that damage your relationship with Trecheon."

Matt sighed. He slumped forward. "The worst part is, I *do* love him…
I just don't know if that's romantic or not." He shook his head. "Sometimes
I don't even know what the difference is."

Ouranos chuckled slightly, filling Matt's mind with a bright rainbow.
"I would tell you that you will know the difference when you see it, but I
do not believe that I would know it either." He met Matt's eyes. "But I can
tell you two things."

Matt perked his ears.

"I have seen your mind, brother," Ouranos said. "I have seen your heart
when you hug him or kiss him or even think of him. I do not know if your
feelings are romantic, but they are strong and they are love… and you need
not run from them."

Matt flattened one ear and wrinkled his snout.

"However," Ouranos said. "You need space and time to work through
those feelings. You need not rush. Perhaps now… perhaps with this
future… you will have that." He smiled at Matt. "You just have to convince
him to come home."

Matt's shoulders dropped and he sighed. "I do." He stood. "So wish
me luck."

"May the Sisters smile upon you, brother," Ouranos said. "With the
Seal and the Veil at your sides."

Matt looked up at Charlotte and Neil, one last time. Something strong,
warm, and comforting filled his heart looking at them. He managed a smile,
then turned and jogged toward the palace.

CHAPTER 59

...Is Where The Heart Is

Trecheon sat on one of the wicker couches in the gardens, hoping the flowers and cool breeze and gentle bird sounds would ground him. So far, no luck.

The hell was he supposed to do? Take Philip and go back to his shop like nothing ever happened? They lost so much. *So much.* And he still had more to lose.

He still had to say goodbye to Sacha and Matt.

He still had to watch his friends and the loves of his life leave while he stayed here.

He still had to face so much of this alone.

He leaned forward, staring at the ground. Damn it. Damn everything.

"Trecheon."

Trecheon turned. Matt stood there, his brow furrowed and his ears pinned back.

For an awful, terrible, selfish moment, Trecheon thought *at least Matt didn't sacrifice himself.* He pushed the thought aside, guilt eating at his heart. Thank Draso Matt hadn't heard that. He stood and jogged to Matt, wrapping his arms around him. Matt held him close, resting his head on Trecheon's.

The thought came back, though slightly differently. *Thank Draso you're safe. Thank Draso I have you.*

But what am I supposed to do when you leave?

"Trecheon," Matt said again, holding him tight. "…Come to Zyearth with us."

Trecheon immediately leaned back, looking Matt in the eye. "What?"

"Come to Zyearth with us," Matt said. "You and Philip. You can live with Sacha and get work with the Defenders and get Philip into a great school and get his own Gem eventually and…" He grasped Trecheon's hands. "And I don't have to worry about you being here on Earth, a thousand lightyears away, wishing and hoping that you're safe and knowing there'd be nothing I could do if you weren't." He gripped Trecheon's shoulders, just past the mounts, where Trecheon could feel his grip. "I've been trying desperately to find a way to stay here with you, but that wasn't the right move. Because that'd never be permanent. It'd never be enough time. I need you closer." He met Trecheon's gaze with desperate eyes. "Come home…"

Trecheon stared at him, his body buzzing, a thousand questions running through his mind. Could they pack up everything he owned and bring it with them? What would happen to the shop and his workers? What about all Neil's stuff? Would his bikes work on Zyearth? Would Philip even want to leave? Would either of them fit in on a whole new planet?

…Would this relationship have a chance if he left his hellish past on Earth?

But how could he really leave? Earth was his home. This wasn't just moving across country, or even to a new part of the world. It was a whole new *planet.*

But then he looked closely at Matt. That brave, powerful, confident Guardian. The alien who had become such a close friend. The quilar he fell in love with.

Scared. And scared for him. *For him.* Despite all his power and magic and strength... he was scared as hell. That kind of fear could only be born out of love.

Maybe this relationship had a chance after all.

Trecheon looked deep into Matt's eyes, searching his feelings the best he could without a Gem bond. He couldn't be certain, but he thought he found a... a spark.

You're an assassin, his brain spat at him. *You don't deserve him if you can't even tell him.*

"Trecheon," Neil's voice echoed in his head, distant yet close all at once. *"Promise me you'll tell Matt how you feel when you see him next. You two deserve happiness."*

He should have responded to Neil. Just said anything. One more conversation with Neil. But he hadn't. He left it in the air. And now Neil was gone. And he'd want Trecheon to do what he had asked, more than anything. Maybe being on Zyearth... maybe being away from his rotten past, in a new world, a new society, a new life... maybe he could fulfill Neil's wish. He could finally share that with Matt.

He took a deep breath. "Let... let me ask Philip. It's a really big change."

Matt flicked his ears back. "I know. I'm asking too much."

Trecheon held up a hand. "Let me ask Philip. But if he's okay with it... I'm happy to move to Zyearth."

Matt's eyes lit up like a child at Christmas. "Really? You mean that?"

"I do." Trecheon smiled.

Matt grinned widely and he pulled Trecheon in a deep hug. He kissed the top of Trecheon's head, longer and deeper than the first time, sending sparks down Trecheon's spine. "Thank Draso…" Trecheon held him tight, basking in the moment. But soon Matt pulled away. "I should talk with Lance about starting the immigration processes actually. Ouranos is coming too, and we gotta name your sponsors."

Trecheon lifted a brow. "Ouranos is coming?"

"Yeah." Matt rubbed his chin. "Honestly, we have enough Zyearth natives that we could probably invite all our allies here if they wanted… I doubt they'd all come, but I should ask anyway. We have the sponsors for it."

"Sponsors?"

"Part of Galactic Accord immigration policies," Matt said. He rubbed his head. "Fire and ice, I'll have a lot to teach you about that, actually. But we have time." He gripped Trecheon's hands. "Finally, we have time."

Trecheon smiled at him. "Do what you have to. I'll go talk to Philip."

"Right." Matt grinned again. "I hope you'll be coming home, Trecheon." He kissed Trecheon's forehead, sending another shock through Trecheon's body, then took off before he could say anything.

Trecheon watched him run off, his ears flushing. Matt had kissed him. *Kissed him.* Multiple times, without hesitation. And each tiny intimacy hit home just how much he loved Matt. How strong that love had become.

Draso, please let this relationship have a chance.

I hope you'll be coming home, Trecheon. Home. That had a nice ring to it actually.

Home.

He entered the palace to look for Philip.

CHAPTER 60

CARRY YOUR ROOTS

Leah wandered the palace, looking for Zeke. She couldn't take this uncertainty anymore. She couldn't hold this off any longer.

She needed to ask Zeke to come to Zyearth. The thought of leaving him here after everything that had happened... she couldn't do it. It wasn't an option anymore.

Of course, that meant convincing Andre to come to Zyearth, and by extension, Chadwick. That... might be harder. With everything going on, she hadn't had a chance to bring it up with Andre again. And Andre hadn't come to her either.

Knowing her luck, all of them would reject the idea. But she had to try. She couldn't leave Zeke here.

She couldn't leave *any* of them here...

She found Zeke in the gardens, on a bench by the golden ArchDragon fountain. Staring blankly.

He looked so… broken. He had a normal pair of Athánatos style pants on, in green. A green similar to Neil's jacket. The long diamond fabric loin cover was lined in white. Unusual for male clothing. Typically that was something seen on more feminine clothing. Perhaps something to honor Natassa. He wasn't wearing a shirt, but he did have his prince's chain on. It lay close to the neck, drooping down almost to his belly. He fiddled with the green jewels hanging from the chain.

His eyes wouldn't focus. He just stared… empty.

Leah chewed her lip, her heart aching. But she shook her head, trying to focus her thoughts. *Okay, remember what you rehearsed. All the good reasons to go, all the reasons why staying hurts too much, the fact that Andre was… thinking about it. You got this. You…*

A soft scent of hot cocoa hit her nose. Zeke looked up and met her eyes.

Her entire speech melted away and she ran for him instead, every aching moment from the last few days hitting her full force.

Zeke stood and grabbed her, holding her tight, stroking her head. "I know…" he said. *I know.*

She sobbed in his arms for several minutes, drowning in the pain. Everything was so unfair, so unbalanced, so *wrong*. No one deserved this…

Everything was wrong…

She couldn't ask him to leave. After everything that happened here, to his home, his family. He needed to be here. It wasn't right to ask him… she couldn't be that selfish. The ache in her chest doubled.

"Leah," Zeke said quietly. "I want to come to Zyearth with you."

Leah's eyes flew open and she leaned back, staring at Zeke. "…What?"

He smiled gently. "I… I know you've been meaning to ask me. I've felt it through the bond even though you've tried to hide it."

She hunched down, her ears burning.

"I've been thinking about it," Zeke said. "…A lot. I have found so much here on Athánatos. Family, a home, peace. But also pain. And this pain has taught me one thing above everything else. Home isn't a place. It's the ones I love." He pulled Leah close, leaning his head on hers. "You are my whole heart, Leah. I need to be where it beats."

Leah smiled, tears building in her eyes. She buried her face in the fur of his chest.

She wasn't going to lose him. He was going to Zyearth.

He was coming home.

Zeke gently kissed the top of her head. *You're my home.*

And you're mine, Leah said. She leaned back, wiping away tears, her grin taking over her face. But then she slowly frowned. "…But what about Andre?"

"What about Andre?" Leah turned to see Andre and Chadwick walking up to them. Thankfully after everyone had calmed down, the healers were finally able to buckle down and get Chadwick the healing therapy he needed and he was back to full strength. He smiled at them. Andre grinned. "Sorry to interrupt such a tender moment, but Matt and Ouranos want us all in the audience chamber. You two okay?"

Zeke flattened an ear, and the quiet, subtle ion smell of a pot just about to boil hit Leah's nose. Hesitation. "Uh yeah, I um…" His shoulders stiffened. "I uh… I told Leah that I'm going to Zyearth with her…"

Andre leaned a hand on his hip, still grinning. "Oh yeah? 'Bout time you settled that, asshole. Been leaving Leah worried sick you'd say no."

Zeke flicked both ears back now. "Really? That's all you have to say about it? I'm leaving Earth!"

"Yeah, well, good thing Chadwick and I are too," Andre said.

Leah grinned and clapped her hands. "You are?"

"We are," Chadwick said. "It's time my family finally went home. Once I get some things settled and find a suitable employee to take over the shop."

Andre eyed him, wrinkling his nose. "Tell me you're gonna give it to Jorge and not Squeegee."

Zeke raised an eyebrow. *"Squeegee?"*

"Don't ask," Chadwick said. "It'd be an embarrassment for all of us."

Andre smiled. "But yeah, we're emigrating. Someone's gotta school the Defenders on why healers are so friggin' important. Might as well be me. 'Sides, I hear Zyearth has the most beautiful sunsets." He winked at Leah.

Chadwick smiled. "Come on, let's go see what Matt and Ouranos want." He shared a quick kiss with Andre, then walked toward the palace. Zeke squeezed Leah and followed him.

Leah threw her arms around Andre's middle and hugged him tight. "I'm so glad you're coming home."

Andre hugged her back. "Home, huh? I like the sound of that." They headed for the palace. Andre walked slowly. "Honestly, as much as I wanna say me going is because of Zeke… there's a hell of a lot more to it."

Leah perked her ears. "Oh?"

"Yeah." Andre wrung his hands. "I keep thinkin' about Drifa and Kaoru. How all they've ever known is pain. I wanna make that better for them. But I don't know shit about summons, and it ain't like I can learn here. Zyearth will fix that. And…" He stared up at the sky. "I want 'em to see real peace."

Leah smiled. "Zyearth will be that for them."

He nodded. "Hey uh… is Zyearth all fuzzballs like you, or are there humans too?"

Leah giggled. "A few, especially around the Defender Academy. All kinds. Base humans, sar humans, fae humans."

"*Fae* humans? Like Irish fairies or something?"

Leah laughed. "Yeah, kinda. There's also centaurs and androvox, and Erdoglyan paleofaunos. Dinos, basically, but don't call them that. We have a robust intergalactic student program. All kinds of creatures study there."

Andre's eyes grew wide. "Can I?"

"Well yeah, of course," Leah said. "It's for everyone." She rubbed her chin. "I don't know when we'll get home, but we can always start you up on the next trimester."

Andre nodded. "It'll give me time to get a job and get loans anyway."

Leah flattened an ear. "Loans?"

"For school."

Leah laughed. "No, no, school is free. We just gotta sign you up. It's a little more complicated for newcomers, but I'll help you through it."

Andre stared. "Wow. Free?"

Leah nodded.

Andre stopped entirely now. "Can I train to be a doctor?" He frowned. "Or does that require a healer's Gem?"

Leah shook her head. "Doctors and healers are different jobs. We have regular doctors too. You're in for a ride with all the anatomy though. But yeah, you can be a doctor."

Andre's mouth turned up in a smile. "Good. Chadwick needed one desperately and we didn't have one. 'Sides, after all this death and pain, I need to focus on healing."

Leah gave him a side hug. "You'll make a fantastic doctor." The pair headed into the palace.

CHAPTER 61

PROPOSAL

Trecheon wandered the palace, his heavy heart dropping weights into his stride and slowing him down.

He should be looking for Philip. That's what he told Matt he was doing. But instead, he wandered toward the guest living quarters.

Toward Sacha.

He had hardly seen her since the wedding prep started. Didn't even speak to her after Neil's death. Both of them had crashed in the bed and slept, wordlessly. Their only real interaction had been at Theron's wake. He wasn't sure why, but it felt like… shame.

He couldn't do that to her. Not if he was going to Zyearth. Not after losing so much.

…Not after Neil.

He just needed to talk with her. Just for a bit. Then they could find Philip together. She'd be a part of this after all.

Just a little talk.

He found her in their guest room, sitting on the bed, staring blankly at the floor. Some soft music played in the background, and she had a scented candle lit, making the room smell of honeysuckle. Her knitting lay on the bed, the yarn bowl on the table. But she clearly hadn't touched it. Trecheon frowned. He knocked on the door frame. "Sacha?"

She looked up.

He crossed the room, took her hands, and pulled her up into a hug. She held him tight, burying her face in his shoulder.

He rubbed her back as she shook, searching for any words of comfort. Nothing would be perfect, but anything would be welcome.

But as he held her, as he silently thanked Draso that she was safe, that Matt was safe, everything hit him like a rocket.

Neil wasn't safe.

Neil was gone.

He pulled her tighter, his body racked with aches and fear and pain, from his ear tips to his toes, as everything hit him at once.

Neil. Was *gone.*

Tears welled in Trecheon's eyes. He buried his face in Sacha's neck and cried.

Everything… all the pain, the damage, the fear, the losses he had experienced his whole life overflowed at once. The war, losing his arms, seeing so much death and destruction. The Shadow Cast, Theron, and watching them both rip apart the Athánatos people. And the losses. His father and mother, who he didn't even remember. Grandma Solana, who he did, but now he couldn't even remember what her voice sounded like.

His sister, Ayumi, vanishing after Granddad's disappearance.

Granddad Ryuichi, who left a scar so deep, he'd never fully recover from it.

Christian, throwing himself at the mage king and dying for his troubles.

His pack in the war… Anthony, dead with his leg severed from his body. Clarissa, Ryota's first love. And… and Ryota too. Dead by Theron's hand.

Rebekka. Just the thought of her name sent painful aches through his chest.

Natassa. Charlotte. Facing down enemies they had no chance of fighting, but facing them anyway.

And Neil… oh god, Neil…

He wasn't sure how long he cried in Sacha's arms. The world melted away from him, drowning him, killing him…

"…I'm so sorry."

Trecheon opened his eyes.

Sacha snuggled into his neck. "I am so sorry, Trecheon… I didn't want this for you. This wasn't what was supposed to happen when the Defenders came here. We were supposed to *fix* everything, damn it." She gripped his shirt. "We're *Defenders*. We *defend*, we *fix*, we *help*, and *damn it, look what happened?*" She sobbed. "Neil should be here with us… we should be celebrating a wedding…" She tightened her hug. "I was supposed to make life better for you…"

Trecheon lay his head on Sacha's, trying to calm his breathing. *But you have… in ways I could never express… you've given me hope, life, love…*

I wouldn't be here without you.

He kissed the side of her head. "Sacha… will you marry me?"

Sacha leaned back, her eyes wide. "What…?"

He gripped her hands and kissed them both. "I don't have a ring or a… a coil or whatever, but… You have made my life better. Hell, I wouldn't have a life if you hadn't come into it." He pressed her hands against his forehead. "I will miss Neil with everything that I am. Probably for the rest of my life. But… he'd want me to live my life. Move on, when I'm ready. However long that takes." He met her eyes. "He'd want us to celebrate a wedding. If you'll have me."

Sacha made a choked sound halfway between a laugh and a sob. She managed a smile, despite the tears and furrowed brow. "You're right… he would." She pulled Trecheon into a gentle hug. "Of course I'll have you, hun… always."

Trecheon smiled. "So… that's a yes?"

She pulled back and cupped his face in her hands, her smile overcoming the tears. "It's a yes."

Trecheon smiled now. He pulled her close for a kiss. Not a long one, or a passionate one. It was one of… reassurance.

Everything hurt. But it wouldn't hurt forever.

Sacha pulled back. "You know that means you'll have to come to Zyearth with me."

"I know," Trecheon said. "Matt already asked me."

Sacha snapped her fingers. "Damn. Beat me to it. Always a step ahead."

"Except where romance is concerned," Trecheon said, rolling his eyes. He wiped his cheeks free of tears. "…But he kissed me."

Sacha raised an eyebrow and smirked, a little of her normal self fighting to the surface. "'Bout time. Are his lips as salty as they look?"

Trecheon shrugged. "Wouldn't know. He just kissed my forehead."

Sacha giggled. "Well, it's a start." She poked Trecheon's chest. "Just so we're clear, getting engaged doesn't mean you get out of talking romance with Matt."

"Good," Trecheon said. "Because I'm hoping going to Zyearth will finally give us that opportunity."

Sacha kissed Trecheon's forehead. "I hope that too, love."

Izzy slid in the open doorway. "Hey you two, Matt… oh, I'm sorry, I hope I didn't interrupt something…"

Sacha gave Trecheon a sideways squeeze. "Nothing much. Just us getting engaged."

Izzy's eyes widened and she grinned. "Wait, really?"

Trecheon smiled and nodded. "Yeah, really."

Izzy squealed and hugged them both. "Does that mean you're coming home with us, Trecheon?"

"Yeah," Trecheon said. "If I can get Philip on board. I haven't actually asked him yet."

"Well, you'll have your opportunity now," Izzy said. "Matt's gathering everyone to talk about that." She gave Trecheon another squeeze. "I hope you're coming home."

"I hope so too," Trecheon replied.

"Take your time, but Matt's meeting us in the king's chamber," Izzy said. She hugged Sacha one more time, then took off.

Sacha leaned her head on Trecheon's shoulder. "So you really mean it then. You want to marry me. It wasn't just some spur of the moment thought."

"I mean, it *was,*" Trecheon said, wrapping an arm around her. "But I meant it with my whole heart." He kissed her forehead. "I need to hang on to joy. The journey was too long and painful not to. You're that joy. You, and Philip, and Matt and all the people Zyearth has brought me."

"Good," Sacha said. "Glad you're finally giving in to that." She kissed along his jaw. "If you're up for it, we should celebrate later. But only if you're up for it. Joy can come in little spurts. Doesn't have to be all at once."

"I gotcha," Trecheon said. "Can't promise anything intimate, but I wouldn't mind sleeping next to you. Just so… so I know…"

"So we know we're all safe," Sacha said. "Always."

CHAPTER 62

A SAFE HOME

Izzy sat on one of the wicker couches next to Roscoe and took his hand. She leaned against him, so grateful that with everything that happened, Roscoe was still safe. He rubbed her arm and pressed little kisses to her head every now and then.

Every seat in the room was taken, and many still stood, making everything feel a little stuffy. Sami and Darvin sat on the couch next to her and Roscoe. Leah, Zeke, Andre, and Chadwick took up the floor pillows, cuddled near each other. Ana and Angus stood next to them. Ana looked longingly at Leah, but didn't make an effort to move closer.

Ouranos and his family stood near the throne. Embrik stood nearby, his arms wrapped across Melaina's shoulders. No one sat on the throne. It felt… wrong, considering. The Archons, including Misty, now Mistik, stood in a semi-circle around the throne, holding their bodies stiff. The new Mistik's fur was covered nearly head to toe in azure blue, with only a few black streaks covering her snout, eyes, and fingertips.

Jaden stood near Alexina, arm wrapped around her. He stared off into the middle distance, still holding a frown, his mind clearly elsewhere. Still trying to recover from Charlotte's death. Izzy frowned. He was going to need a lot of time for that.

Time they finally had, thank Draso.

Baltazar stood not far from them, with half a dozen sentries, spears and swords in hand, though no one really worried about threats anymore. Baltazar fiddled with the bracelet on his wrist, containing his Soul Jewels. Theron was dead, but the damage he caused still lingered and all the sentries remained as Drifters. Though Neil's strength with the Veil left them bridged to their souls, they'd never have a chance to get them back. The sacrifice was too great. But at least they'd lead normal lives.

Dami stood several feet away, staring at the ground, arms crossed, ears flat. He hadn't said a word since Charlotte's death, though Izzy could see his mind was quite occupied.

Trecheon and Sacha stood along the back wall, with Philip beside them. Izzy couldn't help but smile, even if it was sad. They'd make a great family. Neil... he could rest easy. Philip was safe. And hopefully coming to Zyearth.

Matt stood next to Ouranos, gripping his hand. Gentle, soft bells echoed in Izzy's ears. Soothing. Safety. It calmed her considerably.

She wasted so much time running from the bond...

But we're here now, Matt said, catching her eye and smiling. *Let's make the most of it. Love you, Iz.*

Izzy smiled back at him. She cuddled next to Roscoe. *Love you too, Matt.*

Ouranos took a deep breath. He squared his shoulders, nodded to Matt, then moved in front of the throne. He lifted his head and addressed the group.

"Athánatos is finally safe," he said. "It took many great sacrifices, but… we are finally safe. However." He lowered his gaze. "The scars of our sacrifice still linger. The weight still too much to bear. And I know many are seeking an escape." He closed his eyes a moment. "Myself included."

Archon Bouldrik stepped forward. "My Lord, what do you mean?"

"I mean I am leaving Athánatos," Ouranos said. "And making my home permanently on Zyearth."

Several gasped. Archon Dustrik stepped forward. "Lord Ouranos."

Ouranos lifted his hand. "I know many believed I would take the throne after Natassa. But I will never wield the title of Basileus. My father beat it to the ground and tarnished it. Neil and Natassa resurrected it… and died wielding it. It holds too much pain, and… and I do not entirely trust myself."

"But then who will lead us?" Mistik asked.

Ouranos smiled lightly. "I have asked Embrik and Melaina to take on that role. They have agreed to it." He held out his hand to Embrik. Embrik smiled and took it. "My Archons, you now follow Basileus Kyros and Basilea Melaina. And you will be better for it."

Embrik… no, Kyros, lay a fist across his chest and bowed.

The air shimmered with elemental magic as the eight Phonar summons fluttered down from the sky, appearing as their anthropomorphic forms, and kneeling before Kyros, their wings mantled. Excelsis shook his feathers, sending embers into the sky. *The Phonar recognize you as Basileus,* he said. *May Athánatos grow strong under your rule.*

Sisters bless you, the other Phonar called, filling the air with bits of magic.

Kyros nodded to them. "Thank you."

Excelsis stood. *While we are gathered here, and while we know Athánatos to be safe, I wish to announce that the Phonar are also leaving.*

Ouranos stepped toward Pax. "Pax, my friend. You all have been with us since the moment of our births." He took the bird's clawed hands in his. "Life will be bleaker without you."

Pax leaned forward and pressed his forehead to Ouranos'. *And mine without you, my Prince.*

"Where will you go?" Alexina asked. She gripped Kyrie's taloned hands.

Kyrie shook her feathers, sending floating snowflakes into the air. *Our oath commands that we find suitable summoners outside the royal family, should this bond break,* she said. *We will travel the universe and see what we can find. Though Judgement is Sealed, we have seen that seal is not permanent. She will appear again, and we will need to be ready.*

"Archángeli," Zeke said, stepping forward. Archángeli smiled and wrapped their wings around Zeke. Zeke hugged him. "Thanks for taking care of me all these years."

Thank you, my prince, for giving my life as a summon purpose, Archángeli said. Leah and Andre walked up to them, and Archángeli hugged them both. *It brings me great joy to see you all forming such an unbreakable bond. Take care of one another.* They looked up at Andre. *You will make a fine summoner, my friend. Drifa and Kaoru are better for it.*

Andre smiled. "Thanks. Take care, okay?"

"Archángeli," Leah said, frowning. "I… we learned in your journals that you're all Wish Dusters. But we never figured out what your Wishes were."

Archángeli frowned. *For all the memories that have returned to me, that one is still absent,* they said. *Perhaps something else we will uncover in our time looking for new masters.*

Leah flicked her ears back. She held him tight. "I hope you do. Take care of yourself."

Archángeli smiled. They stepped back and as one, the Phonar rose to the sky, trailing their elements. *Thank you all.*

They vanished into the clouds.

Kyros watched them fly off, then turned to the Archons. "My friends, I hope I will be acceptable to you as Basileus. I know I am not Natassa or Ouranos, but I want to do what I can for our people. Be a servant-king, as Neil was. He provided a great example." Melaina gripped his hand and nodded, but still didn't speak.

Bouldrik watched them a moment, then smiled and returned the bow. "More than acceptable, my Basileus."

"I agree," Electrik said. "Though this leaves us with a dilemma. Who will take the title of Embrik?"

Kyros turned to Baltazar. "I was rather hoping Baltazar would take the title."

Baltazar perked his ears, eyes wide. "Me? My Lord, I…"

Kyros walked to Baltazar and gently gripped his shoulders. "I have seen your loyalty, Baltazar. You fought for your Basileus. You followed him and Natassa into the greatest dangers with only the intent to protect them with your life."

Baltazar flattened his ears. "But… I failed."

"But you never gave up," Kyros said. "You have proven what you are willing to do for Athánatos. That, to me, is enough to earn the title. And I do mean *earn,* Baltazar. This is not given lightly."

"But…" Baltazar frowned. "I do not even have my soul."

"You do, my friend," Ouranos said. "As surely as I had mine. Because someone willingly sacrificed to bridge it for you. Take that gift and hold it close."

Baltazar stared, quiet, but he nodded. "If this is your wish, I accept it with grace."

Kyros smiled. He placed his hands on Baltazar's head. "Then I bestow the title Embrik." His hands glowed slightly, and in a move that looked like paint flowing over their fur, Kyros' dark red fur washed away, replaced with black fur and a burnt orange pattern on his quills and face, similar to Zeke's coloring. Baltazar, now Embrik, looked over his body as the jet black of his fur transformed to Kyros' old dark red, leaving streaks of black on his arms, face, quills, and chest. Kyros pressed his forehead to Baltazar's. "As the Sisters command, you leave your birth name behind and take on the name Embrik, to embody the role and responsibilities you take on. Do you accept this?"

"With my whole being," Baltazar said. "I take the name Embrik."

"Then it is done." Kyros stood back, smiling. "The red suits you, my friend."

Baltazar smiled. "Going by Embrik will take some time to get used to."

"As will Kyros," Kyros said, laughing. "It has been centuries since I used that name. But we will adjust. As we always do."

Jaden gave Kyros a sideways hug, smiling sadly. "Love the new look. Congrats to you both." Kyros hugged him back.

Izzy smiled. A little joy was okay.

Damianos stepped forward. "While we are discussing titles..." He turned to Electrik. "My apologies, Father, but... I hereby renounce my claim to the title of Archon."

The moment he said it, Dami's bright yellow fur melted away, leaving only solid black. Izzy gasped, covering her snout with her hands. Dami stared at the ground, tears forming. "I… I am sorry, but I cannot stay here any longer after all this, I…"

"Oh, my dear, sweet son." Electrik stepped forward and pulled Dami into a hug. "There are no apologies here. Not after all this." He pressed a gentle kiss to Dami's forehead. "I had wondered if this would happen. The pain is too much. But there is no shame here. You must do what you need to to protect your heart."

Dami didn't speak, but he hugged his father tight, little tears running down his face.

"But one more thing, my son," Electrik said. "You may reject the Archon, but you do not reject family." He leaned back and pressed a hand to Dami's forehead. "You always have a home here."

A bright, yellow star pattern erupted on Dami's forehead, with little sprinkles of yellow falling down over his fur like sparks from a shooting star. Electrik formed a little lightning in his hand and passed it to Dami. Dami formed a fist and the lightning traveled around his body, catching in his fur before vanishing.

"Thank you, Father."

Izzy sighed. After all this hell, his reaction made sense. At least he got to keep his magic. One more on the bus to Zyearth, then.

"Actually," Matt said, stepping forward. "Dami kind of brought up what I want to talk about. I know a lot of us feel like this place, even just Earth as a whole, holds too many painful memories. For some of us, like Ouranos, it's too much. So Lance and I spoke with the Galactic Accord Immigration Department and we're approved to take anyone who wants to move to Zyearth with us."

Ana and Angus perked their ears. Ana stood. "Really? Any of us?"

Matt nodded. "No one has to make a decision right now, though I know some of us already have. And with everything that's happened, it'll be a while before we even leave. Close to a year maybe. But we want you to know, anyone is welcome."

Izzy glanced around the room, trying to get a feel for who might be interested. She halfway expected Philip to reject the idea. After all, he'd been uprooted more times than anyone should. But his eyes grew wide, he grinned, and looked at Trecheon expectantly. Trecheon smiled and nodded, which got a big hug from Philip.

Izzy smiled. Good. Two more coming home.

Ana flattened her ears and furrowed her brow. "What ah… what does the immigration process look like?"

"I wanna know too," Andre said. "Didn't think about that when I signed up for this."

"I'd like to know more about getting settled there, if you don't mind, Guardian," Chadwick said.

Matt smiled. "I figured that. Anyone who's interested, hang out for a bit. I'll do my best to explain. And tell you a little more about Zyearth."

"I will tell you from experience," Ouranos said, smiling. "It is magnificent."

Many hours and a meal later, everyone had gone their respective ways, likely with a lot on their minds. From what Izzy could tell, it was a definite yes from Trecheon, Philip, Zeke, Andre, and Chadwick. Jaden would come home too, Alexina with him, now that she was home and free. Angus was curious, but didn't seem terribly interested, despite being an alien himself, and Ana was… hesitant. Considering her heavy anchors here, Izzy couldn't blame her.

But she kept looking at Leah. Maybe that alone would drive her to Zyearth.

Dami surprised them all.

"I am grateful for the offer, Matthew," Dami had said. "But I must decline, for now at least."

Matt flicked an ear back, but he nodded. "It's fine, Dami. Though I thought you weren't staying on Athánatos?"

"I am not," Dami said. He pulled a folded sheet of paper out of his pocket. "Ana… she restored Neil's coat after his death. I had offered it to Philip, but he said I should have it instead. And in the pocket, I found this. Neil called it a 'bucket list.' A list of things he wanted to do before he died. He did not get to do any of them." Dami took a deep breath. "So I will do these things in his honor. That necessitates me staying here. For now."

Matt smiled. "I think that's honorable, Dami."

"Hey Dami," Ana said. "I can help set you up for anything you need to do for that list. We have the resources." She smiled sadly. "One last thing I can do to make up for what I had done to Neil."

Dami smiled. "I appreciate it and will take your offer. But I will reiterate as Neil had so many times that it was Ackerson who pulled the strings, not you. Let go of that guilt. For him."

Ana rubbed her arm. "...Yeah. I hope someday I can."

The pair of them had walked off to talk about how to get Dami set up for his bucket list travels.

That left only Izzy and Matt in the room. Tired, but hopeful. Izzy stared up at the skylights. The stars were just poking out.

"I kissed Trecheon."

Izzy shot her head down and eyes grew wide. "Really?"

Matt nodded. "Nothing special. Just the top of his head. One forehead kiss. I was… I wanted to see if I could get him to tell me his feelings for me. Or… or maybe test my own, I dunno. The first time I had to really force myself but the other times just came naturally." He frowned, pasting his ears back, his eyes glassy.

Izzy frowned. She looked him in the eye. "And… that's somehow made you sad."

He blinked rapidly, his eyes unfocused, staring at the floor. "No, not that, it's…" He stared up at the sky, a tear running down his face, his brow furrowed deeply. "I kissed Trecheon… and I can't tell Neil about it. I can't tell Natassa or… Charlotte."

Izzy furrowed her brow now. "Oh, Matt…"

"And I keep playing in my head how they'd all react," he continued. "Neil would laugh and tease me about me daring to call that 'kissing.' But then he'd be all full of real, solid advice about how to move to the next step. Natassa would do that giddy squeal she does when she's really happy, clapping her hands and jumping in place before hugging me. Charlotte…" He choked. "Charlotte… she'd…" He shook his head. "She teased me my whole life, all in good fun, but she'd know this wasn't the time or the place. She'd take me out for coffee at some quiet, hole-in-the-wall place, as private as could be, and just let me gush. No advice, no extreme reactions, just… a listening ear. A safe space. And when I was ready, she'd offer all the encouragement she could muster." He turned his head, tears flowing stronger now. "But that's never going to happen now." He stared up at the sky. "I know that these random bouts of grief come with death, and I know it'll get easier eventually, but right now, the pain is almost more than I can bear."

Izzy hugged Matt around the middle, resting her head on his shoulder, trying to keep her voice steady. "I know. It's not fair and it's not right." She leaned back and placed her hand on his chest. "But Matt... Neil, Natassa, and Charlotte are all right here. In your heart and mind. Because that's the impressions they left on you. That's why you can predict what they'd do for you." She sighed. "It's not the same as having them here. But their love left echoes. And we can cling on to that."

Matt took a deep, shuddering breath. "Yeah… you're right." He sat down hard. "It's too much, Iz. Dealing with all this loss and… and trying to see where my heart lies."

"That's why we need to get you to Zyearth," Izzy said. "Away from all this. In a place of safety for once."

He sighed. "Yeah. Safe."

"Come on," Izzy said. "Let's see if we can find some dessert. You can tell me all about your kiss. No judgement. Okay?"

Matt met her eyes. He nodded. "Okay."

CHAPTER 63

Leave Nothing Behind

Ten Months Later

"Holy hell," Izzy said. "That gave me a *fright.*"

Trecheon and Matt looked up from the box they were packing in Trecheon's tiny living room. Izzy walked out of the spare bedroom carrying, of all things, a unicycle.

Trecheon flattened his ears. "Oh god, where'd you find that?"

"Way back in the walk-in closet of your guest room," Izzy said. "Where the hell'd you get it?"

Trecheon rolled his eyes. "Granddad bought it for me."

"Really?" Matt chuckled. "Why a unicycle?"

Trecheon rubbed his temple. "When I was about ten, Granddad and I had a huge argument," he said. "I told him I was going to run away and join the circus. And I hounded him for *months* about it, even printing out pictures and pamphlets and leaving them all over the house. Granddad finally had enough, and told me I could, but they wouldn't take me until I turned eighteen."

"Ha!" Izzy said. "Did that shut you up?"

Trecheon waved a hand. "I continued for another month, but eventually dropped it." He took the unicycle from Izzy. "He bought this for me on my eighteenth birthday and told me I could either join the circus or join the army. It's a good thing I had already applied for the Marines or I might have taken him up on the circus thing."

"Did you ever learn to ride it?" Izzy asked, grinning.

"Hell no," Trecheon said. "People break their necks on these things."

Matt leaned on a stack of packed boxes. "I'm surprised you kept it all this time."

"I kept everything Granddad gave me," Trecheon said. "As much as I could, anyway. It was all I had left of him."

"Hmm," Matt said. "Let's make sure we don't forget any of that then."

Trecheon suddenly smirked. "Hey Matt. Ten bucks says you can't ride this thing."

Izzy burst into giggles.

Matt tapped the box, one corner of his mouth turned up. "What good is ten American dollars to me?"

"Fine," Trecheon said. "I'll buy you sushi from that fancy place downtown you keep talking about. But I'm upping the stakes. Ride the unicycle and juggle."

Matt lifted a brow. *"Juggle?"*

"You heard me, asshole."

"Tall order," Matt said. He stood up and stretched. "Throw in a boba from that place we visited last week and you're on."

"Deal," Trecheon said, and shook Matt's hand.

They brought the unicycle to Trecheon's garage. Almost all of Trecheon's personal belongings were already packed up. The only things lining the walls were full toolboxes ready for the new owner to take over. Trecheon grabbed a bag of apples from the fridge in his office and passed them to Izzy.

Matt climbed on one of the empty toolboxes and Izzy brought the unicycle to him, grinning. Matt leaned down and steadied it. He stared at Trecheon. "You're really sure you wanna go through with this?"

"I've got cash to burn," Trecheon said, crossing his arms. "Not like I can take it with me to Zyearth. Doubt I'll need to use it though. You won't even get your ass in that seat."

Matt shrugged. "Your funeral." He slipped onto the bike seat, still holding the toolbox, and steadied his feet on the pedals. The wheel quivered madly under his weight.

Trecheon flicked his ears back, a sudden panic blossoming in his chest. "Hey… you sure you really wanna try this? People really do break their necks on these things."

"You asked for it." Matt pushed away from the toolbox.

Trecheon's heart leapt.

Matt wobbled all over the place, waving his arms with a dramatic "Whoaaaaa!" nearly falling off.

Trecheon moved to steady him. "Matt, get off the damn thing before you kill yourself!"

But Matt crossed his arms and peddled backwards, perfectly balanced, a big grin on his face.

Trecheon perked his ears. "What?"

"Izzy, apples please," Matt said. Izzy threw six apples to him, one after the other, which he juggled with ease, all while peddling in a tight, backward circle. "Guess we have sushi tonight. Better call and make a reservation. Also, I like the wintermelon lemonade from that boba place."

Trecheon sat hard on a damaged office chair. "Okay, what the hell. How'd you do that?"

Izzy laughed. "Matt learned how to juggle and ride a unicycle back in fifth grade," she said. "Won the school talent show that year."

"Wait," Trecheon said. "Zyearth has *unicycles?*"

"You'd be surprised how many similar things we have," Izzy said grinning. "Yours is a little different in the seat and wheel design, but that's it. Took Matt a while to learn, but he mastered it pretty quick once he got the basics down."

"And guaranteed that I'd never get another date for a school dance," Matt said. He tossed the apples high into the air while bouncing on the tire. "Black Bound *and* I can ride a unicycle? Loner city."

"You've kept up that skill since *fifth grade?*" Trecheon said. "You're almost 70!"

"It's good for practicing balance while using magic," Matt said. He activated his Gem and swirled the apples in a vortex around his head with his wind magic. "I have my own unicycle and everything."

"Shut the hell up," Trecheon said.

Matt grinned. "Ask Izzy."

"He really does," Izzy said. "Though he tries to hide it."

"Loner city," Matt said. "I'm stigmatized enough."

Trecheon leaned back in his chair. "Good god, I've been played."

"You set yourself up, Trech," Matt said, laughing. He took a dramatic bite from one of the apples while still juggling, then quickly slid off the unicycle and passed the remaining apples to Izzy. "I'll get this in the truck," he said, winking.

Then he pressed a quick kiss to Trecheon's forehead and walked out.

Trecheon's heart fluttered.

Izzy grinned and nudged Trecheon. "I saw that."

Trecheon let the smile take over. "He's been doing that more frequently," he said. "Every day we get closer to leaving. I haven't really gained the confidence to kiss him yet, but… on Zyearth. I hope." He gripped the bag of apples, but he frowned, just slightly. "Izzy, you're in his head. Think we have a chance?"

Izzy smiled. "Yes. The best of chances." She picked up a box. "So let's hurry and get you two to Zyearth so I can start teasing both of you without worrying I'm gonna break something."

Suddenly Philip came barreling down the stairs with Sacha walking slowly behind him. "Hey Dad, can I get some cash for a sundae at Suzy's?"

Trecheon perked an ear, but he smiled. "Yeah, grab it from the petty cash jar. And bring us back brownies."

"You got it!" Philip snatched a handful of bills.

Sacha smiled at him. "Want me to come with you?"

Philip paused. "I kinda want a little time to myself actually. Hope you don't mind, Sacha."

Sacha's face twisted slightly. Her disappointed face. Something few people really picked up on, Trecheon realized. But she smiled just the same, a little stiff. "It's fine, go on. I'll see you at dinner."

Philip smiled back, gave a cheesy salute like Neil used to, then tore off down the alley toward Suzy's.

"Don't eat too much!" Trecheon called after him. "Sushi tonight!"

"Got it, Dad!" He vanished around a corner.

Sacha sighed.

Izzy frowned. "He's still kinda distant, huh."

Sacha shrugged. "Can't blame him. He's still recovering. We all are. Just… gotta be patient."

Trecheon frowned. He hugged Sacha. "Give him time, sweetheart."

She squeezed him. "Yeah." Sacha sighed again. She rubbed her arm. "I worry Philip still sees me as the scary tiger who stabbed his foster mom in the neck with a broken arm. Maybe I should ask him about it sometime. I want him to know he can talk to me about anything. Draso knows we're in this for the long haul." She grinned. "But hey, he's calling you Dad now, right? Progress!"

Trecheon chuckled. "Not sure if it's progress, but I suppose it's something. Wasn't really expecting that when we started this whole thing but it feels… right."

Izzy smiled. "Neil would love it. And it makes Philip happy. That's what matters."

"I'm gonna grab another box," Sacha said. "Be back in a sec." She trotted up the stairs.

Trecheon sighed.

"He will come around, Trech," Izzy said. "It hasn't even been a year yet and he's far more familiar with you than with Sacha. You'll get there."

"I know," Trecheon said. "At least we'll have the space and time to work it out now." He picked up a box and they headed outside toward the truck.

Matt was still in the back of the moving van. "Here, pass those up and I'll get them settled." Trecheon passed his box to him.

A black car rolled up to the space and a man in a white shirt, black pants, and a black jacket came out. "Hey, this Red's Garage?"

Trecheon nodded. "It is, but we're temporarily closed while the new owner moves in. You might have better luck on the next street over."

"Damn," the man said. "You Mr. Red? Trecheon Omnir himself?"

Trecheon chuckled. "You say that like I'm some kind of celebrity. Yeah, I'm Trecheon."

"Good to know." The man crossed the distance between them in several large strides.

Then he pulled out a shiny golden badge.

FBI.

Trecheon froze, eyes wide.

"Trecheon Omnir," the FBI agent said, pulling out a pair of handcuffs. Several more agents got out of the car. "You're under arrest for the murder of Felicity Fawn and under suspicion of being the serial killer known as the White Assassin." He gripped Trecheon's hand and swung it around his back, cuffing him. "You have the right to remain silent. Anything you say can and will…"

The agent's voice faded while Trecheon's mind overloaded. No. *No.* This couldn't be *happening.* He was almost there, he was almost completely *free.* Oh, why did he let his guard down, why did he say his name? Why did--

He looked up.

Matt stared down at him, eyes wide, his jaw loose in shock.

Trecheon's heart threatened to exploded. No, *no, NO,* not *Matt* he wasn't supposed to know this, wasn't supposed to find out like this! He tried to speak, tried to apologize or deny the claim or do anything to save the situation.

The agent pulled him toward the car. Trecheon couldn't take his eyes off Matt.

Everything slipped away. His freedom, his chance for escape… his relationship with Matt.

Oh, god, Matt knew he was a killer. He was exactly what Matt thought he was when he had pressed that sword to Trecheon's throat all those years ago.

He was everything Matt hated.

He struggled to breath, struggled to think. As they shoved him in the back of the car, his eyes still locked with Matt's, he could only get one thing out.

"I'm sorry."

Then the door slammed and they drove away.

THE END

R. A. Meenan was born in London during the golden age of science fiction, but somehow time traveled to the Modern Era (some say a mad man with a blue box was involved). She was dropped on the doorstep of a house owned by anthropomorphic cats and though they were disappointed she didn't have furry ears and a tail, they took her in to teach her the ways of elemental magic. After setting fire to her furry cat friends' tails one too many times (final score – fire: 2612, cat's tails: 0) they called an exterminator and sent her out on her way.

Others would call this "going to college" and "getting a job" but she disagrees.

Now an adult (physically, not mentally), she ride-hops intergalactic military spacecraft, combing the outer reaches of space and time, writing science fiction and urban fantasy stories based on her experiences. She's also hoping to find the perfect cup of coffee and a better way to grow dinosaurs. Humans kind of look at her funny, but she's managed to make herself an honorary ambassador for furry and anthropomorphic aliens and space dragons.

She carefully feeds and brushes her wonderful husband Joe and the pair have four furry children (which are really cats, but don't tell them that) and a human child named after a video game character. She also spends her spare time teaching essay-writing haters, molding them into people resembling Actual Students and Lovers of English.

She may not win the hearts of stiff military men or students who want good grades for no effort, but she certainly captures the spirit and imagination of time travelers, magic users, nerds, Students-In-Training, and fantasy lovers. Welcome to her nonsensical world. We hope you like it here.

You can email R. A. Meenan at r.a.meenan@zyearth.com. Check out more of her works at www.zyearth.com. You can also follow her on BlueSky at @zyearth.com.

If you enjoyed this book, consider reviewing it at the retailer where you purchased it!

Enter the World of Zyearth

Liked this book? You can get FREE Zyearth short stories when you sign up for the newsletter at Zyearth.com! Here's some sneak peeks:

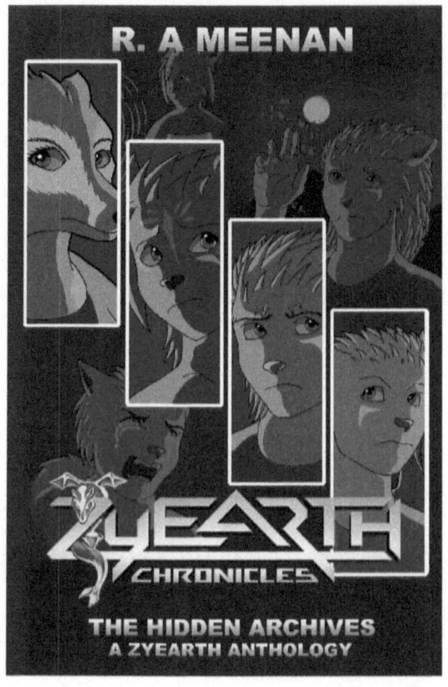

Five stories from the world of Zyearth...

Two rivals falling in love. An artist discovering a horrific secret. A Guardian saving a prince. A genocide survivor discovering his lost wife. A soldier just trying to survive.

Greetings, Traveler. Your curiosity has led you to the Hidden Archives, where I document stories important to the history of the Defenders of Zyearth.

These stories are short, often tragic, sometimes humorous, but they may reveal connections, hidden knowledge, or special insights to the greater Zyearth world, and therefore must be protected.

Read on, Traveler, if you dare, and if this does not satisfy your curiosity, know that I add to the Archives frequently. There may be many more stories for you to discover.

Go forth and may Draso shine upon you.

Get more information by signing up for the newsletter at Zyearth.com!

Glossary

Learn more about the World of Zyearth at Zyearth.com!

Zyfaunos: Zyfaunos are anthropomorphic animal-like bipeds. All zyfaunos have similar characteristics -- plantigrade or near plantigrade legs, human stance structure in the spine, humanlike eyes and sometimes lips, generally short snouts, and have humanlike, five fingered hands, usually with tiny, somewhat sharp retractable claws instead of fingernails. Zyfaunos tend to have the same height range as humans, with a few extreme examples of very short or very tall species. All zyfaunos can interbreed regardless of the individual's species. Unlike most faunos, zyfaunos are not always "traditionally" colored, and often have unnatural colors in their fur, such as red, blue, green, purple, and others. Though relationships are rare, humans and zyfaunos can produce children. Zyfaunos are named as such because the DNA strain originated from the planet Zyearth and Zyearth has the purest forms of this species.

Quilar: Quilar are perhaps the most unusual of all zyfaunos, as it is unclear what animal they evolved from. They have several key characteristics -- catlike ears and snout, slightly humanlike lips, though usually black or dark pink, humanlike feet and hands, tails, and quills of various lengths on their head in place of hair. Quilar quills are hard, though not usually sharp like a porcupine or hedgehog. Instead of fingernails, quilar have tiny retractable claws on each hand. These claws are not very sharp and are mainly used for scratching. Quilar can be divided by color and physical characteristics into three different categories.

Zyearth Quilar: Zyearth quilar have very short, very soft fur and generally longer, thicker quills on their heads. Their snouts are short and flat and many even have human-like lips. They tend to have catlike ears and human-like eyes. Quilar are the most human-like of all faunos. Human-faunos relationships usually involve a quilar. Zyearth quilar tend to have browns, whites, blacks, and grays for their colors. Jason, pictured on the previous page, is wearing the Defender Elemental uniform colors, indicating his status as an elemental user.

Jason is modeling a Zyearth quilar. Jason's fur is soft golden brown.

Earth Quilar: Earth quilar are physically very similar to Zyearth quilar, though their colors tend to be more vibrant. They also generally have streaks of color in their fur and quills while Zyearth quilars tend to be one solid color.

Trecheon is, reluctantly, modeling an Earth quilar.

Athánatos Quilar: Athánatos quilar are typically taller than their Zyearth and Earth kin. They have ears that bend backwards and more animal-like tails and feet. Their snouts are short and flat and like other quilar, they can have human-like lips.

Ouranos is modeling an Athánatos quilar here.

Focus Jewels: Focus jewels are found on many different planets throughout the universe. The term refers to any jewel that can be bound to a user's skin, soul, or lifeforce that grants supernatural powers. Sometimes focus jewel power only grants simple powers, such as long life, but others exhibit more extravagant powers.

Lexi Gems: Lexi Gems are focus jewels bound to the user's soul and grants users several powers. Average Gem users are granted long life, up to four hundred Zyearth years, and slow aging. Advanced users develop "Gem  Specialties" through the Gem "breaking" usually after a stressful, dramatic, or difficult event in the user's life. Military personnel are the most likely to have broken Gems and most Gems break in training.

There are a variety of specialties that users can develop. The most common specialty is healing, followed by elemental fabricators and manipulators, and a select few specialize in cloaking and shielding. Users are usually granted only one specialty, though a rare few have two. In the case of a duel specialist, both specialties are significantly weaker than those in a single specialist.

Lexi Gems are usually about the size of a user's fist. Gems often take on the colors of their users in one of several forms, but they lose their color if the user doesn't touch their Gem for extended periods of time or if the user dies, which also results in the Gem's bond breaking with their user. Gems can be used again by another user after a previous user has died.

Ei-Ei Jewels: Ei-Ei Jewels, like Lexi Gems, are focus jewels and are the source of magic and power for a member of the Athánatos tribe. Ei-Ei jewels are small and they are fused to the skin of the user just around the edge of their eyes. Ei-Ei jewels also come in pairs. Each eye has one set of the pairs. There are three jewels, but all of them work together to properly function.

The first jewel, the Mind Jewel, is yellow, representing the sophia flower, a symbol of wisdom. This jewel set keeps the user's mind fresh and free of deterioration. They even protect against mind aging issues like Alzheimer's and dementia.

The second set, the Body Jewel, is red, representing the purity of blood and flesh. This jewel set keeps the body from deterioration. Athánatos tribe members are immortal because of this jewel, but they are not invincible.

The final set, the Soul Jewel, is the color of the users eyes, representing the user's soul. This jewel set keeps the soul pinned to the body. Together the three sets make the user immortal.

Wishing Dust: Wishing Dust is created from ground up focus jewels and is used by applying the dust to the eye while making a "wish." Wishes are very specific, detailed spells that do one thing really well, but with a cost. Wishing Dust users are called Wish Dusters.

Wishing Dust is very volatile and a majority of attempted users wish too large for the wish to compensate. If the wish cannot properly compensate, the user will go insane and physically rip themselves apart trying to remove the dust. If a wish goes wrong, the user will always die. There is no saving them. Because the dust is so powerful and so deadly, most major civilizations in the universe have banned it. As a result, Wishing Dust is mostly found in black markets and smuggler's groups.

Wishing Dust comes in a variety of colors and will add a light, very subtle dusting of that color to the user's eye. It's difficult to identify a Wish Duster until they've used their magic. Common wishes include magic tracking, object manifestation or enhancement, body morphing, and various magical defenses.

Continuum Stones: Continuum Stones are a pair of magical stones that manipulate time and space. They're almost exclusively used by the zyfaunos bat species of Vanguard from the Tribus continent. Users wear the stones attached to the skin in the inner parts of their ears.

Most Continuum Stone users live beyond their biological lifespans, but how long that is depends on their time powers. Powers are granted randomly as the user grows.

Time powers include healing, which reverses time on the user's body, scrying, and very temporary time freezes, with limited range. Each one has their own down sides. Too much healing can put a user outside of time, which takes time and effort to fix. Scrying is very imprecise as a whole. Time freezing robs the user of time off their lifespan – one hour for every second of frozen time.

Space powers include telekinesis, or the ability to lift things with the mind. Telekinesis users can only lift objects that they would otherwise be able to lift with their own strength. Teleportation, or space jumping, which allows users to jump 50 or 60 feet from where they stand. This is very energy intensive and needs a long recovery time between jumps. Finally, gravity manipulation, which allows a user to increase or decrease gravity on an object or in a small radius for a very short period of time. This is also energy intensive and cannot completely negate natural gravity, which means a user cannot eliminate gravity completely and send someone into space.

Jewel Shards: Jewel Shards are a relatively new focus jewel discovered on the Paleofaunos-inhabited planet Erdoglyan. Jewel Shards are pointed cone-shaped jewels and bound physical to a user, usually grafted onto bone or teeth and held in place with ornate metal holders. As they are a permanent fixture, they're often on the face or snout and positioned to face forward like a unicorn horn.

Jewel Shards manifest a single elemental magic, one of the main seven elements. The inhabitants who own jewels call themselves the

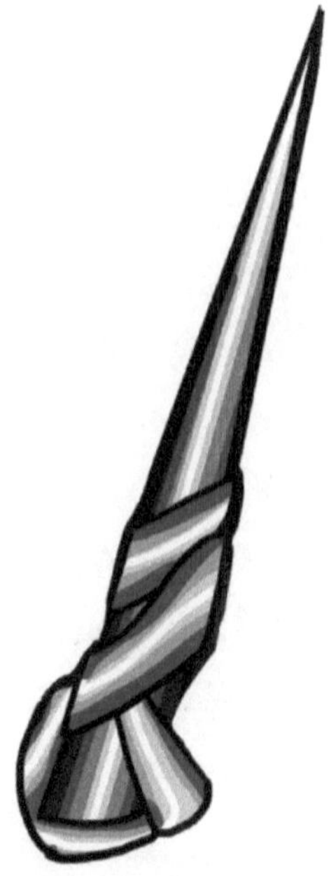

Forged and name themselves off the element they have. For example, "Fireforged" or "Lightningforged." The element it manifests will also determine its user's remaining lifespan. Some shorten the lifespan, such as lightning, which only grants 30 to 50 years of life after binding. Others lengthen it, such as stone, which can grant up to 350 years of additional life after binding. Some claim the element manifested is a reflection of the user's personality, though this has yet to be proven.

Jewel Shards are powered by UV rays. If they are left uncharged for too long, it causes psychosis in the user.

Blood Crystals: Unlike other jewels, Blood Crystals are shaped to look like things, typically something that their users find solace in. Blood Crystals are unique in the sense that they need two or more users to work properly. When bound, users will borrow magic or energy from their partner (called the Bleeder) and use it to create massive, destructive spells. Blood Partners can kill each other if they're not careful with how they pull magic.

Blood Crystals are highly regulated by Galactic InterPol because they were once used to bring people back to life, though very temporarily. The process is all but forgotten now, except for the knowledge that in order to use a Blood Crystal to revive someone, someone else had to be sacrificed.

Defender: The Defenders are a military group run by a small country called Zedric on the continent of Yelar on the plant Zyearth.

Guardian: Guardians are an essential part of the Defender military. Guardians are high ranking, highly trained individuals that perform tasks that average Defenders aren't trained for. There are two important types of Guardians.

Master Guardian: The role of Master Guardian is usually held by two people at the same time, often a former Golden Guardian pair. Master Guardians have a duel task – they are both the head of the Defender army and the leaders of the country of Zedric. Master Guardians must be smart, strong, courageous, and influential. Master Guardians are usually in office for life, though there are checks and balances that can remove a Master Guardian if the governing Assembly or the people of Zedric feels like they are not properly performing duties, and some Master Guardians choose to retire. Master Guardians are generally considered by most Defenders to be the most powerful zyfaunos of their time.

Golden Guardian: Golden Guardians are a team of two Defenders specially trained to handle delicate situations and complete covert and difficult missions that need small strike teams. Golden Guardians are selected by the Master Guardian of their era, and are given an extra five years of special training beyond typical Defender training. Usually the team has one healer and one elemental user.

Defender Pendant: Defender pendants are worn by all Defenders, regardless of their position in the army or Academy. They carry holographic identification cards and are the most common means of communication among Defenders. The pendant also carries several symbols. On Zyearth, a legless dragon is a sign of peace, so the Defenders made the legless dragon the center of their pendant. The dragon's  neck is tucked under, a classic move that prevents strangulation in battle. This represents defense. The outstretched wings are a sign of openness and welcome. Finally, the Gem at the dragon's side represents the world of Zyearth, since nearly all native Zyearthlings are bound to Gems.

www.ingramcontent.com/pod-product-compliance
Lightning Source LLC
Chambersburg PA
CBHW061035310726
48969CB00004B/966